K. Kristen Callihan

she's worn neon skirts, ʼ be retui... (although never all at once) and can quote John Hughes movies with the best of them. A lifelong daydreamer, she finally realised that the characters in her head needed a proper home and thus hit the keyboard. She believes that falling in love is one of the headiest experiences a person can have, so naturally she writes romance. Her love of superheroes, action movies and history led her to write historical paranormals. She lives in the Washington, D.C., area and, when not writing, looks after two children, one husband and a dog – the fish can fend for themselves.

Visit Kristen Callihan online:
www.kristencallihan.com
www.facebook.com/KristenCallihan
@Kris10Callihan

Kristen Callihan

SOULBOUND

The Darkest London

piatkus

PIATKUS

First published in the US in 2015 by Forever,
an imprint of Grand Central Publishing,
A division of Hachette Book Group, Inc.
First published in Great Britain in 2015 by Piatkus

1 3 5 7 9 10 8 6 4 2

A CIP catalogue record for this book
is available from the British Library.

ISBN 978-0-349-40609-1

Printed and bound by CPI Group (UK) Ltd, Croydon, CR0 4YY

www.piatkus.co.uk

*For my family, who loves and supports me,
even when I'm tucked away in my office for
hours on end. You are my reward
at the end of a long day.
And*

For my readers, always.

SOULBOUND

Prologue

So kiss me sweet with your warm wet mouth,
Still fragrant with ruby wine,
And say with a fervor born of the South
That your body and soul are mine.
—Ella Wheeler Wilcox

London, November 1885

She had always been attracted to death. Sought it out for reasons inexplicable to even herself. But it wasn't supposed to end this way. And now she was dead. Of that she was certain. She felt the stinging tug of the knife as it pulled through her flesh. Her life's blood, hot against her skin, cool as it spread in a crimson pool about her still body.

Just before she died, the grizzled, grinning faces of the thugs around her began to fade, the world turning a muddy brown. Eliza's last breath left with a soft, soundless puff.

And now she was dead. She had fought so hard and so long to live. Done ugly things to remain alive, to *survive*.

She'd come to London to find her distant family. They might help, offer her solace. And she hadn't even had the chance to look, set upon by bad men barely an hour after she'd disembarked and stepped upon English soil.

Rage surged up within her. She refused to be cut down like this, by these...mindless thugs. Her body was still, a heavy, foreign thing now. No longer hers to command.

Again came the rage, but the black pall of death was stronger. Before she could think, she was simply gone.

No. *No!*

Eliza blinked, light wavering around her. And then she was back, standing in the alleyway. Alive. Before her, two women fought the men who had murdered her. She *had* been murdered. Hadn't she? Yet here she stood, idly watching as these lovely, properly dressed women, one wielding a sword, the other a baton, fought like masters. Eliza nearly laughed. She was going mad. That was it. Madness had at last claimed her.

And then all was still. The men fled, limping and bloodied. And she was left with her saviors. Eliza didn't know what to say. She felt...odd. No, she corrected, she didn't feel at all. There was, in fact, a decided lack of any feeling. She wanted to think further on it, but the pretty blonde woman was kneeling next to a body, crimson blood soaking into her fine, butter-yellow skirts.

Eliza stared at the sight, at the body of another blonde woman, her plain brown skirts in disarray, her throat cut, her brown eyes wide and sightless in death. *She looks like me. The dead woman looks exactly like me.*

"No pulse," the young lady murmured, pressing her fingers against the woman's pale throat. "They gutted her. Poor dear."

"No!" The shout tore from Eliza. Fear, so violent she

wanted to scream, rose up within her. She knew that body was hers. And yet... "I cannot be dead. I refuse to go. Not like this. Not from the likes of them." Again came a flash of ire and need. The need to live.

The pretty blonde glanced at the woman with dark hair and hesitation rose high in her blue eyes. But her voice was calm as she addressed Eliza. "I'm afraid you are dead. I am very sorry we did not arrive sooner."

The hell I am. Eliza wanted to stomp her foot. In fact, she tried. The action made not a sound. "If I am dead, then how is it that you both see me?" She peered at the women, struck by a strange new fact. "And why do you both glow?"

"You are seeing our spirits," the dark-haired woman said. "Just as we see yours." Around them, the breeze began to stir, and it carried the sound of moaning.

Oh, but Eliza did not like that sound. Despair and urgency lived in that sound. Nor did she like the way the shadows in the corners of the alley seemed to stir, as if impatient. *Stay away from those shadows.* Eliza refused to cower. But she wanted to.

The brunette sighed, the sound full of pity and heavy sorrow. "There is still a chance to move on. You must feel it. I suggest you take it, lest you be stuck here just as they are."

She didn't need to explain who "they" were; Eliza could feel them. When she couldn't even feel her own feet. These beings, whatever they were, exuded cold. Such cold. Eliza glared at the shadows, daring them to come closer. She'd make them sorry. Gads, but they gave her a chill. She tried to rub her arms for warmth and felt nothing of her body, only their desire to take her. "I feel it," she admitted to the strange ladies. "Like someone is plucking

on my sleeve." She shuddered. "I...I can't! I don't want
to die."

"Well, who does?" the blonde mused.

Eliza decided she did not like her very much.

The woman tilted her head and eyed Eliza in a calculating manner. "Would you really rather stay? Even if it
meant you never died?"

Something inside of Eliza leapt with warmth and tight
urgency. Hope. "Is this a true question?"

"She has spirit," the blonde said to the brunette, who
frowned and looked Eliza over.

"She's a strange one," the brunette murmured.

Rather the pot calling the kettle. "Says the woman who
rushed in like a crazed banshee and beat down three full-
grown men," Eliza retorted.

"She's in shock," the blonde said with a smile.

The brunette's lips twitched. "Likely you're right."

What a pair, these two. "I agree." Wouldn't anyone be in
shock knowing they'd died? No, she would not think of that.
Or of the increasingly loud moans coming from the shadows. "Can we move on please?" Hadn't they said something
about her staying here? Hope took on a sharp edge and made
her want to reach out and shake one of these odd women.

The brunette ignored her entirely but focused on her
friend. "We could..."

"We could," the pretty blonde agreed.

Saint's preserve her, Eliza had had enough. Perhaps
if she simply tried to get back into her body...The brunette's words halted her. "You'd be a slave. For however
long He deems."

A new chill went through Eliza. As if she'd had this
conversation before. As if she were on the cusp of...
something. "Who is 'He'?"

"The man who can give you back your life," the blonde said without preamble.

Well...She supposed...That strange, almost anticipatory discomfort within her soul grew. "Will it involve..." She couldn't finish, but being women, they understood readily.

"No," said the brunette emphatically. "You merely have to find other willing spirits for him."

Other spirits? "For what reason?"

"Well, there is the rub," said the blonde a bit sadly. "Only he knows. Some, he allows to return to their bodies and live life out as we are now. Others, he takes with him. Though he promises no harm will come to them, no one here knows what happens to those souls." Her blue eyes grew solemn. "You will not know until it is your turn."

Eliza's body lay before her, its once-pink skin now bone white and going an ugly grey at the edges. Her life's blood had begun to congeal and blacken. She looked pitiful, lying there in the muck. Abused and abandoned. She glanced back at the two women staring at her with quiet expectation. They did not appear to be evil. Had they not just tried to save her?

But perhaps they were witches who laid in wait for such opportunity. After all, if Eliza were not mistaken, these properly dressed and uncommonly pretty women appeared to be some sort of soul harvesters. A gruesome job. Eliza would be a fool to trust them. But she'd come all this way, risked death to escape. The only thing left for her was to remain dead or take fate by the hand and see what it would bring her.

Oddly, she wasn't afraid, but excited. Eliza took a deep breath, uncomfortably aware that she didn't actually breathe anymore. "Fine. I accept."

She wasn't certain what she expected to happen but the two women dickered about for a moment, discussing how to accomplish this supposed miracle. "Ought we not hurry?" she asked them, if only to expedite the process. The moans from the shadows were growing impatient.

"Your body is safe for now," the blonde assured, even though her gaze stayed resolutely away from it. With a sigh, she then pressed her hand against her heart and murmured words too low for Eliza to hear. But the effect was instantaneous. The cold alleyway grew hot and thick with the smoky scent of myrrh and something dark and delicious. She'd never smelled the like and yet it felt right, this scent, a comfort. Lord but she could draw the fragrance into her lungs all day and never tire of it.

The women seemed less enamored of the scent, for they frowned and fidgeted as though agitated. Eliza might have made a further study but her eye was drawn to the spot just next to the women. There, a shadow formed, completely black, with a density that gave it a tangible depth. Its hazy edges grew sharp and distinct, taking on the shape of a large doorway.

Foreboding raced through Eliza as her attention stayed riveted on that spot. "What is it?"

"Hush."

Someone was coming; she was sure of it. Footsteps echoed, the sound hollow and far off. The fragrance in the alley grew thicker, richer, until Eliza thought her mouth might water. If she had a mouth, that was. Then he appeared, larger than life and handsome as dark sin.

Good gravy, it figured she would have to die in order to rest eyes upon a man so stunning. Tall, with the lithe grace of a warrior, he walked towards them without care. His coal-black hair fell over his brow as if he'd just risen from bed. On a boyish face, this might look slovenly, but this man…His features were carved by a master, a big and bold aquiline nose, strong, slanting cheekbones, and a stubborn chin, shadowed with an evening beard. He was the most overwhelmingly masculine male she'd ever seen.

His deep, dark voice poured over them like hot milk. "My delicious daughters." Daughters? "My most lovely creations. How may I be of service?" He smiled at the two women, bringing Eliza's attention to his mouth. A bitable mouth.

A flush of unwanted heat went through her.

The blonde, now blushing spoke. "My Lord, we have one who desires to join."

And then he looked at Eliza. Beneath thick, dark brows that slashed over eyes of stunning gold, he hit her with the force of his gaze, and Eliza's world turned on its end. Him. It was him. She blinked, not understanding why he felt so very familiar, so very right. It didn't matter, for his expression grew covetous and calculating, and she feared she'd need all her wits with this one. Fate, it seemed, had just played a very nasty trick on her.

Aodh, son of Niall, former knight and one-time terror of Ireland and Great Britain, now known as Adam, king and creator of the GIM, took one look at the little spirit wavering before him, and his entire existence ground to a halt. Had he not lived centuries devoid of a single, pleasurable feeling, he would not have been able to hide his surprise. As it was, he barely remained standing. A rush of pure, exquisite emotion punched through him, battering him about like a cork on a monster wave.

Holy God. It almost hurt, this feeling. He allowed himself a small breath. He was *feeling*. After all these years.

Heat and throbbing below his waist had him biting back a laugh. His cock was rising. He'd actually forgotten that particular sensation.

The female spirit was eyeing him as if he might soon bite. She was right to worry. He wanted to bite. But the glow that surrounded her form distracted him. He stared at it, disbelief, hope, and emotion writhing within him until he feared he might double over. That glow, soft gold mixed with sharp silver. The light of her soul. He did not have to glance down at his body to see the exact match of her soul's light to his.

It was *her*. After all of these years. The endless searching. He'd found her. Why, then, did a strange, desperate rage fill him now?

"Your name?" he asked of her. Tension rode his frame hard.

The spirit narrowed her eyes, her gaze sliding up and down Adam's form as though inspecting something distasteful. Perfect. Wonderful. They were off to a grand start.

Her voice, when she spoke, was clipped, with the flat tones of a Yank. "Eliza May."

"Mmm." It came out as a dubious rumble. Adam flicked his attention to Mary. "I'll have a word with you, sweet Mary Chase—"

"And you are?" Eliza May cut in, her translucent hands upon her hips. Like a little fishwife. *His little fishwife.*

Again the anger, the helplessness. He didn't want to need her. Didn't like the urge that rode him hard and demanded he fall at her knees and weep with relief. He found himself snapping. "Not to be interrupted, treats."

The lass's pert chin lifted. "I've a right to know your full name, sir."

Oh, but she would be interesting. Of that, he was certain. Adam put on a smile meant to chill and sauntered over to the hovering spirit. The temptation to touch her was too great. He traced the line of her cheek, and a shiver licked over his skin. She was warm, solid, to him at least. For at this moment, she lived in his realm. She didn't even realize she'd passed into it and that what the lovely Miss Chase and Mrs. Ranulf saw of her was merely a spirit, barely clinging to their world. "My Lord and Master, My Irresistible Liege," he murmured, while his cock throbbed against his trousers. "Pick whichever one you want. Then shut up. I am speaking, and not to you."

He was being a bastard, unworthy of the knight he once was. And yet he couldn't seem to stop himself where she was concerned. She'd turned him into a truculent, possessive child. In truth, if he didn't have her spirit bound to his soon, he was likely to break down and cling to her skirts.

Unhinged, Adam turned his attention to Mary—he had things he needed to discuss with the lass—but he stopped as he spied Eliza's body laying bloodied and battered upon the cobbles, her skirts still rucked up, a pool of blackening blood widening about her head like a macabre halo.

Had she been violated? A new sort of rage lit through him. So strong that the dark alleyway was illuminated with golden light, and he knew his eyes were glowing.

Eliza, seeing the direction of Adam's gaze, swished to hover over her body as though she might hide it. "Don't look at me, it." Her teeth bared in a snarl. "At my body."

Her pride was a feral and beautiful thing. *My sweet dove, if I could, I'd tear those who hurt you into pieces.*

"Why?" he asked mildly, as if he wasn't aching for violence. "It's dead. And if you want to keep it, it's also mine."

Mine. Mine. Mine. It was a rampant refrain in his head.

Eliza flinched, her mouth gaping before snapping shut. "I thought... They said that you wouldn't want..."

And like that, his desire wilted. She feared him. With good reason. The poor lass had just been abused. Adam was better than this. Usually. Still, the disgusted look in her wide, brown eyes irked.

"Devil take it. I quite literally have beings knocking against each other for the opportunity to have me."

Even now, ghosts stuck between worlds gathered, straining along the periphery of the alleyway as though held back by an invisible wall. The silent, wraithlike figures twisted and undulated in unmistakable entreaty. They always did. Thanks to his curse, almost all beings craved his touch and attention. Except this one. His supposed fate and savior. Adam glared. "I've no interest in unwilling, prissy misses."

The lass sneered at him. "Oh, how the other ghouls must envy you."

Wee smarmy... Adam took a step in Eliza's direction. "Let us get this over with. Will you swear fealty to me?"

"What would I have to—"

"Yes or no. Right now, Miss May."

He *needed* her capitulation. Now.

Eliza May glanced between Mary and Daisy, her expression unsure and pained. She'd get no help there. His lovelies were forbidden to talk to her at this moment. It was his law. "Tick, tock, Eliza."

"All right." She drew herself up, all five and a half feet of sweet curves and bitter resentment. "I swear it."

The triumph that filled Adam was absolute, yet not at all the satisfaction he expected. No, he feared. Feared that she'd somehow slip through his fingers and be lost to him again. Unacceptable. "Excellent."

With a flick of his wrist, he'd conjured a thin, golden chain and struck. The chain coiled around Eliza's spirit and her body. Adam gave the chain a lazy tug, and Eliza flew into her body. A great gasp broke from her lips as her body arched off the ground and then flopped back, struggling against the golden bonds like a fish in a net.

He felt her pain. He felt *everything*. Finally. Freedom. Finally, it was in his grasp. All he had to do was keep Miss Eliza May by his side. Forever.

Chapter One

The young man stretched out upon the table struggled to remain still. That much was evident in the way his taut, bared flesh twitched along his muscled thighs and lean abdomen. As the whitening of his wrists where they were bound with crimson satin ropes to the table, and in the way his narrow hips shifted ever so slightly, a tiny thrust upwards as if that one restrained action would bring some relief to his member.

Eliza tried not to look there, at the obscene, angry length of him, bobbing about with each breath he took. Nor did she want to meet his eyes. She did not want to know what lay behind them, if he was in agony or in ecstasy. She settled for studying the pale length of his flank, smooth near his buttock, furred with blond hairs along his thigh, now glistening in the dim glow of the room.

"This one is wonderfully obedient, is he not?" murmured a feminine voice in her ear.

Eliza forced herself to stir, and she swore the tight clench of her corset threatened to put her off her turtle soup. "He has lasted longer than the others." A benign statement but the only one she could muster. For there had been others. A parade of young and beautiful creatures looking for sensual pleasure in the hands of Eliza's Auntie Mab and her court of fools.

At Eliza's side, Mab's ivory skin was luminous and without line or flaw, her auburn hair holding glints of gold, bronze, and copper. An ageless beauty that did not seem natural. Unless you took into account that Mab was fae, an immortal.

Fairies. Fae. Eliza had never paid myths much mind. In Boston, one was far more likely to hear stories of the Headless Horseman than those of little winged creatures. How very misinformed she'd been. Fae were beautiful, powerful, and able to alter their appearance to pass as human. Mab confided it took a measure of power to maintain, and that once their bodies were destroyed here, the fae must return to their lands to regenerate. Decidedly strange creatures. And, according to Mab, Eliza had their blood running through her veins.

A year ago, Eliza would have thought her aunt mad if she'd claimed to be one, save Eliza had once been chained to the demon Adam long enough for the wool to be irrevocably pulled from her eyes. This brave new world was not the bland, colorless life she'd once lived amongst normal society.

Around her, fine gentlemen and ladies ate a grand feast at the fifty-foot long white marble table. Candlelight and crystal turned the world into glitter and gold. Wine flowed

with the generosity of Bacchus, servants dressed in emer-
ald green ready to refill a glass should it lower even an
inch. Which made for sloppy drunkenness. A respectable
lord tossed a chicken leg across the table, and the room
erupted into laughter as it landed with stunning precision
directly between the large globes of a countess's breasts.

The countess merely plucked the little limb from her
bodice and bit into the meat with pearly teeth.

Eliza took a bracing sip of wine and immediately
regretted it, as a low burn traveled down her throat.
Sticky-sweet smoke drifting from hanging brass burn-
ers made her head light. And the poor lad laid out before
her, desperate for attention, seemed to give a silent sigh,
his body growing ever more tense. At Eliza's side, Mab
chuckled before leaning forward to trace a path with her
tongue along the young lad's ribs. He moaned in response,
his pale length arching. A mistake.

Mab lifted her riding crop and snapped it down on
tender, unprotected flesh, eliciting another moan from
the man. "Silence." She whipped him again, much to the
room's amusement. "I did not give you leave to make a
sound. Or to move."

And so he tried again to behave. Mab turned to Eliza,
and her dark eyes were alight with glee. "A sturdy hand,
Eliza. They relish it, you see."

Yes, she saw very well. Mab was grooming her. It had
happened slowly, the fall into this particular niche of
debauchery. It had been lovely at first, being given costly
gowns of the finest silk, velvets, and cashmere, living in
Mab's luxurious home, eating rich and luscious foods
every day. And the parties. Endless parties. No one to tell
her that she was too loud, too brash, clumsy, frivolous.
No one stalking her for favors she did not want to give.

Eliza was free. To be herself, to indulge in whatever whim pleased her.

But then came the cruelty. Eliza had seen enough of the world to understand that those who begged to be tied up and whipped did so in the pursuit of pleasure. They'd come to the wrong place. For Eliza suffered no illusions now; Mab's pleasure derived from the pain and suffering of others. And the lad upon the table would soon end up like those who had come before him. Dead.

Unable to take another moment, Eliza pushed back from the table, her voluminous, aubergine satin skirts undulating as she rose.

Mab's delicate auburn brow lifted. "Surely you are not leaving."

Eliza could make many excuses. She chose the one most likely to repulse. Leaning down, she whispered in Mab's ear. "Privy."

Her aunt's pert nose wrinkled. "Horrid, the human body." Her pale hand waved in lazy fashion. "Go. And be comforted in the knowledge that soon you will not suffer such indignities."

Why? Eliza hadn't the courage to ask her. It seemed her courage had left her on the day she'd fled the demon. She ought to have fought him for her right to live free.

Cool damp swarmed her as she stepped onto the stone terrace that ran along the back of the house. From inside, ribald laughter continued, a trilling sound that scraped her nerves. But here all was clear and still. Eliza hugged herself close. She did not want to be in this house, in this life. And though she was likely as foul and morally wrong as they were, she did not *want* to be. She could run. Again.

Always running. Since the age of fourteen when her

grandfather Aidan died, she'd been running from things. Some nights, it felt as though she were running towards something. But she'd never found it. Only death and entrapment. Oh, but she knew death.

She had died once. Years ago. Of that she was certain. She'd felt the sting of the knife as it pulled through her flesh. And seen her life's blood spread in a crimson pool about her still body, and known with cold certainty that she'd suffered a mortal wound. It hadn't been a dream. It had been real. And yet she now lived. Because *he* had given her life anew. "Him, he," that is how she thought of the demon who'd held her captive for a time, linking her wrist to his by an enchanted golden chain. Never think his name, much less utter it. To give voice to a name, even in one's secret thoughts, was to give it power. Eliza May had enough sense to know this.

Yet, try as she might, the memory of the demon, that darkly handsome fiend who oozed sensual heat and temptation, never left her. Not for a moment. Such a strange demon, the one who created an entire race of supernatural beings. He'd called them Ghosts in the Machine, the GIM. Humans who, like her, had been struck down before their time yet refused to go gently into that cold night. The demon had given them immortality, the ability to roam free in spirit form, and a clockwork heart to bind them to him for a period of time. It seemed a fair bargain. Yet she'd received no such heart. He'd wanted something else from her. Her very soul. Her capitulation. Just like the other man she'd run from.

The demon's roar of rage and pain, the one she'd heard the moment their connection had been broken, still rang in her ears. Her cousin St. John had whisked her away so quickly that she'd only been treated to a mere second of that sound. Yet it haunted her all the same. Because it was not the shout of a man who'd easily give up.

Why did he want her? They'd gotten along like tar and sand, stuck together because of circumstance, an irritant to both each other and those who had the misfortune to be around them. And still he'd been determined to keep her.

How strange it all seemed now. Like a nightmare. She was no longer chained. She was safe. Aunt Mab assured her that the demon would never come for her. That once the chain had been broken, he could never find her again. Cold comfort.

Eliza's fingers dug into her skirt, and the fabric made a hushed rustle. *He* had given her gowns too. In a rainbow of colors, a buffet of textures. And she'd turned away from every one of them, too fearful that she'd be drawn by his enticements.

You wouldn't even be here were it not for me. No, you'd be rotting in an unmarked grave, forgotten and unavenged. Because the GIM did that for you as well, didn't they? Striking down those who hurt you. And what thanks do I receive? Silence. You agreed to be mine. Mine!

The worst of it was, she *had* agreed. She simply hadn't realized how much it would chafe to lose her freedom. From the moment he had her, he'd kept her chained by his side, his mood always angry, always looking at her as though she ought to be giving him something more. Yet he'd refused to tell her what. He'd grown more sullen, and she'd stopped speaking altogether. And then two men had come for her. Friends of her aunt. They'd saved her.

And she'd escaped *him*. Her stomach clenched. Guilt was a terrible thing. No, she would not think of it. Or of his guinea-gold eyes framed by thick, black lashes. Accusing eyes, filled with rage and pain.

As if beckoned by her wayward thoughts, a lone, mournful howl rent the night. Every hair upon Eliza's body stood on end as she straightened. Heart pounding, she glanced toward the back at the windowed doors, where everything was warmth and light. Had it come from within the house or from outside?

Past the grand hall that ran along the back of the house, she could see a small slice of the dining room. Mab's party was still in full swing. Not a flinch or concerned face in the room. Had she imagined the sound?

A mystery solved, as another wailing howl rang out. Such pain and misery in that cry. It wasn't human, that howl, but sounded as if made by a dog. And it had come from the direction of the kitchen wing. Had a dog found its way inside and been hurt? She couldn't fathom how, but nor could she remain here and ignore the plea for help.

Slipping back inside, Eliza crept past the dining room and into the main hall. Once outside the kitchen doors, she stilled. Where now? The echoing quality of the sound made it difficult to discern its origins. With only the light of a few sconces lit along the walls, the hall was filled with shadows. Silence was a weight against her skin, warring with the sound of her blood rushing through her veins. The tall case clock by the salon door tick away.

Eliza's shoulders slumped, and she let out a slow breath. Perhaps she had... A yelp, high and aggravated. Most definitely that had come from the kitchens.

She hadn't taken two steps when she heard someone coming. If there was one good talent Eliza possessed, it was to trust her instincts, and now they cried out for her to hide. Ducking behind one of the decorative Doric columns that graced the main floor, she held still as someone passed. Who, she could not discern, and she was in too great a risk of discovery to peek out and look. The footsteps were heavy; however, the beat between them far enough to suggest a long stride. One of the footmen? Yet she'd never felt a prickle of warning when they were near.

Eliza waited a full minute after the steps had faded and then headed for the kitchens. Once there, Eliza could do nothing more than hope for another sound from the dog to help guide her. Yet nothing stirred. Standing in the center of the room, she turned full circle, her gaze scanning the area. Had her senses not been on full alert, she might have missed the thin but delineated cracks that ran along the wall by the root pantry. A hidden door, not fully shut.

It was not a surprise to find that the door opened to a dark stairwell leading down. Eliza had read enough gothic novels to expect such a thing. Which of course meant that going down those stairs was likely to lead to trouble.

The sounds of Mab's party drifted along the night. She ought to return there. A sane woman wouldn't try to discover what lay beyond. Unfortunately, Eliza had never been very good at taking the safe course of action. A lantern hung upon a hook on the wall just inside the stairway. She plucked it free, lit it, and ventured into the unknown.

Counting each step she took, Eliza pressed her palm against the damp stones for balance. Within the small orb of lamplight, she felt safe, but beyond and behind, there was only darkness and the fear that something would soon leap out of it.

The whimpering grew in strength as she descended. Until she rounded a curve, and then it abruptly stopped. She did as well, hovering in the stairwell. Too silent. As if whatever it was that had cried out now held itself quiet.

Cold air ripped through her lungs, and her pulse beat an insistent *Flee, flee, flee* against her throat. Yet she knew that what lay beyond needed help.

Eliza let out a small breath and continued down, her hands shaking so badly that the light wavered. The bottom of the stairs opened up into a long, low corridor. Following it, she soon turned right and found herself in a circular room carved from stone. The walls were composed of cells, barred with steel that shone bright and new against the surrounding rot. They all appeared dark and empty.

She stood in the center of the room, ears buzzing, heart racing. Nothing stirred. Not a sound. A faint scratching from a cell to her left had her nearly jumping out of her skin. Peering into the darkness, she crept forward.

The light of her lantern led the way, stretching forward, slowly illuminating the small cell and what lay inside, a glossy, black hind leg bent at an awkward, painful angle, ribs protruding from an emaciated canine torso. Eliza's breath caught. The beast moved, a slight adjustment that had its head lifting. Yellow eyes glowed in the dark. A low, warning growl rumbled and then broke on a whimper. And the dog slumped back down, ignoring her, though it did not close its eyes.

Yes, it was a dog, or a wolf. Eliza could see that now. The largest dog she'd ever seen. Slowly she approached it, stopping just short of the cell door. Chains dug into its fur, cutting in some spots. From what she could see, the dog's left hind leg and right foreleg were badly broken, a clever cruelty that prevented it from lying comfortably in any position. Gouges riddled its body, and they oozed with blood that matted its dark fur.

"You poor thing," she whispered past her fear. It

occurred to her that there might be a very good reason for the beast to be locked up. Perhaps it was mad, a killer. But nothing could excuse the treatment it had received. If the dog was a killer, it ought to have been put down. Not brutalized and left to suffer.

That thought alone prompted her to set her lantern down before kneeling near the bars. The dog's yellow eyes tracked her movements without bothering to lift its head. If anything, it seemed to be resigned to its fate. But its body shivered, and she knew it was fighting the pain. She shivered in sympathy.

"I want to help you."

A soft snort came from the dog's snout, as if it understood her words and thought very little of her abilities to do so.

Eliza glanced around, searching for something to strike at the lock, when she noticed a ring with a key hanging from a hook on the wall. She hurried to it, only to stop. She needed supplies. Turning around, she spoke to the dog. "I'll be back soon."

Determination gave her speed. No longer afraid of what lurked in the cellar, she hurried to the kitchens, pilfered the cupboards for food, collected Cook's medicinal kit that he kept on hand for household emergencies, and then grabbed a stack of freshly washed hand linens. By the time she returned to the cell, she was breathless.

"Now then," she said in a low voice, as she opened the cell door, "we'll get you sorted."

The black dog, however, had other opinions on the matter and began to growl, a steady menacing snarl that curled its upper lip and revealed a set of wickedly long fangs.

"It's all right," Eliza said. "I am going to help you."

The dog's snarling intensified. He was chained against the floor but had enough reach to bite her if she came too near his wounds. Which wouldn't do. Crooning softly, Eliza opened the green bottle she'd removed from the medicine bag. Mindful of the fumes, she soaked a rag. As if the dog knew precisely what she was about, it snapped and writhed, only to cut itself short with a yelp as the frantic movement jostled its leg.

Eliza took advantage and threw the chloroform-soaked rag over the dog's massive head. Enraged, it struggled to free itself, but the drug did its job. Soon enough, the dog fell still, and its breathing turned slow and steady. Eliza waited, counting to one hundred, before moving close. She dared not move the rag just yet, but took the time to try out the sole key on the padlock that held the dog's chains to the cell. But it did not work.

"Damn all," she muttered, before setting the key ring aside. Frowning, she studied the dog's leg. She knew nothing of resetting bones. Especially for a dog.

"No matter," she muttered. "First things first." She'd clean those weeping wounds. Eliza rested her hand upon the dog's hind quarter where the fur was slick and damp. But no sooner did her palm make contact then a great puff of glittering dust rose up around the dog, obliterating it from her sight.

Eliza coughed and sat back on her haunches to get away from the swirling dust. Just as fast as it had appeared, the dust dissipated. A strangled sound escaped her. There, on the stone floor, lay not a dog but a man. Long, muscular limbs, broad shoulders, narrow hips. He was battered and wasting away now. Muscles stood out like thick hemp ropes beneath too-tight and too-pale skin. Skin that was slashed and bleeding.

"Jesus, Mary, and Joseph." Gaping down at his badly broken leg, Eliza found herself too shocked to move.

The heady scent of myrrh and heated male flesh surrounded her with dizzying effect. She knew this scent. The torment of it and how it made her breath quicken and her nipples tighten. No, no, no. It cannot be. With a trembling hand, she reached out and plucked away the linen that covered the man's head. Her heart turned over in her chest as her insides plummeted.

"You!" Her shout echoed in the small space.

Gold eyes peered at her from under a mop of black hair. His rich, dark voice was weaker now, slurred and stilted. But it still had the power to unsettle.

"Hello, dove. Did you miss me?"

Adam.

During his seven-hundred-odd years stuck in this life, Adam had been tortured numerous times. He'd like to think that, eventually, he would become accustomed to the pain. No such luck prevailed. Agony held him in a tight grip from the tip of his big toe to the top of his head. For months now, he'd been battered and humiliated by the fae bitch. His life had become this cell. This pain.

And now there was the added ignominy of having *her*, She of the Accusatory Stare, the very one who'd landed him in this hell, looking down upon his ruin. He wanted to snarl again. Instead, he tried to steady his breathing and concentrate upon the cold floor against his skin so that he did not cry out for mercy.

Eliza May—and oh how he'd struggled not to even think her name during these many months—stared at him out of liquid brown eyes, her expression haunted, as though he were a ghost. The irony nearly had him laughing. "So then," he managed through his teeth, "no rejoicing in this reunion?"

Her pretty face scrunched up in a scowl. "I thought you were a helpless dog."

"I gathered." That she preferred a mangy dog to him didn't burn in the slightest. Not at all. Adding insult to injury, his stomach gave a great gurgle of hunger that echoed throughout the cell.

Her lips quirked, a smile she quickly smothered. "I brought some sausages. I thought the dog would like them." With a tentative hand, she offered him one.

Instantly, his mouth watered, and he grabbed it from her, his pride nothing in comparison to his physical needs, it seemed. Not meeting her gaze, he devoured his food in hard, greedy bites. His eyes nearly watered with relief. Pain was one thing; starvation was another.

Golden waves of hair slithered over her shoulder as she tilted her head and regarded him. "Why are you here?"

"What can I say?" He grunted as a shard of pain lanced through his broken ribs. "There are times a man longs for a good cell to rest in after a rousing bout of torture."

Her scowl grew, the plump curve of her lower lip pushing outward. "Think you're funny, do you?"

"No." He was too tired to spar anymore. Wet stones pushed against his cheek, and he closed his eyes. Just for a moment.

The sound of silk rustling filled the silence, and then her scent—light and sweet like roses in this filth—grew stronger. Adam's eyes flew open just as she moved closer. He did snarl then. "Do not touch me!"

Paling, she halted. "I'm trying to help, you oaf."

"I do not want your help."

"Perhaps not, but you need it."

He sagged again, panting through the pain. "For the entirety of our association, you've wanted nothing more than to get away from me. Pray, do not change the pattern now. Go on with you. Get out."

The smooth curve of her jaw tightened with a stubbornness that he'd grown far too familiar with. "At the very least, let me give you something for the pain—"

"Out." He could not bellow as he wanted to for fear of alerting the fae bitch or her cronies. But he infused all his hate and frustration into the words, snapping his teeth at Miss May. "Get the fuck out of here."

Abruptly she stood, and he closed his eyes. He wanted her gone, but he didn't have to see her walking away from him. Again. Her retreating footsteps echoed, and then blessed silence descended. He drifted in a haze of pain and fevered thoughts. Eliza. Her scent, her heat, the golden glow of her soul's light. Even now, when the light of all other souls was hidden to him, he could see the faint illumination of hers. Like a mockery.

A soft touch upon his shoulder had him flinching and his eyes flying open. "What the bloody—"

"Don't you go cursing at me, or I'll…I'll…" She left the threat hanging as she eased next to him, and he lost the will to protest. The cool rim of a glass touched his lower lip. "Drink," she ordered.

Bitterness flooded his dry mouth and numbed his tongue. He swallowed it down. A concoction to ease his pain. He did not resist when she offered him another cup, this time of fresh water. In the dull light of her lantern, Eliza's pale hair glowed like a nimbus around her heart-shaped face.

"Now then," her voice trembled in the dim, though she did an admirable job of hiding it, "I'm going to clean you up."

"No." He grasped her wrist, staying her progress. When she stared at him, mutiny in her eyes, he sighed. "Lass, if you help me anymore than you have, they'll know. And we'll both suffer for it."

"Surely my aunt—" She bit her bottom lip, a little wrinkle forming between the wings of her brows. "She knows about this, doesn't she?"

A dry laugh escaped him. "Dove, she's the one who does this to me." Repeatedly.

Eliza's perplexed expression deepened. "She must have a good reason."

"Oh, aye," Adam drawled. "She's a demented bitch."

The fine bones of her wrist shifted against his firm grip. He wanted to loosen it, but his hand wouldn't obey. He liked touching her. Too well. How could he not? He *felt* her. He hadn't been privy to pleasurable feelings for centuries until she entered his life.

"Tell me why she does this. Why are you chained down here? Why were you a dog, for heaven's sake?"

"Do you know this is the most you've spoken to me in all of our acquaintance?" He couldn't keep the bitterness out of his tone. He'd waited for months to hear her speak to him. Now that she finally was, he both reveled in the sound of her blunt, flat American voice and resented her for making him wait so long to hear it.

She made a scoffing sound. "Because we are conversing now. Before, you talked *at* me, as though I were a dog."

"Untrue and unfair," he protested weakly.

Something close to a smile hovered at her lips. "Stop trying to deflect and answer me."

Warmth and a small bit of numbness worked through his body. Adam let his head rest on the floor. "I'm turned into a dog because she believes that causes me humiliation." It didn't, but he wasn't about to let Mab know that. When he was the dog, his pain was somehow more bearable. Unfortunately, the animal had no qualms about voicing its pain, which had brought Eliza to him. "Only the touch of a fae will turn me back, usually for torture."

"I am not fae."

Adam made a crude noise. "Oh, aye? Not of Mab's blood, are you? Forgive me if I spoke in error, and yet, here I am, a dog no longer."

"That is debatable," she grumbled.

"As to why she does this," he continued as if she hadn't spoken, "she is fae, ye ken?" Christ, his Scots hadn't emerged in a good five hundred years, but weakness and days without food or water had his tongue slipping. Adam swallowed hard and tried to focus. "You do understand what she is?"

Beneath his fingertips, her pulse beat faster. "Yes, but she saved me ... from you."

He snorted. "Do not start that up again." He'd go mad if he had to justify himself once more. When she gave a stiff nod, he went on. "Fae are friends to no one but themselves."

"She's my aunt. Why should I believe you over all the kindness she's shown me?" Oddly, her voice lacked heat. If he didn't know better, Adam would suspect she was merely trying to get a rise out of him. Bollox, her tactic worked. He wanted to shake some sense into her.

"I'm the one lying here broken." He let out a sharp breath. "She isn't your aunt; she's your grandmother and the fae queen." Eliza started to protest, and he spoke over her. "I have never lied to you, and I won't start now. It's true, and what's worse, if you stay here in her sphere, you'll soon be sorry for it."

"Why would I?"

"Because she'll find a way to use you for her own gain." With an odd twinge of regret, he let her go and then rubbed a tired hand over his face. "More than she already has."

"I don't understand how you came to be her prisoner. You are known—widely, I might add—as a great and powerful demon."

He took a bracing breath. "I'm not a demon." Adam caught her gaze and held it. "I'm a man, lass. I don't drink blood, nor use it to take on another's identity. All that's been said about me is a lie. Thought up and circulated by me as a means of protection. I'm cursed, ye ken? Cursed by Mab to remain immortal, heal when I am injured. I had uncommon strength, the power to create life, to take a soul unto me, or to destroy the life I create. Aside from that, the only skill I had was the fighting abilities I learned as a mortal man and my wits. What little there was left of them," he added with a wry smile.

His smile faded as he watched her. "I'm giving you this truth as a sign of goodwill, dove. No one on earth, save a few key fae, knows. Should the supernatural world gain this knowledge, this hell I'm in now would be what you Yanks call a cakewalk."

Her nose wrinkled. "Demons are said to be tricksters. How do I know if anything you say is true?"

He snorted. "First, I don't know where you've picked up this hate and distrust of demons, but you've been misinformed. They aren't all bad. Will Thorne, the man who helped set you free, was a demon."

She had the good grace to flush at that, though her chin remained set.

"Second," he added. "Had I these great powers anymore,

were I a demon capable of taking on another's form through blood, do you honestly believe that I'd be here?"

Eliza's stubborn frown grew, as if she didn't believe him. "That is my point exactly. So then, how—"

"Enough questions. I'll no' answer another. Just go before you're caught."

They glared at each other for a long moment.

"I'll go," she said finally.

"Saints preserve us, she does know how to obey."

"But I'm returning," she said, ignoring his quip and giving him a hard stare. "I want answers."

Adam gritted his teeth against the urge to shake some sense into her. "You want answers? Open your eyes and *see*, lass. Pay attention not only to what Mab says but what lies beneath her pretty words. Look for the signs. Promises she'll talk you into, pacts she'll suggest you enter, yet somehow make it seem as though it was your idea all along. Knowing the bitch as I do, Mab will have already found ways to use you for her own ends."

Something flickered in Eliza's deep, brown eyes. Fear? A realization? He didn't know. But he drove his point in. "If you have any care for your own skin, do not let Mab know you've seen me."

Chapter Two

Eliza had thought that, having lived in Boston, she knew city life. Watching the endless stream of cabs, carts, omnibuses, pedestrians, peddlers, beggars, and urchins from behind the window of Mab's well-appointed carriage, she realized she knew nothing. This was a true city, with its maze of avenues crisscrossing each other, buildings looming on either side in seemingly limitless supply. Coal soot and smoke had painted the buildings a dark, gloomy grey. That was, the small bits of buildings that weren't papered in advertisements. London was absolutely covered in billings and posters promising this and that. Only the boys who slapped them up with a quick brush of wet paste did so in a haphazard fashion, covering old adverts with impunity, so that one slogan bled into the other. One might read of "Mr. Solomon's hair tonic, guaranteed to be" "the finest dinner you shall ever serve your family!" Or of "Olly's ladies face cream" to promote "quick and lustrous hair growth."

London was ugly and foul and vibrant and beautiful all at once.

"What has you smiling, child?"

Mab's curious question had Eliza turning from the window and pushed her thoughts away from bearded ladies. Mab, her aunt and savior, sat opposite her. Mab who tortured men in her basement.

"London, I suppose." Stiff with doubt, Eliza gestured toward the grimy streets. "It's like nothing I've ever seen." As if to punctuate that fact, a man in lime green plaid velvet stomped down the street. On stilts.

Mab's pretty face wrinkled. "It's horrid. Too congested. One cannot properly breathe in this infernal place."

"Then why do you remain?" Eliza knew Mab had a home in the countryside. Several homes, apparently.

Her aunt's gaze slid away. "I've business here at the moment."

Eliza's fragile hold on levity crumbled. Did Mab mean Adam? Eliza did not want to picture him chained up, his body ravaged, his eyes filled with pain. He was there for a reason. Mab had shone her nothing but kindness, opening up a world of freedom and independence, while Adam had kept her prisoner for months without an ounce of remorse. Yet the itchy, ugly feeling within her remained.

He'd been tortured. Eliza hadn't the ability to justify that and live with herself. And she found herself studying Mab again. There was a soft, green glow about her that grew brighter when she was content. After Eliza had died, she had begun to see the glow surrounding persons.

"You glow," she found herself saying.

Mab's red brows lifted with amusement. "Pardon, dearest?"

Eliza flushed. "I see a greenish glow about you at times." Her aunt watched her in silence before answering.

"And out there"—she waved a slim hand towards the streets—"do you see anyone else glow?"

"Yes." Eliza did not need to look. "All the time. Greys, blues, reds, and yellows." Every color of the rainbow, actually. Everyone she encountered appeared to have a colorful glow about them. The hues changed, though some were similar. And it was enough to give Eliza a headache if she focused too hard on them. She'd learned, by sheer will, to let her gaze go soft or to focus on objects instead. It made it easier to bear.

Mab leaned in, resting her elbow upon her crossed leg. "You are seeing the light of a person's soul."

Eliza glanced at the window. Yes, she saw the light of souls. But that wasn't the only thing she saw. Spirits, wavering misty grey forms drifted here and there, moving through solid objects. Moving through people. Ghosts. She suppressed a shiver and turned back to Mab.

"I see spirits as well."

It was Mab's turn to shiver. Her gloved hands clenched. "Do you now?" Mab glanced about as if fearful there was one nearby.

"All the time. All over London." Truth be told, they were in greater numbers now. And always watching Eliza, as if pleading for her to hear them. Oddly, they did not frighten her. But they filled her with sorrow. Why did they linger when others did not? Where, for example, were the souls of her family? Did she even want to see them? No, she did not. It would be too painful when she could not truly have them in life.

"A word of caution, dear child," Mab said tightly, her creamy skin pale. "Do not engage the spirits. Fae are not meant to interact with the dead." Fear crept into Mab's eyes. All the more shocking because Mab never quailed.

"Do I see these things because I died before?" she asked Mab.

A moue of distaste marred Mab's cool beauty. "No. It is the demon's doing."

Eliza's shoulders hit the cushioned squabs. "He did this to me?"

"You are essentially GIM without the disgrace of a clockwork heart. No doubt, he thought to do you an honor." Mab's eyes darkened in disgust. "Or perhaps he figured that, as you were already chained to his side, he did not need to control you by means of your heart as well."

Eliza stared blindly down at her lap. Her hands, covered by the finest kidskin gloves money could buy, were clenched into fists. GIM, but not. She wondered if her spirit could leave her body as well, but did not want to try it. Horrible visions of being unable to get back into her flesh made her breath quicken. He'd made her as he was?

"He's never tried to find me," Eliza blurted out. Because Mab had been insistent that Adam would try. It was the sole reason Eliza was constantly watched by one of Mab's servants whenever they went out. Only now Eliza knew that to be a grand lie. How could he come for her when Mab already had him?

Across from her, Mab showed not the slightest hint of discomfort. She merely shrugged. "Demons are mercurial beings, pet. Best not to dwell on it." She gave Eliza a bright smile as she leaned in and squeezed Eliza's hands with just a bit too much force. "You have my word that he will never touch you again."

It was easy to bite her lip and nod, affecting the countenance of a girl much relieved and not a little frightened. Easy, Eliza thought, to lie.

"Come now," Mab said brightly. "Enough talk of distasteful things. We are here, and we shall have a lovely time at this party, meeting new people and eating sweet-meats, just as you wanted."

Eliza hadn't wanted to go to this garden party. All the tittering and social niceties made her head ache. It had been Mab's suggestion. Hadn't it? Frowning, she let herself be handed out of the carriage by a liveried footman and took a deep breath of smoky London air. Her bodice squeezed back in protest. Eliza smoothed a hand down her skirts, made of pure white silk foulard. The fabric cost more than most laborers made in a year.

"Eliza, dearest." Mab gave her a small smile, the gesture managing to look both welcoming and impatient. "Let us join the party." She turned, without waiting to see if Eliza followed, her grass-green skirts swaying as she made her way up the front stairs of the grand town home.

Follow Eliza did, she had little choice. Endless parties. New gowns. And Eliza falling deeper and deeper into Mab's debt. Was that what Mab wanted? For Eliza to be beholden to her. Well, she already was, now wasn't she?

It was difficult to stand idle when everything inside of her screamed to turn and run, to get away from Mab, from London even.

Damn the demon, he had put this suspicion and fear into her. Her agitation did not improve as they made their way through the fine London townhouse and into the garden, a lovely English garden with meticulously trimmed hedges and beds of newly blooming flowers marching in orderly rows.

Around her, women swarmed and converged into little groups to chatter. Mab loved this, the attention, the laughter and adulation. Eliza had long since noticed that Mab seemed to soak these things in as a flower might the sun.

Oddly, when it was all done, Mab would return home and indulge in her more private proclivities. It was as if these social outings gave her the energy to fuel her hidden cruelties.

Run away. That is what Adam had advised. Eliza did not want to believe Adam. Not truly. And yet she felt ashamed. She knew precisely why she stayed with Mab. Until this moment, her entire life had been composed of "have nots," forced to live on meager sums, clothes that needed constant reworking, winter nights that left her shivering because coal supplies had to last for months, until, finally, she'd been too poor to feed herself and she'd done unforgivable things. Deep inside of Eliza, there was a hateful, shameful lust for luxury.

From an early age, she'd coveted fine things. Sparkling jewels, silky textiles, luscious foods, costly items that she could never hope to possess, all called to her. Mam had called her a magpie. She used the moniker with affection. But Grandda Evernight had always frowned upon her roving eye. Only once had she heard him mutter that Eliza was too much like her grandmother. As she'd never met the woman, Eliza couldn't feel offended on her behalf, but it stung nevertheless. It made her feel wrong and unsettled.

Was Mab truly her grandmother? And the fae queen to boot? Eliza snorted softly to herself as she walked along the shadowed path, the air fragrant with the scent of loam and sunshine. It all seemed so normal here. When her life had become anything but. Fairies, demons, men who could raise the dead, and men who could turn to shadows. Tales, if told around normal folk, that would have her packed up and sent to Bedlam. And yet she'd seen it all with her own two eyes.

As she drifted past the gentlemen's beverage table,

laden with all the tempting drinks deemed too strong for weak women, Eliza plucked up a glass of champagne and drank it down, letting the cool, tartness of it sooth her parched throat, not caring if anyone saw her do it.

"Swallowing nearly an entire glass of champagne?" said a male voice at her side. "I'm shocked."

Eliza knew that voice and found herself smiling. St. John Evernight returned it. "And in public, no less." He glanced around, taking in the crowd, all dressed in their finest as they ate their picnic food off of china plates and used silver to cut their fruit. "What will these crows think?"

"Perhaps they'll banish me from ever attending another function," Eliza said hopefully. And then she touched his arm. "It is good to see you again, Sin. It's been too long." Months, in fact.

When he'd first introduced himself to her, he'd called himself "Sinjin." Or that's what she'd heard him say, yet most of their acquaintances called him Sin. Later he'd explained that the English pronounced the name St. John as Sinjin. Thus, his friends and family called him Sin. An apt nickname, for he was constantly seeking out some form of mischief.

"English society is a bore," Sin answered now. "If it were up to me, I'd be rid of it completely."

"I'd hardly call the fast crowd that runs with Mab proper society." Eliza thought of the disturbing dinner Mab has hosted last night. "In truth, I'm fairly certain you could do anything in her house and she'd not turn a hair."

At her snide tone, Sin's green gaze searched her face. "What troubles you, cousin?"

In a distant way, they were cousins, his grandmother being first cousin to her grandfather. Only she'd grown up in Boston, and he in Ireland.

She edged closer, hesitation warring with a need to confide in the only person she trusted. "I saw *him*."

Sin, along with Will Thorne, had been the one to rescue Eliza from Adam. Instantly Sin's nostrils flared. "Did he come after you?" He looked around the sunny garden as if expecting Adam to jump from the hedgerow and attack.

"No, nothing like that," she assured. "He cannot harm me. He's injured. In fact he's—"

"Stop," insisted Sin. "Don't say another word." Sin's skin took on a pasty hue. "Not until I explain one thing." On unsteady feet, he came closer. "I'm bound, by a vow, to tell Mab if there is a danger of you consorting with Adam."

"What?" Eliza's voice rose too high, she knew. A few heads turned, censorious frowns shooting her way. Sin hissed his displeasure, and Eliza struggled to temper her tone. "Why? And what do you mean you 'vowed'?"

But Sin merely shook his head. "If you do not want her to know, do not tell me."

Eliza frowned. If she wanted Mab to know she'd found Adam, Eliza would have gone directly to her and asked why he was chained and tortured. But Eliza hadn't said a word. For the first time, she looked upon Sin anew, taking note of the agonized guilt that shadowed his eyes. Perhaps he'd finally let her see it.

Her insides turned. "Sin," she said carefully, "ought I have a reason to hide things from Mab?"

He grimaced, a mere twitch of his lips, before pasting a pleasant, carefree expression upon his face. He picked up a glass of champagne and made a show of taking a sip. "At this moment," he answered as though speaking of the weather, "I've no reason to believe Mab would cause you harm."

That did not mean she wouldn't, Eliza realized with

a racing heart. Inside of her silk gloves, her hands grew cold and damp. The urge to shout and cry nearly bubbled over. "Why," she managed, "did you not tell me?"

He glanced away, his throat working. "I could not." His pained expression returned to her. "I have watched over you as best I could."

The sun came out, a rare occurrence for London, its rays a harsh yellow light, and Eliza blinked away a hazy blur of frustration and hurt. "I'd have preferred the truth."

"I know," he said softly. "I can only strongly suggest that you never agree to a blood vow with anyone you do not implicitly trust."

She made a pretense of putting on a pleasant face, but still she did not look at him. "I don't even know what that is."

"You must learn our world, Eliza," Sin murmured. "We are not like humans."

When she looked up swiftly, he gave her a false smile even as his tone remained serious. "You are more than half fae, even if you've yet to believe it. Which means you can be bound by a blood vow. I am an elemental. Thus, I too can be bound." Sorrow lined his handsome features. "Once bound, your vow is irrevocable, no matter how much you regret it."

Eliza took a step away from him. "I think I'll take a turn around the garden." Her voice was wooden.

He frowned. But then nodded. "I understand," Sin whispered. "I do."

"No," she ground out. "I don't think you understand at all."

Loneliness smothered her as she walked along an abandoned garden path. She'd thought Sin would be her one ally in this strange new world. She thought she could trust him. Enough. She was becoming downright maudlin. "Pity is for the weak," she whispered. Especially if that pity was applied to one's self.

"Yes, Eliza, it is." The familiar masculine voice sent a shard of terror through her middle.

Eliza whipped around, her voice lost in shock. From out of the shadows, a figure slipped. And her dread increased, her insides threatening to heave. The man was of a towering height, his hair pale blond, and his eyes a deep, endless brown. Those eyes had once smiled at her, promising her the world. And she'd believe in them, just as gullible as the endless young men who laid upon Mab's table like offerings.

Through dry lips, she found her voice, weak as it was. "Mellan."

Mellan Marbury. Leader of the Black Death gang in Boston. Now her personal nightmare. She almost let out a laugh. And here she'd thought her demon captor was a bastard. She'd clearly forgotten what true bastards were.

His gaze, cold as ever, raked over her, lingering on her breasts, and his thin mouth curled. It was not a look of lust or even appreciation but of ownership, as though he believed he was entitled to do anything to her. Eliza did not flinch, even as her mind screamed at her to run. Gods almighty, she'd faked a death, traveled across an ocean, and he'd found her.

Mellan tilted his head, the angle extreme, calling to mind a crow about to peck at its prey. "You do not seem happy to see me, pet."

She knew that tone. A fist would be accompanying his words soon enough. Eliza found she didn't damn well care. "For once, you've correctly assessed my feelings, Mellan. Is it too much to hope that you'll also turn heel and leave this instant?"

His slow chuckle was nails against glass. "I have so missed your sense of humor, Eliza."

"I have no sense of humor where you are concerned."

His patience vanished like smoke, and he took a hard step closer. "Your constant sassing wears thin." His teeth showed with an ugly grin. "Here on in, I'll be taking my pound of flesh for each snide remark."

"I expected nothing less," she snapped back as though her insides weren't churning. "Only I do believe our acquaintance has come to an end."

"Is that what you believe?" He chuckled. "Dear girl, you know so little. It's pitiful, really."

They glared at each other, laughter and the gentle murmur of conversation drifting over the garden, when the light scuff of a shoe sounded.

"Ah, Eliza," said Mab—her savior. Mab's doll-like face plumped with a smile as she looked toward Mellan. "I see that you've found Mellan. Excellent."

Eliza's heart nearly stopped as she gaped at her aunt. "You...you know this man?"

Mab cocked her head, exactly as Mellan had done. "Know him? Why, my dear girl, he's my brother. And your kin."

The bottom dropped out of Eliza's stomach. As if Mab hadn't just voiced something utterly horrible, her expression grew beatific, and she gave Mellan a pleased nod. "I believe he's been most desperate to see you."

For an endless moment, Eliza simply stood, her hand pressed tight to her middle, her mouth open and silent. "I...How..." Her breath hitched, and her hand curled into a fist. "Aunt, you do not understand—"

Mab's little nostrils flared in irritation. "I assure you, child, I understand perfectly well. Mellan has kept me apprised of the situation, and shame on you for running from him. That is not the mark of honor." Her eyes were hard and unyielding. "I realize that you yearn, as all fae do, to be independent. But a child of my bloodline has certain duties, and certain customs must be respected. Make no mistake, Mellan shall be your husband."

"You've healed nicely."

Adam refused to react to the sly finger that slid along his chained arm and lingered along his collarbone. The very bone the bitch had broken in three places last night. Mab hummed, a pleased sound, as her touch moved to his nipple, and Adam ground his back teeth together. Given the choice between enduring her touch or meeting her gaze, Adam picked the latter.

Her beauty was flawless, an elegant rose in perfect bloom. And beneath it, foul rot. She smiled at him, her plump lips revealing black fangs. She liked to bite him with those fangs. Hard, deep bites in his most sensitive places. Bitch.

"Such hate in your eyes, Adam." Mab sat back on her heels and tutted. "When your freedom could be gained by simply loving me."

Unable to hold it back, he snorted with disdain. "Love? Is that what all this is about? Your undying need to be adored by those who refuse you?" He would be ill. He imagined splattering her fine satin dress with his vomit. An entertaining image, that. But Adam would not give her the satisfaction of seeing the depths of his feeling.

Mab stood, her small nostrils flaring. "Always so very proud, Aodh. To your downfall." With the tip of her boot, she forced his chin up. Her eyes held the satisfaction of victory. "One day, you shall gladly kiss these boots."

He ought to remain silent. If anyone knew how maddening silence could be, it was Adam. Eliza had given him a hard dose of that particular treatment for months. It had nearly driven him to madness. Often times, he'd pictured himself tearing apart a room, rage and hopelessness over her refusal to engage with him pushing him to the edge. Yes, Mab would detest a mutinous silence.

Unfortunately, Adam detested holding his tongue with equal measure. He simply could not do it. Which is why he found himself affecting a pleading voice, strongly laced with acidic sarcasm. "Oh, Mab, please spare me another round of torture. I cannot possibly stand another moment."

Her lips pursed as she glared down at him. "You think you're so cheeky. We'll see who's laughing when I finish flaying your skin."

One of her favorite methods. Bile surged upward. "If memory serves," he said as though his throat wasn't burning, "that would be you."

After all, the bitch had cut his tongue out during that particular session so he hadn't been able to join in. And while Adam would rather not think on that time, or experience it again, he'd be damned if he'd let that show.

Her eyes narrowed, their color flashing from human brown to a fae's pansy purple. "I clearly need to be more creative with my tricks."

He simply stared back, tired of her games, tired of everything.

"Silence, is it?" she intoned brightly. "No pithy replies?"

"Perhaps you ought to tell me what I should say." He shrugged his aching shoulders. "Write a script for me to read."

The smack across his face was so quick and hard that his head rattled against the wall. It took all his control not to snarl at her, to try to rip free from his bonds. A useless endeavor at any rate. And she watched him, her eyes alight, as if waiting to devour his anger. Her rapt expression crystallized to icy disdain when he did nothing.

"What do you want of me?" he asked. "Truly? Are you not tired of this game you play?"

Her little fangs flashed, black and needle sharp. "To beg."

He sighed, letting his head rest against his arm. "I will no'. Best you kill me now, fae."

For a clean, bright moment, he thought she might, as her arm raised and black claws sprung from the tips of her fingers. One good and true swipe and his head would topple. Some wounds even an enchanted man did not come back from. But she collected her wits and took a visible breath.

"Too easy, Aodh. By far." Mab's lips lifted in a cruel smile. "There is another way to earn your freedom." Her tone and the bitter twist of her lips spoke of reluctance. "Return what you stole from my people."

Ah, yes, Adam's stolen artifacts. It always came back to that. When he'd been a knight, charged with collecting heathen artifacts for the Church, he certainly did not view his quest as theft. Now, he simply had no desire to give Mab what she wanted. He smiled, with teeth. "I did not offer them up when you first threatened to curse me. What makes you believe I shall now?"

Her red curls bounced as she shook her head. "Why would you not? You prefer to live this way? Prefer being a dog on a leash?"

Adam merely raised a brow and stared back at her.

Mab sniffed. "Fine. Have it your way. This shall hurt you far worse than it hurts me."

The bitch actually believed she was amusing.

Smiling, Mab strolled across the cellar and picked up a hammer. Adam eyed the thing, sick dread spreading through his gut.

"Tell me"—she hefted the hammer's weight, testing it with a light smack against her palm—"where is the Horn an Bás?"

Surprise hit Adam. The Golden Horn an Bás, the horn of death. It was said that to hear its notes was to be instantly struck down. No being of this earth or of the fae could fight its power. Death to immortals.

Adam nearly laughed. He bloody well wouldn't be hanging like a side of beef on a hook if he had the horn. But it wouldn't go well for him at all were he to admit that. Then again, it wouldn't go well for him either way, so he was bolloxed.

Best to irritate the bitch and let her vent her frustration until she tired. So Adam grinned with teeth. *"Nuair a thiocas an bás ní imeoidh sé folamh." When death comes he won't leave empty.* The Irish had used that proverb in regard to him at one time. He'd relished it. Now, he gloried in the frustration and rage gathering over Mab's too pretty countenance.

"Lest you want *an bás* to come for you now," Mab said lightly, "you'll tell me where it is."

"Best you go fuck a goat."

And that ended the conversation. Mab's narrow boot heel stomped down upon his gut. Absently, Adam watched the crescent-shaped bruise bloom, growing darker as blood seeped below the surface of his skin. Adam did not know where the horn was. But that triviality was not going to stop him. If the fae wanted it that badly, he was going to get it. Somehow.

Chapter Three

Eliza had returned. Adam could scent her drawing closer, feel her vibrancy light up the pitiless grave they'd left him in. He kept his eyes closed and remained still, barely daring to breathe. It hurt to breathe at any rate. Perhaps she'd see him sleeping and leave. It would be better that way.

The rustle of her skirts and the scent of luscious pears surrounded him, his senses stronger now as he was a dog. The ruff along the back of his neck lifted, his skin prickling beneath the fur. The urge grew worse as she knelt down next to him and the silk of her gown settled over his hind quarters.

"Lord above but you look worse for wear." A soft, tender hand settled upon his hip bone, and he whimpered. Damn dog reaction.

A massive shiver scattered agonized shards of pain throughout him as he dissolved and then reformed as a man. It took a moment for his vision to clear, to focus in on the perfect oval of her face. Concern pulled the gentle arches of her brows together, and the pink curves of her lips puckered into a small pout. He wanted to lick, suck, and bite those lips, feast on them as if they were sweetmeats. He also wanted to shove her bodily out of his cell and out of his sight.

He settled for remaining as he was, sprawled upon the ground, his arms wrenched high overhead by the chains that bound him. Her hand had not strayed from his hip, and while it was one thing for her to touch him there when he was a dog, it was quite another to feel her palm resting upon his bare skin. The muscles along his lower abdomen tensed, a sweet-sharp pain. With a lazy air he knew would irritate her, he glanced down at her hand.

"Planning on moving that hand lower, sweets?" He allowed himself a leering grin. "There is one part of me uninjured. Yet I can assure you it aches all the same."

As expected, she snatched her hand away. He ought to rejoice but missed the touch too much.

She let out a little huff. "You really are the most mercurial demon—"

"Mercurial?" He laughed and immediately regretted it when his body seized in protest and the open wounds that crisscrossed his chest began to weep blood. "Dear girl, my temperament is as steady as they come."

She snorted but her gaze strayed to his chest, and that beguiling pucker returned to her mouth. "When we first met, you acted the insouciant ass. Then you changed, becoming a brooding, snarling, cold, unfeeling—"

"You've made your point," he cut in. "And if my mood was less than appealing, it had all to do with the dour, silent weight attached to me." She had driven him half mad with her silence. Had she expected him to be happy about it?

Her pretty cheeks darkened. "It's a good thing I left you then. You are *far* more pleasant now."

"Sarcasm, Miss May, is not the mark of a lady." He rather loved her unladylike barbs, but wasn't about to confess it now. When storm clouds gathered in her eyes, he spoke again. "Why are you here? Pleasant a distraction though you may be, you appear far better dressed for a party."

She was utterly lovely in her bronze satin gown that both hugged her curves and offered them up for one's delectation, a hothouse lily both delicate and luscious. Tiny garnets glittered in her hair and at her throat, bringing out the velvet-brown color of her eyes. Eyes that were focused on his chest. Her fingers twitched over the folds of her skirts. And while Adam would like to think that her attention was due to pure feminine appreciation of his male form, he knew better. She could not stand to see a being in physical pain.

"The party has yet to begin." Still eyeing his wounds, she rose and went for the leather doctoring satchel she'd brought before. "And I wanted to visit you."

"Oh."

Eliza May did something he thought he'd never witness: She laughed. It was a husky sound, full and round and wonderful. Her eyes crinkled, going triangular in shape with her mirth.

"I never thought I'd see the day," she said, still grinning, "that the great and fearsome Adam of the GIM was reduced to a single exclamation."

He wanted to scowl, but could not. Not when humor lightened her fine features. It did not help that her gaze slid down his unclothed length, and his cock began to take notice. He did not mind her seeing him naked. Not that there was much to boast of at the moment. He'd had better days. But her stare was altogether too probing for his comfort. And he rather thought now was not the time for his roger to be waving about and begging for attention.

"Keep staring," he told her, "and I'll assume you like what you see."

Slowly, she stirred as if waking from a dream and met him head-on.

"I don't."

Adam blinked. Right then, the lass certainly wasn't one for false praise. A scowl drew at his mouth despite the fact that he bloody well didn't care what she thought. "You don't." He managed to fit a world of skepticism into those two words.

And her rosebud of a mouth twitched. "So certain of your charms."

He wasn't. "I am."

Eliza shook her head, a patronizing gesture if ever he saw one. But her answer was not. "It seems wrong." Her voice was soft then, thoughtful, and it held all of his attention.

"Wrong?"

"Yes. That I should see you unclothed this way."

The tight unease in his belly grew. Shame. He felt ashamed. And he hated it. "Lass, it does not bother me in the least if you see me without clothes."

That earned him a ghost of a smile. "I'm certain it doesn't. But it still feels wrong. It'd be one thing if you undressed for me." Adam studiously ignored the heat elicited by that image as she went on. "If you'd done that, I could feel free to be annoyed or disgusted."

Oh, well, don't hold back, lass. His glare grew in

strength. Not that she noticed. Her bloody, pitying look remained.

"It isn't your choice to expose yourself. Thus I cannot view your body with anything other than a sense of unfairness and anger that Mab should treat you in this manner."

He couldn't say a damned thing to that. In truth, he couldn't even look at her. He wanted her out of his sight. He wanted to be out of hers. Desperately. A first, and it did not feel like a victory.

"Tell me why you're here, dove." Then perhaps she'd go and leave him in peace.

"Why did you treat me as you did?" Her voice was calm, quiet, and yet it rang like a shout between them. He ought to have expected the question, but it surprised him all the same.

Adam braced himself against flinching. Inside, however, an uncomfortable feeling coiled like a knot. All those months he'd held her captive, he hadn't wanted to tell her the truth. The utter rot of it was that he'd been embarrassed and afraid. Afraid that she'd laugh in his face, embarrassed that he needed her, based on nothing more than a bloody curse. A man ought to have a choice over who his life mate should be.

But he couldn't say all that now. Not with Miss Eliza May staring a hole through his skull. Flushed, he cleared his throat. "As I said before, I was cursed."

One delicate golden brow lifted. An annoying prompt to continue. He scowled. "I'd lose possession of my freedom if I did not find my soul's other half in the allotted time frame."

Her silence was smothering, making it harder for him to get the words out. "I had a saving grace, however. It was prophesied that my soul's mate would be one who died before her time yet stubbornly clung to life, and that I'd know her upon sight." He shifted his arms, trying and failing to alleviate the ache in them. "The light of her soul would match mine."

For a moment, she simply stared. Her voice, when she spoke, was crisp as burnt toast. "And you can see the light of souls."

Before he'd been stripped of his powers, yes. Adam merely gave a curt nod. Eliza's eyes narrowed, her sweet mouth turning down at the corners. But she said nothing, forcing him to finish his confession. "It is why I created the GIM, you see. In return for their immortality, they had to bring me stubborn souls who refused to die."

"So you were searching all this time for—"

"You." He met her eyes. "Your light is an exact match to mine."

With those words, Eliza cocked her head as if he were a particularly odd object she'd happened across. And never had he wanted to rage and snarl as much as then. It wasn't as though he wanted to need her. Or that he loved her. Hell, he barely liked her.

He opened his mouth, the temptation to say all that and more too great to resist, when she spoke over him. "And you think we are soul mates?" A sharp, half laugh cracked through the air. "Are you mad?"

"Madam," he ground out, "you cannot begin to fathom how much I wish I were."

"Oh, I believe I have some idea," she said, rising with a rustle of petticoats. "Let me see if I have this correctly. You believe me to be your soul's mate, and, as a result, your first course of action was to put me in chains and force me to be by your side henceforth."

When put that way... Adam stared back, unspeaking.

And Eliza made an unladylike snort. "Well, isn't that simply brilliant thinking on your part." She paced before him, her skirts snapping around her legs with each brisk stride. "Certainly, the best way to court a woman is to keep her prisoner."

"I wasn't trying to court you. I was trying to secure you."

At his mulish retort, she halted and spun round to face him. High color stained her cheeks. "Secure me?"

Hot, uncomfortable regret made it hard to answer. "I was not thinking clearly."

"Obviously."

He shot her a look. "I only knew that, after hundreds of years, I'd found you. I wasn't going to risk losing you."

With a huff, Eliza leaned against the cell wall and crossed her arms over her chest. She looked him over with the cool detachment he'd become accustomed to. "One would think," she said after a moment, "that I'd know it if you were my soul's mate." Her nose wrinkled. "A ridiculous notion, at any rate."

He concurred. However... "And yet when you ran away, Mab took claim of me because you had rejected our bond."

Her mouth fell open, her eyes going wide as tea saucers. "Bond. Is that what... you blame me?" Again she laughed. "Good Lord above. You needed my acceptance, and yet you treated me like a slave. You *are* mad."

And what could he say? Those had not been his finest hours, driven by a sort of madness that had sound logic fleeing in the face of a base, nearly animalistic need to claim what was his.

From the moment she'd opened the cellar door, Eliza knew it was a mistake to visit Adam. Nothing in his behavior proved her wrong. Yet she found herself unable to leave him now. Not when he lay prone and bloody, needing aid, even though she knew he'd never admit to it. Now that he'd confessed, her head was reeling. Soul mates? Impossible. Ridiculous.

"I don't believe in soul mates." She hadn't meant to speak, but, then again, it was best to tell him straight out.

"Neither do I," he shouted, his swift ire shocking her into silence, as he glared a hole through her head.

"Then why—"

"Because I saw your light." He bared his teeth when he growled out the words, reminding her of a wounded animal. "I took one bloody look at you and began to feel again. Do you understand what it means to feel nothing that is good or real?"

She did. She'd felt it for a mere twenty minutes when she'd first died. To live that way for centuries was an endurance she did not want to contemplate. But he wasn't finished with her. His tendons stuck out like thick ropes as he strained towards her. "I was bloody desperate, you ken? I was promised my suffering would ease upon finding this elusive soul mate, and lo' you arrive with your bloody golden glow, making me bloody feel again. So, aye, I'll play the fool. I'll believe whatever I damn well have to, if that's what it takes to find some measure of peace."

Well then. Eliza licked her dry lips. "All right. Neither of us believes in this farce—"

"Oh, I believe in it," he cut in, rather snidely. "I simply don't like it. Do you suppose I fancy being beholden to a woman who loathes me?"

"For good reason."

He rested his head against the grimy wall and sighed. "Fair enough. Now, what do you want?"

Biding her time, Eliza soaked a length of linen with cool witch hazel. Under the slashes of his brows, Adam's deep-set eyes narrowed, and a low growl of protest rumbled in his throat as she came near.

"I...don't..." His ruined pectorals twitched. "Need help."

Gently, she lowered the cloth onto his chest. His body tensed, ropy muscles bulging in response, and then he let go with a sharp breath. His tension eased on a sigh. "Better," he rasped.

Eliza prepared another cloth and assessed how she could best help him. Two separate lengths of chains, each attached to heavy cuffs around Adam's wrists, held him fast. Secured to a set of rings driven into the stone cell wall, the chains had been pulled tight and forced his arms up over his head so that he was stretched out and barely able to move.

"Lean forward, if you can, and let me see to the rest."

With a muffled grunt, he complied, tilting his big body towards her. She was able to reach around his neck and drape the cloth along his shredded shoulders. So set was she upon her task that she did not consider how close she'd brought herself to the man. Not until the heat of his breath ghosted along her neck.

Every hair upon her body stood on end, and she froze, aware of her own breath and of the way her breasts brushed against his chest. She dared not turn to meet his gaze. It did not matter. Awareness lit between them. Of his cheek and hers mere inches apart. Of his scent, that delicious amber and myrrh scent. It had her eyes fluttering, wanting to close if only to heighten her sense of smell. He made a small, strangled sound, barely audible, and yet it struck the core of her.

Get away. Get away now! But she could not.

Unwanted and uninvited heat coalesced between her legs and spread outward, up her torso and down her thighs. Her eyes closed then, as she held herself very still for fear of leaning closer and pressing her now heavy breasts against him. And it disgusted her. She could not be attracted to this man. Not him. Anyone but him.

The sound of his indrawn breath and the feel of his lips brushing her neck had her eyes snapping open. Her body tensed further.

"Are you..."—she swallowed past a wave of heat— "smelling me?"

He was silent for a moment. "Aye." Defiance shaped his tone, and then it went husky as he inhaled again. "Aye, dove. I cannot resist. Your sweetness is a ray of sunshine in this hell."

Craning his neck forward, he drew in another deep breath, and a low, rumbling groan escaped him. "Gods, but I could drown in the scent of you and not be sorry for it."

The realization that she'd nearly arched her neck to give him better access finally snapped her out of her heated fog. Eliza reared back. And Adam regarded her through lowered lids, not at all repentant, but as if daring her to come back to him.

"That is enough," she said, wishing the words came out steady and firm. "I'm not here to—"

"Get me off?" he supplied lightly, a wicked gleam entering his pale amber eyes.

She gritted her teeth. "Yes, that."

He mocked a shrug but then winced. "Fair enough, sweeting. But as you continue to ease my pain, while ignoring the place I need soothing most, I cannot help thinking you mean to tease me." His hips shifted the slightest bit.

The urge to slap him was high, but Eliza sank into herself where it was calm and nothing could affect her. She'd learned that from him. Nothing like being chained to a man to teach a woman about self-preservation. When she spoke, her voice was a shard of ice. "You're trying to drive me off, aren't you?"

He seemed to flinch in surprise before sagging a bit. "Yes." Mulishly, his gaze slid away before returning with renewed defiance. "Though I did not lie. Your scent is an addiction. I want more of it."

No, she would not react. "And yet you want me to leave."

At this, he let out an exasperated snort. "Gods, woman, can you no' get it through your head? If they find you with me, you'll be in a world of trouble. As will I." His outstretched arms tensed as though he was straining to break free. "What I cannot understand is why you keep returning. Is it amusing you to see me this way?"

"What? No."

"Have you a death wish then?"

"No." Her hands fisted her skirts. "I—"

"What?" he snapped when she hesitated. "Out with it, girl."

"Do not bark at me! Nor am I a girl."

Adam paused his attack.

For a long moment, they simply glared at each other. And then the wind went out of Eliza's sails. "I cannot live amongst these people and keep my sanity."

"That's the first reasonable thing you've said yet."

She found herself fighting a smile. "Surely not the very first."

He clearly fought one as well. "I'll concede. You've said a few more."

Eliza laughed, short and soft. Then she looked away, a sudden burning in her eyes making her fear she'd soon weep. And she abhorred weeping. "There is a man. He... his..." Hell, she hated to even say the bastard's name. "His name is Mellan."

Adam's swift intake of breath had her turning back to him. He'd gone bone white, his lips peeled back in a macabre sneer. His eyes hid nothing, not to her at least.

"You know this man, don't you." It wasn't a question. Not when he wore that look.

"Yes." Adam's sneer turned to a snarl. "He's a right, ruddy bastard. The question is, how do you know him, lass?"

Her icy fingers clenched. "I knew him in Boston. I— my grandfather Aiden died. I didn't have a dime..." She trailed off, disgust and hot humiliation writhing within. "Ah, well, you know such tales, I suppose. I needed safety and security."

"And you sold yourself. To him." Adam's words whipped like a lash.

Eliza glared at him. "He pretended to care, wanted to be my protector. I was naive and foolish." It was a sad testament that she'd rather Adam believe she'd sold her body than confess the reality of what Mellan had her do. There were worse things than being a whore. "Before I knew it, he claimed that he owned me." Eliza pinned Adam with a stare. "Sound familiar?"

The man had the grace to flush. He grumbled a bit but said no more.

"I ran from Boston to get away from him. And now he's found me." Bile burned up her throat as she thought of it. "Worse, Mab claims he's her brother, and that I am to marry him." The very idea that she'd marry her uncle... Good God, that Mellan *was* her uncle, made her ill.

Adam had grown utterly still, his golden eyes roaming her face as though he saw everything all too well. "Mab is your grandmother," he pointed out softly. "Which makes him your granduncle."

"Oh, well that makes it much better, thank you," she choked out.

His big body sagged. "What have I to do with all of this? Tell me."

She drew in a bracing breath, regrettably, since the room was foul. "I'm leaving. And I'm taking you with me."

His response was not what she'd expected. Rearing back until his thick head hit the wall, he scowled fiercely. "No."

"What do you mean 'no'?"

An imperious black brow rose. "Need I give you a definition of the word?"

Eliza sat back on her heals, a huff of shock leaving her lips. "Why on earth are you fighting me on this?"

His narrowed gaze slid away. "There are some things a man cannot outrun. Nor a woman. They will hunt you down, and believe me, they will make you hurt for your desertion."

"Which is why I need your help." *Thick-headed demon.*

"Have you had a good look at me, lass?" His shoulders bunched, all those sinewy muscles of his chest tightening as one lovely landscape of repressed strength. "I'm not the knight in shining armor you need."

"No, but you are the only one available."

Eliza pressed her sweaty palms onto her thighs. Even so, it took her a full minute to find her voice, one in which he stared her down as if waiting for the obvious. "Will you help me?"

A lock of black hair fell over his brow as he gave a pointed look towards his shackled wrists. "A bit hung up at the moment, dove."

"You are hilarious," she deadpanned. "Really, you ought to consider vaudeville." She leaned in, coming closer to him than she'd like, but it certainly caught his attention. His gaze darted over her face as she spoke. "You know Mab's ways, how she thinks. And you know London's underworld. Help me and I will set you free. Don't, and remain here as her plaything."

His eyes narrowed, his lips compressing. "If I am to help you," he said after a long, pained moment, "then I want something in return."

Of course he did, calculating demon. Because she still feared he was a demon.

"I should think my freeing you is enough."

Golden eyes, full of irritation and dry humor, pinned her. "Freeing me benefits you, as I cannot provide assistance otherwise."

Annoying man. Eliza crossed her arms over her chest. "I could find someone else to help me."

"Go ahead then," Adam said with a shrug. "And good luck to you on your search." With that, he closed his eyes and said no more.

Silence stretched between them.

"You aren't moving," Adam observed, his eyes still closed.

Blasted, no good rat...

"What is it you want?" she asked.

His eyes snapped open, his gaze spearing her with its intensity. "I want another bargain with you."

"You cannot possibly believe I'd be so stupid as to make another pact with you."

"This one you'll make fully informed." The corner of his eyes crinkled with the devil's humor. "I'll even give you more than ten seconds to decide."

"Oh, really?" she drawled, not wanting to smile.

"Mmm..." The sound came out like a deep purr. She imagined a lion doing much the same. Before he pounced. "A full minute."

It was tempting. Too tempting, to ask him what he wanted. Curiosity had always been her downfall. Hers was rampant. "State your terms, demon."

"'Adam'," he corrected firmly. "You call me Adam or—"

"My Lord and Master, My Irresistible Liege?" she offered, tossing the words he'd once said back at him.

Against the sooty grime on his face, his teeth flashed white and strong. "You remember, dove."

He was doing it again, using his charm to distract her.

"Adam," she warned.

Her use of his name seemed to please him for heat entered his eyes, and he suddenly seemed closer. "I want you."

Eliza rather feared she had made a horrible gurgle of shock. "'Me.' But why? Do you..." She blanched. "Fancy me?"

Abruptly he snorted. "No, not particularly, though you're pretty enough."

"Do not strain yourself with praise, sir."

"You want sweet words now?" His thick lashes cast shadows on his cheek as he blinked up at her, the picture of innocent confusion. "When here I thought honesty was what you admired."

"If you don't have feelings for me," she ground out, "then why do you want me? Just look at us, constantly at each other's throats like baited bears."

"I want the possibility of you," he said softly.

Eliza's mouth fell open. But he simply held her gaze, his expression, for once, perfectly serious.

"My curse is irreversible. I will never know peace unless I am accepted by my soul's mate. By you, as it happens."

A heavy mix of guilt and something close to sorrow filled her chest. "It might be trickery, you know. Mab might have led you to believe that I was your soul mate."

"Then why was she desperate to get you away from me?"

"Because I'm her kin?"

The chains rattled when he shook his head. "Believe what you will. Doesn't matter." His chin lifted in that stubborn way of his, that months of watching told her she'd never persuade him otherwise. He confirmed it when he spoke again. "I want my peace, Eliza. To feel whole, happy, free. That is all I've ever wanted. Seven hundred years, I've searched for it. And if there is even the slightest possibility that you can give it to me, then I am willing to risk everything to get it."

Horribly, tears prickled at the back of her throat. She cleared it. "That is a terrible burden to place on a person. What if I cannot come to…"—she faltered, unable to even say the word *love*—"to accept you?"

His hard expression did not alter. "Then you don't. It won't work unless your affection is freely given, regardless."

"And what of your affections? You expect me to come to care for you while you outright dislike me?"

The corner of his lush mouth curled. "What I am asking for is a chance. I help you and you stay with me during that time. A clean slate, no more viewing me through the lens of the past. And I shall do the same with you. We start anew. Partners in this quest."

"How long?" Knowing his sly ways, he might drag out this "quest" endlessly.

He grinned again, as if he knew precisely what she was thinking. "One month."

"A week."

"Not enough time. I have to heal to be of any use. One month."

"That number was already deemed unacceptable. Two weeks."

"Three."

Eliza sat back on her heels, while Adam merely stared at her as though he had all the time in the world. "Fine," she said. "Three weeks. I free you and you help me." She gave him a warning look. "I'll need your word that you will help me, that this"—she waved her hand between them—"isn't merely a way to trick me into freeing you."

"This business was your idea, woman," he said with affront.

"Nevertheless, I'll need your word."

His nostrils flared with a sharp exhalation. "My word then." Eliza did not look away from him, and he glared back in obvious exasperation. "What now?"

"I'm merely considering if I ought to trust your word," she said.

A low growl rumbled in his chest as he bared his teeth. "I keep my word, whether I want to or not. My word is my bond. Honor, Miss May. Unlike you, I have it."

"How dare you—"

"How dare you?" He craned forward, the muscles along his shoulders bunching. "Not so long ago you broke your promise of fealty. To me!"

"Oh yes, how quick you are to remind me." Eliza leaned close, grinding her teeth to keep in a shout. "You enjoy being quick, don't you?"

His thick, dark brows furrowed. "What in the bloody blazes are you talking about?"

"You gave me all of ten seconds to make a choice." Eliza's fists ached from clenching them. "And what a choice. I was dead, my body sliced open, my blood on the ground. I would have done anything, *anything*"—she thumped her fist to her chest—"to get back my life."

"So that makes it better?" he snapped back in outrage. "Desperation gives you leave to go back on your word?"

"No. That is not what I meant."

"Then you agree that you bloody well have no honor—"

"You never explained what was involved. You never said I'd be chained to you, like some animal, for the rest of my days," Eliza shouted. "I was told I would be a GIM. I was ready to serve you in that manner. You knew full well that's what I believed. If anything, you swindled me!"

All at once, he sagged, though he still eyed her with resentment and distaste. Well, she had a healthy helping of those feelings for him too.

"Tick-tock, Eliza," she mimicked. "You rushed me because you didn't want me to think things over."

When he broke eye contact, his hard jaw twitched.

"I'm correct, aren't I?" Ire and a red rage surged up within her. "And you have the brass to sit on your high horse and talk of honor. Well, let me tell you something, demon. There is little honor in forcing a person's hand. Or using your power to coerce those weaker than you."

A black scowl twisted his face as he glared at some distant point. "Fine. May I continue, or have you more complaints to heap upon my head?"

"Please do continue," Eliza granted.

His golden gaze flicked back to her. "I want to kiss you."

"No." The word burst out of her with force. "Absolutely not."

Unfazed, Adam shrugged. "Unless you have something to offer in exchange for your freedom, Mellan and Mab will, as you say, merely hunt us down, and you'll be back to where you started."

"Then I shall find out what he wants." Eliza straightened her back. She could do that. She must. Like hell was she going to kiss this demon.

Adam simply gave her a slow, wicked half-smile. "Fortunately for you, lass, I already know what he wants. What they both want. More than controlling you. More than torturing me, even."

"Then why in blazes haven't you used it to secure your own freedom?" Eliza blurted out.

"I'm only alive because they cannot break me into revealing where this item might be." The belligerence burning in his eyes was gone in a blink, replaced by a look of pure cunning. "However, I might be persuaded to help you use the knowledge. All I require is—"

"Fine," she snapped, irritation getting the best of her. "I'll kiss you."

Silence fell, and Adam stared at her with those eyes of his. Devil's eyes. Eyes that made a woman forget herself. Heat rose up over her breasts and crawled along the back of her neck. Eliza grasped her skirts, her fingers twitching. She would kiss him. Kiss a man who had brought her nothing but irritation. Maybe she'd bite him to boot.

His chest, gleaming with sweat, rose and fell in a soft pattern. A bead of perspiration broke free from the top of his shoulder and ran down along the firm rise of his pectoral muscles, straight toward the dark nub of his nipple. All this time arguing with him, she'd forgotten his state of undress. Not so now. She'd have to press up against those hard muscles, touch his skin. Eliza wrenched her gaze back to his face, and his sinful lips curled in a knowing smile.

"You know," he said casually, "I believe I shall pass for the moment. I'd rather it be when you aren't wearing such a sour face. Kills a bloke's ardor, you realize."

Eliza blinked. And then his meaning hit her. "Why you...rutting...cheap, trickster..."

He laughed, a flash of even teeth. "Come now, Eliza, fret not." He stopped then, that obnoxious smile growing and heating with promise. "I'll take that kiss soon enough."

She rose to her feet in a rustle of skirts. "And I'll be sure to bite that wicked tongue when you do!"

She marched out of the cell, slamming it behind her, as he began to laugh again. Bastard. She might just leave him here to rot after all. His laughing taunt echoed through the dark. "Now that I know tongues are involved, I'll be sure to collect."

Chapter Four

Eliza climbed the stairs, irritation with Adam still so high that she did not take proper heed. Not until she walked directly into Mab's path. They locked eyes, and Eliza's skin prickled in utter terror.

"I...I heard a dog howling." Not a lie. "I thought..." Eliza gave Mab what she hoped was a shocked look. "I did not expect to find the demon."

It seemed an eternity ticked by as Mab's gaze bore into her. Eliza did not flinch but let herself show the confusion and the questions that she'd first felt upon finding Adam. She'd learned long ago that, when telling a lie, walking as close to the truth as possible was the best course of action.

The silence between them grew as taut as corset boning. And then Mab spoke. "And what did you feel when you saw your tormentor trussed up like the pig that he is?"

Horror. Sorrow. "Satisfaction." It was the emotion Mab wanted, and Eliza was going to give it to her.

Mab's unmoving expression broke into one of pleasure. "Ah. And did you express this satisfaction to our guest?"

"No. I left." Eliza straightened her spine. "The very sight of him sickens me."

"Hmm..." Mab flicked a glance toward Mellan, who'd strolled up to her side, his gaze narrowing darkly on Eliza. However, Mellan merely gave Mab a nearly imperceptible nod and slipped past Eliza, going down to the cellars. Eliza's heart pounded in protest. What would he do to Adam? Guilt hit hard. Adam had warned her. And she hadn't listened.

Mab linked her arm through Eliza's and guided them across the hall. "There was a time," she said, "when humans believed in the fae. They feared. Superstition wasn't to be mocked but to be heeded. And because of that, we grew strong."

"Strengthened? By superstition?" Eliza couldn't see how.

The corners of Mab's plump lips curled. "Superstition led to vigilance. Humans took precautions. They protected themselves from the likes of us. They thought of us constantly. Now?" Her slim shoulder raised a fraction. "Science and logic have turned us into nothing more than silly myths. Something to be ignored." Pansy-purple eyes flashed with irritation. "And our power fades."

Despite her stern inner lecture not to react, a shiver ran through Eliza. Mab felt it, for she gave her a gentle, encouraging pat on the hand as they walked up the stairs, their skirts rustling. "But all that will soon change. We shall regain our glory."

"We shall?" Eliza wanted to keep Mab talking of things other than Adam. But she did not like the idea of Mab having any more power.

Perhaps it was written on her face, for Mab gave her another pat. "Do not fear power, my darling. Once you learn how to wield it, it shall become your greatest joy."

"Mab, are you truly my grandmother?"

Mab's lips tightened. "The demon told you that, did he?" She sighed. "'Grandmother' makes me sound so very old." With a moue of distaste, Mab touched her flawless cheek. "I do not look old, do I, dearest?"

"Not at all," Eliza murmured by rote.

With a pleased expression, Mab shrugged. "Well, all right, then, I am your grandmother. Though I rather liked being your Auntie Mab. It had a lovely ring to it."

"And you are the fae queen?" Eliza pressed, as if her blood did not run cold.

"Now that," Mab said with a grin, "is a title I've been longing to proclaim. I did not want to reveal all too soon, lest you be too awed by my glory, but, yes, I am the fae queen."

And not a bit vain, Eliza thought with a mental roll of her eyes.

Mab tilted her head and smiled, coy and just a bit evil. "I shall make a proper fae princess of you yet."

That was what Eliza feared most. But she said nothing as Mab stopped at the door to the ballroom where two young, handsome footmen in brilliant green satin livery stood at attention. "Now, your first lesson."

Mab gave a regal lift of her chin, and the footmen swept open the doors, revealing a glittering world of diamonds, silks, and flickering candlelight. The sickly sweet scent of lilies thickened the air, wafting out and curling around Eliza.

"Revenge," Mab said, "and how to exact it."

The crowd of richly dressed ladies and gentlemen turned as one. And as one, they all bowed in deference to Mab as she glided through the parted throng. Eliza followed; she had little choice, still snared as she was by Mab's tight grip.

They were all young, this crowd of people. Young and beautiful. Not a single face marred by lines or time. It ought to be pleasing to the eye, but it struck Eliza as wrong and unnatural. *They are all fae.* Her supposed people. And she wanted to run as fast as she could from them.

Mab led her to a dais, upon which sat three large, gilded chairs. "Sit."

Knees shaking, Eliza did as bidden. Eyes watched her, curious, cunning. But she paid them little heed. Her mind was on Adam.

Adam's world was a little darker when Eliza left. Oh, he'd taunted and teased, wanting her to leave, but now that she was gone, he missed her. Wanted her back.

He thought of their bargain, and anticipation quickened his blood. They would be partners. And she had promised a kiss. That, he *would* collect. His mind sifted through the possibilities before settling on a less pleasant thought. Prince Mellan. The fae prince's presence in London was unsettling. He'd been banned from this reality for centuries. Which meant the fae had found a way to move with ease, and in greater numbers, between worlds. Somewhere, a crack had formed. More agitating, Eliza was promised to Mellan. Like hell.

For that alone, Adam would have agreed to anything she demanded. Because he'd be damned if that bastard would have her. But she needed to feel as though she'd fought a fair bargain with him. Adam hadn't let her be an equal before now. And it was wrong of him. From now on, he'd keep his wits about him and plan ahead.

So he'd follow Eliza's plan, get her the hell away from Mellan, and find that damn horn to use as a bargaining chip.

Sighing, he eased himself into a more comfortable position, or at least one that relieved at least some of the strain upon his ribs. The cloth Eliza had set over his genitals slid sideways. Dark humor had him fighting a smile. So very considerate, his Eliza May was, to cover him. The smile faded. She'd seen him at his very worst. And the humiliation burned.

Thus, when he heard the scuff of a shoe, he did not know whether to laugh or sob. She'd returned. It had to be her. Mab never visited at night. From the corner of his eye, he caught a flash of long, blond hair.

"Back for more, dove?" he drawled, a smile growing despite himself.

It quickly died a swift death as a shape stepped from the shadows. Pale blond hair that fell in a straight line, eyes like cold death. Mellan. And he did not appear pleased. "I do believe you were expecting someone else, Aodh."

Adam's eyes went to the collar in Mellan's hand. Whatever was in store for him would not be pleasant. Adam forced a grin. "Think of the devil and he shall find ye."

Chapter Five

The wait was not long for Eliza. The doors of the ballroom opened again. And the blood left her face. She could feel it draining. Feel her skin growing cold.

Mellan strolled in, his hand around a chain that led to a collar. Adam. Proud, cheeky Adam, now leashed like a dog. Utterly nude and covered in grime. Adam did not follow but matched Mellan's pace, his gait steady and strong, and Eliza realized with a start that he'd been healed.

She glanced at a smug-looking Mellan and realized that the fae bastard had healed Adam for this purpose. To parade him through the crowd of cooing and tittering onlookers. To break Adam once more.

"Ah," said Mab. "Our entertainment has arrived."

Eliza wanted to slap the woman.

Chains still encircled Adam's wrists, and when Mellan stopped him before the dais, two servants came and pulled those chains taut.

Mellan gave Eliza a mocking bow. "My dear Miss May, I do believe you've met our pet."

As it wasn't a question, Eliza didn't answer. Adam did not meet her gaze but stared straight ahead.

Mellan frowned, not liking her lack of reaction. "Is this not the demon who had the audacity to enslave you?"

Murmurs went through the crowd. Eliza felt herself flush. What happened between her and Adam was no one's business. But she could not say that here. "It is."

"You? Blood kin to both myself and Mab?" Mellan looked around the room in outrage. "He dared to chain my future bride."

That went over well. Now came the shock that she was supposedly promised to Mellan. Her bloody *great-uncle*. Eliza ground her teeth together but managed to keep a placid expression.

Mellan held out his hand, and a servant placed a rather large bullwhip in his grasp.

Bile rushed up Eliza's throat. She would be ill. Her lips and fingers went numb. Whipping. Gods. Her own back began to burn. Through a haze of despair, she saw Adam's long arms drawn wide. He caught her gaze and held it.

Horror raced through her. She did not want this. Never had she wanted this for him.

Mellan was speaking, his voice a buzz through the rushing sound in her ears. "Let us show dogs what happens when they disobey."

The crack of the whip seemed to lash through her. Adam's body flinched, his lips turning white. But he did not shout. Golden eyes burned into her. And she did not look away. *Watch me. Focus on me, not the pain.*

Eliza did not know if he heard her plea. But his attention stayed on her.

"He watches you," Mab murmured in her ear.

"Perhaps he dreams of revenge," Eliza whispered

lightly. She suffered no illusions about what would happen if Mab thought she and Adam had reached an accord.

"Perhaps."

Again and again the whip fell, till blood splattered and sprayed across Mab's white marble floor.

Adam grunted now with every strike. He had to be in agony.

Eliza sat like stone within her chair, unable to do a thing. *Make it stop. End this.*

And then it did. Mellan, sweating now, lowered the whip. Blood flecked his once-pristine white shirt and dotted his pale brow. "I think," he said, catching Eliza's gaze, "that I take too much, when really the pleasure ought to go to you, Miss May."

He stretched out his hand, offering her the whip. It hung like a dark snake, the ends glistening with Adam's blood.

Her heart beat so hard within the cage of her ribs that it was visible upon the swells of her chest. Mellan's gaze lingered there, his nostrils flaring as if he were taking in the scent of her discomfort and enjoying it. Lust crept into his eyes as he lifted his head. Bastard. Eliza drew in a deliberate and steady breath.

She forced herself to look at Adam, let her eyes rove over his battered and unclothed body. God, but he was magnificent, the way he refused to cower but stood as straight as the chains would let him, every tight and sinewy muscle bunched and ready for a fight.

Grimy sweat ran in rivulets down the valleys of those muscles, and along the taut wall of his chest and abdomen.

Mellan walked in front of Adam, turning a bit and pointing toward him with the whip. "He is unmarked here."

Dear God. Despite her resolve, her gaze dipped lower. Adam's sex hung heavy and thick below a thatch of ink-black hair. Strong thighs bracketed it, but would provide little protection against the whip. Already a few telling pink stripes marred their furred expanse from where the whip had lashed around his legs. Should Eliza take up the whip, she'd be striking him where he was most vulnerable. The cruelty of it gutted her.

But she could hardly refuse to engage in this little "revenge." It would call suspicion down upon her, and likely lead to an even greater torture for the demon.

The silence drew out and pressed down upon her shoulders. And she felt Adam's gaze upon her, the weight of it greater than Mab's stare or Mellan's taunting smile. She raised her eyes, and their gazes clashed. What did he feel at this moment? She could not tell. He gave nothing away. With a calm strength she did not feel, Eliza spoke.

"Physical pain is child's play," she said, not looking away from Adam. "Even humans excel in dolling it out."

A rumble rippled through the crowd.

"Explain, my dear," said Mab in a soft voice.

Eliza gave a negligent shrug, all the while aware of Adam's eyes upon her. "Whipping lacks imagination."

Mellan's golden brow lifted. "Oh? And what would you suggest to liven the festivities up?"

"The demon endures too well. To a tiresome degree." Her back tightened as she met Adam's eyes once more and held his stare. "I suggest humiliation instead."

Eyes of deep, angry gold held hers. A snare from which she could not free herself. From a distance, it seemed that Mab's voice came at her. "Is this not a humiliation?"

"No," said Eliza, still locked in Adam's wrathful glare. "It is giving him what he wants, an outlet for his rage.

True humiliation would be him chained at my feet, as I was chained at his for all those dark days."

A pulse jumped in Adam's strong throat. The only indication of any emotion he might have felt.

As for the crowded room, a murmur of approval broke out.

"Oh, my dear child," said Mab, chuckling with delight, "how proud you have made me."

Mellan bowed low. "As you wish, my lovely."

No, she did not wish. If anything, Eliza wished herself far from this spectacle. She wanted to go home. To Boston. But if she thought about her old home, she'd cry. So she stiffened her spine and glared at Adam. "Come, demon, at my feet where you belong."

The long length of his body tensed, but his expression remained unreadable. The servants release him, and Mellan gave his chain a hard tug, forcing Adam forward. And then, as if deciding not to fight, he moved of his own volition.

It did not matter that he was hobbled, that the chains forced him to shuffle his steps, he walked towards her as if prowling. She swallowed past the lump in her dry throat and lifted her chin in a show of defiance. It did not help. Dark humor lit his eyes, as if he knew precisely how she was affected, and reveled in it.

He stopped before her chair. Eliza gave him a long, bland look and then met his eyes. "Sit." She was proud that her voice did not waver.

The very room seemed to still as he stared at her, his expression blank, his body a tightly coiled wire, and then with utter grace, he knelt at her feet.

Eliza's insides recoiled. He was so close, too close, the scent of his blood and sweat surrounding her. His gleaming chest, gently rising and falling with each breath, within touching distance. Part of her wanted to push him away, and yet, perversely, she found herself fighting a smile. *Well played, sir.* But Mab was watching, and so Eliza grabbed a length of golden chain that ran around his neck and yanked him down at her side. "I said 'sit.' "

She suspected he toppled only because he allowed it. But he made as if to move away from her, and she gave the chain a rough jerk. "Stay."

Though his jaw bunched, he did not move again, but heeded as a dog might. Revulsion churned within her belly. It did not matter what had passed between them, degrading another soul sickened her. Did he know this? Did he understand what she was trying to do? And did it matter?

Adam remained on his arse, still utterly unconcerned by his nakedness. Other men might have appeared vulnerable. But he wore his nudity like armor, letting the world see the strength and fluidity of his body.

"Well now," exclaimed Mab happily, "shall we have some dancing?" At that, the musicians started up, and the crowd began to waltz.

Eliza looked on, pretending to be content, pretending to preen. But the heat of Adam's body next to her thigh unnerved her further. She ignored it. And him. Yet she wished him to hear her unspoken promise. *I will get us out.*

Every inch of him screamed for mercy. Each breath Adam took threatened to have him fainting. His back had been flayed to nearly entirely raw meat. And yet he sat at Eliza's feet with a sense of odd pride.

It grew when she nudge him roughly with her boot. "Do not crowd me, demon." So cold her voice, her gaze barely straying to him, as though she found the mere sight of him distasteful.

He almost grinned. Ye gods, but she was clever. He'd known the second she glanced at the whip that she was loath to touch it. Even before that. She'd gone white as French linen the moment she understood what Mellan meant to do. Lucky for her, Mab and Mellan had been too engrossed in wanting to see him whipped to notice her expression. Had they done so, they would have realized, as he did, that she could no more torture another than she could stop her heart from beating. He'd wondered what she'd do; she had to have known she was caught between the whip and retreat.

But her choice had stunned him. It was so simple, so brilliant, her move. She'd understood Mab's need to humiliate him. And played the fae bitch perfectly. For that alone, Adam would have knelt at her feet. Eliza had no clue that he'd shown her his deepest honor in doing so. She thought he was mocking her. Nor could he afford to enlighten her. So he played his part, making her force him down, to curl up at her feet like a dog.

As for Mab, she'd never understood that humiliation only worked if a man was unwilling. Having Eliza see him beaten by the prat Mellan? That was humiliating. But having Eliza whip him while knowing it was killing a bit of her soul with every strike? That would have been true torture.

On the other side of Eliza, Mellan sat. Adam did not need to see his face to know that his little torture session had not ended but was merely delayed by Eliza's cunning. Mab might have been satisfied by his humiliation, but Mellan wasn't. And he'd make Adam pay for it.

Chapter Six

"Demon? Adam?" The female voice was a soft hiss. Smooth hands touched his shoulder, awaking a world of hurt.

Adam tried to shrug it off. Only to receive a pinch on his earlobe in return. With a growl, he turned, capturing a slim wrist and hauling a body close. The female landed upon his battered body with a huff. Bad idea. That hurt. A lot.

Adam forced his eyes open. Still clinging to the wiggling mass of warm woman, he thrust her away as he tried to sit. "Quiet," he muttered. "My head aches something fierce."

Eliza scrambled back, her pretty face twisted up with irritation. "I was simply trying to wake you."

"I'd rather sleep." Now that he was awake, he was in pain. "Well then, what is it?"

Her gaze went to his shoulders, and he knew she thought of his back. And though it was dark, far darker than usual—she'd brought only a small torch by her side—he noted the pallor of her skin and the way she flinched.

"I am sorry," she blurted out. "For tonight."

"As am I." Adam gave her a weak smile. "I'll just as soon leave all whippings behind."

"Yes, well, I meant...for the other..." She grimaced.

"You did well, lass. Did right."

Her mouth opened in a little circle of surprise, but she quickly shut it. "I'm going to get us out of here."

"As you said." Adam wanted to laugh at her huff of impatience. "Though I'm thinking we'll be better guarded from now on." He glanced at the door. "How is that you've come here again? Eliza, you must take better care—"

"I made myself vomit," she cut in with another grimace. "Took syrup of ipecac." Her mouth twisted wryly. "I'm not certain you know, but fae have a decided revulsion for sickness."

"I've yet to meet anyone who is fond of it, dove."

She nearly grinned at that one, her cheeks plumping. "Well, upon hearing mine, they quarantined me in the guest wing. As for guarding the door, it is two in the morning now." Eliza leaned in a bit. "Did you know that fae become lethargic at night? Those guards can barely keep their heads up. Slip a bit of valerian into their nightly tea..."

"Clever. So we leave now?"

"No." Eliza came closer, bringing with her the scent of woman. "We need to do this carefully. We need a plan."

Of course. Adam knew better. He'd never gone into battle without a plan of attack.

"First off," Eliza said, "how do we get you out of those chains? I cannot find a key. Second, we'll need some method of transport. You're weak as a babe now."

Humiliation curdled in his stomach. He pushed it away. There was a way to move forward. The best way. But it relied on her. Would she help him once again? What he would suggest was far worse than a mere promise to give him a chance. Likely she'd see it as a trap. And it was, of sorts.

Her gaze was a hot hand sliding over his skin, and sweat broke out at the base of his neck. He clenched his hands, conscious of the chains pooled upon his lap and the way they rattled with the slightest move. Those bloody chains, they drained him of his strength even as his body fought to heal itself.

Taking another breath, Adam forced himself to face her, to appear as though her answer did not mean everything.

"Yes, as to that. We have a predicament, dove. Two actually. Mab has a key, likely held in her rooms, but that will only unchain me from the wall. These"—he refused to glance at his wrists—"will be harder to be rid of."

"So how—"

"Which," he cut in, "leads us to the second issue. I saw the way Mellan looked at you tonight. It is clear that he has a greater interest in you than expected. He won't stop until he makes you his."

She flushed at that, her chin dipping. "You don't know that—"

"I do." Adam had heard the desperation in Mellan's voice. It matched the one in his own soul. "And I believe you do as well."

He almost smiled at the way her sweet mouth pursed. She wanted to argue, but couldn't. Eliza was stubborn as the year was long but she had a streak of honesty that rivaled any knight's. Proven when she squared her shoulders. "Fine, he does appear to be ... insistent."

To put it mildly. Adam assumed a restful pose, when he was anything but. His heart was pounding now. "It is clear he wants something from you." Adam smiled when her neck turned pink. "Aside from your feminine charms."

"I can't imagine what it would be," she said, her lithe frame tight.

He shifted a bit, and the chains rattled. "The fact remains, you are vulnerable. You accepted his suit, forced though it was, which means he has a claim on you."

Eliza puffed up, the plump swell of her bosom lifting beneath her tatty shirtwaist. "As much as he'd like to believe otherwise, he has no claim on me. A lady may reject a suit at any time."

"We are not discussing human society. We're speaking of fae law." Adam pinned her with a look because he could sense she wanted to avoid the truth. "He can force you into a fae marriage, and there wouldn't be a damn thing you could do about it."

She crossed her arms over her chest. "What do you suggest then?"

Oh, he didn't want to smile, though sheer nerves made his lips twitch. Nor did he want to hear yet another rejection from her. But there was no going back. "The only way to get out of his reach is to make yourself unwed no longer. Take a husband." He stared her down, noting the growing horror upon her face. "Take me."

For a thick, silent moment, Eliza fought to find her voice. When she did, it burst forth as a near laugh. "Oh, well played, sir. You had me walking down that trail of deceit once again."

Adam's scowl was a fearsome thing. The harsh lines of his handsome face made it so. Golden eyes narrowed to mere slits as he growled, "'Tis no jest, Miss May, nor a line of deceit."

"Oh? Take *you* for a husband?" Her pulse thudded at the base of her throat. "And to think I was beginning to believe you were truly trying to help me. When all you were doing is finding another way to bind me to you."

A snarl left his lips as he sat upright. That he was chained against the wall in no way diminished him. Likely he'd appear as regal as a king in any situation. "Enough," he said. "Gods, but you accuse me of conceit." He leaned forward a bit, his big fists clenching. "I am helping you. The curse does not abate unless you truly believe me to be an essential part of your soul. Marriage is not that bond. It is merely a contract between two persons."

"For someone who professes to believe in soul mates and destiny, you've a rather dim view of marriage."

Adam sighed expansively. "This modern world makes confusion where there need not be any. Do you honestly believe that speaking a few vows to one another assures everlasting love?"

The scorn in his voice scraped along her nerves.

"No, but—"

"Love," he spoke over her, "is feeling, how you treat a person, not spouting pretty words."

"Words matter." Eliza did not know why she pressed, nor what it mattered if he did not agree.

He appeared equally confused, his thick, dark brows knotting, a little M-shaped groove forming at the bridge of his noble nose.

"Words, actions, feeling, they all matter, demon." She gave a humorless smile when he scowled. "Else you wouldn't take offense when I call you 'demon.'"

Adam's jaw bunched, the cords on his neck visibly growing taut. "May we kindly address the matter at hand?"

"I thought we were."

His straight, strong teeth snapped together with an audible clack before he spoke with a near growl. "Fine then, let us compromise. We can be handfasted instead."

"Handfasted?"

"Yes," he said with exaggerated patience. "We join hands and pledge our commitment to one another. To the fae, a handfasting is as good as marriage. The only difference is that a handfasting has an end date. It is a way for a couple to see if they would truly enjoy being married. If they do, they'll take marriage vows." His expression grew shuttered. "If not, they part."

"And..." Eliza licked her dry lips. "What would our expiration date be?" She could not believe she was even considering it. Nor did she want to examine precisely why she wasn't running from the room and his offer.

Adam pursed his lips. "Three weeks. Just as you promised me before."

Dully, Eliza nodded, not agreeing to his terms but his logic. She flicked her gaze back to his, catching the way he'd tensed, and then relaxed when her focus was on him. He must not want her to see how much this agreement meant to him.

"How does this benefit you?" she asked.

He seemed to solidify as if turning to stone. Oh, but his eyes. So many thoughts running behind those strangely beautiful eyes of his, calculating, weighing odds, possible scenarios. It was right there, for anyone to see, and yet he wasn't an open book of a man. He chose to let others see this, that was equally clear. He let one know that he was thinking things through. Which somehow made it worse. For it was equally clear that, when he reached a decision to act, he'd have the upper hand.

When he spoke, his voice was a deep well of sound within the quiet. "It benefits us both. The chains." His nostrils flared a bit as he glanced at the irons in distaste. She understood, far too well, his hatred of them. "Just as the chain I used on you was unbreakable by anyone save those who had my magic within their blood, so is this enchanted to prevent an easy escape. These chains are worse. Not only do they leach my strength, preventing me from healing at my normal rate, but…"

He cleared his throat, his fists rhythmically clenching upon his lap. Oddly, for once, she did not resent him in this, but empathized. Especially when his tone grew tight. "Mab wants me to be hers. And only hers." A flush worked its way over his sharp cheekbones. "Therefore…" A strangled sound of sheer embarrassment broke from his lips, and he ducked his head, the chains clanking as he pressed the heels of his hands against his eyes. "Bloody hell. They cannot be broken by anyone but my bride, aye?"

It was her turn to utter a strangled sound, as an odd, twisted warmth bloomed over her. Embarrassment for him. Incredulity and a simmering rage toward Mab. "Are you saying," Eliza got out, "those chains are some twisted version of a chastity belt?"

An abrupt, awkward nod was his answer.

Eliza found herself leaning against the slick, icy stones of the cellar. Numbly, she gripped her bent knees as though it could somehow anchor her. "You had to have known this from the beginning."

Adam's wide shoulders bunched. But he raised his head. "Aye."

"So then, you knew your only hope of escaping those chains was to somehow convince me to be your bride."

His mouth went stiff. "If I had said this to you when we first bargained, you'd have turned tail and run. Am I manipulating your emotions?" Again he nodded. "I learned my lesson, coming at you with brute force. Now I proceed with caution. And Eliza?" He leaned in. "Never forget that my endgame matters most to me. But that does not mean we cannot work together to get what we both want."

"Well," Eliza said, a little unsteady, "you certainly do not sugarcoat your words."

"I can no longer afford to." Adam did not move. "Will you accept my offer?"

Eliza's gaze drifted to her lap. The truth was, she'd been hedging by purposely needling Adam. She knew it. He most certainly knew it. The ire that sparked in his golden eyes said he'd played her game long enough.

Damnation, but her insides twisted and clenched. Her heart beat a hard pace against the base of her throat. "Always bargains and deals with you," she muttered.

His large body shifted, a nearly imperceptible move of his lean hips. She was too attuned to him to miss it, and her skin tightened in response. Fight or flight. She'd done both. His stare held the weight of the world, and her shoulders ached under the strain.

"When will you realize, Eliza? You have the power. Between us. You always have."

Licking her dry lips, she took a deep breath and lifted her gaze to his. The face that looked back at her was hard and so very masculine that, taken in parts, his features were almost too blunt, too large. Put together, they created a tableau that took one's breath and stirred one's blood. He'd belong to her. This bold, charismatic creature who incited lust in nearly every being he came across.

A heated dizziness threatened to send her crashing down. He claimed to be her other half. She, who'd crept through life, escaping notice of everyone she could.

Husband. She would call him husband. It wouldn't mean anything. Merely an arrangement.

His deep voice rumbled. "Tick-tock, Eliza."

"Do not rush me," she snapped, her breasts heaving against her bodice in her agitation. "You are always rushing me."

His hawkish gaze strayed to the motion, and his fine nostrils flared. He did not bother to look away, but spoke with rough, barely restrained patience. "Make your choice."

A shiver worked its way over her, drawing her skin up tight, beading her nipples. Eliza pressed her spine against the opposite wall. "All right. Let us do this thing."

He closed his eyes for all of one second, the look upon his face that of extreme relief mixed with wild triumph, and then he blinked, the mask of indifference falling back in place. But she'd seen. And it terrified her.

More so when he spoke with rough command. "Come here, then."

"Now?" She barely kept the question from being a squeak.

His lips curled up at one corner. "That is the general idea, dove." He raised his hand and held it out to her. "Come," he said softly. "Do the deed quickly and you'll have no more cause to dread it."

"Don't we need a witness?"

"No. Pledging ourself and leaving proof of the binding will be enough. It was in the old days, so shall it be now. We'll be needing a bit of your skirts."

Together, they managed to rip a length of her clothing

free. "In gothic books," she said as Adam helped her tear at the dress, "the heroine always rips her petticoats with such ease."

"Aye, well, the hero always manages to get neatly shot in the shoulder, so..." He began to shrug but winced. "We'll use the chains, as well." He laughed short and without humor. "Seems fitting, does it not, dove?"

She couldn't help but laugh as well. "Oh, very."

Adam's hand clasped Eliza's more firmly, sensing perhaps her desire to bolt, and began to wind the strip of her dress and a length of chain around their wrists. Eliza could not look away from Adam now. If she did, she might miss something, as though Adam were an illusionist, capable of playing a sleight of hand with her very soul. And yet, he seemed nervous, the pulse at his throat visibly beating, his eyes steady upon their hands, and then on her as if he too feared he'd blink and his hopes would be gone. It was that fear mixed with hope that softened her towards him.

Without thinking about it, she gave his hand a small squeeze. *We do this now. Together.*

As if he read her very thoughts, he took a sharp breath, the muscled expanse of his chest visibly lifting, then nodded. "Together, Eliza, we can change our fates."

Chapter Seven

Sweat dotted Eliza's brow and trickled down her back as she made her way to bed. Her knees shook, making each step an effort. Dear God, the blood trailing down Adam's back, the wet slap of the whip against his flesh. And having to endure him kneeling by her feet.

A shaky breath gusted past her lips. She fretted over what she had to endure, when his plight was so much more dire. And he'd born it nobly, telling her he was *proud* of her quick thinking. Hardly. She was ashamed. And though their relationship had not been based upon kindness, Eliza wanted nothing more than to return to where he was kept and give him some comfort. Even if that comfort was nothing more than staying by his side in the cold darkness.

"You do not fool me, girl."

Eliza halted so abruptly that her skirts swung forward around her trembling legs.

From out of the shadows, Mellan strolled, his hands tucked into the deep pockets of his pin-striped trousers.

Such a casual stance for a man whose eyes radiated dark menace. Eliza kept her back to the wall and her attention on him. He was known to strike without warning. Having been on the receiving end of his blows, Eliza had little desire to experience such an attack again.

"I would not presume to fool you, Mellan." She would. But it was best not to antagonize.

A soft snort left him. "And yet here we are." Spreading his arms, he smiled. And it chilled her blood. His smile dropped. "Mab might be arrogant enough to believe your little performance, thinking that she has you in line, but make no mistake, Eliza, I know you far too well."

The soft scuff of his shoe sounded in the hall as he stepped forward, his voice going lower. "You spared the GIM maker's pain."

Eliza quailed. And what could she say? Swallowing hard, she held her chin up. "I've had enough of violence, which is why I left you."

"You have developed a fancy for him."

"I'd rather say that you've developed an unhealthy obsession over him."

Mellan made a noise of amusement. "Clever, having him sit at your feet. But then you always did like having a man pay homage to you."

Her stomach protested. "I do not recall having received any homage from a man."

In a blink, he was before her, pressing her against the door to her room with his body. "Shall I give you a demonstration now? See if it stirs any memories?"

Eliza had quite enough of those where he was concerned. And every one of them made her sick with shame. "No. Simply find another girl. There must be plenty who want you."

"Now, Eliza, where is the fun in having a woman who wants me?" His fae eyes grew dark purple. "I'd much rather break a resistant lass."

"You did break me, Mellan." She glared up into his face, even when everything inside of her wanted to run away, to cry like a small child might. "My association with you has brought me nothing but death and sorrow."

He flashed his black fangs. "You haven't begun to understand the meaning of sorrow, little girl." Like a rattler, he struck, his claws digging into her scalp as he clenched her hair. "You'll do what I say, when I say it. Without question."

Hadn't she always? She'd died for this man. Ironic, considering she wanted nothing more than to kill him instead. Well, no more. She'd run away with Adam and find a way to be rid of Mellan.

His cold eyes bore into her. "You will never be free of me." She did not flinch, did not blink, when the sharp edges of his fingernails scraped lightly along her jaw. His voice grew soft, beguiling. A prelude to sin that had her insides turning to stone. "I own you."

"Apparently the GIM maker has a prior claim on my soul." The words were out before she thought them through. And she gasped as she realized what she'd said.

Mellan, too, blinked in shock, but was quicker to recover. "So then," he murmured, "you believe he is your soul mate?"

"No." She stood taller, bracing her spine when she wanted to cower. "But he does. Mab does. And if you did not, at the very least, fear it might be true, you wouldn't bother with Adam either."

Slowly, he chuckled. "Smart girl. When there is a glimmer of belief, there is cause for concern." He tugged her hair, just enough to make her wince. "Which is why we shall eradicate the situation."

Eliza's throat went dry, her voice coming out in a croak. "Eradicate?"

Mellan nodded, not taking his eyes from hers. "You shall destroy the GIM maker."

"No." The denial shot out of her with such force that the sound echoed in the dim hallway.

With a snarl, Mellan grasped her hand and squeezed until her bones ground against themselves. "I know you, Eliza. You'll seek to bargain with Adam, thinking you'll be free."

Her breath froze, her heart plummeting to her belly.

"Oh yes, I know," he went on in a smooth murmur. "And I will let you free him. For he will lead you to a prize I've been coveting." Mellan wrenched her hand up to hold it before her face. "Let him take you, and when I have my prize, you will use this hand of death, the very one you used to kill countless others, and you will take Aodh's life. Or I will cut that pretty head from your shoulders and place it on my bedroom mantle."

Vivid. And yet he was not exaggerating; she'd witnessed firsthand how he decorated his lair in Boston. Heaven help her if Mellan realized she was handfasted to Adam. On this, Adam had agreed that the fae prince should not know of it until they were well and gone.

Mellan could clearly see the fear in her eyes, for he nodded. "Now, if you're a good girl, and do as I say, I shall allow certain liberties once we are wed." He tilted his head as if considering, his yellow hair sliding in a sheet over his shoulder. "I think I can agree on letting you continue your outings with Mab, and perhaps a trip or two abroad."

As if her whole life were decided. With him. The pulse at the base of her neck throbbed. Kill Adam and gain some glimpse of freedom. Refuse and die.

"You once told me that my skill would not work against the supernatural."

"It will not work against me. You aren't strong enough." The corners of Mellan's eyes crinkled in true humor. "Or did you think I'd forgotten how you tried to end me?"

And what a disaster that had been. Her powers simply did not work on Mellan, and he'd made her suffer for days afterward, all the while laughing at her foolishness.

Wisely, she refrained from answering the question. "And yet you think I'm strong enough to attempt Adam?"

"Oh, I most certainly do. Nor is he a true supernatural, but merely a man cursed."

Eliza had grave doubts. Her power did not work that way. It was shoddy and gun-shy at best. She had terrible control and, until now, Mellan had sent her after weak spirits, men foolish enough to be caught unaware. Adam was neither of those things.

"I am surprised," Mellan murmured, "that you did not try to do so when he had you chained. Like chattel."

Hypocrite. Eliza suppressed a glare. "Whatever magic was in that chain dampened my strength." Nor, Eliza reflected, had she wanted to try. Even then, she could not bring herself to kill. She'd been forced to do it enough as it was.

"But now he is the one chained and weak." Mellan flashed his fangs. "Easy pickings, Eliza."

For a moment, Eliza allowed herself to picture the deed, to envision Adam's golden eyes going lifeless and dull. Whatever he was to her, he did not deserve that. No one did.

Tears burned hot in her eyes but did not fall. They only fell when death was coming. "If Adam is my soul mate, I will not be able to take his soul without destroying my own."

"Well then," Mellan said through a creeping smile, "you had better pray that he is not."

Eliza lay in the dark. The bedding around her was a cloud of silk. Comfortable, perfect, the very luxury she'd often dreamed of. But she could not draw a clean, free breath. She thought of Adam's flesh, slashed, his blood flowing. She'd done nothing to help him, but watched his torture, as they all did. This was the life she would live? This is what she'd become? A fanciful creature, intent on nothing more than her own pleasure? And now that Mellan had found her, he'd use her as a plaything and then toss her away. After she killed Adam.

Her first kill had been accidental. She'd been young and terrified, alone in the world after her grandfather had died. Easy prey for predators. And when she'd walked back from the market one day, her once-kind neighbor had cornered her in the alleyway behind their row houses. Even now she remembered the stink of his breath and the grip of his sweaty hands, and it filled her with a queasy revulsion. She'd screamed then. That strange, ugly, odd scream, her hand rising to grasp his chest. And he'd simply died before her eyes.

Eliza hadn't felt relief, only a bone-deep terror. And then Mellan had appeared, as always, moving from dark shadows into the light.

"Dear girl, you're frightened." He'd stroked her cheeks with a tender hand, this lovely, strange man. "When you should rejoice. You did this. You have the power to walk amongst the foulest creatures and never fear again."

How seductive it sounded back then. Come live with Mellan, be one of his crew, and all she had to do were some little favors for him.

Eliza tossed in her bed, her stomach roiling. She hated herself for agreeing those first few times. And then, when her soul grew black with the grime of her sins, Eliza had told him no more. And he'd made her pay.

He'd beaten her and ground her will into dust. For so long.

Her whole life, she'd felt a bit like a cork in a vast sea, men's expectations batting her here and there. She did not mind going where the winds took her but she wanted a sail, oars, and rudders. She wanted a say. And she was damn well through with being under the thumb of another's will. The truth slammed into her like a rogue wave; if she wanted a say, she needed power.

"And I'm not going to get any by sitting on my ass," she muttered, rising to her feet. No, she needed a plan.

Chapter Eight

Sin's insides grew uncomfortably tight as he climbed the wide, red carpeted steps of the theatre. All around him people followed, making their way to their seats while chatting and softly laughing. Anticipation was a palpable hum, thicker tonight, for Londoners loved good gossip, and this performance promised to offer up a tasty meal of it. For Miss Layla Starling, the young, beautiful, and extremely wealthy heiress, was in attendance. With a suitor. Until now, she'd managed to evade the marriage noose. Despite the fact that she was unfortunately American, she'd received a staggering number of offers. And turned down every one.

Sin did not want to admit to the relief he felt every time he heard of her refusals. Nor did he want to admit to feeling as though his knees were cut out from under him when he thought of Layla finally marrying. Which was unfair of him. Layla deserved to be happy. She deserved to live a rich, full life. And if that included marriage, then so be it. As for him, he could not offer those things. He would never be normal, never be anything but a freak in her world.

Why then was he following her to the theatre? Irritation was a prickle at the back of his neck as he entered his brother-in-law Archer's family box and took the seat closest to the rail. In the quiet hush of the luxury box, he let himself watch Layla. She sat in a box opposite him and one tier lower.

Seeing her sent a pang through his chest. The oval of her face was a cameo against her mahogany hair. He remembered when that hair had hung in snarls, from when they'd climbed trees, bits of leaves caught in the silky mass. He knew she had a smattering of freckles across her nose, like cinnamon over cream. He knew that, when she smiled, she'd reveal a front tooth that was just a bit crooked. And that her eyes would appear forest green, amber gold, or dusky brown, depending upon the light.

He knew *her*. Or had. Tonight, she was resplendent in pale pink satin, trimmed with chocolate brown ribbons. Despite her vast wealth, the only adornments she wore were small pearl earbobs and a brown satin ribbon about her slender neck. His fingers itched to touch the nape of her neck where he knew it'd be warm and soft, to tug the ribbon free and set his mouth to the place it had rested.

Foolish thoughts. He forced his attention to the man at her side, the one sitting so attentively, watching both the gathering crowds and her at the same time. He was older, with black hair and dark eyes. Yet there was an air of timelessness about him, as if he could be in his twenties or in his forties. But it was the "otherness" about him, as if the man stood apart from the rest of the crowd, that bothered Sin.

Or perhaps it was jealousy. When the man set his

gloved hand near Layla's, Sin's back teeth met with a click.

"And who are we staring at?" said a female voice at his ear.

Sin loathed the muffled yelp that escaped him. He turned his head to properly glare and found the cool, jade eyes of his sister smiling back at him. "I'm purchasing a cowbell for you," he groused as Lady Miranda Archer settled into the empty seat at his side.

"You'll have to discover a way to make her wear it," said her husband, Lord Benjamin Archer, as he took the seat next to Miranda's. Amusement lit his pale gaze. "I'd take care. She's liable to singe off your brows."

Both Miranda and Sin snorted as one. Miranda could, in fact, burn a man's brows off with a thought. But then, so could Sin.

"What are you two doing here?" Ordinarily, he'd be pleased to see them, but this was his night, and he did not want to share Layla with anyone.

"Why, I'm certain I don't know." Miranda blinked, her eyes wide and innocent, her voice falsely vapid. "Archer, why are we here? I've plum forgotten."

Archer settled back, crossing one long leg over the other. "I believe it had something to do with attending the theatre, love."

"Very amusing," Sin muttered.

"So..." Miranda leaned forward, craning her neck in the direction of where Sin had been looking. "What lovely lady has caught your attention, then?"

"No one." Sin's cheeks burned. "And would you please sit back? You're going to attract attention." Miranda always attracted attention. Beautiful as she was, it couldn't be helped.

Her lips curled in a smile. "Afraid your ladylove might see?"

"Stop pestering the lad, Miri."

Good man, Archer. He, at least, understood discretion. But then Sin caught Archer's evil smile.

"It's clear," the bastard said, "that he's near wetting himself with worry. And I'd hate having to explain the spoilt upholstery to the management."

"Arse." Sin turned his attention to the empty stage. "The both of you are unmitigated arses."

Miranda elbowed him softly. "Miss Starling is quite fetching, is she not?"

Sin lurched upright, and Miranda smiled. "Oh, come now, your study of her was fairly obvious, dearest."

"Miss Starling?" Perhaps he could play the ignorant buffoon.

Apparently not. Miranda gave him a chiding look. "All of London is talking about the young heiress. The richest girl in the land, who has the audacity to be an American." Her smile grew teasing.

"Nothing the ton loves more than a wealthy anomaly," Archer added with a certain dryness.

Miranda gave him a little kiss on his cheek. "Never fear, Ben. You'll always be London's most infamous moneybag."

Archer rolled his eyes, but wrapped an arm about her slim shoulders, tucking her closer to his side. Sin was grateful for the distraction, hoping they'd become engrossed in each other, as they tended to do, and forget about him. No such luck graced him. Miranda turned her too-keen attention back to him.

"I do not blame you for noticing her, brother. Miss Starling is quiet lovely." She gave him a saucy look. "If I didn't know better, I'd say you've developed a tendré."

Gods, but he could feel himself blushing. Damn it all to hell. The air unnaturally heated as his power threatened to slip his control, and he took a calming breath. "I know her, is all." He cleared his throat. "Or knew her. Long ago."

"Then go speak to her," Miranda urged. "You are too isolated as it is. Make friends, Sin." Concern marred her smooth brow. "You know I speak from experience when I tell you that cutting yourself off from the world won't help."

It was a known fact that on every third Sunday, in Mab's household, three-quarters of the staff had the day to themselves. It was also known that Cook made a cherry trifle for those unfortunate few who must remain behind. It would be simple enough, then, for Eliza to sneak into the kitchens and give the trifle a liberal soaking of opium syrup. There was a risk that the staff might imbue too much and not fall asleep but perish, but given that many in Mab's employ were of fae blood, Eliza did not believe— or rather she fervently hoped—it would not kill them.

More difficult, however, was finding a means of escape. Hope came by way of the spirits seller who made a monthly visit to the house to deliver ale and mead. Eliza took the risk to speak to him.

"You shall be called back here," she told him, "because the barrels you are delivering now shall meet with an unfortunate accident."

When the driver, a crabby, grizzled man of an indeterminate age, scowled, she spoke on before he could protest. "It shall be done. However, you stand to earn one hundred pounds if you help me with a delicate matter."

Still frowning, the man scratched the back of his head, sending his cap over one eye. "An' what's to be done when the mistress of the house puts the blame on me? I'll be expected to pay for them 'faulty' barrels. An' I want no trouble." Despite his protests, his expression that said he could be persuaded.

"One hundred pounds on top of your expenses." Eliza shrugged. "Or I could simply damage the barrels and leave it at that. I doubt anyone in the house would believe the blame lies upon my shoulders."

The man harrumphed. "Mad chit, you are." But he was listening.

It was a plan filled with pitfalls and holes. Everything could go wrong, but Eliza was taking that chance. Mellan had helped. No, he'd not open the doors for her; Mab would not know his part in things. But he'd given her Mab's key to the chains that bound Adam to the cellar wall and then taken Mab out for the day.

Eliza hated that she must put her faith in Mellan's promise that he'd keep Mab away and that she had to believe the one man who had every reason to crush her beneath his boot.

Mellan's eyes had borne into her. *Do not fail me, Eliza. And do not think for a moment that you can cross me and live.*

Now, when escape was upon her, Eliza's palms were so sweaty that it took her three tries, her hand slipping from the key, to turn the lock on Adam's cell door. He lifted his head, his eyes a dull copper color in the dingy light, but he made no move to rise.

"Dear God," she muttered as she took stock of him, "what did she do to you this time?"

He was black and blue, more slashed than whole. He grunted as he made an effort to sit. "Another productive visit."

Eliza shook, the key clinking as she slipped it into the lock that attached his chains to the cellar wall. Damnation, but she'd expected him to be in better shape than this. The moment the chains clattered to the floor, Adam took a deep breath, his wide chest lifting. He rubbed his wrists, still bound by the cuffs and the heavy lengths of chain attached to them. Flushed and fevered, he gazed up at her. Every fear within her came to a standstill. She forgot to breathe. Why was it this man affected her thusly? How could he heat her blood and make her heart stutter with merely a look? Worse, why did she want to hold him close and tell him how sorry she was that theirs was a relationship that would never come to pass?

"What is it?" he rasped through dry lips.

Eliza licked her own. She could hardly admit that she was meant to kill him. "Nothing." Her voice sounded raw, cracked. "I've brought you some clothing." A grimace twisted her face, for Eliza had not been able to provide very good ones; she'd had to pick through the footmen's limited off-duty clothing.

She managed to gather up a cotton work shirt that had faded to a dull grey color and a pair of horrible red, black, and yellow plaid trousers. Boots were harder to find. The only size she thought might fit being a mismatched set, one with an appallingly large hole in the sole. Never mind, they'd get him a proper pair later.

He eyed her selection now without comment and then reached past the undergarments to pick up the trousers. He proceeded to tug them on, gritting his teeth as he moved. His struggles made the muscled plane of his abdomen bunch and his cock slide along his strong thighs...Eliza forced herself not to watch.

"Help me with my shirt," he ordered, his eyes averted.

His short tone did not annoy her, for it had to be difficult asking for assistance, and with a certain degree of gentleness, she eased the paper-thin rag over his head. The thing smelled of cabbage and soot. Eliza did not want to contemplate what little beasties might be hiding amongst its folds.

Adam gritted his teeth and pushed his arms through the sleeves, the bulk of the chains he wore making the process unwieldy. By the time they were finished, Eliza buttoning up the collar with deft hands, a sweat bathed his skin.

Shaking inwardly with sympathy, she lifted his arm over her head to settle around her shoulders. The cold chains hit her arm, a marked contrast to the warmth of his skin beneath the thin shirt.

"We haven't much time," she said. "Can you stand?"

"I'll crawl if I have to." But he managed to lurch to his feet, dragging his broken leg along as she walked them out of the cell. It was slow going, the chains clattering, his body leaning onto hers.

"Remember the knot?" he managed to say.

"Yes, I've got it." Eliza pulled the length of her gown they'd used to handfast from her pocket. Adam had tied the silk into an intricate Celtic knot. A symbol of their joining. They'd leave it here now to send a message. Eliza had grave doubts that Mellan would honor their handfasting. But she had to try, nor could she now explain to Adam that Mellan was privy to their escape. Such a mess.

Before she could drop the knot, Adam took the thing and rubbed it across his bloody brow.

"So they know you are mine," he said, making her flush.

"Lean your bad hip against me," she ground out, dreading the walk up the stairs. He had a foot in height on her and, even in his emaciated state, was a great deal heavier than she was. There was no help for it. Either they made it out or they would suffer.

Servants lay pell-mell around the house, their slumberous snores breaking up the eerie silence. Adam glanced at them as she shuffled him along, and his full, split lip quirked. "Devious, Miss May."

"Necessary, Mr..." Eliza trailed off, realizing she did not know his last name or if he even possessed one.

"Once upon a time," he rasped, "I was called Aodh MacNiall. But that man has long been dead to the world."

They said no more; it was clear that talking drained his strength. At the back of the kitchens, Mr. Albright, the driver, set down a barrel of mead before looking around in a frantic manner. When he glanced back at Eliza and Adam, tilted drunkenly at her side, his eyes went as wide as dinner plates. She supposed seeing over six feet of bloody and battered and chained male would do that to a person.

"Jaysus. You didn't say nothing about..." The driver swallowed hard and shook his head. "Hurry up, then." Sweat peppered his grubby brow and he wiped at it with a dingy rag. "First sign o' trouble and I'm off. Blunt or no." He did not dare look upon Adam, as if doing so would somehow make him more accountable. "Get him in the cart, lass, afore someone sees." The driver hurried off to finish his delivery.

The small trip out of the house and to the waiting cart felt endless. Eliza's back was so tight that she feared a sudden movement might make it crack. The vivid image of them taking a tumble and sprawling on the pavers flashed in her mind before she pushed it away, and, bending her knees to take more of Adam's weight, she gave his long, unwieldy frame a desperate shove. Coupled with his own, albeit weak, efforts, the man fell into the cart, only to lie prone and panting just inside of the cart door.

Sweat ran down her spine and over her brow as she roughly pushed his legs farther into the cavern of the cart. Good gravy, he was heavy. Wiping an arm across her forehead, she hopped in behind him, having to crawl over his body to get fully inside. Once there, she tugged on his hips and shoulders, edging him along. Adam's eyes fluttered open, thin slits of pale amber. With a grunt, he heaved himself along, trying to help her. She did not want to think about the noise they were making or the time that had elapsed.

Nausea churned in her belly, threatening to rise up her throat. She couldn't think about getting caught. She *would not.*

"Lie still," she whispered in his ear when he attempted to move again. Thankfully, he did so immediately, though Eliza suspected that he'd simply run out of strength. Hunched against the side of the cart, he shivered, his mouth pinched, his knees drawn up to his chest. Damn it, but he was far too injured for her liking. They ought to have waited until he'd healed further.

"Shit," she hissed under her breath. With quick movements, she hunched over him and heaved a barrel in front of him, blocking his upper body from view. Another barrel had to be moved to hide his legs. By the time she was finished, the world around them was a dark cocoon and her arms burned with exertion. She could only be thankful that the big, wooden barrels were empty of mead or ale.

On a suppressed sigh, she pulled off her cloak, draped it over Adam, and then sat back next to him. Her pulse knocked against her throat, her heartbeat visible at her breast. Every inch of her ached. Fear had her body twitching with the urge to run. They were barely covered from view. Anything could go wrong. Mab could decide to return and pay a visit to Adam.

Eliza ground her teeth together. *Stop thinking. Now.*

Footsteps echoed out in the courtyard, followed by a man's voice. "Then it'll be next month, sir?" The driver.

"Best to make it two weeks," came the butler's voice. He must have returned early, which meant he'd soon find the staff drugged. "We've been going through mead like washing water, this incident aside."

"You'll be hearin' no complaint's from the likes o' me." The two shared a chuckle. Too close to the cart.

Eliza tensed so hard that she shook. At her side, Adam stirred. Immediately, she put a quelling hand upon his sweaty shoulder. She kept it there, feeling the blood seep through the shirt and willing him still as a single set of footsteps grew louder. The cart shook as the driver heaved an empty barrel into the back of the cart.

The barrels next to Adam's body were pushed hard against him as the driver adjusted his load. Though Adam hadn't opened his eyes, nor made a sound, pain pinched his features. Eliza's hold gentled, trying to soothe, even though a sick, dreadful terror had her by the throat.

She held her breath as the driver secured his haul with ropes, going about his work as though he hadn't a care in the world. She wondered if he saw them hiding or if he'd done his best to cover them further. She dared not look. But the interior of the cart grew darker, the air heavy and muted.

Moments seemed to drag on endlessly in which the driver fussed about and then walked away. Silence stretched, broken only by her thundering heartbeat. And then suddenly they were moving. Eliza dared not breathe a sigh of relief; she'd save that for when they were well and truly clear of this house.

But as the minutes rolled on, she allowed herself to rest against the high slat-board wall of the delivery cart. Beside her, Adam dozed, his brows drawn and his complexion pale. She'd have to wake him; she didn't know where to go. But there was time yet.

Eventually, the card rolled to a stop. And then the driver's disembodied voice drifted through the weak light. "Where to then?"

Eliza moved to shake Adam awake, but his eyes flicked open, and he answered quick but quiet. "Houndsditch, by way of the Rag Fair."

There was a pregnant pause from without, which made Eliza think Houndsditch wasn't a favorable destination. Adam confirmed this when he added tightly, "You'll be well rewarded." Even half dead, his tone brooked no argument.

The driver's sigh was audible, but he'd been given enough cash from her to know they were good for it. "Righto."

They were off in a tick. And the small space in which they hid fell to silence. Eliza allowed herself to be lulled by the rocking of the cart. But her unease didn't entirely fade. Would she ever feel safe again? Was she insane for helping Adam? Believing in his tales?

"I am sorry."

The words were so softly spoken that, for a moment, Eliza thought she dreamed them. But, by the expression upon Adam's face, she hadn't. "I am," he said a bit stronger now. "For chaining you." He visibly winced. "Having been on the restraining end of one, I can safely say that doing so to you was possibly the worst decision of my life."

She could not help but frown. Some things were harder to forgive. "I won't argue with you, if that's what you're after."

A line formed in his lean cheek, evident only when he was amused or regretful. She knew that much about him, even though they'd barely interacted with each other. And she was struck by the strangeness of how she seemed to read this man so well. Why him? Not for one moment did she entertain the idea that he was her soul mate. Such ideas spoke of fate. And she wasn't one for fate but a woman who made her own way through the world. Actions determined one's destiny not the other way around.

"Ah, Eliza May, believe me, lass, arguing with you is the last thing I want." He glanced down at his wrists, raw and oozing around the thick cuffs that bound him, and a furrow worked between his thick brows. "I was afraid, aye? Centuries I'd been searching and my time was nearly up. I saw you and..." His muscled shoulder lifted then dropped. "I've always been a man of action. It seemed best to secure you by my side where nothing could take you away."

Eliza sank farther down the side of the lumbering cart. The heavy canvas cover rubbed against her hair and threatened to smother. She hated the dark, hated feeling trapped. "I understand," she said at last.

One of his brows kicked upward, and she gave him a crooked, half smile. "I didn't say I approved of your actions. But...well, I'll forgive you for them."

When he sat up straighter, his attention more intent, she rushed onward. "We are in this together now. To be at odds is counterproductive."

Through the strained silence, he cleared his throat. "Do not forgive me, Eliza, unless you mean it." He turned and faced her head-on. "Regardless of where we stand, I'll not argue with you or treat you with disrespect. But I'll no' harbor false hope. That I cannot tolerate."

Eliza found herself turning as well so that she might see him better in the muffled dimness. "What is it that you are hoping for?"

The thick fan of his black lashes swept down, hiding his gold eyes. "That we might..."—his cheek twitched—"be friends."

Her breath hitched, and in the dark, she rested a hand against her belly. Friends? Could she be friends with him? Protest surged forth, hot and deep. How could she even think it? And yet, she'd been the one to offer forgiveness. Had she been merely performing lip service?

He waited quietly, not pushing, not backing away. The cart dipped and bounced along the road, making his big, rough body sway. He was a patient man, but also capable of cold cunning. Capable of torturing as well. She remembered the shadow crawler Darby that Adam had ordered about like a slave and ultimately killed by simply stopping his heart. All without batting an eye. And yet, even though he'd chained her, she had never feared for her physical safety.

He'd never even raised his voice to her, save that one time when her never-ending silence had pushed him past patience.

"You agreed to be mine. Mine! And now you act as though you've been tricked. I gave you life anew. I look

after your every comfort, for all that you ignore it. What do you want of me? What?"

"*Freedom.*"

Eliza flinched at the memory. At the desperate anger that had sharpened his tone, and the pleading that had been in hers. And what had his answer been? No. He would not give that which she yearned for most.

Bitterness was a fist punching against the inside of her ribs. Part of her didn't want to look at Adam, big, strong wreck of a man, whom she had freed. She'd taken him out of hell, at the risk of her own freedom. The bitterness within her grew.

"I don't know if I can be your friend," she said, not surprised at the waspishness in her voice.

Though he clearly tried to prevent it, his expression fell to disappointment. For a long moment, he visibly swallowed, several times, as though tasting his own bitterness. "Do you...might you be able to one day? To truly forgive me?"

Gods, but he shocked her. He wasn't one to beg. He certainly had no reason to with her.

"Why does it matter to you?" she found herself asking. "You no longer need me to avoid Mab. What's done is done. I won't help you more or less based on friendship."

He adjusted his position, the numerous wounds making his movements jerky and stilted. Focusing on one of the barrels they were squeezed between, he spoke in a low, almost irritated voice. "Not everything is about the fae witch. What lies between us, Eliza May, is ours alone."

Chapter Nine

Torture had changed him. For the first time in his life, Adam did not think in terms of the future but focused on the here and now, or rather, focused on escaping the here and now. When he'd made his bargain with Eliza May, he wanted only to get away. Get away from Mab, regain his strength, and exact his revenge. Lofty goals for a man who'd been chained these past months. Now, as the wagon rolled to a gentle halt and the sounds of Eliza stirring caught his attention, grave misgivings roiled around within him.

They were in front of a GIM public house. Early as it was, it would not yet be filled with patrons. But there would be witnesses enough. And he would have to ask for their help. He'd have to tell them who he was, and they would see the pathetic state he now lived in. Humiliation was a bitter taste in his mouth, and he nearly squeezed his eyes closed.

But Eliza needed him sharp. So he did what he must and hauled himself to sitting. Well, a half slump. Hells clamoring bells, he was a pathetic wreck. A king no longer. Breathing too fast and light, he struggled to find a steady voice.

"I'll..." He swallowed down a fist-sized lump of humility. "I shall need your help quitting the cart."

A tiny wrinkle formed on Eliza's smooth brow. "Well, of course you will. Your leg is broken, as are a number of your ribs and left arm." *Silly man* was implied.

"I am healing," he added with a touch of acid. "There is that, even though it is at a snail's pace."

"We need to get those blasted chains off so you can heal faster."

"No truer words, dove."

She shoved a pair of lumpy, mismatched boots onto his feet, and he wanted to laugh. Paired with the plaid pants and tatty shirt, he looked no better than a court jester.

They ought to have used the back-alley entrance. Even on this shadowy, dismal street, lined with crooked houses that sagged in on each other, he garnered too much attention. "Act as though I'm a drunken sot," he murmured against Eliza's neck.

She shivered, but she began to vocally chastise him. "I ought to have stayed in Boston with mother. You're a no-account lout and hanging three sheets to the wind to boot. Just look at yourself, barely able to walk, and here you are seeking out more." She hissed in disgust.

"Shut yer hole an' do as yer told," he said in a loud slur.

Muttering and grousing, Eliza all but stumbled them into the small, dark pub. All heads turned their way. And then the barkeep did a double take. "Sire?"

Adam looked the man over. Alan Brown. GIM age: eighty-seven years. Death age: twenty-nine. Cause of death: knife to the gut after his fellow thieves took exception to Alan's portion of the take. Souls owed Adam: three.

"Mr. Brown," he said with as much dignity as a man who was heavily leaning on a slip of a girl could muster, "I've a favor to ask of you." He glanced about the room, taking in the familiar faces. He knew them all. Of course he did. They were his children. "Of all of you."

Mr. Brown's mouth hung open like a dead cod's before he regained his wits and snapped it shut, immediately coming out from behind the bar to bow before Adam. "Sire."

Adam could do without the display. Which was a first. He repressed a sigh. "Rise, Mr. Brown." When the man did as bided, he continued. "Miss May and I need to be out of sight for a while." The understatement of the year. However, he'd be damned if he begged for a soft bed and a cudgel blow across the brow so he could find blessed oblivion.

Fortunately, it was obvious what Adam needed, and Mr. Brown sprang into action, snapping his fingers at the barmaid, who bustled over and gave Adam a kind smile. "This way, sir." Anna Smith. GIM age: seventy years. Death age: seventeen. Cause of death: strangulation after rape.

He kept his voice low. "Thank you, Miss Smith." And though it gutted him to do it, he let her slip her shoulder under his free arm so that she might help Eliza bear his weight. Thus supported, they moved as an awkward group toward the back of the room. As they went, every GIM in the room stared on, silent and questioning. He'd answer them later.

Adam caught the eye of a slim young man, all but hidden in the shadows by the bar. "Jonathan Moore, I'll ask you to keep watch outside."

Quick as a tick, the man nodded and slipped out the door. Good lad.

Brown hurried to open a door that led to a set of narrow and rickety stairs. Wonderful. Adam swore he heard Eliza mutter much the same sentiment under her breath. But when he glanced down at her, her face was serene and her attention set on their destination.

"We'll get you set up in—" Brown stopped midsentence, his gaze focused on a spot just to Adam's right. And Adam inwardly cringed, realizing that Brown was listening to a spirit. One Adam could no longer see. Brown's eyes narrowed, and he turned back to Adam expectantly. When Adam merely returned his look, Brown obviously realized his predicament, and the man's wispy brows lifted a touch. Inside himself, Adam died a little more. But Brown was polite enough not to make a fuss, only got to the heart of the matter. "Fae spotted coming down the road."

A ripple of palpable tension ran through the room. Fae were rare enough that most immortals feared them. Misinformation mixed with heinous stories of torture helped that fear along. Rather brilliant of the fae, Adam thought with grudging admiration. For now the mere mention of them had others cowering or looking over their shoulder.

However, the GIM had very real reasons to fear the fae. A GIM could not see much less pull a fae's soul from his body. Adam knew this fatal weakness was due to the fact that his magic was connected to a fae curse; thus they were the only supernatural immune to the GIM's power. The only recourse was to fight them hand to hand with iron and hope to strike a killing blow.

"Come," Mr. Brown said. "We haven't much time."

*   *   *

Though a frisson of terror raced up Eliza's neck, she remained steady as the GIM around her snapped into action. Two men stepped in between Eliza and the young barmaid to take hold of Adam. They wedged their shoulders beneath his arms and, with a shocking display of deference, half carried him towards the other end of the pub. The barmaid touched Eliza's elbow.

"Follow me, Miss."

Eliza followed, pretending that her heart wasn't in her throat, that she didn't hear the agitated whirring of the girl's heart or see the way the gentle glow around her body had darkened to a coal-smoke color.

The room grew darker as well. Outside, just visible through the latticed, bottle-glass windows, a thick, greenish fog had rolled in. A shiver tickled Eliza's skin. It was as if the fog were sentient and searching for prey.

The two GIM led Adam to the back wall of the pub. The walls were constructed of wide slabs of wood so old that they were blackened and glossed over with smoke and grease. Hammered into the walls were intricate bands of iron forming a pattern of crosses interlocked with fleur-de-lis. Rather lovely, but odd. It was if they were inside of a cage.

The woman caught Eliza looking and dipped her head in close. "For the GIM, a fleur-de-lis represents mind, body, soul. I've no idea why Adam favors the cross pattée."

But Eliza did. It was a knight's cross.

A GIM touched the center of a cross, and a door, completely hidden by the pattern on the wall, swung open. A crawl space, no bigger than a kitchen pantry, greeted them. "There's a tunnel that leads to an exit about a block away," said one of the men. He pointed to a hook on the wall. "Pull that there and it'll open." The pained tone of his voice made it clear that he thought it unlikely Adam would be able to move.

"I'd rather fight," Adam said, "short as that battle would be."

The GIM grinned with satisfaction. "Aye, sire, I'd expect nothing less from you."

Though they set Adam down with care, the GIM hurried now. Eliza was handed in a moment later. She shuffled over to Adam's side, where he'd begun to slump down the wall. He wouldn't last much longer. As she needed his help, anxiety rode through her at the thought of him expiring. He'd promised that he'd soon heal, but it didn't appear likely.

Adam leaned against her, a slight touch, not one to be noticed by the GIM helping them, but she noticed.

"The iron ought to deter them from messing about with the walls," a man murmured before unceremoniously shutting them in.

The room fell to utter darkness, not even a slant of light showing beneath the hidden door. A moment later, she heard the fae enter the pub. Worse, she felt them, like a burr under her skin, making it prickle and her heart beat faster.

"You there," said the unmistakable voice of Mab. "Are you the proprietor of this...establishment?"

"Aye. Can I be helping you with something, Madam?"

In the cramped space, Eliza sat, arm pressed against Adam's arm. The hard heat of his shoulder and biceps held her attention for one moment before Eliza concentrated on the words drifting in, on Mab's voice.

"My granddaughter Eliza May has gone missing. She

was last seen in the company of the coward Adam of the GIM while boarding a wine wagon. My servant followed the wagon as far as Houndsditch." There was a pause, as if Mab wanted to let her words soak in. She continued on in a measured tone. "As this is the closest GIM hovel, reason stands that they have come here in search of sanctuary."

An awkward silence descended before one of the GIM spoke. "It takes naught but a pair of good, working eyes to see that they aren't here, Madam."

Heels clicked against the floor. "If you'd like to keep your eyes, GIM, you'll watch your mouth. I've no patience for your cheek. I know very well that you are likely harboring them."

"Madam," said the man quickly, "I wouldn't touch the—"

Mab's irritated snarl shot out.

"—walls," the GIM finished. "The iron runs throughout, Madam."

"Yes, I see that," Mab snarled. "And I can well guess why. Now you mean to tell me that you are friend to the fae?"

Another voice piped up, a woman's. "We never said we were. Surely you can't blame us."

Footsteps sounded as Mab prowled the room, trying to detect where Eliza and Adam might be hiding. Mab's voice rang out, heavily laced with pomp and false graciousness. "You ought to be bowing down to me in gratitude. Your creator Adam has no power over you anymore. I have freed you all."

Beside her, Adam let out a harsh breath that sounded overloud in the tight enclosure. With the tips of her fingers, Eliza touched his forearm. It was enough to distract him. His breath evened out, but his body remained as stone against her.

"Freed us?" came a snide reply. "Were you under the impression that we were slaves, then?"

A ringing silence followed. "Were you not beholden to his will?" Mab trilled out as though shocked that anyone would dare suggest otherwise.

A woman spoke. "We were given the choice to serve. That is not slavery."

Adam's head turned, making the slightest noise, and Eliza could feel the force of his gaze upon her. She was glad of the darkness that hid what would surely be recrimination in his eyes. Yes, all right, she's accused him of being no better than a slave owner. But, admittedly, the GIM had not been bound in chains as she had.

"A choice of death or servitude hardly seems much of a choice at all," said Mab.

"And yet we'd gladly make the same choice to serve Adam again," said another man.

Beneath Eliza's fingertips, the warm skin of Adam's forearm twitched.

"Enough," snarled Mab, loud enough that it rang through the small space in which they hid. "Adam's reign is over. He is an enemy of the fae. Bring him and the girl to me, and you shall be rewarded beyond your wildest dreams."

Silence.

Anger and a deadly coldness laced Mab's next words. "Harbor him, and you shall suffer beyond all endurance."

Eliza found herself leaning just a bit closer to Adam. He radiated warmth, though she feared it was feverish. At the moment, it did not matter, for she was growing so cold, so very cold. Deep within her, a shiver began, and with it came the urge to give in to that strange, unnatural laughter that always arrived when death grew near. *No, no, no. She could not do this now.* Eliza ground her teeth together and tried to push the urge away.

Outside, another voice rang out. "Threats, is it?" said a man. "Oh, now there's a rich incentive to betray our creator. To be sure—" His words were cut off with a gurgled sound of pain.

Adam lurched, as if he'd rise, and Eliza clutched his wrist. It gave her the distraction she needed. Turning her head, she pressed her lips to his ear. "You cannot help him." She mouthed the words for fear of being overheard. "You will merely make them all suffer."

He gave a jerky nod. In the dark, Eliza's hand slid into Adam's larger one. Their fingers intertwined. As if one, a tremor rippled through their bodies. An awareness, an acknowledgment. Of what, Eliza did not know, but she felt connected to him. That this broken, wounded man would keep her safe was ridiculous. They had never been in greater danger.

"Don't like what you see?" Mab said. "Then give the coward up to me. He is mine now. As is the girl. They are my property."

Another agonized cry rang out.

Eliza's chest quaked as she suppressed the horrible laughter that wanted to rise. Gods, but Mab was killing the poor GIM. Tears burned in Eliza's eyes.

Next to her, Adam sucked in a soft breath, as he too reacted to the sounds of the GIM's torture. Sweat and blood soaked his shirt. He burned too hot, but he remained still as the sounds of a man being slowly, methodically tortured came from without. Grunts, muffled screams, the grumble of protests so obviously bitten back by the rest of the GIM, for they too must have known it was a lost cause to retaliate in the face of the fae queen.

But for Adam, it was worse. On the next shout, he jerked against Eliza, trembling, not from fear but rage. He was close to cracking. Without hesitation, Eliza wrapped an arm about him and drew his head down to her shoulder. He let her gather him up, let her hold him tight, hold him back.

With each shout and moan from the outer room, he flinched, his muscles twitching as if feeling the hits. And she could only close her eyes, rest her head against his, and pray that he did not move. Hot tears ran down Eliza's cheeks, her chest heaving with suppressed sobs.

The footsteps without stopped. Directly before their hiding spot. Silence.

Adam's grip upon her hand tightened. Eliza dared not breathe, but her heart pounded so loudly that she feared they would hear it. The brush of a large, male thumb against her knuckles was a small but needed comfort.

"For the last time," said Mab, as though she were speaking to recalcitrant children, "give me the coward Adam and his concubine."

More silence. Then the scuff of a shoe. "Madam," said a woman softly, "we've nothing to reveal. Adam is not here. Nor is this girl of whom you speak."

"Well, then," said Mab lightly, "I'll leave you with this little reminder." Her tone turned hard. "I shall check in regularly. I expect cooperation."

They did not hear Mab go, but Eliza could feel it. As if a dark weight had lifted from her shoulders, leaving behind a deep ache. Yet they remained silent and unmoving. Until finally, Adam let out a great, rasping breath. "Never again," he whispered so softly that she could barely hear it. He pressed his forehead against her shoulder. "Never again will I remain hiding while one of mine suffers."

Regret formed a lump in her throat. "No," she croaked. "Never again." With the very tips of her fingers, she touched his sweat-slicked hair, but did not stroke it. She didn't have the right. And so her hand fell. "I'm sorry I made you do it. I was afraid." The confession hurt her pride, but it had to be said.

She felt him flinch and then lift his head. "No," he said in a strangled voice. "No, you were in the right. I'll not see your safety sacrificed for my pride."

Beneath her hand, his skin was clammy, his body leaning into hers. Slumping. Eliza had little further warning before he fell against her breast.

Chapter Ten

Sin sprinted into the house and took the stairs two at a time. His breath burned in his throat, not from exertion but from fear. No sooner had he reached the middle landing than a door crashed open. A blur of movement, a snarl, and then a claw-tipped hand had him by the throat and slammed him into the wall.

Ian Ranulf, fangs extended, his human face stretching into lupine lines, snarled again as he squeezed Sin's throat tighter. Shit and bloody, fucking hell. Ian was turning werewolf on him. Sin hung limp, trying not to fight back, trying to calm even as the walls began to rattle and his power surged under his skin. Another man burst from the room.

"Ian," Archer shouted, deep and powerful. "Stop. It is Sin."

Ian's eyes, more animal than human, narrowed. A snort of hot breath hit Sin's face. At his side, Archer eased closer, his expression stern. "He is your brother-in-law. *Daisy's* brother."

At the sound of Daisy's name, Ian winced, a forlorn sound escaping him.

"Let him go, Ian."

Ian blinked. In an instant, his face rearranged into a fully human visage. A deep breath, a shocked look, and Ian abruptly let Sin go, stepping back as Sin staggered.

"Apologies," Ian bit out. Still pale with sweat darkening his long auburn hair, the man was a mess. "I reacted... badly."

Leaning against the wall, Sin rubbed at his neck until he could find his voice. "And mine," he rasped. "I should not have charged in as I did." No, it was never wise to rush into a lycan's lair. Especially not the king of the lycans. And not now of all times.

Ian nodded, a sharp, distracted gesture, and then looked away. His body was already turning back to the door from whence he'd sprung. A grim Archer gave Sin's neck an assessing glance. "You'll live." His shoulders sagged. "Come along, then."

As if going to the gallows, the three of them entered the bedroom. The lights were turned low, and a fire crackled cheerily behind the grate. But an air of desperation and sadness filled up the space.

Ian strode toward the bed, every line of his body tense and agitated. Sin did not want to look; a small, frightened part of him wanted to turn tail and run. But look he did. A lump filled his throat.

Still as death and twice as pale, his once vibrant and happy sister Daisy lay upon the bed. He knew she was not dead, they'd have told him, but he could not make himself believe she was truly alive. Not when her breast lay unmoving. Not when her once-glowing skin had gone utterly dull.

Christ.

Ian knelt by his wife, taking her smaller hand in his. Slowly, Sin approached, the bed looming larger and his sister growing smaller. A rustle of skirts caught his attention. Miranda rose from a chair at the other side of the bed. Her green eyes were listless.

"Sin."

"Miranda," he got out. And then he was at the foot of the bed.

Miranda came to stand next to him, and she caught up his hand with hers. He clenched her cold, damp fingers as if they were a lifeline. He'd just found his sisters, and they'd come to mean the world to him. He could not lose one now.

"How . . . what . . ." He took a breath. "What is wrong with Daisy?"

It was Archer who answered. "Her spirit is not here."

Daisy was a GIM, her spirit able to travel from her body at will. That she'd left her body should not have caused anyone concern. There had to be more. "For how long?" Sin asked.

"Going on twenty-four hours now," said Archer.

Long but not exceedingly. Sin frowned. "I don't understand."

Miranda sighed. "She's never been gone for this long, and when she left this time, she simply . . . collapsed."

A strangled sound came from deep within Ian's chest, and he pressed his head against Daisy's breast as if it might rouse her. The intimacy of it discomfited Sin, but he could not look away.

Ian cleared his throat. "She's been fatigued lately. Unable to stay awake."

Which *was* odd. Daisy was immortal, her body stronger than three men's. Nor did she need to sleep for as long as a human.

"The other night," Ian went on in painful slowness, "she went milk-white, looked at me, and then..." He closed his eyes tight. "She was gone."

"Did you see her spirit?" Sin asked, cautious now because he did not want to aggravate Ian's lycan side. When a man was half wolf, his animal tended to lash out when threatened. But because Ian was a lycan, he was able to see spirits whereas the rest of Daisy's family could not.

Ian shook his head, sending the sweat-damp strands of his shoulder-length hair tumbling about his face. "Which is the most frightening. She was simply gone...Christ." He curled over Daisy once more, murmuring something in her ear while smoothing her golden curls with a trembling hand.

From below came the sound of the front door opening. Archer cocked his head and then sent Ian a look. "I believe it is Jack." Not exactly subtle, his way of warning Ian not to attack, and Ian made a noise of annoyance.

"I know," he murmured. "I recognize his scent just fine, thank you." He ought to; Jack was Ian's foster son.

A moment later, Jack entered the room, his eyes wide and worried, his massive frame taking up the whole of the doorway.

"Piss and shit," Jack whispered as he saw Daisy. But he did not rush in; he had his wife, Mary, at his side, and she clung to him with a pale hand. No, it was Jack who clung, slowly guiding her as if she were made of spun glass. It was then Sin noticed how unsteady Mary was, her grip knuckle-white on Jack's massive forearm.

"Let me have a look at her," Mary said in a weak voice.

Ian leapt up and stepped aside. "Do you know what has happened? Where she might have gone?" Like Daisy, Mary was a GIM.

Mary settled on the bed beside Daisy and rested a

hand directly over her heart. Daisy and Mary both had clockwork hearts made of gold. And in the tense silence of the room, it became exceedingly clear that one heart barely clicked away while the other worked hard and fast. Mary's eyes closed, and she seemed to be gathering her strength, while Jack set a bracing hand on her shoulder. He looked as if he'd soon be ill.

Sin's insides plummeted.

"Tell me, lass," Ian snapped, his eyes wild.

Mary flinched. "The GIM are dying."

It took the air out of the room.

"The youngest," she went on in a wooden voice. "The newly made. They're simply vacating their bodies—"

Ian howled then. The big lycan snatched his wife up and gathered her against his chest, her arms and head flopping sickly as he huddled down with her in a chair, his eyes going lupine and feral as he glared around at them, daring another to get closer.

"Da," Jack started, but Ian snarled.

"Don't," he shouted. "Don't tell me she's dead. Her heart still beats. Her heart still beats!"

Mary made a cooing sort of noise before speaking slow and steady. "Yes, it does."

Ian gave her a brusque nod, but he did not let Daisy go, only cupped her head to his shoulder.

Jack ran a hand through his short hair. "Some are like Daisy. Their spirits are gone but their bodies remain as if waiting. And others..." He put his hands back on Mary's shoulders, drawing her near.

"Are weakening," Mary said with a sad, wane look. "I...I am so very tired. Nor can I leave my body."

"And Lucien," Ian asked. "What says he?" Lucien was the leader of the GIM in London.

"He believes it has to do with Adam," Jack said, and Sin's insides lurched.

Fuck, fuck, fuck. Sin wanted to scream and feared he'd be sick on the carpet.

"Adam has gone missing," Jack was saying, his voice coming at Sin as though through water. "Lucien has been trying to contact him but he's simply disappeared."

Sin ground his teeth together. More than anything, he wanted to tell his family of what he knew. That, acting under Mab's orders, both he and Will Thorne had stolen Adam's woman. That the demon Adam, creator of all GIM, was likely enraged and in some trouble with Mab—for Sin knew taking Eliza from Adam would somehow hurt the demon; otherwise Mab would not have bothered.

God, but he wanted to tell them all. And yet he was blood bound by Mab. He literally could not speak a word of it to anyone. His mouth simply would not be able to move.

Fucking hell. He did not deserve to be in this room. He was shite, a stain on a better man's boot. Breathing between clenched teeth, he raked his nails along his scalp and fought the urge to simply run. A soft squeeze on his arm had him starting. He'd forgotten he held on to Miranda.

Her fine green eyes, the same shade as his, looked up at him with gentle compassion. He looked away.

"Poppy and Win are on their way home," she told Jack. Poppy was the eldest sister and the leader of the SOS, a society who guarded the supernatural world. She and her husband, Winston, had been on holiday in Egypt.

Ian snorted. "Not much they can do."

"No," agreed Archer. "But Poppy wanted to be here..." He grimaced. In the event that Daisy died.

Ian's nostrils flared, but he looked to Jack and Mary. "I

want you both living here until we understand what is happening. The lass needs rest and you"—Ian stared pointedly at Jack—"organize the lycan. They can see spirits, aye? Well, they can damn well search this bloody city for Daisy."

Jack nodded. "The SOS is doing all they can to get to the bottom of this." Jack and Mary were directors in the SOS. "I've regulators working round the clock…" Jack trailed off, his expression frustrated. It was clear that all their efforts had been for naught.

No one looked to Sin. Why should they? They believed him nothing more than a frivolous young man. They never entertained the idea that he was their greatest traitor.

Eliza was not certain how she knew something had entered her room, but awareness stole over her skin like a hand slipping into a tight glove. All at once, her body tensed and her breathing grew short. The covers hissed over her frame as she abruptly sat up and took stock of the room Mr. Brown had provided her. Pale blue moonlight gave the room a ghostly glow, making what was once innocuous chairs and tables appear to be squat and sinister beasties.

"Fluff and stuff," she muttered, perspiration cooling her brow. But her pulse beat hard against her throat.

And then she spotted it. A spirit. The lady moved from her perch upon Eliza's writing chair and glided forward. She was a lovely creature, all rounded curves and winsome features. And though she was transparent, her golden curls and the deep green of her fashionable gown were easy to discern. The woman's lips moved as she walked. She was talking to Eliza.

Eliza held up a hand. "I cannot hear you."

At this, the woman's wide blue eyes narrowed in both

confusion and irritation. She made to talk again, this time moving her arms with emphatic motions.

"I still cannot hear. I'm sorry." Eliza frowned. The woman was familiar. Just the sight of her caused Eliza's innards to lurch. And then she knew. "You... You're one of the women who tried to save me."

Two women had appeared and fought off her killers with skill that she'd thought only men possessed. The blonde woman was named Daisy. She'd been the one to call forth Adam. And then it had all gone wrong.

As though she were corporeal, Daisy settled herself at the end of the bed.

"Why are you here?" Eliza asked, then flushed when Daisy scowled and gestured from her mouth to Eliza's ear. Right, she couldn't tell her. Eliza settled back against her pillows and regarded her guest. Perhaps she ought to resent Daisy. The woman had led her to Adam after all, but she had also tried to save her. Daisy had clearly been shocked by Adam's treatment of her, that much Eliza had seen before he'd placed her in some odd sort of spiritual limbo. Daisy hadn't been in contact with her until now.

"Are you in need of something?"

Daisy's shoulders lifted on a silent sigh, and she nodded. Sadness seemed to weigh her down and darkened her spirit's light, making the lines of her body fainter.

Eliza worried the corner of her lower lip. "I can't imagine what I could do for you. Why not seek me out tomorrow? You know, in the flesh?"

Daisy made a face, and Eliza bit back a smile, but it faded as their gazes clashed and a realization stole over Eliza. "You cannot use your body?"

Slowly Daisy shook her head, fear and sorrow filling her lovely eyes, and her form faded even more. Eliza reached out, ready to hold her hand, when she remembered Daisy was a spirit. "Why come to me?" she asked her. "I cannot do anything to help. I'm not even a GIM."

Squaring her shoulders, Daisy leaned close and carefully enunciated one word: Adam. Eliza saw it clearly upon her lips, and she went cold.

"Adam?" she repeated, just to be clear.

Daisy nodded.

"He's asleep in the other room." Guilt and shame hit Eliza anew as she remembered Adam toppling to the floor. What would Daisy think of Eliza's part in her creator's captivity? Or if she learned of what Mellan wanted Eliza to do? Then Eliza decided she did not care; she had her reasons. But Daisy was weakening by the second, her shape flickering in and out as though shadows moved through her body. Her round face scrunched up with concentration. Frantic now, the spirit shook her head, waving a hand over her eyes and ears and then pointing down to the ground.

Following this strange pantomime, Eliza spoke slowly. "You've tried to ... He doesn't see you, does he?"

One sharp, pained nod.

Eliza slumped back. "He said he'd lost his power."

Daisy simply stared, her diaphanous body growing pale, whispery white. Her mouth worked more words: Help him.

"I am." As much as she could.

Desperation and terror twisted Daisy's pretty face into a macabre mask. And as she flickered out of existence, she said her last word. *Please.*

Chapter Eleven

❧〰️✦〰️❧

As with every moment of his new and miserable life, pain coursed through Adam's body, making it throb. Even in the dark, he recognized the pain, as if it had become an extension of himself. However, something was different. Softness cradled him, and warmth enveloped him. It felt so bloody good that he did not want to move for fear it was a dream. It had to be. Or perhaps one of Mab's tricks, a new method of torture.

A muffled creak, as though someone sitting in a chair had stirred, had him tensing. Only when his eyes opened did he realize that they'd been closed. That he was in a bed.

The room was dark, heavy curtains drawn and the weak glow of a bedside lamp casting flickering shadows along rough stone walls. And then he saw her, tense and too pale, and sitting in a chair next to him.

"Eliza." He hadn't meant to say her name, but it burst out of him in a rather pathetic croak. Pathetic too was the relief he felt upon seeing her.

She'd been reading a book, but upon hearing him, set

it aside and picked up a glass of water. She moved to the bed, bringing her clean, sweet scent closer, and offered him a drink. The wall of his abdomen ached as he shoved up on one elbow and drank deep. Cool, clear water washed down his parched throat. His hand shook only a little as he passed the glass back to her.

"I have some broth for you as well," she said, gesturing to a table at the other end of the room where a tray sat.

He eyed the soup bowl with displeasure. Where was a good slab of beef when a man wanted it? "I've not had my teeth pulled. Am I to be offered pap next?"

"Pap?" She blinked in confusion.

Right, she was a Yank. "Food for infants..." Adam waved a negligent hand. "Never you mind." He surveyed the room again. "Where are we?"

"With the GIM, of course." Her brow wrinkled as she peered down at him. "Or did you think that they'd turn us away?"

They'd have every right to. But he didn't voice the obvious, only moved to sit back. She stopped him with a fleeting touch on his shoulder before leaning over him to adjust the pillows. Adam closed his eyes and simply breathed her in, letting her warmth seep into his bones. Should he look at her now, at the smooth arch of her neck or the soft rise of her breasts, he'd pull her into the bed with him. And then what? He was too weak to do what he wanted with her, and she'd surely clout him.

Thankfully, Eliza was quick and soon stepped away from him, giving him room to breathe without fear of drowning in her heady scent. He leaned back, never taking his eyes from her.

"Believe it or not," she said, a smile forming in her dark eyes, "you're much improved."

He wanted to snort, but his ribs hurt too much. "So then, not so much resembling a man trampled beneath a carriage's wheels? Now, that is an improvement."

The smile reached her lips. "Battered but not wrecked."

Heat rushed through his blood. She of the Eternal Frowns was smiling at him. But then he remembered how she'd last seen him, as a weak, crumpled coward, held in her arms. Running a tired hand over his face, Adam surveyed the room before glancing down at himself. He wore a worn yet soft work shirt, and it lay half undone, exposing a swath of his chest. The infernal chains remained. That had to be dealt with. Among other things.

Eliza tidied his covers before refilling his glass of water and generally fussing about, doing everything other than look him in the eye. She smoothed her woolen skirts as she sat once again. Only then did her brown eyes meet his. "Do you feel better?"

He gave a slight nod. "Have I been out for a fair bit?"

"All night. It's going on noon now. I drew the drapes so that you might sleep." She picked a spot just above his shoulder to study with undue attentiveness.

"What," Adam said in a firm tone, "are you hiding from me, Miss May?"

Her pretty, pink mouth opened like a blooming rose. Then abruptly shut. "Tell me, what is it that Mellan wants?"

"You only ask after Mellan's desires," he said carefully. "Not Mab's?"

Her gaze slid over him and then flicked away. "I know what Mab wants from you."

The tartness in her tone had him grinning. "She wants many things. One of them being power over death. All fae want that because death frightens them."

"Well, it frightens me too, if I'm honest," Eliza retorted.

"You have fae blood, love."

She did not like that; her nose wrinkled and her eyes narrowed. Adam thought it prudent to move on. "Mab was under the impression that I know the location of a weapon called the Golden Horn an Bás. It's thought to call the dead and command them. I've no idea where this weapon is, or if it's even real," he added when Eliza leaned forward in anticipation.

With a little huff, she settled back. "Well, that won't be very helpful."

"I do, however," Adam said with a small smile of satisfaction, "know the location of an object Mellan desires."

At this, Eliza went oddly stiff, her mouth thinning. Adam watched her as he spoke. "My sword. The one I used when I was a knight those many centuries ago. He fears this sword because it is one of the only objects that can actually kill a fae."

The chair beneath Eliza scraped over the floorboards as she lurched to her feet and paced over to the curtained window. She did not peek out of it but leaned her head against the thick woolen hangings.

"Eliza," Adam said softly—when really he wanted to shout—"tell me what it is you hide from me."

Her shoulders tensed on an indrawn breath. "He wants me to kill you."

Little surprised Adam anymore, but the confession kicked him in the gut just the same. "And how are you to accomplish that?"

Slowly, she turned and pinned him with her dark brown eyes. "He said for me to free you, and that you would lead him to a prize he's been coveting. And then..." She trailed off, biting down on her plump bottom lip.

As for Adam, he felt as though he were made of lead. It took effort to speak. "So our bargain—"

"I made that bargain with you before he demanded this." Her cheeks paled. "He was not fooled when I refused to whip you, and he became suspicious."

With a jerk of his head, Adam nodded. It eased him to know she hadn't initially sought his help as part of Mellan's plan. Though the thought of Mellan sending Eliza on a fool's errand to presumably cut off Adam's head with his own sword had him seeing red. How could the bloody fool possibly think Eliza could go up against a seasoned fighter? "And are you?"

Eliza frowned. "Am I what?"

"Going to kill me." At this point, Adam did not know if he'd try to stop her. He did not think he could bear defending himself against her.

She lowered her head, her lashes fluttering down as well. "I suppose I deserve that." When she looked at him, her expression was composed but hate burned in her eyes. It was strong enough to have him flinching. Her smooth voice flowed over him. "There is only one being I long to destroy, and that is Mellan." She leaned in a little. "You promised to help me be free. Then help me be free of him, and I shall…"

"What?" he whispered. "Do whatever I want? Give yourself to me?"

Her nostrils flared, but she did not waver from her fierce stare. Adam waved a hand. "Be at ease. I thought I made it perfectly clear that I have no interest in having you under duress."

Eliza merely blinked, still not moving, and Adam resisted the urge to fidget in his bed. "What is Mellan to you, Eliza? An old lover? What is the connection?"

She flinched. "We never…He'd hint at wanting that, use it as a threat to scare me. But, no, thank the gods, no." A fine flush covered her cheeks. "There was a man or two, young lieutenants in his gang in Boston, when I wanted basic comfort." At once she stopped and took a breath and gave him a glare. "Not that it is any of your business."

Adam laughed a little, holding up his palms. "You'll find no judgment from me. Although, in the fairness of truth, the idea of Mellan touching you revolts me, if only because I hate him. Thus it is more the notion of being offended on your behalf, lass."

She smiled then. "In the spirit of honesty, Adam, I feel the same outrage over Mab on your behalf."

He found himself grinning like a fool. Were he not weakened and in pain, he'd pull her into the bed with him. The moment between them grew thick and taught, and his breath quickened, despite his wretched state, but she broke from his gaze and a frown worked its way across her brow.

"So then, Mellan wants some old sword of yours."

"Old," he scoffed. "You make it, and me, sound like a dusty relic."

Almost as if she had no control over it, her gaze went to his bared chest. He felt it like a soft glove stroking his skin, and his gut tightened with sweet pleasure. Lord, if he got his hands on her, let him not unman himself by going off like a lad. Adam cleared his throat. And so did she.

"There's more," she said. "Last night, I had a visitor."

Adam scowled. "Who? Are you hurt? What happened?"

"Nothing like that." She eyed him. "It was Daisy. The woman who called you to me?"

"Ah, yes, Daisy Ranulf." He quite liked the saucy wench. In truth, there was much about her that reminded him of Eliza. "Did she want to see me?" Adam really didn't want to be seen in this condition. But Daisy was his child just as any other, and he would not turn her away.

"Yes." Eliza's expression was grim. "Adam, she was

stuck in spirit form. She could not return to her body, and..." Eliza sucked in a breath. "Adam, the GIM are ill somehow...Did you not notice how wane they all are? I've been talking to them. They say there are those who have simply vacated their bodies and died."

All these months, Adam had known fear and rage. But it had been directed toward his own predicament. Now his chest constricted as a lump rose within his throat. His children. Ill. Dying.

Rage without an outlet or hope of recourse was a terrible thing. It turned in on itself and ate away at one's soul. A man could wither under such emotion. Adam ground his teeth, taking a ragged breath as he stared up at the rough-beamed ceiling. "I cannot help them."

"What?" Eliza's question was a breath of outrage.

His chains clattered as he punched the mattress. "Have you gone deaf? I cannot do a thing. I've lost my power. Nor do I know why this has occurred." Adam blinked rapidly. "What am I to do, Eliza? I'm no longer their king, but a mere man."

"You are our king still," said a voice from the doorway. Mr. Brown, the proprietor.

He looked at Adam as though he was a source of salvation. Weariness weighed down Adam's body. "No, I cannot help you." He lifted his head and took in the GIM hovering at the door. It seemed the whole of the inn had crowded forward, wanting to hear his confession. Pain turned to regret. "The fae bitch spoke true. I am without power." Slowly, he eased to standing, swaying a bit with the effort. "To harbor me is ill advised."

A ripple seemed to go through the room. They knew what he was saying. He was giving himself up to their care or letting them turn him over to Mab.

"Can you no see our souls? Or hear our thoughts?" said a young woman, her brow furrowed as she looked up at him.

"No." The word punctured the taut silence. It hurt to say. More than he'd expected. He'd ruled them with utter conviction. But no more.

Instead of sneering, however, the woman's lashes swept down as if his confession wounded her. "Which explains why you don't realize that we would never hand you over."

And as a lump of emotion clogged Adam's throat, a fine-looking man with a youthful face but a world-weary voice spoke up. "Were you to hear our thoughts, you'd know. You are our sire. Now and forever."

The clothes Mr. Brown brought Adam were not of good fit or high quality. Adam hadn't wanted that. "I need to appear working class," he'd told the GIM.

The assumption being that Adam would attract less notice that way. Eliza rather thought he could not be more wrong. A fine specimen of a man without window dressing simply made the architecture of his body that much more appealing. No matter how dull and shapeless the cut of his trousers were, they could not hide his massive thighs, nor the length of his legs. The wrinkled white work shirt worn open at the collar with the sleeves rolled up to his elbows merely drew attention to the strong column of his throat and the ropey muscles along his forearms.

They were going out today. They had two objectives now. Meet with an oracle and obtain the sword from Lucien Stone. In that order.

"If Mellan expects you to lead him to your sword, that means he's following us."

"Logic would assume so." Adam, having apparently

decided to put on a jacket, proceeded to secure the top button of his collar.

"Then why on earth should we go to retrieve it? You are not at your best." Eliza winced as he frowned, and she hurried on. "I'm sorry to be blunt about that, but it does concern me."

"Concerned about my welfare or my ability to protect you, Miss May?"

"I'll leave that to your imagination, or rather you may let your rather large conceit decide.

"I'm being serious, Adam"—his chest lifted at her use of his name—"why go after your sword with this threat hanging over our heads?"

He was silent for a moment, and she dared not lift her head to meet his eyes. With a distinct step backwards, he put a small distance between them. "We need it for these." He lifted his wrists and the chains clanked loudly. "The sword is a fae weapon, Miss May. Coated with iron, unbreakable, and capable of killing a fae warrior. I stole it long ago when I was a knight." He grinned, showing his bold, white teeth. "Didn't realize what it was at the time, but you can be sure I'll not be giving it back."

"And this sword will cut through your chains?"

"By your hand?" He glanced at her hands, resting in her lap. "Yes."

"And the sword is with Lucien?"

"It is on Lucien's barge. However, that is being watched," Adam said.

"Can Lucien not simply bring it to us?" Lucien was Adam's right hand. Eliza had watched him when she'd been with Adam before; the GIM was charming, crafty, and loyal.

Adam had looked pained then. "If anyone could find

him. But he's gone off somewhere, and I'll not trust another with retrieving the sword."

"Then why not retrieve it before we go to the oracle?"

"You've endless questions, Miss May," he said mildly.

"Yes, and you're constantly fueling more of them." Eliza sat in a chair, unwilling to move until she was satisfied. "Answer them."

Adam grunted. Clearly being ordered to talk was not something he liked. "The sword will keep. The oracle will not. I want to get there before someone else does."

Eliza lurched upright. "Is the oracle in danger?"

"Every oracle is in danger, dove. But the more likely case here is that Mab or Mellan will persuade the oracle to lie to us." He shot her a look. "I'd rather have my information untainted, wouldn't you?"

She made a noise of agreement. And the corner of his mouth tilted upward. He really was a fine-looking man.

Adam, in the act of slipping on a brown wool vest and buttoning it up, caught her gaze and stilled. The golden eyes of a hawk pinned her. "Why do you look at me so?" he asked in his dark, coffee voice.

Eliza willed herself to remain light and unaffected. "And how is it that I am looking at you?"

He peered at her, his head canting just a bit. "As if you find me amusing." Oh, but it was clear he did not find *that* amusing in the least. And he could not have been more wrong. Obviously, he hadn't the faintest notion how charismatic he was. The GIM that cared for him could hardly keep their eyes off of him. True, he no longer possessed that odd, overwhelming sexual pull that his powers had given him. This was more subtle, but no less potent. Adam, the man, was one of those rare persons who others would always long to be near.

And, by God, he was magnificent.

"I was thinking," she said, "that you'd have been better off dressed in those horrid plaid trousers. At the very least, you'd look ridiculous."

His scowl grew, but oddly so did the color upon his high-cut cheeks. He was blushing. How charming. Eliza found herself smiling, and he grumbled low in his throat at the action. "I bloody well despise those trousers, and why the bloody hell would you want me to look ridiculous?"

"You stick out like a candle at midnight as you are now."

His gaping mouth abruptly snapped shut but his flush darkened, turning his golden skin ruddy. When he spoke again, it was gruff. "I'm dressed as a common laborer. No one pays them any mind."

They will if the laborer looks as good as you do.

With brusque movements, Adam tucked a limp, grey neckerchief around his collar and began to tie it. In front of her, as if she were his wife. A blush stole over her cheeks, and she counted herself a ninny. She'd seen him unclothed so many times now that, were she to close her eyes, she could still map the lines of his strong body with neat precision.

"You're tying that neckerchief all wrong," she observed.

He snorted in amusement, "It's a poorly cut lump of cloth, Miss May. Ugly clothing, ugly fit."

Though she ought to stay put, Eliza moved to help him with his collar. One end was sticking up at an odd angle and would not settle no matter how he fussed with it. Gently, she smoothed it, aware of his proximity and the warmth of his big body. He watched her, his gaze lowering to her lips. As if greedy for his attention, they seemed to plump up, becoming sensitized to every light brush of his breath.

She felt her body slow down, growing hot and languid,

wanting to melt against him. Eliza tried to fight it, taking steady breaths. As she began to tie the rather horrid cloth around his neck, she spoke in a low, and not altogether steady, voice, "One would think you've never dressed yourself before."

"Mmm..." His voice was a deep rumble. "Or perhaps I'd rather you helped me."

Her gaze flicked up, shocked. She started to speak, but the door burst open. Adam and Eliza flinched as one, and his hand came to the small of her back. In trod a young serving girl holding a tray of food. She caught sight of Eliza and Adam standing close, and she halted.

"Begging your pardon, my lord. I..." The girl went pink in the cheeks and promptly lost the power to speak further.

Eliza took the moment to move away from Adam, noting how his fingers tensed as if to hold her back, but she eluded him and went to the window. A tremor went through her hand as she gripped the heavy curtain. The man was too potent. Too tempting.

An opinion she gathered the young GIM shared, for the girl merely stood, gazing at Adam as if he were something of a god to her.

It did not help matters when he gave her a graceful nod of the head, his deep voice mellow with command when he addressed her. "Good morn, Miss Annabelle. I see you have something for us?" He eyed the tray that was presently tilting at an alarming angle.

Cups and crockery rattled as Annabelle righted the tray. "You'll be wanting your breakfast, then?"

"Breakfast would be most welcome, my dear." Outwardly, Adam gave no indication of insincerity or impatience. Indeed, he had that rare ability to make every person believe that his attention and interest rested solely on them. Eliza, however, knew better. She did not miss the tight rein he kept on his body. Or when his gaze flicked to hers, communicating in seconds his amusement over being interrupted and how he wanted to get her alone. The knowledge connected them on a level that disturbed her, and yet made her feel somehow as though she were finally precisely where she ought to be.

Eliza took a quick breath and turned her attention back to watching Annabelle.

Annabelle's flush grew in depth and hue as she set the tray down. "Well, then"—the GIM bumped into the doorway—"I'll...be going." The poor girl was a lovely shade of magenta as she fled the room, slamming the door behind her.

The corners of Adam's eyes crinkled as he went to latch the door. "She's developed a bit of a tendré for me, I'm afraid." His wide mouth twitched. "Or for the king of the GIM, rather."

Eliza swallowed down a snort. "Doesn't everyone who meets you?" The quip was out before she could think better of it.

The latch clicked shut. Adam glanced at her from over his shoulder, and his mouth quirked. "Everyone but you."

He strolled across the small space between them, his gaze rapt.

"You never gave me the chance." Eliza pushed past him, seeing the question forming on his lips and not wanting to answer.

But he followed, close on her heels, the looming wall of his body providing warmth in the cold chill of the dim room. "And if you'd had the chance?"

Eliza stopped. Behind her, Adam stood, his chest not quite touching her shoulder blades, but near enough to feel his heat. Not turning, she stared up at an intricately carved cuckoo clock that hung upon the wall and she pretended that warmth wasn't blooming over her breasts. "A moot point as that time has come and gone."

Gently, but with clear purpose, he caught hold of her elbow and turned her to face him. His expression was stern, his brows drawn over eyes of deep gold. God, but he was too much for her. Every time she looked at him directly, she could barely breathe. He was like the sun, blinding her, making her want to both turn away and look upon him endlessly. When he spoke, his voice was deep, almost urgent. "And if you had the chance now?"

The press of his fingers seemed to burn through her sleeve and into her bones. She could lie to him. Drive the wedge between them deeper. He stood, motionless, waiting for her answer. Eliza took a breath, aware of her ribs and breast pushing against her corset. "I am drawn to you."

His nostrils flared, his lids lowering in a lazy, leonine way that was pure sin. "And I to you."

A river of heat snaked down her center. He drifted closer, his broad chest nearly touching the tips of her breasts. Eliza fought the urge to put a hand up to stop him. "It's merely attraction." Her voice was too faint, too unsteady. "Attraction does not mean that we are..."

"Meant for each other," he supplied, low and dry.

"Yes, that." She raised her chin and pinned him with a quelling look. "Attraction is not so precious. It happens all the time."

Again his gaze roamed her face. It felt like a caress. His wide mouth went soft. He stared at hers for only a moment before meeting her eyes. "Not to me. Not until you."

The intensity of his statement—the way he looked at her, as if willing her to understand how it could be between them—made her dizzy, unable to breathe. She spun away from him, her skirts swishing. "I cannot believe that." Idly, she ran a finger over a battered dressing table, leaving a dark trail as dust clung to her skin. "I'm certain you've had many women."

Cold amusement lit his voice. "I was a Templar Knight, dove. I took a vow of celibacy when I was naught but eighteen years, and before that, I was a squire, and before that a paige. Always in training to be Templar."

Her breath stuttered. And she could not help but look at him. "Surely at some point, you must have felt—"

He shook his head. "Better not to allow yourself to let those feelings in, when there is no chance of releasing them. I channeled it into aggression, used it in battle. I've never known the pleasures of a woman. Never allowed sin to rule me."

"Oh…" Heat, swift and sure, rushed through her limbs. A virgin. He was a virgin. *Oh, my silver stars.* He'd confessed without shame but the look in his eyes, the hot need that darkened his eyes, told their own story. Seven-hundred-odd years this man had gone without release. He was through with waiting. Should Eliza offer, he'd take her without pause.

She tried again, for she could not fathom this man, so very strong and virile, not leaving a swath of broken hearts in his wake. "But afterwards, when you lived as the king of the GIM?"

His smile turned bitter. "Dear old Mab was quite creative with her curse. She unmanned me while making me irresistible to others."

The cruelty of it lanced through Eliza's middle. But she did not want to pity Adam. It seemed an even worse insult. "You once told me that you'd fallen in love with a girl at a May Day fair." It felt like ages ago, when she'd been his captive, and he'd taunted her with that tale. But she remembered every word he'd spoken to her.

"I lied." He did not appear sorry for doing so. In truth, there was a slight smile upon his lips. She needed to stop looking at his mouth.

"And I'm supposed to believe you now?" she said with more irritation than she felt.

His head canted as he peered at her. "Confessing one's virginal state is hardly something a man would do unless it were true." She merely returned his look. And his wry smile grew. "I was trying to rile you up then. To get you to acknowledge me."

"And you aren't now?"

"No. You're acknowledging me quite well at the moment, dove."

Her cheeks heated.

A soft, dark chuckle rumbled in his chest. "I was told," he went on, "that when I found the other half of my soul, I'd feel again. In all ways." Adam pushed off from the wall he'd been leaning against and took a step closer to her, careful, however, to hold her gaze, as though he did not want to frighten her off. "And I do."

Her mouth went dry.

"I've nothing to lose now, lass. So when I say that my want of you was one of the reasons I knew I'd found you"—slowly he reached out—"you can believe it."

The warm, rough tips of his fingers grazed her cheek. Eliza jerked back, stumbling on her skirts as she edged away from him.

"Perhaps my attraction toward *you* is merely Mab's magic, making you irresistible to all beings."

"You find me irresistible?" His husky, laughing question had her shooting a glare over her shoulder.

With his smiling mouth and eyes brightened with glee, irresistible was definitely the word for him. Damn all.

"Just so you know," he said, "I find you quite fetching as well."

"Isn't that the point?" She tossed up a hand in irritation. "I cannot know if this attraction is because of Mab's curse upon you. And you cannot know if what you feel is out of some strange, misplaced gratitude or if it is simply another one of Mab's tricks. Nothing feels real."

His smile faded, but he did not appear offended. No, he was calm and rational as always. "I've lost my powers."

A huff broke from her lips. "What has that got to do with anything?"

"I no longer possess an unnatural ability to attract others. So what you do or do not feel for me has nothing to do with Mab."

Eliza edged back. "I've noted a good number of ladies, and a few gentlemen, gravitating towards you." She gave a pointed glance towards the door. "Even now."

He took one small step closer. "I never said I was without natural charm. Perhaps they merely want me for me."

She harrumphed. "You've an answer for everything, don't you?"

"A man learns a thing or two during seven hundred and twenty-nine years of life." His eyes flashed with a hint of his former GIM glow. "Or he ought to."

"Either you are not listening to me or are deliberately misunderstanding."

"Educate me then, love."

His easy capitulation annoyed her. She wanted a fight.

Perhaps that way, he'd stop looking at her as though she were an especially tasty treat.

"I do not believe in soul mates," she said. "I do not believe that this attraction we feel has anything to do with fate or anything deeper than a simple surface interest. Mine based on the fact that you come wrapped in a pleasing package, and yours perhaps due to some misplaced gratitude because you suddenly feel something you've been denied for hundreds of years." When he kept on watching her with that self-same, easy smile and heated want, she stomped her foot. "We've been at odds since we met."

"You are correct," he said. "I've fostered an intense dislike of you for the past year and a half."

That ought not to sting. But it did.

He wasn't finished, however. "I like you better now."

Horribly, she liked him better too. Somehow he'd drifted closer without her knowing it. Stopping beside her, he leaned his hips against the windowsill and crossed his arms over his chest. The stance ought to have diminished him. It only made his shoulders appear broader and highlighted the bulge of his biceps beneath his plain coat.

"You should kiss me," he said.

The breath left her body in a rush of air and a raspy "What?"

His gaze drifted to her lips. "How else are we to know? Kiss me. And find out if your want of me crumbles to dust or grows."

A gentle throbbing started low in her belly, traveling downward. They stood so close, a handspan apart, close enough that his smoky scent and powerful warmth enveloped her, compelling her to move closer still. She planted her feet, refusing to give in.

His hands grasped the edges of the sill, holding it tight,

as though he needed an anchor as well. "You'll be in control. I'll not touch you, nor try to stop you from pulling away. I vow it." He spoke softly, forcing her to strain her ears and edge toward him. "Put your lips to mine, sweet dove. See if you like my taste."

Her mouth went dry, her lips parting. *She wanted. She wanted.* It was perverse, this need. He'd chained her, kept her at his side without a care of how she'd felt about the situation. To even consider this...

Her heart beat hard and strong within her chest. Adam's own chest rose and fell with greater speed. Half-sitting as he was upon the wide windowsill, they were nearly eye to eye.

Trying to buy time, Eliza looked him over with a deliberately bland expression. "Was this entire conversation simply a trick to get me to kiss you?"

He grinned again, the pink tip of his tongue just visible between his even teeth. "Absolutely."

"I thought you did not want to kiss me." Eliza scowled at the memory of him outright rejecting her.

"That was before. This is now," he answered easily. "Now, I want that kiss." On a deep breath, his lids lowered, his gaze somnolent and hot on her mouth, his voice rough and urgent. "Kiss me, Eliza."

She was going to. She had no resistance when it came to him. This close, he seemed immense. Not just in size, but in presence. Vitality sparked along his skin, drawing her like a magnet to his firm flesh.

Not daring to meet his gaze, she studied his mouth. It tempted her. So finely shaped, the upper lip just slightly bigger than the bottom, as if it were swollen. Dark stubble of the day's growth framed that soft mouth of his, and she wanted to feel the different textures of his skin. As if bidden, her fingertips drifted up and grazed along his chin, just beneath his lower lip. Rough, silken.

His breath visibly hitched, and a puff of warmth escaped him and ghosted over her skin. Her hand slid down to his chest to press against the rapid beat of his heart. And then she was closer.

Their lips nearly touched, but he halted. "I've not done this before, so you'll—" His breath caught when, unable to resist, she brushed her lips against his, the contact fleeting but capturing all of her attention. A spark of heat lit through her. She wanted more. "Have to..." He groaned, opening his mouth to let her lap at his upper lip with the tip of her tongue. "Guide me."

Part of her had kissed him simply to shut him up, call his bluff. And yet...A whimper of want echoed in her mouth as she leaned into him, her lips melding with his. Heat and need suffused her, as she delved farther into the warm depths of his mouth. He tasted divine.

That she knew more than he, that she was teaching him, gave her a heady, erotic, little thrill. Eliza tilted her head, the tips of her fingers cradling his jaw as she enjoyed his mouth. He made a murmur of approval, his slick tongue twining with hers. A quick study. Adam's breath came in disjointed pants, his lips following hers, seeking and nuzzling.

How very good it felt to kiss this man. Her head swam with pleasure, and she pressed her body into his, until there was no space between them. The hard length of his cock seemed to throb against her lower belly. And Eliza moaned.

At the sound, tremors rent Adam's body and his mouth surged forward, capturing her lower lip in a suckling kiss. "Let me touch you," he whispered, tasting her mouth in a series of urgent nibbles. "Let me, Eliza. Release me."

She wanted that. Her skin seemed to stretch and tighten

with the need to feel his hands upon it. But it wouldn't end there. She'd soon want him inside of her, filling her up. Madness. Her mouth shaped the word even as she kissed him. "No."

A half laugh, half groan left him. "Evil, wee besom."

She could not help but smile against his mouth. "Wiley, wicked demon."

He huffed, and she pulled back a little. The corners of his eyes crinkled as he smiled, the lush curve of his top lip touching hers. Little shivers of pleasure danced along her spine as he spoke. "I told you, dove. I'm no demon."

"Mmm." She moved back another step, taking herself away from temptation. But her hand lingered on his cheek. "You are to me. Burning hot and the devil's own temptation."

His nostrils flared, the need in his eyes almost pained as he leaned in, his lips parting. She held him back. An illusion, for even with the cursed chains draining his strength, he was far from helpless. In truth, she was in more danger of succumbing to him than ever before. "We'll be late for the oracle."

Weak, weak argument. His expression said as much. But Adam glanced down at his bound wrists and then back up at her. "You want me, Eliza May. Deny it all you like, but I'll be using that knowledge, dove, and you'll not be evading me for much longer."

Chapter Twelve

Rain came down with steady determination, as if its sole purpose was to wash London clean. A failed effort. The streets grew thick with sticky muck that covered boots and ruined hems, and coal-leaden rain left grimy tracks along all that it fell upon. It was slow going for Eliza and Adam as they made their way from the GIM tavern down to Fleet Street.

Tension coiled tight upon Eliza's shoulders as they wove past equally downtrodden pedestrians. She'd kissed Adam, and kissed him well. His promise still rang clear in her head, and with it, a dark anticipation that tightened her nipples and made her lower belly ache. She tried to ignore it in favor of the practical, such as not being taken by the fae.

"This is foolish," she muttered.

"It is necessary," Adam retorted beneath his breath.

"It's only a matter of time before we're discovered. People are staring as it is." She gave a quelling look to a man who gaped at them and then she huddled closer to Adam's side. She had to; he hadn't yet the strength to hold himself up, and there was the nuisance of his chains to contend with. The blasted things rattled and clanked with each step he took, and it was Eliza's job to hold their length tight within the folds of her skirt to keep them as quiet as possible.

The corners of Adam's mouth twitched. "If anyone asks, we'll say I'm playing the part of Jacob Marley at the local theatre."

"*A Christmas Carol*? In April?" she hissed. Another glance over her shoulder confirmed that people were watching them pass. They might not see the chains hidden beneath Adam's sweeping great cloak and Eliza's unfashionably voluminous skirts, but they certainly heard them.

Adam merely shrugged. "Very well. Perhaps you have a penchant for clattering chastity belts?"

Eliza made a noise of disgust. "I rather think that would be your proclivity."

"What? To wear one?" He appeared so utterly horrified that she snickered.

"I meant asking women to wear them. Wasn't that just the thing back in your days of jousting, old man?"

He snorted. "Those chastity belts are a myth, you realize? Made up in this century, likely by some bored lord in need of titillation." He slanted her a sly look that was far too effective at warming her skin. "However, I'm willing to play that game if it pleases you."

Her cheeks were surely red, and she ducked her head as yet another man walked by and gave them a curious stare. "What would please me," she ground out through clenched teeth, "is to be off the streets. We're exposing ourselves to attack."

"Fae cannot tolerate London rain. Its polluted nature irritates their skin." He glanced at her from beneath the thick fringe of his black lashes, and his golden eyes lit with amusement when he caught her rubbing at her damp cheek. "Tuck yourself farther back under the umbrella. We are almost there."

A flush of annoyance rushed through Eliza. She did not like seeing proof of her fae blood. Her annoyance grew when Adam slid her a knowing look. "Elementals are born of fae blood, and they are some of the most brave and noble beings I've ever come across."

Which was all fine and dandy, except she wasn't an elemental. Evil ran through her veins without any of the benefits. Eliza pushed the thought away, not wanting to be a Sulky Sue.

Thankfully, they reached a rather decrepit doorway. A peeling sign that read *The Daily Tattle* hung woebegone overhead, the board swaying slightly in the rain. "The oracle is a reporter?" Eliza asked as Adam opened the door and ushered her, rather clumsily, inside.

He caught her surprised look and made a small noise of acknowledgment. "It makes perfect sense to me. After all, who else is in a better position to warn us of future woes than one who chronicles the stories of our present folly?"

"I don't know," Eliza muttered. "I pictured a gypsy woman leaning over her crystal ball."

"What a pedestrian imagination you have, Eliza."

His white teeth flashed in the dim light as she scowled, but then he turned his attention to their surroundings. A darkened and narrow stairwell stretched upward, and Adam muttered a ripe curse under his breath. She knew how badly he hated his weakness. Likely, he'd never been anything less than extremely fit his entire life. Until now. She'd seen that frustrated rage and fearful helplessness in the eyes of soldiers back home. Good men who'd lost limbs to grapeshot and cannon balls and now struggled to find some sense of their former selves.

Glancing down at her feet, she frowned. "Horrid shoes," she said with bitterness. "I declare they've worn a hole clear through my foot."

Adam leaned heavily against the crackled plaster wall, a faint sense of amusement lighting his austere features. "Got yourself a blister, did you?"

She gave an exaggerated grimace, as she went on in a blithe tone. "Only a small one. Go on without me, I'll just rest here a moment."

His expression grew softer. She knew perfectly well he was on to her. They both knew. But neither of them addressed the truth. Instead, he offered her his arm. "Lean on me," he said in a soft rasp. "And we'll climb the stairs together."

And if, in truth, Adam ended up leaning into her, letting her shore him up as they limped up the stairs, it was nobody's business but theirs. Nor did she take notice when he panted upon reaching the landing. Instead, she pulled out a kerchief.

"Here," she said, wiping the sweat from his brow with brusque strokes. "You are filthy. I thought Mr. Brown gave you leave to use his bath."

Tall as he was, she had to rise up on her toes to reach him, and his hand settled upon her waist to steady her. Eliza ignored the little kick his touch set off inside of her. Quietly, he watched her, his face bent towards her so she might clean him. But she felt the weight of his stare, the strange tenderness of it.

What on earth was she doing? He did not need fussing over and certainly not by her. She took a hasty step back, pocketing her kerchief.

"There." She made her voice bright and cheerful. "All better."

He watched her for a moment more, his expression solemn, then cleared his throat. "Come along then, mother hen."

His fingertips found the small of her back as he led her into the inner press office, and she realized that, no matter what his mood or predicament, he acted the gallant knight first and foremost. And though the chain leached his strength, he moved with the grace of a warrior.

Cheaply dressed Adam might have been, yet as soon as they walked into the cramped newsroom, a man hurried over not with an intent to eject them from the premises but with clear deference. "May I help you, sir?"

"We are here to see Mr. Michaels."

Mr. Sean Michaels, it turned out, was a cheerful Irishman of medium height with hair the precise shade of Christmas gingerbread. It curled around his ruddy face and highlighted the color of his brilliant blue eyes.

"Have a seat, then." He hastily cleared stacks of yellowed papers from the bentwood chairs in his small, chaotic office. Towers of paper and books tottered higgledy-piggledy and threatened to come crashing down as Eliza and Adam took their seats in the little area cleared for them. "Here we are. We'll have a spot of tea and a fine chat."

Bold as you please, Adam threw back his cloak and the blasted length of chains clattered around him. Michaels's brows rose. "That's quite a ... spiffing outfit."

Adam laughed, deep and full. "Eliza insisted I wear them. She finds the chains titillating."

"Horrid man," she whispered, barely resisting the urge to pinch him, even though part of her fought a smile.

Adam shrugged at Michaels. "They are merely part of a garden variety curse. Pay them no heed."

"If you say." Michaels caught a folder midslide and tossed it into a corner. "I'll get us that tea."

In the time Eliza had to give Adam a dubious look, the young man returned, carrying a plain, wooden tea tray, laden with a clunky crockery teapot and three mismatched earthenware teacups. "Were this a social visit," Michaels said as he set the tray down, "I'd ask you to do the honors, Miss May. As we've a bit of work to do here, I'm afraid I must be pouring the tea. Milk or sugar?"

"Both," Eliza and Adam said as one. They glanced at each other in mild surprise before Eliza turned her attention back to Michaels.

He went about serving them with surprisingly graceful movements. The aroma of good, strong, milk-in-first Irish tea filled the office and made Eliza aware of how very cold and weary she'd become. Gratefully, she accepted the hot mug and, not standing on upper-crust manners, wrapped her icy fingers around the heavy bowl of it.

"Drink it while it's fresh and hot," Michaels said as he sat himself behind his desk. The eerie greenish light of rain-soaked London shone through the rice paper shade covering his window and set his curls aglow.

Eliza took a bracing sip and sighed.

"A Yank who appreciates her tea," Michaels said with a small smile. "Now that is something I like to see."

"A Yank, yes," Eliza answered after taking another sip. "But three-quarters Irish to boot."

"Well"—Michaels' eyes crinkled—"we won't hold that one-quarter against you, now will we, lass?"

Adam set his cup down with more force than necessary. "As charming as discussions of ancestry are, I do believe we are here on other business."

Michaels simply grinned, his ruddy cheeks plumping up like autumn apples. "There's been talk, speculation that you disappeared because you fell in love. But, until now, I didn't believe it."

"Shouldn't you know the actual truth," Eliza couldn't help but ask, "seeing as you are an oracle?" She didn't want him running on about Adam being in love, at any rate. Nor did she care to have Adam correct his error. Their odd relationship was uncomfortable enough without others knowing about it.

Michaels glanced at her, his blue eyes mischievous. "Oracles aren't omniscient, Miss May. We've limitations just as much as the next supernatural." Not to be distracted, Michaels turned his attention back to Adam. "That's it then? You've lost yourself in a woman?"

Adam relaxed into his chair and draped an arm along the back of Eliza's, looking for all the world like a man at perfect ease, despite the reporter's nosy questions. "As a matter of fact—"

"The GIM are growing weak," Eliza cut in. "Do you know why?"

Michaels scratched beneath his chin. "Speculation is all I can give you on that."

Some oracle.

"Illuminate us," Adam drawled.

"Well..." Michaels looked Adam over. "Their power is tied to their sire, is it not?"

Which meant that as Adam grew weaker, so did they. Eliza wondered if Adam knew this all along, for he waved a lazy hand. "Speculation, to be sure." But Eliza knew

Adam well enough to see how much the weakening GIM upset him.

"We are here," Eliza hurried on, wanting to smooth over the moment, "on account of me. I'm Mab's granddaughter."

Michaels lurched upright, his teasing manner falling away. "You're serious?" His skin paled but his cheeks turned crimson.

"As the grave," said Adam, his catlike eyes gleaming.

The young man ran a shaking hand through his curls, sending them into disarray.

"Tell me," Eliza said in a softer tone, "about the fae."

"What? You're Mab's granddaughter. I cannot possibly tell you anything you don't know better."

"I know nothing." Eliza clutched the edge of his desk. "I didn't even know my true kin until a few months ago. Adam seems to think you are the best person to tell me, so...please?"

"Of course, of course." He poured himself another steaming cup of tea, then took a gulp of the hot brew, his eyes watering. With a deep breath, he sat back. "Here's the thing, Miss May. Fae, demons, lycans, elementals, angels, gods, goddesses, they're all interconnected with mankind. It's a bit like the chicken and the egg. Did humans create the myths or did the myths come before the humans?"

"You mean no one knows?" Eliza found that hard to believe.

"Aye, well, according to the angels, who are the oldest beings anyone knows of, the humans, with their powerful imaginations, gave birth to all but God. But that in itself is dicey because what you'd think of as God is the collective power of human consciousness."

Michaels steepled his fingers and pressed the tips to his lips. "Theology aside, we do know that fae, in particular, did grow out of myth. No other being is as closely linked to human thoughts. And, to be quite frank, this brasses the fae off something fierce. They hate that humans have so much control over them."

When Eliza frowned in confusion, he leaned in close, his voice becoming emphatic. "You've no notion how powerful human belief can be. Nor how much it effects the Others. That is why being seen and acknowledged means so much to them. They have power because we gave it to them.

"Over their existence, the fae have had many incantations, distinctions made by humans wishing to expand and explain the myth. They've been the Seelie Court and the Unseelie Court, Trooping Fairies, Solitary Faires, Light fae, Dark fae, Tots, household fae. Mab, your grandmother, holds great power simply because she's so well known in the human world. Every time someone orates Mercutio's speech about Mab or some poetically inclined sod recites Shelley's Queen Mab, she gains strength."

"I don't understand," Eliza said. "These beings are real. They're stronger than humans, capable of killing them, yet you say humans created them and feed their powers."

"Yes. Human thoughts and beliefs took on a consciousness and corporeal bodies. They are entirely their own creatures now. But they still feed off of the power of human belief. This is why so many supernaturals want to expose themselves to human society. They are of the opinion that humans, once realizing the truth, will give them a surge of power because their belief will be absolute."

"Well, won't it?"

"No," said Adam, his deep voice so resonant it seemed to tickle her skin. "Because there is the power of disbelief as well. Humans have a great capacity for disbelief. We'll tell ourselves that what we see isn't real. Now more than ever, when science and reason hold greater sway than myth and faith. To come out into the open would be catastrophic. Humans would either explain the Others away, fight them to the death, or shut down mentally. Likely a little of all. The result will be the weakening and needless deaths of countless supernaturals."

Eliza grew up in the aftermath of a great war. She knew quite well the toll it took on a society. "And Mab wants exposure?"

Adam turned his attention on Michaels. "Mab knows the power humans have over her kind. Thus she both fears and hates them. However, she's cunning enough to know that she's better off feeding the myth of herself than destroying it. What she wants is power over supernaturals, not humans."

"Aye." Michaels sat back. "But the trick is finding something stronger than immortality."

A dark smile curved Adam's lips. "Don't you know what that is?"

Eliza didn't but she rather thought they both did, given the way Michaels smiled too.

"Pray, end my suspense," she clipped out.

Michaels answered first. "Death. That which is already dead cannot be defeated."

Adam crossed one leg over the other. "As I am certain this information will be circulated all through London's underworld soon enough, here are the facts. For the past six months, Mab has tortured me, first for the fun of it, but recently to discover the location of the Golden Horn an Bás, which I supposedly took hundreds of years ago while pillaging Ireland." Adam waved an idle hand. "Rot, all of it. But if Mab wants it, then so do I."

"So then, you want to find its true location before Mab can?" Michaels shook his head. "You know finding lost items is beyond my talents."

Adam regarded him for a quiet moment, then spoke, his voice low and serious. "Sean, I am asking this as a friend."

Michaels's ruddy skin flushed. He glanced at Eliza. "He saved my life once, you know."

"Are you GIM?"

"Never got that far. He stopped a killer's knife before it slid into my gut."

Adam shrugged. "There are times when I liked to roam as a normal man. And murder has never set well with me."

Michaels laughed. "Right then. I'm still beholden to you, and I'll do what I can. Finish your tea, the both of you, and we'll see what we can see."

They did as told, and Michaels collected their cups. Peering into Adam's cup, he studied the dregs. "You'll not be liking this, old man."

"That surprises me very little." Adam leaned forward. "Out with it."

"You've no future."

"What?" Eliza burst out.

"His future is naught but a muddle. I cannot see anything more than a vague sense of him possessing the horn. But...even that appears wrong and off." Michaels took Eliza's cup. "Let's see yours."

Instantly, his pleasant face smoothed out. He glanced between Adam and Eliza, his expression wary. "I'll need to be speaking to Miss May alone."

"Absolutely not," Adam spit out, his chains rattling as his hands clenched.

"Why?" Eliza asked just as quickly.

Adam growled at her, but she gave him a quelling look.

Michaels ran a hand through his ruddy hair. "If I tell you both, it might alter the course, and believe me, friend," he said to Adam, "you do not want that to happen."

Abruptly, Adam stood, his jaw bunched, his teeth bared. "If you seek to play me false—"

"It's no trick, Adam." Michaels appeared tired just then. "I swear it on my mam's grave."

They stared at each other for an endless moment, and then Adam nodded abruptly. He turned and pinned Eliza with a look. "That goes for you as well, Miss May. Try to cross me and—"

"It would behoove you not to threaten me, *dearest*. Such behavior does not prompt accord."

Oh, but she could see him swallowing down a snide retort. "How kind of you to remind me, *sweets*," he ground out. With a last warning look all around, Adam moved to go, but then stopped and bent close to her. His hot breath fanned her skin, drawing up little prickles of sensation. She thought he might threaten her, or complain further, but he did nothing of the sort. His soft lips pressed gently to the hollow below her ear.

With that, he was gone in an irate clatter of chains and general male huffing.

Eliza found Michaels grinning.

"Oh, do have a laugh at my expense, Mr. Michaels. When I'll be the one forced to live with his temper."

At that, Michaels cleared his throat. "Right." He scootched closer, holding her teacup. "Here's the thing. I see Adam in possession of the horn, but only you, Miss May, appear to be able to use it."

"Odd." She peered into the cup, seeing nothing more than a jumbled mess of wet tea leaves.

"Yes," Michaels agreed. "Odder still, you'll only know how to use the horn when you let Adam into your heart."

Eliza reared back at this. "Is this some trick?" Her heart pounded. Eliza didn't hold it past Adam to use this oracle for something so low. She knew how ruthless he could be, damn his golden eyes.

"A trick," Michaels parroted.

"Yes, a way to get me to… accept him," she hissed.

Michaels laughed shortly. "I do not know what goes on between you two, but I assure you that it is no trick on my part."

"But why do I need him to use the horn?"

"I do not know. An oracle can state what might occur if one follows a certain path, but not why one must behave as one ought."

"Rather irritating that," Eliza groused.

His blue eyes took on a soft light. "I've heard as much. And you're wise to keep your trust close at heart, Miss May. Lies make our world go round."

"Then why," she said, "should I trust you?"

"So don't, then." Michaels set the cup onto his desk and slouched back in his chair as though he hadn't a care. "But I'd advise that you not tell Adam of my reading. Because there is one truth on which I think we can agree. If that demon wants to claim you, he'll do anything in his power to achieve it."

Sin had turned hiding into an art form. Which saved his sorry hide more than once. Of course, all the household had taken to hiding when Eliza had flown the coop with Adam. Mab's once-fine house now lay in chaotic shambles, torn apart by the mistress's own hands. With the temper of a recalcitrant child, she'd lashed out, screaming her displeasure.

Now, as Mab met with Mellan in the parlor, Sin hid behind the plethora of enormous potted palms and ferns that turned the room into a veritable greenhouse, and listened in.

"How difficult is it to find two weak and powerless humans who have run away from me?" Her screech had the delicate teardrop crystals in the wall sconces tinkling.

From his lazy sprawl upon a green velvet chair, Mellan gave her an annoyed look. "Weakened Aodh might be, but he is hardly powerless. Nor are they mere humans. You keep forgetting this."

Mab tossed a length of scarlet hair over her shoulder. "They are as pathetically mundane as any human, Mellanhov."

"And yet they elude you, Mabella." Mellan grinned with evil glee when she snarled, baring her little black fangs at him.

"I want every GIM in London cut down until Aodh gives himself up. Slaughter them all, the unnatural creatures."

Sin ground his back teeth and willed himself to remain frozen. If he moved the slightest muscle, he would be detected.

"The lycan king's mate is a GIM," Mellan said idly. "So his subjects stand with the GIM. It would be unwise to make further enemies with the lycans."

Mab flopped down into a chair. "Their numbers are few."

"But fierce."

She shot Mellan a glare. "Are you attempting to irritate me?"

"Merely guiding your wayward thoughts back to solid ground." Mellan's thin lips curled. "Irritating you in the process is not without its enjoyment." His smile fell. "You've always been too possessive of the knight. Aodh is a lost cause, pet. He'll never be yours."

It seemed the very air stilled, then grew so humid that the walls beaded with condensation. Around Sin, the plants began to grow, leaves coiling and crackling as they wound around his face and slithered over their pots. Mab's pretty human countenance fell away, her fangs growing long and her eyes flashing purple. Mellan simply looked back at her.

For a moment, Sin thought Mab's temper would explode. But then she gave Mellan a syrup-sweet smile. "And you believe Eliza will be yours, do you?"

"You think I have a care if she doesn't want me?" He laughed, dark and slow. "It matters not if she ran off with Aodh. I shall track her down. It is but an eventuality."

"Mmm..." Mab examined her black fingernails, her mouth in a saucy tilt. "And then what? You claim her as your bride and our kingdom is secure?"

Mellan's eyes narrowed. "As you well know." It was clear that Mellan knew she was baiting him. And just as clear that he'd let her. To a point. His utter lack of fear intrigued Sin. Everyone feared Mab.

Mab lifted one red brow. "A rather difficult task," she said silkily, "given that she and Aodh are now handfasted."

While Mab's displeasure had heated the air, Mellan's had a decidedly different effect. It froze. With the force of a blizzard, icy air swept through the room, cracking mirrors and destroying the plants in an instant. Had Sin not been an elemental capable of frost, he'd have died.

Slowly Mellan stood, his skin pale blue, his hair turning snow white. Ice gathered around Mellan's temples and over his brow, forming a crown.

Hell, Sin thought, as shock speared through him. Bloody hell.

From her seat, Mab's eyes went wide, her lips parting as if to take back her words. Sin had never seen her afraid.

"Repeat yourself, Mabella," Mellan said in a terrible voice, so deep it vibrated throughout the room.

Mab pulled an object from her skirt pocket. It was a rag, bloody and tied in a Celtic love knot. "This was found in Aodh's cell. It is Aodh's blood. I can smell it. There can be no doubt that Aodh has handfasted to the girl."

Mellan's roar shook the house.

"Who is laughing now, Mellan—" Mab's words were cut short from the force of Mellan's blow.

"Stupid cow. You know nothing."

"It does not matter if the girl joins with Aodh. He has already ceded his powers to me. He's lost."

"As it is, I cannot wed her if she's handfasted to Aodh. Our laws forbid it, as you damn well ought to know."

Her eyes slid away. And Sin understood at the precise moment that Mellan did. Mellan shouted his rage, shaking Mab as though she were a porcelain doll. "You want to kill her! Foolish chit. Always letting your lust blind you. The girl means everything."

"He is the one with potential," Mab shot back. "She is just a balm to his ego. And yours, apparently, oh great Unseelie Prince."

With the flick of his wrist, Mellan flung Mab across the

room. The rosewood secretary exploded as she slammed into it.

"Idiot! If they truly bond, you'll not be able to kill one without destroying the other. Two millennium I've waited to find the means to control death, and thanks to my sister's base needs and vanity, it is in danger of slipping past me once again."

Chapter Thirteen

By the time Miss Eliza May exited Michaels's office, Adam was ready to smash his fist through a wall. It did not help that Eliza merely gave him a pleasant smile and announced that she was ready to depart.

He tromped through the press office and led them outside. For a while, they walked in tense silence. He hated silence between them. Hated it almost as much as being left in the dark where she was concerned. Adam could hold his tongue no longer.

"Tell me what the oracle said." Adam was reasonably certain the words sounded like a request instead of a plea. He'd be bolloxed if he ever pled for another thing in his life. Especially from her.

Eliza fussed with her wrapper, drawing it farther around her slim shoulders. The rain had stopped, and she'd hooked the handle of her umbrella over her forearm.

"Well?" he snapped out.

She was acting as she'd done when he'd chained her those many months ago, settling back into herself, shoring up those bloody defenses that, once in place, he knew he'd have a snowflake's chance in hell of breaching. He ground his back teeth, fighting the urge to smash his fist into the side of the brick wall they were walking past.

"Eliza, if this is about your orders from Mellan—"

"Oh for the love of...I already told you that I have no wish to do as he says. It has nothing to do with that, Adam."

Only slightly appeased, he searched her face. "Then what?"

She sighed. "Michaels told me to hold my own council."

Adam was going to kill Sean bloody Michaels. Turn around and stuff his fist right into the man's gob. Maybe pull his tongue out for good measure.

"Why? Why would he tell you that?"

Eliza uttered a little, incredulous laugh. "I rather think answering that question would be counterproductive to his original request." She glanced at him. "And you need not growl. It won't change my mind."

"I was not growling." Adam halted and turned to confront her, and, yes, growl in displeasure. Instantly, she lifted her chin and met his glare without flinching, her face pale against the dingy backdrop of the alleyway they'd been traversing. He'd become too isolated. It must be so, for her lack of deference to him both unsettled and made his insides warm. For centuries, anyone who came into his sphere either rushed to do his bidding or rushed to get the bloody hell away from him as quickly as possible. He'd had enemies. But no equals.

Some of the starch melted from his shoulders, and he fought a sigh. "You promised to be mine. As such, there should be no secrets between us."

The rosebud of her lips went tight. "Yours? Hardly."

"We are handfasted. Which is as good as declaring yourself mine." At least until his time was up. But he wasn't about to make that distinction. "Hiding things from me is hardly a fortuitous start."

Eliza's velvet-brown eyes flashed with ire. "If that is your logic, then you are mine as well."

She couldn't know the heady satisfaction those words had on him, else she wouldn't have flung them with such enthusiasm. He felt himself grinning. It was not a nice smile but one of primal satisfaction, and he took a step closer. Not that Miss May noticed. Her voice grew in agitation as she continued her rebuttal. "Regardless of who owns whom, every person has a right to keep secrets."

"Secrets imply lack of trust. What good is joining together if we cannot trust one another?"

Her slim shoulders lifted on a sigh, and she glanced away. Guilty. "What Mr. Michaels told me had nothing to do with you. It was about me." Her gloved fist pressed against her sternum as she met his gaze once more. "It was about my life."

Something hot and writhing seemed to go through his lower gut. "Are you in danger? Tell me that at least, Eliza, or I will not give you a moment's peace." He wouldn't be able to.

A soft chuff of air left her. "No." The thick fan of her lashes swept up as she stared into his eyes. "Adam, upon the souls of my family, I give my word that I will not betray you."

The simplicity of her declaration, the unexpectedness of it, took the breath from him, and it shamed him that he hadn't made certain things clear.

He sank to his knees before her. She gave a little squeak of surprise when he pressed his forehead between the soft pillows of her breasts. But she did not push him away. Adam knelt, his neck exposed, his hands at his side. "What kin I had have long since turned to bones. I'm no longer a knight but a broken-down shadow of that man. Hardly worthy to be your champion."

He glanced up then, forcing himself to meet her eyes. "But Eliza May, your champion, I am. Upon the souls of the only ones that mean anything to me, my children, the ghosts in the machine, I swear, while there is breath left in my body, I will protect you."

She went quietly pale, her soft lips parting. But it wasn't her voice that cut through their fraught silence.

"Now that's a rare sight round these parts, a man servicing a tart."

Every battered muscle in Adam's body tensed as he slowly turned, still on his knees.

Two street thugs ambled into the small alleyway. Both were tall yet wiry in the way of street criminals. And despite the friendly smiles they wore, their eyes held no pity, only a low simmer of lust and violence.

"Never been one for tipping the velvet muff meself, Pike," the bald one said to his blond friend before his eyes roved over Eliza. "But I'm of a mind to try it with this here toffer."

An old but familiar rush of sheer energy lit through Adam, the desire to kill. It hit him so strongly, he could barely see through the emotion, but he held it at bay. Blind rage only hurt a man in battle, making him sloppy and vulnerable.

"We've no blunt," Adam said in a voice that carried. "I suggest you walk away while you can."

"While we can? Oh, that's a fancy cant, comin' from the man on his knees," Blond said with a sneer.

Pike's face split into a grin. "Mayhaps we work our payment out on the mort. What says you, Jim? Care to grease your wick between those buttered buns?"

Eliza's hand drifted down to Adam's shoulder. He did not know if she sought support or wanted to offer it. But he knew quite well what she thought. Here he was, stuck on his knees, a broken fibula and radius, cracked ribs, and the chains leeching his strength. What protection could he provide, no matter how pretty his words were?

"A true man doesn't take from a woman," said Eliza, her tone far from afraid.

Pike snorted. "You'll be bowin' to me before the night is over and working the gutter lane."

Another, stronger wave of black rage crashed over Adam. He'd kill Pike last, let the man realize what was coming for him. Jim, he'd merely damage. Not taking his eyes off Pike and Jim, Adam rolled his shoulders and his cloak slid off, revealing the chains coiled at his sides.

But the men merely grinned like cats cornering the canary. "See," said Pike, "I told you I smelled fae magics on 'em." His eyes flashed mustard yellow before going full black.

Oh, hell. Demons.

Eliza saw it too, for her grip on him tightened painfully. "Adam…"

"There's a good price on yer head, GIM Maker," said Jim. "An' hows we's hears it, you ain't got no powers what to stop us with, what with them chains keeping you in check."

"Eliza," Adam said, not taking his eyes from them, "run away, and don't look back."

"We've got ourselves a runner, Jim."

"Time for running has passed." Adam lashed out, the

thick chain on his wrist snapping like a whip, wrapping itself around Jim's neck. The man's eyes bugged out, his hands flying to his throat. Adam yanked the chain, and Jim's feet left the ground as he hurtled forward. Adam's fist met with his face, crunching bone. Jim flopped once and then went limp.

A blur of movement caught Adam's eye. Pike, recovering from the shock of the moment, rushed him. Adam rolled into the charge, catching Pike's legs with his shoulder. The thug toppled over him and landed flat on his back. With a roar of vengeance, Adam twisted and slammed his elbow into Pike's throat, crushing his windpipe. Pike gagged, his arms flailing, trying to rise. Adam grabbed a handful of greasy hair and wrenched the head hard. A sharp crack rang out, and Pike went limp as a doll.

It wasn't enough. They'd soon rise, and he hadn't a weapon to truly destroy them. For now, there was only silence, the feel of his breath rushing in and out of his lungs and the foul stench of demon bowels letting loose. Then Eliza stirred, a bare flutter of skirts and a soft, gurgled sound of shock. He was not at all surprised to find her still standing there.

Adam shoved the body away from him. Eliza's brown eyes were round and glossy against the pale of her usually honyed skin. Golden strands of hair fell about her face. He could not read her expression. Was she disgusted? Frightened?

Warily, he reached out to her. "Help me up?" His voice was soft, even as his heart beat hard and painfully. Aye, he could incapacitate two demons, and yet he hadn't the strength to stand. Or maybe he simply needed to know she was still willing to touch him.

Eliza's gazed darted from his outstretched hand to the

bodies on the ground and back to his eyes. It was then he took note of the gun she held. Pointed directly at his heart. Cold flooded his veins. "Do you plan to use that, Miss May?"

She blinked, then glanced down at her hand, and her lithe body jerked as if she'd forgotten about the weapon. "I...you...It went so quickly." Licking her pink lips, she lowered the weapon. "I was going to shoot them. But you took care of them first."

Tenderness swelled within his chest. "If it pleases you, the next bastard who tries to assault us is yours to vanquish."

Making a face, she tucked the pistol into her skirt pocket, then took hold of his hand. Her fingers were ice cold, even through her gloves. "I realize the women in your world are warriors, capable of killing without turning a hair." She eased her shoulder beneath his arm, and together they stood. "I'm afraid you'll find me lacking. I hate violence and death. I wouldn't even have a gun, save Mr. Brown thought I might like to carry some protection."

She was cold, so cold, and shivering. Adam turned her so that she was tucked against his side, and wrapped his arms about her before she could protest. "And still you were willing to shoot those men."

She was stiff for a moment, then relaxed, her arms slipping around his waist as she trembled. "I'm even less willing to become a victim."

Brave, strong lass. He pressed his lips to the satiny crown of her head. "I've hacked off so many limbs, beheaded numerous men, that I have long ago lost count of my deeds." His mouth curled in a bitter smile as he thought about those long-ago battles. "And yet the sight of blood used to make me vomit."

Eliza gave a start. "What?"

"Vomit. Every single time. My brother knights called me Scourge and Purge."

She was still for a breath and then burst out laughing. Just as he'd hoped.

"Come, now," he said, "we've got to move. These two won't stay down for long."

To punctuate his statement, a low groan came from the demon named Jim.

Eliza's eyes widened. "I thought you killed them."

Adam hurried them down the alleyway, his leg screaming in protest. "Unless you take their head or destroy their hearts, they will rise again."

She jostled him as they moved onto the main lane. From the mouth of the alleyway, the two demon men emerged, their eyes yellow and enraged. Adam's grip on Eliza tightened. "Come, they are up and following."

Her steps quickened, dragging Adam along. He was panting now. No help for it.

Adam grunted and forced himself to focus not on the pain but getting them to safety. "We'll go through the Rag Fair." The GIM safe house was at the far end. If they could reach it, the GIM would scare off the demons. Unlike the fae, demons were susceptible to the GIM's powers.

Adam simply had to get Eliza to the GIM first. They entered the hot chaos of the Rag Fair.

Chapter Fourteen

Life and noise surged around Eliza like the incoming tide. She'd never been in the presence of so many people at once. They surrounded her, calling out prices, shouting to one another, laughing and carousing. It was a discordant song that had her head reeling. The fair was an open-air market, hemmed in on both sides by buildings. Canopied stalls lined the walls and, along the ground, vendors had set up areas by simply placing their wares upon tatty blankets. And everywhere, people were purchasing old and very worn clothes.

Adam gave her arm a squeeze. The pair of demons he'd beaten to a pulp were now healed and snaking through the crowd to close in on them.

"Bloody hell," Adam muttered, his limping gate growing worse.

Eliza slowed and reached for her pocket.

Which caused Adam to stumble. "What are you doing, woman?"

"Hold a moment," Eliza murmured, and before he

could protest her stalling, she pulled the gun from her pocket and raised it in the air. "Home rule! Free Ireland!" Her voice bellowed out over the crowded streets, and then she shot the gun in rapid succession.

The crowd scattered like pigeons, shouting and crying.

"Christ," Adam snarled, grabbing Eliza's arm and wrenching it down to hide the gun. "Don't dally when you've started a riot."

Already, a wave of humans, trying to flee, was rushing toward them. Adam pulled her around a coffee monger's cart just before it toppled under the onslaught.

"It will slow those bastards down, at the least," Eliza said, bracing Adam up once more.

"Aye, and trample us to boot."

"It seemed a good idea—"

Something large and hard slammed into her shoulder, tearing her from Adam's grasp and sending her reeling.

"Adam!"

A rotund man lumbered past as a swarm of people swallowed Adam up. Eliza struggled to get back to him, but it was no use, she was swept along in the opposite direction. Elbows and shoulders knocked her about, and it was all she could do to stay on her feet. Eliza shoved her way towards the walls that made up the market's main square. With a great push against a young man's side, she stumbled into a small alleyway.

Sweating, she leaned against a wall and tried to ease her breathing. Adam was out there, hurt and possibly trampled. The magnitude of how much that distressed her was shocking and made her throat ache. For all their strife, Eliza had felt oddly safe and right knowing that he was in the world, that he lived somewhere, even when she hadn't been near him. If he were to die, if the golden light of his soul were to go dim, she'd be bereft.

The wrongness of his demise struck her to the core, and her chest began to quake with the mad urge to cackle like a harpy.

"No," she whispered, terror clutching her heart. She knew that laugh. Hot, acid tears burned in her eyes. "No, no." Adam could not be dead. She would *not* laugh at his death. A small snicker escaped her. Gods, but she was deranged. Why did she laugh near death? She hated herself for it.

A hard hand grasped her arm and spun Eliza around.

"Adam..."

The man looking down at her was not Adam. Tall and wide with bulk, and rumpled beneath a battered coat, the man had the eyes of a killer. The sort of man who took joy preying on the weak. Eliza had spent far too much of her life either facing or avoiding such men.

Their gazes clashed, his flat and cold. Eliza glared back, putting every ounce of her will behind the look. "Who are you?"

"The poor sod assigned to watch your arse."

"What?"

"You heard me. Lord Mellan had me follow you and see that you don't muck things up." The man sneered, revealing a row of brown teeth. "Looks like you have already." He gave a jerk with his head toward the market where people were calming down but still shouting. "You weren't supposed to kill the man until he led you to the sword."

The mention of Adam sent a bolt of urgency through Eliza, and she wrenched free of the man's brutal grip. "You're human." Were he fae, she wouldn't have been able to get free of him, nor would he have smelled like rotten tobacco.

"Well I know, mot." The man shrugged. "Lord Mellan suspected this Adam bloke might notice a fae."

She straightened her spine. "I have to go. As you say, I've a job to finish, and it won't get done sitting here with you." She wanted far away from this man. "If you'll excuse me."

His weathered face split into a jack-o'-lantern's grin, complete with naught but two yellowed teeth hanging from the maw of his mouth. Hot, fetid breath brushed her cheeks. "Why the rush, lamb? The GIM Maker will keep. I've seen to it."

"He'll keep?" Disgust warred with fear. "What did you do?"

"Slipped me shiv into a pair of demon hearts. They won't be chasing him." The man laughed, a rusty, broken sound. "As for your wayward mark, he's likely lying in the gutter where the crowd pushed him."

A sharp breath left her, and she started forward, intent upon finding Adam and helping him.

The man's hand slapped down on her shoulder. "Hold your water. Spare ol' Gus 'ere a piece, eh?"

A familiar feeling inside of Eliza broke loose, quaking like an earth tremor. That dark, ugly, hidden spot within her wanted to reel this tumescent insect of a man into her web and suck him dry.

No, no, no. Do not do this, Eliza. But that giddy, swelling feeling bubbled and rose to the surface. "You have two choices, sir. Let me go and live." Her voice was not her own, now cold and oddly high. She took note of the fact with a detached air, as she glanced down at the grimy hand upon her shoulder. He was missing a nail upon his middle finger. "Or keep touching me and die."

He laughed then, a wheezing sound, sending more of his foul breath into her lungs. "You've got spirit." A rough hand grabbed hold of her skirts, yanking on them, as his eyes went duller. "I like that in me women."

She hit the brick wall with such quick force that she saw stars. And then her mad cackle rang out, giving her attacker pause. It was the last sound he'd hear. When she spoke, it was ice, coating her tongue and lips with frigid cold. "Wrong choice."

His form grew hazy, a grey fog settling over him, or perhaps it was her vision. She did not care. Rage punched into her, giving her strength. Her fingers wrapped around his neck.

Her laughter grew in force, until it sounded more like a screech. He gaped at her, his mouth hanging open, and that strange muddy fog surrounded him, and then coalesced, swirling even as he writhed, trying to break free of her grip. He ought to be able to, yet he struggled, the grey fog growing thicker.

A cold sweat broke out over Eliza, and again came the unnatural, twitching need to laugh or cry. Her chest shook with it, tears forming in her eyes. "No more," she said, and the fog shot free from his body, flying up high into the sunlit sky and evaporating in the next instant. In her hand, the man sank, a suddenly unbearably heavy weight.

As if burned, she let go, and he flopped to the ground, his eyes sightless, and a dark stain of urine spreading over his undone trousers. Dead.

Eliza spun and vomited. Over and over. Until there was nothing left. Pressing the heels of her hands against her eyes, she fought back a revolting laugh. How could she laugh? She needed to be away from this place, away from the body. With wooden movements, she walked out of the alleyway. Ice filled her veins, made her steps stiff. She shivered, too cold, too sick.

He mustn't know. Adam could not know what she'd done. Mellan had used her "talent" for his own gain, and while she did not think that Adam would do that, he might refuse to help her, repulsed by the darkness inside of her. For she also knew that, despite his flaws, Adam was not an evil man.

The Rag Fair's main square had quieted down. People milled about, some in a daze, others talking heatedly about what had happened. Coppers were in full force, ordering those loitering to move on.

Shaking and cold, Eliza surveyed the square, searching for a sign of Adam and fearing the worst.

"Eliza!" His deep voice rang out with such power that several heads turned.

A sob tore from her as she spotted him limping forward, bearing his weight on a thin length of timber that appeared to be a table leg. She thought no more on the oddity, but found herself wrapped up in his arms, her face pressed up against the warmth of his chest. God, but she was cold. So cold. She tucked herself closer to Adam's big body. It was the only solid, real thing around her. She could rest there forever and be happy.

"Eliza," he breathed, hands running over her back. "Thank God."

His heart beat rapidly within his chest, and the scent of his sweat mixed with hers. She'd run to him. The realization stole over her. She'd run across the square and thrown herself at him. And he'd caught her.

"I'm sorry," she whispered. "So sorry I lost you."

"You didn't lose me," he said softly. "I'm here."

And her tension eased. He was here. Alive and whole. And suddenly she felt foolish for carrying on so.

"Were you hurt?" she asked in what she hoped was a calmer tone.

He snorted. "Crippled further, you mean?" The muscles along his chest flexed. "No. thrown about, more like. But I'll live."

The disgruntlement in his voice made her want to smile. He clearly berated himself for his weakened state. Foolish man. He was a warrior. Pure and simple. Eliza had underestimated Adam, smugly thinking herself safe, that she could control him because he was wounded of body and kept weak by Mab's chains. How foolish. He'd dispatched two large and street-hardened demons without even standing. And done it in less time than it would have taken Eliza to unlace just one of her walking boots.

Eliza was able to defend herself against one man, but against a group of them? She was far too helpless, her power only working with one-on-one contact. A group of men had killed her before Adam restored her life. Strangely, she'd never had a man protect her without demanding she be of service to him.

He'd fought for her. And he would do so again. Her champion.

And she was grateful to him. But when he tried to ease back to look at her, she resisted for a moment. Adam, however, was insistent, and pried her from his chest.

"What happened?" His worried gaze darted over her face. "Why have you been crying?"

Damn her weak eyes. Damn him for noticing. "I haven't been crying." She wiped at the sticky wet of her grimy cheeks. "I got coal smoke in my eyes. This blasted city is as foul as the devil's den."

Adam did not appear appeased by her answer. And Eliza spoke before he could. "We've got to get those blasted chains off so you can properly heal."

"It won't be easy now that we've demons looking out for us."

Eliza nodded, but her mind worked through the problem. "I've an idea who can get us to Lucien's barge."

Chapter Fifteen

Eliza looked up at the house. An ugly, cruel, iron-spiked gate circled the massive structure, whose long windows were shuttered against the street. Not precisely the most welcoming home in London.

"This is Holly Evernight's house." Adam did not appear pleased. No, he wouldn't be. As Sin had told Eliza, Holly's man, Will Thorne, had been the one to distract Adam while Sin had set Eliza free.

He'd have to get over it. "Holly is the greatest inventor in London." Eliza took his arm. "And my distant cousin, to boot. Lucien's barge is being watched. Thus we have to figure out how to get to it. Holly might be able to help." Or slam the door in their faces. Eliza hadn't met her, but desperate times and all that.

Grumbling, he hit the door buzzer—a wonderous thing—and they waited. What Eliza did not expect was to see her cousin Sin jogging down the drive, his gaze darting about as though something might soon tackle him. "Eliza," he got out a bit breathlessly before glancing at Adam. Sin blanched but gave him a nod. "Adam of the GIM."

Eliza's heart was beating too fast. Sin was Mab's creature, whether he willed it or not. She could not take chances. "Let us in, Sin." And when he moved to open the gate, she caught Adam's eye. He peered back at her, frowning. *Follow my lead*, she tried to say with a look.

He barely blinked, and she wondered if it was an acknowledgment. She'd have to believe so. The moment they entered Evernight's drive, Eliza rounded on Sin. "Hold him," she said to Adam.

In an instant, Adam whipped one of his chains around Sin's neck and pulled tight. Adam held him fast, his free hand fisted in Sin's shirt. For Sin's part, he did not fight but stood still, his green eyes narrowed and annoyed.

"I'm sorry," Eliza said. "But you've admitted to being bound to Mab. I'd not have come here had I known you were in residence."

Sin nodded as much as he was able. "Choose your words carefully, and we'll have no problems."

"Lad," said Adam conversely, "you're the one with the chain around your neck."

"Oh, aye," Sin drawled, his accent suddenly lilting Irish, "and there you stand, weak as a newly born kitten. I'm quaking, I am."

Adam growled and gave the chain a squeeze.

"You realize," Sin said, "that I'm all elemental. I could freeze you solid before burning you alive."

Adam showed his teeth. "And I could snap your neck before you take your next breath."

"Oh, stop," Eliza said. And then thought about Sin's earlier confession. "You're bound to tell Mab if there is a danger of my consorting with Adam."

"To the letter," Sin said, sounding somewhat pleased, given that chains were choking him. "Since the two of you are already consorting, can we dispense with these?"

"Not yet." Adam leaned in. "You and I both know Mab will be asking if you know where Eliza might have gone."

"Yes," Sin admitted.

"Swear that you'll stay out of her way for this day, and I'll let you go." Adam glanced at Eliza. "After that, it will not matter what the boy tells her."

Sin's dark brows knitted, and Eliza swore she saw flames in his eyes. But he conceded. "I swear." He rubbed his neck as soon as Adam let him go. "You needn't have squeezed so tight."

Adam snorted. "Call it a bit of payback thrown in."

Both men tromped up the drive and Eliza followed in tow, biting back a small smile.

Evernight House was much like any other, if one ignored the strange brass panels on the walls, sporting numerous buttons that Adam longed to push and then take apart to see how the ingenious Miss Evernight had done it. He'd always admired the lady.

It was too quiet here, however. Like that of a tomb. As St. John Evernight led them down a hall, their footsteps echoed in the eerie silence, punctuated by Adam's limping step and the rattle of chains. Adam bit back a smirk. The ghost of Jacob Marley indeed. Eliza was not far off there. Adam would be well and glad to be rid of the blasted things.

A flash of dull grey caught Adam's attention, just before a young woman with black hair strode around the corner.

"What is that infernal racket?" she snapped. "I'm conducting a very delicate experiment—"

They stopped at the sight of Holly Evernight, and she

stopped as well. Her cool gaze moved over them. Her blue eyes hit upon Adam, and she backed up a step. "I know you. What do you want?"

Adam made as graceful a bow as he could, given his chains and a lame leg. "Miss Evernight, please know that I bear you no ill will."

"Perhaps I bear some toward you," Miss Evernight retorted. But she turned to Eliza. "Miss . . . May?"

"Eliza," Miss May corrected, taking a tentative step towards her. "I'd been meaning to visit. Though I'd hoped it wouldn't be under these circumstances. And I do apologize for coming to call unexpectedly."

Holly Evernight's stiffness broke like a tart crust. Suddenly she beamed, her stern features brightening. "And I've been meaning to visit you, to assure that you are well. Please do forgive my rudeness. I've been known to get caught up in my own world."

"Perish the thought, Petal." A man popped his head out from a doorway, his white hair brushing the tops of his shoulders. He had the grin of a man content with his lot in life. Adam knew him on sight: Will Thorne, Holly Evernight's mate, and the demon responsible for freeing Eliza from Adam.

As if he sensed a threat, Thorne caught Adam's gaze, and his entire frame tensed. He stepped into the hall, and his fangs peaked out from the corners of his lips. "What goes on here?"

Miss Evernight lifted her hand, just enough for Thorne to move to her side—which he did in the blink of an eye—and take hold of it. "Dearest," she said to him, "Eliza and Adam are here for a visit."

Thorne's expression was dubious. "Tea with the GIM King, I am honored."

Adam snorted. "Put your fangs away, demon. I'm not here for vengeance."

Thorne merely ran the tip of his tongue over one fang.

"Enough," said Holly, giving Thorne an elbow to his ribs. "Welcome, Eliza." She gave Adam a weak smile. "And you, Adam. I...well, I am not sorry for our part in freeing my cousin, but as the two of you seem to be together once again, I suspect there is more to the tale." Miss Evernight gave a pointed look at the chains Adam could not fully hide beneath his greatcoat.

"Indeed," drawled Thorne. "Lovely adornments, mate. Quite musical."

Adam showed his own teeth. They might not include fangs, but he knew how to use them. "When last we met, you'd turned human. So I gather there is more to your tale as well."

Thorne shrugged. "Got the girl, the witch was banished, and they lived happily ever after."

Eliza snickered by Adam's side. St. John, who had been rather quiet, rolled his eyes. "I see everything is well at hand here. I am going." He kissed both Eliza and Holly on the cheek before walking off.

Thorne frowned after him, but then turned back to Eliza and Adam. "Shall we?" He gestured for them to follow him.

Unlike the gloom in the hall, the library they entered was bright and cheerful. And massive. Books lined the walls, the shelves stretching up to the ceilings. A seating arrangement of buttery leather chairs and couches was set before an ornate fireplace with a deep green marble mantle. Papers, books, metal cogs and coils, and numerous other objects cluttered the floor, the desk before the windows, and even the piecrust table in the corner.

In short, people lived here.

Miss Evernight bade them to sit, stopping to lift a stack of books from one seat and putting them on the ground instead. "Will and I do like to spread out," she said with a wrinkle of her nose.

"It is lovely," Eliza assured her, and Adam felt a pang, for he knew she envied their homey environs. He wanted to give her that. A home. Comfort. He did not know why, but the compulsion was real. As was the need for his own home. *Someday.*

Miss Evernight looked to Eliza. "Tell me, what brings you here? Not that I have cause for complaint. I am happy to have you, please know."

"We need your assistance," Eliza said. "I know it appears odd, my being here with Adam. We..." Eliza shook her head. "Mab is not the beneficent aunt I believed her to be."

Thorne let out a crack of laughter. "Understatement of the day."

Miss Evernight frowned. "I ought to have taken you in with me. For that I am sorry."

"What did she do to you?" Eliza asked. Her discomfort in the subject was clear, but she forged on. "I know it was some foul mischief, but it would help to understand her."

Holly sat back, and almost as though she did not realize it, her hand reached across the space between her and Thorne. His hand was there to catch hers, and their fingers linked. "I was dying, my powers turning on me because I'd been using them too much to help William." Their fingers visibly squeezed before relaxing. "Mab was the only one to offer help. Which she would do in exchange for a price."

Thorne's gaze locked on Adam. "To save Holly, I agreed to take Eliza from you, and forfeit both my immortality and Holly."

A strange sorrow punched into Adam's chest. Despite what the world thought of him, Adam's respect for love was only second to yearning for a love of his own. Tenderhearted sap that he was, he'd often created a GIM simply to spare that spirit the loss of love. He'd certainly done so for Sin's sister, Daisy Ranulf.

"It was hell," Thorne whispered.

Eliza made a sound of distress, which in turn distressed Adam. Yet the tight rage he'd held on to in regards to Thorne eased. He could not hate Thorne anymore.

"This was all because of me?" Eliza whispered before lurching to her feet. All the color washed out of her pretty face.

"Not you," Adam cut in before Thorne could answer. "Because of me." When she shot him a look of irritated disbelief, he wanted to smile, but could not. "She was after me. To take you away from me meant that she'd win my soul."

Thorne leaned in, his chair creaking under him, and fixed his silver stare on Adam. "Look, mate, this isn't our business, but you're here, asking for help and knowing far too much of Mab for my comfort. So I'll ask you directly, what is this curse you're under and how did it happen?"

Eliza perked up with such obvious anticipation that he could barely restrain a smile. He did not care about Thorne or his concerns, but Eliza deserved the truth. And Adam knew he'd no cause to fear that his secret would go farther than this room. He could read that in Thorne's eyes quite well.

"Long ago," Adam started, "I was a Knight of the Templars. After returning from my pilgrimage to Jerusalem, I was sent to explore Ireland under the express orders to gather heathen relics and bring them back to the church." Adam gave a wry smile. "The idea being that they would destroy them, though I knew full well they merely wanted to possess these items because they feared the power within them."

Adam waved a hand. "I thought it ridiculous superstition but did my duty. I'd plundered half of Ireland when I came upon a low hill. The locals called it *sídhe,* a fairy mound."

Thorne snorted. "Let me guess, you did not believe in wee fairies either?"

"No," Adam said with equal humor. "I'd soon learn otherwise, for I'd attracted the attention and the ire of their Queen Mab."

Even all these centuries later, Adam could perfectly recall the visceral shock as the beautiful, red-headed woman with strange purple eyes simply appeared from out of a thick, green fog. "Mab, you must know, loves men. She loves to bed them, but particularly the reluctant ones." Adam kept his gaze away from his audience. "I was most reluctant. She was beautiful, yes, but I'd taken a vow, and there was an inherent evil about her that made my innards recoil."

"So then you offended Mab's pride," Miss Evernight murmured, her tone knowing.

"That," Adam acknowledged, "and I'd stolen from her. Those were her objects, after all. Admittedly I was an arrogant arse, not caring one whit about what I'd taken from the unnatural woman."

Eliza's muffled snort had him sliding her a sidelong

look. She met it with a pointed raising of her brows, as if to say *Am I wrong?* No, she was not wrong to laugh. He still had his arrogance and was not likely to be losing it anytime soon.

He thought of his old self. He'd carried many titles back then, Aodh, Son of Niall of Moray, Knight of the Templars, and upon roaming Ireland, *Cù-Sìth* the harbinger of death. Yet there was one title he'd coveted was never to be his: husband. Aye, he'd killed countless men in the name of God, he'd lived the austere life of a monk, traveled from the verdant mists of Scotland to the acrid deserts surrounding Byzantium, and yet all he'd ever wanted was a wife. A family. A home.

"She held me for seven days," he said in a low voice, recalling when Mab had taken everything from him. "Always trying to get me to submit, to want her. And on the seventh day, her patience ran out."

He'd been chained to a massive stone in a glen, his arms stretched wide, his chest bared to the cold air. Aodh had thought his life was at an end when the fae bitch lifted a stone dagger to his throat. But she merely grinned, her little black fangs glinting in the morning light.

"You are mine, Aodh. I claim your soul, and you shall belong to me." The tip of the dagger punctured the skin at the base of his throat, and hot blood welled up. Mab's cloying scent choked him as she leaned forward and licked. Aodh strained against the bonds, cursing her to hell and back, but she merely laughed and pressed her hand over his heart.

Green light poured from her palm and into him, making Aodh scream in rage and pain.

"Never to die," she chanted, "never to age. Young and mine forevermore."

He felt his soul slipping into her grasp, as if she were siphoning it from his flesh. And yet he fought it with all that he was. He would not go like this. He would not lose his dream, his hope.

But his vision began to fade, only to be brought back when a flash of white light flooded the glen.

Mab turned, a snarl of impatience tearing from her lips. And there, standing calm and straight, was a man made not of flesh but of crystal. Or so it seemed to Aodh. Wings of translucent silver, and wide as tree limbs, arched from the man's back. An angel.

The man glanced at him. *Yes, human. Though you may call me Augustus.* The words rang clear in Aodh's head. Augustus turned back to a seething Mab.

"Aodh's soul is not yours to take, Mabella of the Fae."

"Odd, as I was doing so with great ease." As if to stake her claim, she dug her claws into Aodh's chest.

"And yet he does not bend to your will. Thus you have resorted to theft. Nay, Mab, he is one of the divided. One half of a soul torn in two."

Mab's claws sank deeper into Aodh's chest. "You jest. Be gone, foul angel. This affair is not yours to attend."

The angel merely gazed back. "Can you not sense the emptiness that consumes him? Nor see that dark spot from which his other half was rent?"

Mab glanced at Aodh and then away, her nose wrinkling as though smelling something foul. "If this be so, pray, where is his other half?"

"I know not. Nor does it matter. That she exists is enough."

Aodh did not believe in soul mates, nor love. Not the sort that bound one to another for eternity. Granted, until this morn, he'd not truly believed in the fae or angels, yet here they were before him, fighting over his very soul.

"This human stole from me and my kin," Mab snapped. "Restitution is mine to claim."

"Very well," the angel said placidly. "Claim it."

Aodh wanted to protest, to spit in Mab's face, to call her every foul word he knew. Yet he held his tongue. Instinct told him that he could very well lose it, and he wasn't about to earn more of her wrath. Not when she was grinning like a she-devil and dread crawled over his body.

"Aodh MacNiall, henceforth you are living-death, unable to age, grow ill, or suffer mortal wounding. No longer will you feel the joy of the living. Your male beauty, which you so vainly wield, shall draw both women and men like flies to honey, and yet you will never know the heated flush of desire. The dead shall be your sole companions."

If he could talk, he'd blister the earth with his curses to the foul fae bitch. As it was, he could only hang there and feel his body grow oddly numb, feel the hope leach out of him even as his wounds knitted themselves closed.

The fae's carmine lips curled with clear satisfaction. "Enjoy your immortality, love."

She stepped away from him, and he sagged against the chains that held him, a sob crawling up his throat, despite his resolve to hide it. Already he'd lost his sense of touch. The breeze making the trees dance did not soothe his skin, nor did the light of the sun warm it.

Despair wracked him, and he looked up to find the angel Augustus before him. Silver eyes locked onto him. "Aodh MacNiall, while I cannot spare you from the curse that Mab has spun, I can grant you this. As you have been cursed to live amongst the dead, so shall you be soulbound to them. Death shall be the source of your greatest power and your salvation. Look to the dead to lead you to your soul's mate. She will dwell amongst them. When you find her, you shall feel once more, and you shall love."

"You cannot," screeched Mab.

"And yet I have." Augustus stared at Mab, and it seemed his wings stretched wider, his chest lifting higher. "Do you wish to challenge me in this?"

The fae broke the stare first, her cheeks flushed with rage. "Interfering pest." Mab gave a huff but then glanced at Aodh, her dark gaze calculating. "And if he fails to find his soul mate or she rejects him?"

"Then he remains as he is."

No! The denial screamed in Aodh's mind.

Augustus regarded him with an expression as smooth a still waters. "You have seven hundred years to complete your quest, Aodh, or Mab's curse remains." Kind eyes surveyed him. "Worry not. 'Tis but a drop in the bucket of time."

To immortal beings perhaps, but to Aodh, it was nearly unfathomable. Centuries of hell stretched forth, a bleak, empty road.

The angel held his gaze. "One more gift, to help you on your way." Ignoring Mab's squawks of protest, Augustus pressed the tips of his fingers against Aodh's forehead. "I grant you the ability to create life out of what was once dead."

Light, so much light. Blinding brilliance. It shimmered around him, took his breath, filled him up until it seemed to pour from his mouth, out of his eyes, ears, and nose. Until Aodh became light. Power, a dizzy rush akin to that which he felt in the heat of battle, took hold and settled into his very bones.

When the angel stepped away, his body appeared limned in a silver light that was as pure as any Aodh had seen. His soul. *I see his very soul.* Nay, it could not be.

"But it is," said the angel as though Aodh had voiced his fear. "You shall see the light of every being's soul. Even your own. Your soul's true mate shall have a light that mirrors yours."

Unable to help himself, Aodh glanced down at himself. Golden light, pale as new butter and tinged with glimmers of diamond brightness, swirled about him, and yet, right over where his heart dwelled, there was darkness. His soul, torn and waiting to be filled. The mere idea terrified Aodh. Enough that he found his voice, raw and untested though it was. "And you, angel? What shall you require for this gift you place upon me?"

The angel smiled, fond and amused. "Brave knight, that you be true to honor. Soulbound to death as you are, let them be your army and fight for what is good and true. Pick your children well, Aodh."

Aodh glanced at the fae bitch. Her eyes gleamed with unholy green light, wee fangs sliding down over black lips.

"Aye," he rasped, rage filling his throat. "That I shall do."

Finishing his tale, Adam cleared his throat and glanced about. He'd almost forgotten where he was. Holly and Thorne looked thoughtful. As for Eliza, her face was pale and her expression drawn. He could not fathom what she thought.

But then she glanced at him, and her velvety eyes were moist. "All that suffering for refusing Mab?"

"And for stealing," he admitted. "I cannot deny that."

"Even so," she said, "it hardly seems fair."

"Fair? What does Mab care for fairness? If you are to survive," he went on in a harder tone, "what you must understand about the fae is that they view life as a chess match. Every move they make is measured by how it will affect the final outcome, not the here or now."

He traced the carved whorl in the arm of the chair, watching his finger move instead of facing all of them. "Something I myself forgot. I thought more of what I wanted than of what lengths Mab would go to in order to get what she wanted. I thought like a human, not an immortal."

Silence was a ticking clock, the weight of their collective judgment bearing down upon him.

"We are all pawns," Thorne said softly.

"Yes." Adam glanced up. "But you are not human now. And clearly with Miss Evernight once more."

Holly gave a tight smile. "William remembered me. Mab and I had a little chat, in which I destroyed her mortal body and sent her back to the fae lands." She leaned in a little, bracing her arm upon her knees. "And yet she has returned."

It was Eliza who answered. "She disappeared for a few

weeks in May. Then returned one night, saying she'd been in the country. I'm afraid I never sought to question it. Nor any of her actions."

"She returned rather quickly," Holly said. "I was under the impression that she would need more time to regain her strength."

Adam leaned closer to Eliza. "You see, Mab's mortal body is of this realm. One might destroy that body and yet she lives still. However, she must gather the power to create a new body and return here."

"How did she do it, then?" Eliza asked.

"She leached my powers," Adam answered, then turned to Thorne and Miss Evernight. "She is searching for us and has put a price upon our heads. The demons appear up for the challenge."

Thorne glanced at the chains Adam wore. "Sorry to say, mate, but you're easy pickings trapped in those fae laces."

Not so easy, Adam wanted to protest. But Thorne was correct; while Adam had been able to slow down two low-level demons, he would not survive a fight with a more powerful one.

Eliza fists bunched upon her lap. "We need to get onto Lucien's barge, only it is surely being watched."

"What is it that you had in mind?" Thorne asked. "We have quite a bit of effective weaponry."

Eliza's eyes took on an interested light, but Miss Evernight shook her head, her nose wrinkling as though the idea were horrid. "I've an excellent way to get you onto Lucien's barge undetected."

Chapter Sixteen

Holly had put them in a tomb. A damned underwater tomb. That was, at least, how Eliza saw it. She'd nearly turned tail and run when Holly had guided them down into her dungeon—her cellar laboratory—and then along a dank and cramped tunnel that led directly to the banks of the Thames. Hidden in an abnormally large boathouse was a strange sort of vessel that looked like an overgrown cigar.

Adam had taken one look at it and grinned so wide and pleased that he appeared to be no more than a boy. "A submariner boat. Bloody brilliant."

Though it was Adam who appeared brilliant just then, his dark, sinful handsomeness juxtaposed against his bright smile. Even Holly appeared disconcerted for a moment. She blinked at him, then seemed to shake herself out of her fog. "Yes. I've been conducting test runs. She's seaworthy and sound."

"So this...boat," Eliza got out, "goes underwater?"

Holly gave her a cool look. "You Yanks used such vessels during your civil war."

"Oh, we did." Eliza's breakfast curdled in her belly. "Most famously the *H. L. Hunley*, which sank off the coast of Charleston." Eliza shivered just thinking on it.

"Now, now, Miss May, where is your sense of nautical adventure?" Adam grinned at her. "Surely little girls fantasize about being pirates as well?"

"I'd rather be a highwayman and keep my feet dry," she muttered.

Next to her, Thorne nodded sagely. "My mate is a brilliant bird, but I quite agree. It's far too much like a coffin for my liking."

"I thought you loved coffins, dearest," Holly quipped.

Thorne grinned. He was a handsome devil, with a sharp beauty. Not Eliza's particular brand of liquor, as her grandfather Aiden used to say, but striking to be sure. He caught her gaze and leaned in a bit. "Tell me true, Miss May, are you well?" He glanced at Adam, who was wrapped up in gazing longingly at Holly's nightmarish craft. "If you need assistance—"

"I am well," Holly assured Thorne in a low voice. "And under no duress. But thank you. It is kind of you to ask."

"Of course."

Adam's gaze snapped back to her just then. "Hurry along, Miss May."

As though he could hardly wait to get in the death trap, he all but dragged her to the pier.

For a boat that was supposed to remain underwater, the thing was far too small, perhaps twenty feet in length, and made of iron plate. Eliza's trepidation grew as Holly opened a small, circular hatch and descended down a ladder. Eliza had no choice but to follow. Inside was as expected, narrow and suffocating. The only source of light came from a row of portal windows no bigger than dinner plates and, at the front, a curved window made of glass so thick that Eliza decided it would only be good for seeing what lay directly in their path. Not particularly comforting.

With ill grace, she sat upon one of the narrow seats that ran down the middle of the boat. Able to fit two people each, the benches were spaced in a checkerboard pattern so that the passengers' weight was equally distributed throughout. Or so said a brusque Holly as she finished giving a dockside Thorne instructions on how to release the craft from its moorings and then closed the hatch. The sound was a dull and final boom.

It was fine. Safe. Holly was brilliant. Eliza repeated this mantra as her cousin took the captain's seat and messed about with various nobs and levers. The engine started with a horrible buzz and made conversing impossible. Not that she'd be able to. Adam had crawled up to sit by Holly and was now having an animated discussion, involving his pointing to things of interest and generally grinning about like a child at an iced-cream cart.

Eliza braced herself as the craft gave a hard lurch and then simply sank. Gads, what a sensation. She felt as though she too were falling. Darkness descended as they slipped into the murky waters of the Thames. *Under the water.* Eliza shifted in her seat, trying not to let her thoughts run wild.

The air was hot and stale. Barely moving. Sweat trickled. Holly had promised that the trip would take no more than ten to fifteen minutes. They hadn't very far to go to reach Lucien's barge, but the submarine must move at a snail's pace to avoid debris and detection.

To Eliza, every second felt an eternity. Distantly she heard the deep cadence of Adam's voice, paired with

Holly's lighter tones. But the engine noise was too loud to understand what they were saying. Eliza closed her eyes and practiced taking even breaths.

"You look ill," Adam said in her ear.

She yelped. From the front, Holly sent a worried look over her shoulder but soon set her attention back on her instrument panel.

"You scared the blazes out of me," Eliza said to a still-smiling Adam.

"Apologies." His big frame barely fit on the seat next to hers, and their shoulders pressed together.

"It's all right." Eliza managed to peek at him, not really wanting to open her eyes and remember where they were. "You love this."

"The submarine?" He glanced about as though entranced. "It's marvelous. Miss Evernight is a wonder."

"Mmm." Eliza tucked her clammy hands beneath her thighs in an effort to warm them. "I'd forgotten, you love technological advancements as much as she does."

He gave a start of surprise, and his upper arm rubbed over her shoulder, so much taller was he. "You noticed that?" His voice was soft, and she fidgeted. Yes, she'd noticed. Adam had always appreciated modern conveniences, and during the time she'd spent chained by his side, he'd often pop into factories to watch great machines chug away.

Eliza filled the silence between them. "Holly would make an ideal companion for you." It was the truth. Adam could wax on about cogs and pistons or whatever with Holly, while Eliza would likely fall asleep out of sheer boredom.

She felt him turn in her direction and forced herself to turn as well. His eyes were narrowed, his wide mouth tight, but when he spoke, his tone remained mild. "Aside from the fact that Will Thorne owns her heart, Holly Evernight and I would not do. We are both far too analytical and would bore each other within a week. " Again he studied her. "Is this some sad attempt to drive me off?"

"Hardly." Her laugh sounded false. "I'm merely saying, if you were to look past all this soul mate drivel, you might realize that there are women better suited for you."

"Hmm." He scratched his blunt chin where, even now, dark stubble grew. "And what of you? Perhaps a man such as young St. John might entice? He is, after all, your age and quite pretty to look at. I'm certain many young ladies fall in a swoon whenever he passes by."

Eliza's lips twitched at the way Adam could not quite hide his disgruntlement. "First, you insult me by assuming that appearance is the only attribute in a man that I, no, that my entire sex finds attractive. Second, Sin is my cousin."

"He's a second cousin, at the closest," Adam countered, with an apparent dogged determination to annoy her. "Kings and queens have coupled with closer kin."

She shot him a sidelong glare and found him grinning. "You're teasing me."

The corners of his eyes crinkled. "Aye, sweet Eliza, I'm teasing. Besides"—he leaned in and murmured against her ear in his sinful voice—"you do not want to fuck him." The tip of his tongue flicked her earlobe. "And I don't want to fuck her."

Eliza jumped, her face heating, her breath coming short. "And you presume to know who I'd like to *fuck*?" If he could say the word, so could she.

Adam's nostrils flared on a sharp breath, his expression turning carnal. "No presumptions necessary. All you need do is work up the courage to ask, dove. Believe me, I shall comply."

She wrenched her head back. Arrogant bore. She might have said so. But then the craft turned, sending her tilting and the engines groaning. Eliza's insides pitched. Adam gave her an assessing look, then wrapped his arm about her shoulders and drew her to him. Eliza stiffened. She'd seen him nude, bathed his body, held him up, but this embraced was different. Despite her annoyance with his teasing, his hold was a comfort, his strength warm and solid, his arm secure. And she let herself sink into it, not think of anything else but the scent of his linen shirt against her nose and the delicious fragrance of his body.

All this time, she'd done an admirable job of blocking out that scent. He'd been dirty, blood soaked, and she'd been distracted. She wasn't now. Taking another slow breath, Eliza drew more of him into her lungs. Spice, buttery rich, like Christmas cakes. His body tensed, the pectoral muscle beneath her hand lifting a bit when it tightened. She had the mad urge to dig her fingers into his solid strength. Enfolded in his arms, the noise around them was dulled, the swaying less marked. She'd almost drifted off when his hand moved. The warm weight of his palm glided up her waist, slowly, steadily.

Eliza's eyes snapped open, but she held herself still, her heartbeat kicking into her ribs, her breath going light. Neither of them spoke. They barely moved, save his hand, which drew inexorably closer to her breast. A sweat broke over her skin. Eliza found herself moving ever so slightly forward, into his seeking touch.

He must have noticed, for he swallowed audibly. Though Eliza could not see him, she felt the shiver go down his chest and his thighs twitch. And when his palm finally slid over the swell of her breast, they both took a sharp breath. Eliza's eyes fluttered closed. His hand engulfed her breast, warm, firm, and holding all of her attention. He gave her a little squeeze.

A huff of breath left her, and Eliza turned farther into his touch, burrowing her nose in his lumpy cravat, her fingers grasping the loose folds of his coat. A fine tremor took hold of his body, but he did not stop kneading her breast, exploring the contours of it with his fingers.

The lawn shirt, chemise, and corset she wore provided little padding against his touch, and his questing thumb soon found the nub of her nipple. He made a sound, a low grunt, and his grip around her shoulders tightened, holding her in place as the blunt tip of his thumb rubbed a torturous circle over her aching flesh.

"Adam." It was a plea to stop. Gods, he had to stop. Her sex throbbed now, at once swelling and clenching with the need to be filled. "Holly will see." Eliza whispered it against his neck, not knowing if he could hear. Perhaps that was the point; perhaps he wouldn't and keep going.

But he pressed his mouth to her ear. "I don't care."

And then very slowly but very firmly, he pinched her tender nipple, not releasing it but building the pressure. Eliza gave a wordless cry, arching into him, a shudder of heat wracking through her. She didn't know what she might have done, had the entire craft not come to an abrupt halt. From a distance, she heard Holly's voice, crisp with command. "We've come alongside the barge."

Lucien's barge was, as Adam had said, deserted. And destroyed. Someone had torn through it, throwing furniture pell-mell, ripping silken drapes from their heavy brass hangers. What appeared to be a once-decadent pleasure home was now in tatters.

Adam's strong features took on a fearsome cast as they walked down the narrow hall. "This will not go unanswered." The man who had impudently fondled her breast and given her a wink just before they'd stepped out of the submarine was gone. This Adam stood taller, his broad shoulders practically brushing the walls, his expression fierce.

The passage ended at an ornately carved door. Inside were the remains of a dining room, a fairly large space that took up the back third of the barge. This, too, had met destruction. Adam stepped over a fallen chair, as Eliza picked her way past broken glassware, the floor sticky with spilt wine. No blood, however.

Adam stopped at the bulkhead beam running across the back picture window. Intricately carved fleurs-de-lis decorated the beam. Delicately, Adam ran the tip of his finger along one of the marks. "Long ago, the angel Augustus told me to hide anything of value in a place that will stand the test of time."

That the man before her spoke lightly of conversing with angels had Eliza's head reeling, but she pushed that aside. She'd long since fallen off the map of normalcy. "You remained in contact with Augustus? Even after the part he played in your curse?"

"Of course. I bear him no ill will. He did what he could to help." Adam shrugged. "In truth, I consider Augustus a friend of sorts. One such as I does not have the opportunity to converse with many others."

Eliza did not want to think about Adam's years of isolation. She did not want to pity him, nor did she think he'd take kindly to her doing so. Instead she glanced about. "I'd hardly call a barge a place of lasting permanence."

"That is because you don't know Lucien. The man would never let his home go." A shadow of worry fell over Adam's countenance, but he blinked and the look was gone.

"What if it sank? Or caught fire?"

The corners of his mouth curled in a half-smile. Golden eyes glanced at her from over his shoulder. "You are quite the pessimist."

She felt her face heat. "I'd call it practicality."

That made his mouth curl in a half-smile, but he did not answer. Instead he pulled a pocketknife out, flicked it open, and pushed the tip into a seemingly random place. A panel slid open to reveal a hidden space within the wall. Adam reached into the space and pulled out a long, fairly wide iron box. Clearly, it weighed quite a bit, for it fell to the floor with a decided thud. He grimaced. "Bloody thing weighed naught but a feather when I did not have these bloody chains on."

Eliza knelt next to the fallen box. There was a lock upon the thing, and it did not appear easily broken, nor had they brought any sort of tools to do the job.

Adam saw the direction of her frown. "Not to worry." He knelt next to her and took the box, turning it on its end, and simply tugged it. The entire thing slid open, and Adam smiled at her. "It's built like a puzzle box. The lock is merely for show."

Inside lay a sword, at least four feet long, with a simple cross-shaped hilt that appeared to be made of iron.

"Ah, now," crooned Adam, "here we are, then." With infinite care, as though he were handling a babe, he lifted the sword out, and a sigh seemed to go through him. "Ah, my lovely, it's been far too long."

"Shall I leave you two alone, then?" Eliza's lips twitched. She'd never seen such a look of reverence mixed with old familiarity. It was nearly indecent.

Adam spared her a glance. "Quiet woman, a man's relationship with his sword is a sacred thing."

"So I've heard."

"Saucy wench." But his words held no anger. Almost tenderly, he ran the tips of his fingers over the plain hilt, and his breath visibly caught. "We've been through a lot together, this sword and I. Many a battle won with her in my hand." He grasped the hilt and held it firm. In that moment, his eyes closed, as though it were almost too much for him.

When he opened them again, they were bright with emotion. "I claimed this sword in Jerusalem, after a skirmish. It called to me, felt right in my hand." He made a sound of wry amusement. "Perhaps it was fate, after all, for I later learned that this is a fae weapon, crafted in their world. How it came to be in Jerusalem, I know not, but it has been mine ever since." Adam held the sword out to her, presenting it with two hands. "A fae-made sword ought to cut through these chains like a knife through pudding. Strike the cuffs directly."

Eliza blinked. "What? You expect me to cut them off?"

He looked at her as though she were daft. "Only my bride can cut the chains. Or do you think I'm capable of doing this myself?"

Well, of course he couldn't. Only she'd never wielded a sword in her life. Eliza kept her hands upon her lap. "And if the sword does as you predict, I could end up cutting off your hands in the process." She swallowed reflexively. No, she would not be ill now. Save that for later.

His eyes gleamed with humor. "You're wise to worry,

lass. I can assure, you do not want me to lose my hands."
He grinned broadly, looking darkly handsome, before
sobering when she paled. "Have faith, Eliza. You'll not
injure me. I promise."

Muttering things best not said by ladies, Eliza took hold
of the ancient weapon. The leather-wrapped hilt slipped
against her damp palms, and she fought back a wave of
mad laughter. She could do this. Adam laid his arms across
the iron box and waited for her, his strong, corded forearms relaxed, the thick cuffs around his wrists glinting in
the torchlight. One strike. She'd come at it in a slight angle,
hopefully missing his hands, and, please, dear God, with
just enough force to cut the metal and not through his limbs.

Adam's deep voice came as if from a distance. "Swift
and true, Eliza May."

Taking a breath, she lifted the monstrous sword and
struck. The blade hit with a shower of sparks and the clear
ringing of steel. And then Adam bellowed, his great body
falling back as he clutched his arms to his chest, curling
over them as if in agony.

Eliza cried out in terror, tossing the sword aside, and
flinging herself upon him. "Adam! Where did I hit? Let
me see."

She got as far as touching his head before her caught
her up and tumbled her back onto the ground, his arms—
quite unharmed—wrapping around her as he laughed
with abandon. Shocked, Eliza stared up at him, his head
thrown back, his eyes crinkled into half-moons by his
laughter. And then she broke.

"You complete and utter bastard," she shouted, pounding her fist against the curve of his shoulder. He only
laughed harder, tearing up with it, his solid body shaking
on top of her.

"Oh, but you should have seen your face," he got out between chortles. He pulled back then and made a ridiculous expression of wide-eyed horror. Eliza would kill him now. As soon as she was free. She wiggled against him, trying to get in a good hit, but he held her too close as he laughed on.

"Vile, hateful . . . shitting pig!" Her blows grew to light slaps as a small snort left her. No! No, she would not laugh. But his laughter was too infectious, and she found herself joining in. They lay upon the ground, cackling like loons, until her side pinched. She didn't want it to stop. He was all around her, his body protecting hers, his joy flowing like a warm wave. Nothing else mattered. She needn't think of who they were or what they were doing. She could just be.

Eventually, her laughter ebbed, leaving a pleasant ache within her chest. "That was a terrible thing to do, Adam." But she was no longer truly angry, and her words came out low and easy.

At the sound of his name, a pleased light entered his eyes. "Yes, I know." The way he looked her over, as if luxuriating in the sight of her, sent a small but heated shiver down her spine.

"I'll not be sorry," he said so softly, it was a caress. "You were wound so tight, fear and guilt making those warm brown eyes of yours go cold. I'd rather see them alight with life, even if it means you're railing at me."

His thumb stroked her temple, slower now, and his gaze grew slumberous and hot. "I like playing with you, Eliza."

Everything inside of her became slow and quiet, until each breath seemed to brush along the small space between them. "I know."

He'd been a virtuous knight and an isolated king. When had he ever been a mere man but when he was with her? As for Eliza, she'd never been able to laugh or play with carefree abandon. Not since she was a child.

She did not feel like a child at the moment. The hard press of him against her soft, aching places grew more pronounced. She wanted to spread her thighs, let him sink farther in. He, who she'd resented for so long. Resented, yes, but never hated. She could admit that now. This man, handsome as sin, heady as spiced rum, had always tempted her.

As if he knew her thoughts, Adam studied her face, his lips soft and parted. He leaned in, his attention set upon her mouth, and Eliza's breath grew agitated. Yes, now. Past all logic that told her to retreat, Eliza slid her hand along his shoulder to cup the heated skin on the back of his neck, drawing him closer.

At her touch, a sigh seemed to flow through him. "Eliza."

She loved the way he said her name, as though it were a song. She might have answered with a kiss. Only a sudden cold invaded the room, strong enough to halt her progress. He felt it too, for they turned as one, in time to see a low, rolling fog creeping along the floor. Tinged an ugly pea green, the fog seemed as though it had a life of its own. Adam made not a sound as he came to his feet in one smooth movement. Adam's gaze stayed on the door, but his hand reached for her, and she took it, letting him help her up.

"Eliza," Adam said, his deep voice hard yet steady, "get well behind me."

She did not hesitate. Something was coming for them. Already the room grew icy.

Adam picked up his sword, his grip on the hilt not tight but firm. He stood, feet planted apart, sword at the ready.

At the dark mouth of the doorway, lights flickered and shadows stretched. From out of the fog, dark shapes solidified into the forms of men. Four of them. They were tall and thin, their hair flowing free about their shoulders. Eliza needn't see any more of them to know they were fae; she felt it in her bones.

The leader, a blond-haired man with purple eyes and fangs of black, spoke, his voice soft and melodic. "Aodh, you ought to have known we'd hear the sword as soon as you pulled it free of the iron box."

"You presume that I did not expect your company." Adam rolled his shoulders as though he were settling in, his body now loose and ready. His smile was not kind; it was hungry. "Shall we...converse?"

There was no other warning; the fight simply was. Eliza pushed back against the curved wooden wall as the four fae converged on Adam, long swords appearing in hand and whizzing with silver light through the air.

The thrill of the fight surged through Adam's blood. He laughed with it, even as he sliced and pivoted. God, but he had missed this. Missed the marriage of his body and mind to fight with sword and fists. There were four men, fast and quick. Almost too fast, but the chains had been broken and the effect immediate. He was strong now. As he'd been as a knight.

Adam feinted right, kicked left. And then blocked a jab with his sword. One fae thrust his sword, aiming for Adam's gut. He grabbed hold of the blade, the dull edge made for jabbing, not cutting, and wrenched the weapon from the fae's grasp. Novices, he thought with disgust as he swung around and beheaded one man. An ordinary sword wouldn't have done that, but this was fae iron. It cut through them like they were soft bread.

Sweat trickled down his spine as Adam hacked his way through the fae. His side stung, likely cut, but he didn't slow. Until there was one. Their swords met again and again, a clatter of metal upon metal. Adam backed his opponent into a corner, his blows never ebbing. This he knew. It was rote. Even after all these years. And with an upswing, he caught the fae's sword on the hilt, slicing away fingers. The fae male screamed, dropping his sword and clutching his hand.

Mellan sends me mere boys.

Adam stopped and pressed the point of his sword just at the base of the young fae's throat. The lad stilled, his chest lifting and falling in a rapid pant.

"I've a message for Mellan," Adam said. "I've bested him by this sword once before, and I'll do it again. Come after me and what is mine and I'll cut off his head."

Licking his pasty lips, the fae gave a faint nod.

A soft, feminine scent stirred the air, as Eliza moved to his side. He'd kept Eliza in mind the entire time, knowing precisely where she was and making certain to draw the fight away from her. But he'd never looked her way, the threat of distraction too high.

Adam did not turn to acknowledge her now, but his body seemed to broaden, as if to form a wall between her and the fae warrior. The soft touch of her hand upon his elbow merely heightened the need to haul her out of harm's way. Adam stayed the course.

"I've a message for Mellan as well." Eliza's voice was low yet strong. "We are through. I'll die before doing his bidding again."

A chill went through Adam at her words, and he leaned his weight towards her, letting his shoulder butt up against hers.

"Go on, then," Adam told the fae, gesturing towards the door with his sword. "Before I simply send him your head instead."

The young fae left on swift feet, a mere blur in his terror. If only he'd utilized that speed while fighting Adam, he might have had half a chance.

Winded, his body warm and pleasurably humming with the exertion of the fight, Adam let his sword arm lower and finally turned to Eliza. She glanced down at the bodies littering the floor. Tears stained her cheeks, reddened tracks against her skin.

"Love," he began, taking a step in her direction. But then halted when she opened her mouth and began to laugh.

The sound lifted the hairs upon the back of his neck. It wasn't a natural laugh, but a mad, crazed cackled. Something about it shriveled his insides and drew his cods up tight in terror.

Her neck arched as she threw her head back and howled.

"Eliza!" His shout came from deep within him, and she reacted as though slapped.

With a flinch, she snapped her mouth shut. Wide, fearful eyes met his, and then she turned heel and fled.

Adam found her at the end of the long, narrow hall, just before it opened onto the fore deck. Her slim figure was a dark silhouette against the bright entrance. She stood, hand upon the wall, back stiff as washday starch. She might have simply been waiting for him, but it was the steady way she held herself, as if taking too deep a breath would make her crumple, that had him approaching her with care.

She stiffened further as he stepped near, but she did not turn. Pale sunlight shone down on the tops of her cheeks, giving them a soft peach blush. There was something about the curve of her cheek, the vulnerable delicacy of it, that made him want to cup her there, stroke his thumb along the sweet, cupid's bow of her upper lip.

He shoved his hands deep into his trouser pockets instead. "Would you like to talk?"

For a long moment, she stared off into the distance. "What is there to say?" Her voice was too low, almost defeated.

Adam took a step closer, coming alongside her. At his back, the barge was cold and dark. Fresh air and warm sunlight caressed his face. He closed his eyes to the light and took a deep breath.

And her small, pained words reached him. "I laughed."

He opened his eyes. "Yes."

Their shoulders nearly touched, and he could sense her shiver.

"I laughed at their deaths like a mad woman." A shuddering sigh broke from her. "I couldn't stop myself."

Hands still shoved in his pockets, Adam glanced down at his blood-splattered shoes. He rather thought she wouldn't like it if he made eye contact just now. "And you think this somehow makes you evil?"

He felt her turning. Only then did he do the same. Wide, brown eyes gazed up at him. "Doesn't it? What sort of person laughs at death?" She was almost shrill, panic creeping into her words.

"Are you telling me that you felt pleasure at seeing their deaths?" Adam asked.

Instantly her nose wrinkled. "No. God, no."

He shrugged. "Then you are far better than I. It gave me great pleasure to cleave their heads from their necks."

She made a noise of irritation. "But I laughed—"

"Eliza, love, people have all sorts of reactions when distressed. Some even laugh. I knew a warrior by the name of Godfrey. Brave, strong, skilled with the sword. Wore his flame-red beard long and pointed, and his foes often thought him the devil come to claim their souls." Adam's throat constricted as he thought of his old, long-dead friend. "And he was pious, devoutly so. Yet every time we'd pray after battle, he'd laugh."

A smile lit through him. "He'd try to stifle it. His great shoulders would tense. A gurgle would sound at the back of his throat. And then, a small snort." Adam glanced down at Eliza, and he found himself chuckling. "All it took was that one snort, and he'd go off like a lit fuse. Worse, once he laughed, we all fought not to, too, for the poor bastard had a laugh like a braying ass."

Eliza bit the bottom of her lip, clearly fighting back a smile as well. "I cannot imagine a big, bad knight braying."

"It was how he reacted after a battle. Understand, we'd work up this tremendous energy, victory and the thrill of the fight rushed through our veins. With no outlet but quiet reflection." Again Adam shrugged. "Were we ordinary knights, we might have tupped it out of our system as other warriors did."

Eliza's cheeks pinked, and he leaned in a bit, unable to resist. "Lust, and the instinct to bed a woman, is a common reaction to fighting, you realize."

One of her golden brows rose. "You were making a point about Godfrey laughing," she said tartly.

"We were Templar, sworn to live chaste and in service to God. Godfrey found no more humor in prayer than you find in murder. It was simply his way of releasing. Yours as well, apparently. The problem was that to laugh during prayer was considered blasphemy. Which was the last thing Godfrey meant to convey." Adam thought of Godfrey and lowered his voice. "He might have been sentenced to death. Might have been accused of possession."

Eliza's eyes went wide. "What did he do?"

"Nothing for it, really." Adam shrugged. "So every time he started up, we'd all laugh too. 'Tis one thing to lose a single knight. But to do away with the lot of us would have been too high a cost."

"You protected him." Her voice had a note of wonder.

"Aye, Eliza May, that we did." He reached out and slowly took hold of her waist, drawing her to his side where she belonged. Perhaps it was testament to her being upset, or perhaps she was growing accustomed to his touch, but she did not resist. Adam rested his palm against the warm crown of her head and held her tight. "I will protect you as well, dove. Always."

"Well now," drawled a voice Adam had nearly given up hope of hearing again, "I never thought I'd see the day the two of you would cozy up together."

Adam grinned down at Eliza and then turned his head to greet the man who'd interrupted them. "Lucien."

Chapter Seventeen

⊁⟋⟍⊱

Adam's happiness in seeing Lucien, his right-hand man, was infectious, and Eliza could not help but smile as well as she greeted him.

"Hello, Lucien." Despite her disgruntlement at Adam during the time he'd kept her captive, she'd always liked Lucien. A Southern Creole, the man was utterly beautiful, so finely formed that his features were almost feminine.

As always, he was dressed as a gentleman from the last century, wearing a satin frock coat and tight knee britches paired with white silk hose. However, there were circles under his eyes and a thinness about his mouth.

"Miss May." He made a leg, bowing with grace. "Enchanted as always." He glanced at Adam, and his mouth thinned even more. "*Mon capitaine.* I see you've decorated my barge. I cannot say I approve of the adornments, but our tastes have always differed, no?"

Adam smirked. "Were it you doing the decorating, the adornments would be far more lavish, I'm sure." Adam's grip upon Eliza's waist tightened. She'd been aware that

Adam kept his hold upon her as if she were his. But she did not want to shrug him off, not yet. Not when he was so happy. His voice rumbled over her, the vibrations humming along her side. "But where have you been?"

Lucien's expression shuttered. "Away. I did not realize I was needed until I began to weaken." He leaned against the wall. "You are aware that the GIM are not well?"

"Aye," Adam said softly. "And there's not a damn thing I can think to do about it." His body tensed at Eliza's side. "Other than find a way to destroy Mab."

"Hmm..." Lucien glanced at Eliza, and the look in his eyes was calculating. Eliza eased away from Adam, feeling his resistance in the matter, but he let her go.

Lucien's golden brown brow lifted a touch, but he looked back to Adam. "Her merry little band of fae, I am told, tore through my home."

"It appears so," said Adam.

"Looking for you?"

"That, and she wants the Golden Horn an Bás."

Lucien walked past them in his gliding way, and they followed as he strolled down the dark hall to enter his dining room. He took in the destruction with a jaundiced eye. "I've heard of the horn, but some say it is one of the true myths." With ease, he righted his pearl-inlaid chair and then went to pick up the others littered around his massive dining table. "Other stories insist that it is not an object, but a power, just as the GIM can leave their bodies."

Adam guided Eliza to a chair and held it out for her. Rather macabre for them to be seated around a dining table, considering the bodies on the floor, but she took her seat.

"Mab thinks I know of its whereabouts." Adam helped Lucien pick up other bits of overturned furniture around the table. "However, I am wondering if Mellan is leading her on a goose chase to occupy her while he plots his own little games."

Lucien stopped in the act of righting a wine bottle. "That *cunnard* is here?"

"Unfortunately." Adam glanced at Eliza. "He ordered Miss May to kill me."

Lucien's laugh was slow and full. "Oh very delightful." He glanced at Eliza. "Biding your time, are you?"

"Perhaps I've decided to be rid of Adam's cohorts first." She smiled. "Starting with you."

Undeterred, Lucien winked. "Eye sockets are quite vulnerable. I taught my lovely Mary Chase that when she was a mere GIM *bebé*."

Eliza laughed, until Adam leaned a hip against the back of her chair, distracting her into abrupt silence.

"Mellan wants my sword," Adam said.

"Doesn't everyone," Lucien muttered under his breath before brightening. "And your head, yes?"

Slightly pink in the cheeks, Adam answered curtly. "Yes. But I think what he really wants is a weapon to destroy his sister. With Mab gone, he'll have total control over the throne."

"Which means that he won't stop until he's taken the sword from you," Eliza said.

Adam glanced down at her. The thick, black lashes rimming his eyes made the gold of his irises appear brighter. "Which means we must find a way to destroy them both."

"Or pit them against each other," Eliza countered, quite liking that idea.

His full lips curled in his familiar half-smile. "Or that."

"Until you find a solution to that little problem," said Lucien, "you must leave London. Go into hiding."

"I've a mind of where to go," Adam said. "We'll be

leaving within the hour." He gave Eliza a small nod and then went to dispose of the bodies. It was a testament to his returning strength that he no longer limped and could easily heave a body over his shoulder.

Lucien, however, stayed behind. "I want to give you something."

Eliza sat a bit straighter, the idea filling her with trepidation. The man was a known trickster. "Oh?"

Smiling a bit, he reached into his collar and pulled something over his head. Eliza could see him grasping the object, as if it were a necklace he wore, but the actual object wasn't visible to the eye. With care, he came close, and the faint glimmer of a chain shone in his dark palm. "This is yours now."

Intrigued, Eliza held out her hand, and he slid his gift into her palm. Shining like spider silk was a delicate cord, upon which rested an ornate pocket watch about the size of a silver dollar and seemingly made entirely of translucent crystal. "It is utterly beautiful."

She'd never seen the like.

"It was made for you," said Lucien with surprising gentleness.

Her head snapped up. "Me?" Her fingers curled around the watch, warmth infusing her hands. "But this is... It must have taken time to make this." Years perhaps.

"I believe it took a century." Lucien gave a lazy shrug. "But made for you, it was. Go on, *ma chère*. Put it on and let it rest against your heart where it belongs."

Eliza was wary of doing so, but something about the watch called to her, and it was too great to ignore. She slipped the chain over her head. The instant the watch settled on her skin, it disappeared.

"Magic," Lucien said with a smile. "And protection, so

that no other might see it and be inspired to snatch it from your pretty neck."

Unbidden, Eliza's hand flew to her throat, and she touched the chain as if to assure herself that it was still there. "I do not understand why this is mine."

Again Lucien shrugged. "I am not of a mind to explain at the moment." He gave her a kind smile, however. "Wear it for me and keep it safe? You need not keep it when all of this is over, but for now, do an old Creole this one favor."

"Well, I can hardly ignore the request of such an aged gentleman," she muttered, unable to quell her smile.

"You are as wise as you are beautiful," Lucien said with a jaunty bow. Then, with liquid grace, he flowed into the chair, set an elbow on the table, rested his chin in the palm of his hand, and proceeded to look her over in frank appraisal.

Amused, Eliza settled more comfortably in her seat and returned his stare. Lucien's full mouth pulled into a small smile. Frilly lace cascaded over the grass-green satin of his sleeve, the color offsetting his brilliant jade eyes. He really was extraordinarily beautiful for a man. It was in the deep honey of his skin, the sculpted features, but also the effortless way he carried himself.

His smile grew. "Careful now, *mon fille*, if Adam sees you looking at me in that manner, he shall become quite jealous." Lucien's expression said he would not mind that consequence one bit.

"How could he blame me?" she replied with sauce. "It is like gazing upon a piece of art."

A laugh burst from him, and he slapped his be-ringed hand upon the table. "Ah, but you are delightful." A fine rose tint rode along his cheeks. "I cannot remember the last time a woman had me blushing."

Eliza had hoped her honesty would deter him from his

study of her, but it did not. Glowing green eyes watched her once more. Though the humor remained, his voice was smooth cream. "I did not allow myself to fully look upon you before. He would not allow it."

"But now you may?" she asked, not understanding why he would bother.

He gave a lazy shrug. "You are no longer attached to him by means of a chain. And as he is not around at the moment, I may look my fill."

She spread her arms in an exaggerated fashion. "By all means."

Lucien made a hum of amusement. "He knows not what you are, that much is clear."

His statement drew the air from the room, replacing it with ice. Eliza struggled to breathe, to not jump up and run. How did he know? She wanted to shout the question. Worse, she wanted to beg him to give her answers. What was she truly? What did he see in her? The darkness? The dread?

Somehow her mouth formed words. "And what do you believe me to be, Mr. Stone?"

His eyes gleamed, a mesmerizing brilliant peridot. *"Quarteron. Gens de couleur."*

Though his remark was the last thing she expected, the tension along Eliza's neck released.

"Your golden fae hair makes it harder to detect," Lucien observed. "Then again, *les quarteron* are as varied as they are beautiful."

"I've never tried to hide it, if that is what you were implying." Eliza was proud of her parentage, but to use it for sympathy or gain she would never do.

"No, I do not suppose that you have. Nor would I." Again that wry smile. "Birds of a feather, are we not, *fille*?"

Eliza had known Lucien was *quarteron* as soon as

she'd laid eyes upon him. "I'd say you were more of a peacock to my plain plumage."

Lucien chuckled. "You are exquisite. And this?" He waved an elegant hand along his frame. "Is stolen. Long ago, my body and that of my lover were destroyed. Murdered for being blights against God and nature." For once, Lucien's expression was stone. "I chose to inhabit my lover's body instead of my own."

A pulse of surprise went through Eliza's middle. He saw it, but merely blinked, as if bracing himself for her censure. She did not blame him for that assumption; by English law, what he'd revealed to her could land him in prison. It most certainly would have him spurned by society. Eliza gathered he cared little for either the law or society. As to why he felt the need to tell her, she did not know.

"And your lover?" she asked.

"He chose to move on." Another negligent shrug. Then his gaze pinned hers. "Do I shock you?"

"A bit." She too shrugged. "That you chose his body instead of your own. It is ... odd."

Lucien's lips twitched. She'd surprised him again, it seemed. But his tone was insouciant. "His was far more beautiful. And it was quite an effective reminder of ... many things," he finished quietly. "It was Adam who suggested I go to London, away from the oppression of America." For a moment, he looked lost in the past; then his expression grew thoughtful. "Had Adam understood your family history, he might have treated you differently. Most certainly he would have not kept you in chains."

Eliza had her doubts about that. "My familial origins ought not matter. No person ought to be enslaved."

The gems on Lucien's rings flashed as he slowly drummed his fingers. "You sought to test him."

"Hardly. He ought to have released me from those chains because I asked. And for no other reason."

"This is true, and yet I'm thinking you have not experienced the ribald fear of losing your heart's desire. You do not understand how such fear can shatter logic and make a man do what he might not otherwise consider." With unexpected tenderness, he reached out and cupped her cheek. Eliza stared back, unable to move as the glow in his eyes intensified. "Tell him, *ma chère*."

"Tell me what?" Adam's deep voice sliced through the air like a scythe, and Eliza jumped within her skin. But she was slow to turn her head. His expression was dark; his eyes copper bright in the dim light and fixated on Lucien's hand upon her cheek. A muscle along his jaw twitched. "I assume you are referring to me. Or are there other men you've kept secrets from?"

Lucien, sly devil that he was, did not let go of her, nor look away from her face. "We were referring to you, *mon commandant*. As to what?" He raised a dark brow, giving Eliza a pointed look, and waited.

Eliza glared, not taking her gaze from Lucien either. "I was telling Lucien that he was as pretty as a peacock."

The room fell to heavy silence, Lucien grinning wide and pleased, and the weight of Adam's displeasure pressed against her back.

"Oh," whispered Lucien, "you shall do nicely."

The pocket watch Lucien had given her ticked along with a tiny click, click, click, and then Adam's voice, hard and rough, crashed over her. "Are you going to tell me the truth?"

Fists pushed deep into the pockets of his ratty jacket, Adam forced himself to remain still, to not take hold of

Lucien, the little pismire, and pummel him. He knew full well that Lucien sought to antagonize him. The man was in a mood over some transgression Adam had unknowingly made, and this was his revenge. It had bloody well worked.

"I do believe," said the canny bastard, "that I shall leave you two to your tête-à-tête." Swift as a bird, Lucien rose and gave Adam a bow. Adam waited until Lucien glided past to grab him by the elbow.

Lucien halted, his expression impassive, but there was a challenge in his eyes. He wanted a fight. Adam leaned in, hovering over the slighter man. "I want you to send word to Augustus. You know how to do this, I assume?"

It was almost amusing the way Lucien's face clouded in confusion, save Adam wasn't in the mood for levity.

"I do," Lucien said finally.

"Good. Tell him that St. John is under Mab's control. A blood bond. He may well know. But perhaps not the extent." Adam had thought of St. John when he'd told his tale. The boy likely suffered more than simply heeding the bitch's orders.

Frowning, Lucien gave Adam a short nod of acknowledgment. Adam let him go, giving him a warning glare that conveyed his displeasure and the knowledge that he'd soon lose his temper were Lucien not out of his sight. Smartly, his second in command quit the room with due haste, leaving Adam alone with Eliza.

"What did you say to him?" Her tone was accusatory, as though she'd protect Lucien if she must.

Adam ground his teeth together until his jaw ached. The bastard had been cupping Eliza's cheek with tender familiarity. Touching smooth flesh that Adam ached to... He took a deep breath, fighting off the urge to roar. It did not matter that he knew Lucien had no desire for women; in his mind, Adam could almost feel the shape of his old sword handle against his palms, the weight of it and how much force he'd need to slice it. Clean through Lucien's neck.

Temper, temper. Adam slowed his breathing and brought his attention back to *her.* Whether or not that was wise, he did not know. As always, simply looking upon her was a kick to his gut. From the beginning, he'd felt the primal instinct to claim. A call within that shouted: *mine.* As a warrior, he'd trusted his instincts. They had kept him alive in battle. But the fiend he'd been for centuries had lived by cold calculation and logic. And his mind told him to proceed with caution. Eliza May had softened towards him, but she was still skittish.

As it was, she sat, half turned in her chair, a slender arm draped over the back of it, and glared at him, those luminous brown eyes full of wariness. It had been unsettling to see her and Lucien together, their heads nearly touching. Neither of them possessed the milk-white skin of Londoners. They shared a golden, honeyed glow, as if the sun had blessed them with its favor. Beautiful creatures both, with bold features and full lips. A pretty picture, they made. As if they belonged together.

Though Eliza held the look of the fae as well. It was in the satin gloss of her dark gold curls, and the way her eyes tipped up at the corners, their color so deep brown they held a hint of purple. And she'd been sharing a confidence with Lucien.

"Answer my questions, and I shall answer yours." His voice sounded like rust, his throat raw, as if he had been shouting. "Is this about the fae?"

"No, not the fae—"

"Then what? You will tell me now, Eliza. I am weary of your secrets." As soon as he made the demand, he knew he'd erred.

Her nostrils flared on a drawn breath. "You realize that I am under no obligation to tell you anything."

Adam ran a hand over his tight jaw. "I lashed out in jealousy, dove. You ken? It...you have the unique ability to steal my reason, if I'm speaking true." And wasn't that bloody inconvenient, when he needed all his wits about him.

She held his gaze for a moment, then the starch went out of her shoulders, and her tone went soft. "It was nothing. I suspect Lucien was merely trying to annoy you."

She stood, and the movement sent the light of the sun across her skin. Something glimmered there, a flash that caught his eye. Perhaps he'd seen it because his paranoia ran high at the moment, but Adam could not stop himself from reaching out and tracing his fingers along her collarbone.

Eliza stiffened, but did not back away from him. His fingers snared the invisible chain, and when he lifted it off her skin, the tiny pocket watch dangled before him. Adam stared at it, memories and a strange heaviness clamped down on his heart.

"Lucien gave it to me." Eliza's tone was defensive, if not slightly shaken. She was wary of the watch. Wary of him once more.

"This is mine." *You are mine.*

Her pert chin raised a notch. "Then why was it in Lucien's possession?"

"He was keeping it safe for me." Adam's mind drifted off, thinking of those dark hours when Eliza had first escaped him and he knew he must give himself over to

Mab. It was then he'd placed the watch in Lucien's reluctant hand.

"This is the heart and soul of the GIM. Keep them well. Keep them safe. You are their king now."

Lucien's expression had been grim, angry. *"It is your heart and soul as well. I am but a caretaker until you can retrieve it,* mon ami.*"*

Adam's hand trembled as he lifted the piece higher, the light catching the crystal and sparking a rainbow of color against his dull coat front. "Do you know what this is?" he asked Eliza in a low voice.

"Other than a watch?" Eliza shook her head. "Lucien would not tell me. Only that I must keep it safe." A little wrinkle formed along the bridge of her blunt, straight nose. "He said that it belonged with me."

An odd lump filled Adam's throat. "I suppose it does." The watch would not have allowed itself to be worn by her if it weren't so. "Wear it against your skin. Do not let anyone see or know of its existence."

He knew his expression was hard, unyielding, but she needed to understand. Thankfully, she gave a solemn nod. "I will. But... If it is truly yours, then you ought to have it back."

"No. It isn't safe." He met her curious gaze. "Not when Mab wants my soul."

The pillow of her bottom lip pushed out enough to catch his attention and hold it. "Adam..."

God, but he loved the husky way in which she spoke.

"If I cannot..." She trailed off again, a huff of impatience leaving her. And then her head tilted down as if she could no longer hold it high. "What if I cannot help set you free?" she finished in a small voice.

A real fear. As he could not force her to want him. He ran his thumb along the smooth edge of the watch. "I wish..."

Her gaze was a touch on his skin. "What do you wish?"

Adam's chest lifted on a breath, and he made himself face her. "That we could trust each other. That you would believe it when I told you I'd never hurt or betray you."

Pansy-purple flooded her irises, so fae that something inside him balked, even as he found himself drifting closer. Or perhaps she did. It did not matter who moved, only that the soft rise of her breast brushed against his forearm, that her lips parted, the rosy color and plump curve of them tempting him to taste her again, endlessly.

"And what of you?" she asked. "Will you put your trust in me?"

He wanted to say yes. But he'd been alone, without anyone knowing his truths, for hundreds of years. And his throat closed around the word. "Tell me what you spoke of with Lucien," he found himself saying.

Instantly, her long lashes swept down, hiding her eyes from him. "No." She moved to step away from him, and his hand grasped the watch, holding her in place.

Eliza's sweet mouth compressed, but she did not look up. "Let me go, Adam."

He wanted to. Maybe that was the true way to gain her acceptance, her love. But he could not make his fingers relax. "Why won't you tell me?"

Only then did she lift her eyes to his. "When it ceases to matter, then maybe I will." Her step was so abrupt and swift that the watch slipped from his grasp. And so did she. Again.

Chapter Eighteen

D o you know where she's gone?" Mab's question came out light, almost unconcerned, but the way she pinned Sin with a stare was anything but. She'd flay him alive and enjoy it.

Sin leaned against the doorframe, hands stuffed into his trouser pockets, his heart thudding against his ribs. "No."

"Mmm..." Mab trailed one claw-tipped finger over the green velvet brocade divan where she lay. She'd summoned him to her rooms with the message to make haste. And Sin had complied. Because he could never do otherwise. Mab's eyes turned fully purple as she watched him now. "Are you certain?"

"Madam, you've made certain that I cannot lie to you."

"And yet there are ways to slip around the truth." Again her pointed claw dragged along the fabric, deeper this time, snagging in the velvet and leaving a jagged scar in its wake. A smile curled over her carmine lips. "Isn't there, my sweet meat?"

Revulsion caught him by the cods and held on with an

icy grip. He fucking hated that nickname, and what often came after. Sin swallowed back bile. Fuck it all to hell, he was done. Done being her pawn. "Then I shall put it thusly. I made bloody well sure Eliza May would know not to trust me."

Rage flashed in Mab's eyes. And Sin was honest enough to admit that it terrified him. But he held still. And she suddenly laughed, showing her pointed teeth. "Clever boy. Are we growing into a man now?"

God, would he ever be clean? Or would he feel the taint of his misdeeds for a lifetime?

Mab stirred, drawing his attention back to her. A pale green silk dressing gown encased her slim body, and when she lifted her knee, the silk slid away from her white thigh. A pretty sight. It made Sin's insides heave. She watched him with narrowed eyes as she slowly spread her legs, exposing a wet and waiting quim.

He wanted to die. He knew that now. Die, rather than touch her. And yet a fierce and sudden rage came upon him. He would not let her win. He'd not end himself because of her.

Mab drew a finger along her plump, pink seam. "Come along then, sweet meat. I require release."

He swallowed down his hate and revulsion. Tapped it down deep inside of himself and went numb. She was nothing. His body was nothing but a receptacle for his soul. He told himself this. And it still didn't matter. He still felt everything.

Instead of using the horrid submarine, Adam took Eliza to Kew by way of a pleasure cruise. Dressed now as a lady and gentleman of good stock, they blended in with a large group of people intent upon picnicking at Kew

Gardens. However, despite the gaiety surrounding them, the trip had been somber and silent.

They disembarked without a word exchanged, and Adam set off down the country lane, his back straight and his jaw clenched.

He was angry with her, she knew. Guilt in regards to Adam was a new sensation for Eliza. Before now, her anger or withdrawal from him felt justified. They'd had a horrible courtship, if one could call it that. But the truth of the matter could not be ignored; he was courting her, if only in his odd, managing way. Eliza supposed as a battle-hardened knight turned immortal demigod—and didn't that fact make her head spin—he had much to learn about tender feelings and tact. He'd lived his life either taking or demanding. Not that she was inclined to let him off that particular hook. Adam had been a bastard.

But he was also trying. And he was charming. *Charming the knickers right off of me*, she thought wryly. One kiss had her so hot and bothered that thinking about it left her slick and wanting. If she let him into her body? She wouldn't be able to think straight. In truth, she wanted him. Quite desperately.

She'd hurt him when she'd refused to answer his questions. He was a proud man. Just as she was a proud woman. Had the tables been turned, she'd be stomping about, wanting to brain him with her reticule.

But the proprietary way in which he'd questioned her had irked, and Eliza had not particularly cared to answer him. Even so, the stiff set of his shoulders and his utter silence left her feeling unsettled. She'd elevated silence to an art form in her dealings with him before. Was this how he felt? Shut out and aggravated and craving a mere word or nod of acknowledgment? She swallowed down a lump of ugly emotion, but it still poured out of her with a sharp tongue. "My grandfather was a slave."

Ahead of her Adam halted. The wind pressed his coat against his back, outlining the leanness of it. "A slave," he repeated in a dull voice. "In the States?"

"Yes. On my mother's side. His master set him free upon his death. Later, Grandpa Joseph served as an army surgeon in our Civil War." A distinction of honor, even if he'd only been allowed to operate on his *own* kind.

Adam ducked his head and pressed his fingers to the bridge of his nose.

In the silence, Eliza took a breath. Did he think less of her now? She did not rightly care. Only that, if he did, she'd leave him where he stood, the world and its problems be damned. Typhoid had swept through Boston and wiped out her entire family, save Grandda Aiden and herself. But she still missed Grandpa Joseph, missed them all. And she would never be ashamed of them.

"Lucien recognized me as a *quarteron*. I am a woman of color."

Adam's entire body tensed, and it seemed he squeezed the bridge of his nose harder. Then with a sigh, he turned, Eliza opened her mouth—to say what—she did not know, but he hauled her close and pressed his lips against her temple. "I am a wee shite, Eliza. I know that. An utter shite, do you hear?"

She heard. But he gripped her arms as though he wanted to sink into her skin. "I chained you."

He sounded so woebegone that she nearly smiled, but she stood stiffly in his arms, not wanting to yield to his comfort. "Adam, it ought not to matter. Chaining another is wrong, regardless of who their grandparents were."

"I know," he said in a small voice, his words muffled in

her hair. "And yet I'm compelled to admit that I still feel worse for knowing."

She laughed. "Your honesty is refreshing, at the very least."

Slowly, he backed away. His expression was haunted and contrite. "Please, Eliza. Let us be friends."

His gilded eyes looked at her as though she were everything he'd ever need, and her heart grew soft and warm. She touched his cheek with the tips of her fingers. "All right. Friends."

A lock of dark hair fell over his brow as he gave a sharp nod. "Good." He let out a breath and captured her hand in his. "Very good."

Together they walked down the sidewalk, the sun shining bright upon them. His sword was wrapped in a large satchel that he had strapped across his back, making him look more highwayman than gentleman. "We rest here until my strength is fully restored, and then we shall return to London and set up house."

Eliza halted, her skirts swaying. "Set up house?"

He glanced at her, and the corner of his mouth quirked. "Steady on, Eliza. We shall need a base of operations to wage our war. And then I shall take great pleasure in cleaving Mellan and Mab's heads from their bodies."

"You're very certain of yourself."

"I've never been more motivated, dove." It was not a nice look that resided in his eyes.

"How can you strike against Mab? Does she not own you?" Eliza could not refrain from asking.

But he did not frown as expected. "While we are handfasted, the only one who owns me is you, Eliza."

She ignored the way that made her shiver and followed him once more.

"Decades ago," he said conversationally, "I lived for a time as a clockmaker."

Eliza made a noise of amusement. And he smiled faintly. "Yes, I know. But I really do love clocks. My clockwork hearts are created by magic, but I'd always wanted to know how to do it by hand. And so I learned my trade."

"You enjoyed it."

"Had I my way, I'd have lived my life out doing just that."

Eliza found herself wishing he'd be able to one day.

It felt strange to walk once more along the quaint streets where Adam had pretended to live as a mere man for a few years. Time stood still here, houses and shops being repaired instead of pulled down for newer structures. Even the flowerpots gracing the mullioned windows looked the same to Adam, as if there would always be red geraniums decorating the bookshop or purple pansies hanging in the bakery's window.

The area was relatively safe. Many GIM lived here, mainly because Adam had purchased the bulk of the surrounding property and given them refuge. He had similar hamlets established around the world. And while Adam and Eliza were still being hunted, they'd likely have some warning before a strike.

Mellan had some honor. Now that Adam had the greater claim on Eliza through handfasting, the fae prince would likely bide his time, looking for other ways to entice her to his side.

Not bloody likely. Adam would be damned if the bastard got near her again. He merely needed something to trade. He understood Eliza's ire in being treated as a commodity. Nor did he want to treat her as such. But facts were facts. The fae would not leave her be until they were satisfactorily appeased.

Problem was, Adam had no idea where to find this bloody golden horn. Or if it even existed, for he had a suspicion that Mellan was toying with Mab and using the myth of the horn as his bait.

Despite Adam's worries, a sense of peace filled him as he walked along the cobbled walkway, their stones worn smooth from centuries of use, and without thinking much about it, he caught Eliza's slim hand up with his once more.

He felt the shock of his action run down her arm and into her fingers, turning them stiff. For a moment, he thought she might pull away. But then she relaxed, inexplicably, wonderfully. She moved closer to him, walking at his side, and let him lace his fingers with hers. "Remember," he said out of the side of his mouth, "we are man and wife here."

"What a lovely town this is, darling," she said in a voice that carried.

His contentment burst like a soap bubble. Right. She was merely acting the dutiful wife. He let her hand go.

"The shop is just ahead." He gestured with his chin to the black shop sign that had a clockwork cog and the words GIMSIRE'S CLOCKS painted in gold.

"Gimsire?" Eliza murmured in amusement, her breath warm and soft against his collar.

Adam shrugged, as much as to relieve himself of the prickling heat that her nearness caused. "What can I tell you? I'm abysmal at coming up with names."

"Oh, I don't know," a smile played about her full lips. "It's quite clever to me. Very tongue-in-cheek."

They stopped before the shop window, the faint outlines of clocks visible in the darkened store.

"So you lived as a man here?" She shook her head. "I confess, I expected you to live as a lord, taking up residence in Knightsbridge or some such place."

It amused him to picture that. How very boring it would have been. "As king of the GIM, there were those who would see me topple, and I had no means to defend myself. Do you know, I was forbidden to raise a hand to any but my GIM?"

"So you had to hide?" Eliza said.

"When I came to London, yes. But I took the risk now and then, when the isolation of not living amongst others grew too great. And after all, few would think that a simple clockmaker was really the reviled and feared Adam of the GIM."

"I suppose they wouldn't."

Slowly Adam trailed a finger over the cold glass, leaving a path in the condensation. Inside, his old worktable sat, still covered with cogs and springs, as if waiting for him to return. "I was sorry to leave this place."

She spoke quietly, her body close to his, as though they were in their own world. "Then why did you?"

And there it was, the one thing he never thought about when he was with Eliza: the loneliness he'd felt for so many years. His voice came out in a rasp. "Time, Eliza, has never been my friend." His reflection in the window was pale and watery. "Certain rules regarding my powers made it that I could not remain in this world for more than a few months at a time. It became tedious, keeping this shop and constantly leaving it." Not to mention that it made him soul sick.

He turned and faced Eliza. "I paid a local to maintain the shop, keep it clean, and watch for vandals."

Adam might have closed the shop altogether, but something inside of him could not fully let it go; he'd been happy playing the part of a respectable clockmaker, happy spending countless hours bent over his worktable, devoted to the creation of fine timepieces.

Eliza's brown eyes deepened to purple—something that had been happening with greater frequency.

"What are you thinking?" he murmured, for she looked at him as though she'd seen into his soul.

"That you are surprisingly sentimental." She touched his forearm, the contact sending a bolt of pleasure into his heart. "That you wear many hats. And I wonder how many have seen all of them."

A lump rose in his throat. And he touched her with fingertips that were not quite steady. "Only you, Eliza." And she was the only one who would, the only one he wanted to show his whole self to.

He bent his head, needing to kiss her, but just then Mrs. Wilson stepped out of her tea emporium, her back stooped and her face wizened. Though it ought not be, it was a shock, seeing her now. The woman he'd known as Mrs. Wilson had been a pretty, pink-cheeked widow with an easy smile and generous curves. Adam knew that she'd been perfectly willing to warm his bed. Had he been capable back then, he might have asked. Many a dark cold night, he'd longed for a soft body to help warm him, for a pair of willing arms to ground him to this world. He'd settled for paying her a generous stipend to clean his clock shop when he'd left town.

Through the delicate wrinkles that webbed Mrs. Wilson's face, a pair of bright blue eyes locked onto him. Her thin mouth fell open and remained before she had the presence to close it. "Mr. Gimsire?" Then she shook her head. "Lord above, but you couldn't be, you're a young man."

Adam stepped forward, fondness and melancholy tempering his smile. "I suspect you are thinking of my grandfather, the elder Mr. Gimsire. You are Mrs. Wilson, are you not? Grandfather spoke highly of you."

The old woman blushed. "Sir, you are too kind." She glanced at Eliza.

"Pardon me," Adam said, putting his hand on the small of Eliza's slim back. As though he had every right. Illusions. "My wife, Mrs. Gimsire." He'd lied to humans for centuries. Still the words were hard to utter. And, if the sudden tension along Eliza's back meant anything, they were hard for her to hear.

"A pleasure," Mrs. Wilson said as Eliza murmured her hellos. "And how does your grandfather fare?"

"I'm afraid my grandfather has passed. Just last year." Adam put on a frown, suddenly hating the lies he had to tell over and over. Hating that he never bonded with a community, a set life, but watched the world drift past him while he remained frozen in place.

"Oh," Mrs. Wilson exclaimed with a small, weak breath. "Oh, dear, I'm so very sorry to hear it."

"I ought to have written to you. I know you've been keeping his shop well."

Mrs. Wilson grimaced. "Not as well as I would like, I fear. I'm getting on and there is just myself to..." Her voice drifted off as she searched her reticule for a kerchief. "He shall be sorely missed, young man. In that you can trust."

Adam gave her a gentle nod of acknowledgment. "You were a good friend to him."

"God be with you, Mr. Gimsire." Mrs. Wilson sniffled

into her lace handkerchief, then dabbed her eyes as she ambled back to her shop.

He watched her go and the odd feeling of time slipping through his fingers hit him square in the chest. And he was always on the outside of it.

Chapter Nineteen

An hour caught in Mab's snare and then Sin was free to go. He stumbled out into the mews, the stench of manure and household garbage thick in the damp air. He made it to the coach house before he retched. The force of it doubled him over and lifted him to his toes. The smell of sick burned his nostrils, as his fingers dug into the loose mortar between the bricks. Surrounded by filth, and yet he was the most disgusting thing out here.

His skin crawled with the taint of Mab and the knowledge that he'd let her do those things to him. That his body had enjoyed it in some profane way. With the female responsible for destroying his family. A sob, deep and filled with rage, tore from his chest. The thick ivy that clung to the top of the mews began to crackle and grow, spreading toward his hand. Sin did not bother to rein in his power but leaned against the wall and tried to breathe through his anger.

Above him, the sky was the pasty white of spoilt milk, the light of the sun hidden behind endless layers of clouds.

It hurt to look at that pale, unending sky. And he closed his eyes, trying to breathe past the heaviness invading his chest. Ivy leaves tickled his cheeks and climbed over his shoulders. Perhaps they'd entomb him. Perhaps he could dig a hole in the loamy earth and lose himself in its cool embrace.

"Death is not the only solution, you realize."

Sin froze. That someone would come upon him in this moment and see enough to understand what he was contemplating. Self-loathing and impotent rage made his skin fire hot. He forced himself to open his eyes.

A man stood not far off, his expression placid but his dark eyes keen. Though he wore the fine wool suit of a proper English gentleman, with his bowler hat resting just so on top of his coal-black hair, everything about the man screamed foreigner. And then recognition set in.

"You were with Layla at the theatre." The words were out of Sin's mouth before he could think to keep them in, and he flushed in annoyance. "Miss Starling, I mean." Not much better, that. He'd made it painfully clear that he'd been watching Layla.

But the man smiled kindly, a knowing look lighting his eyes. Smug bastard. "Yes. With Miss Starling. I was hoping you'd join us, but you did not." One shoulder lifted. "Perhaps next time."

Sin pushed away from the wall and glared at the man. "Who are you?"

"My name, for all intents and purposes here, is Augustus. Your sister, Poppy, knows me as Father."

Fear ran through Sin's tired body. Father was the enigmatic head of the SOS. As far as Sin knew, only Poppy had any real contact with the man. "What the devil are you doing with Miss Starling?" Sin would not believe for a moment that the man was actually courting her. Not from what he knew of Father—an ageless man who was gone more than he was around.

"Protecting her."

The length of Sin's body tightened with swift pain. "You'll pardon me if I find that answer less than comforting."

Augustus's black brows rose as one. "Have you reason to believe that the founding father of the SOS would fail at this task?"

"No," Sin said with reluctance. "It's the fact that she needs protecting that worries me." If Layla needed watching, he ought to be the one to do it. The memory of her bright smile hit him hard enough to hurt his heart. They'd been fast friends. Being near her had been his daily joy, his air, until she moved away.

Augustus watched as a hawk might. "You cannot protect her as you are now."

Sin's fists clenched. "How—"

Communication of thoughts are not limited to mere words, lad.

"Get the bloody hell out of my head," Sin snapped, a fine sweat coating his skin.

Augustus bowed his head. "My apologies, Master Evernight." He did not look at all contrite. "However I do believe it important that you fully understand with whom you are dealing when you speak to me."

"Oh, and why is that?" Sin would take great pleasure in making sure this prat knew how capable Sin was in dealing with others.

A thin smile curled the man's lips. "Because I am going to make you an offer you'll want to refuse." Before Sin's eyes, Augustus's olive skin leached of color, more and more until the man before Sin appeared to be made entirely of translucent flesh.

The living crystal Augustus grinned at Sin's stupefied expression. "I'd show you my wings as well, but I fear you aren't yet ready for that display."

"I...uh...you..." Sin's brilliant contribution to the conversation.

"Young St. John, you'll hear my offer." Silver eyes bore into him. "And if you have an ounce of sense left in your head, you shall take it. For I am about to give you everything you deserve."

A twist of fear went through his heart, because he was not so certain what he "deserved" was anything good.

Chapter Twenty

Sin did not quite know what to expect of Augustus's home, but it was not this. He glanced around at the sedate yet finely appointed study in which he sat alone, a glass of brandy in one hand, the crackling warmth of a fire heating his trouser leg. It felt almost normal, as if he'd been plucked out of a nightmare and set down into another dream. It left him unsettled. His hand shook only a little as he took a deep, burning drink of his brandy.

Augustus strolled into the room in graceful ease. "Apologies for making you wait, Mr. Evernight. Cook was in a state over tonight's dinner and Layla is off somewhere, unable to provide her assistance."

Sin shoved up from his slouch, his mouth suddenly dry. "She lives here?" God. He did not want to see her. He couldn't bear it.

As if Augustus knew Sin's discomfort perfectly well—which the bastard likely did—the corners of his eyes crinkled, as he took the seat opposite Sin. "Yes. She is my ward at the moment." He looked down at his hands, the backs of them hatch-marked with fine scars that shone white in the firelight. "However, I shall soon be leaving, and she shall need a new protector."

The arm of the chair creaked beneath Sin's grip. "If you dare suggest that I—"

"Come now, young St. John. You know perfectly well that I am suggesting it." Augustus's gaze was hard and direct. "Do not deceive yourself in thinking that you do not want the position."

A flush heated Sin's cheeks. "Doesn't matter what I want, only what is right. Even if I were in the position to watch over..." He swallowed past his dry throat. "I'm bound." To the bitch. The fine taste of brandy turned acid on his tongue.

A log upon the grate snapped, sending sparks up the flue. And Augustus sat back in his leather chair. "Yes. You are." Black eyes bore into Sin as Augustus's mellow voice flowed into him. "And what would you do to be free? Anything?"

Sin snorted without humor. "Enter another form of bondage, you mean?" He shook his head. "You can go to bloody hell if you think I'll do so again."

"Hell is a state of mind. And you're already there, are you not?"

Sin lurched out of his seat, his heart pounding. The fire in the hearth flared high. "Fuck you, Mr. Augustus."

The man bloody laughed. A soft, rolling laugh. A fucking mockery. And then his expression fell to deadly serious. "Sit. Down."

When Sin did not move, Augustus waved his hand in a lazy fashion. Sin became a puppet on strings, his limbs no longer his own. Down he flopped into the chair, and there he stayed, not able to use his powers or move from his seat.

"Now," said Augustus. "Give your rage a rest for a moment." He leaned forward, bracing his forearms on his bent knees. "The fact is that Mab has never been weaker than at this moment."

Sin didn't know what to make of that knowledge. He was blood bound to serve her. It wasn't as though he could destroy her. No matter how much he yearned to.

Smiling a bit, Augustus continued. "She used up much of her power to hold Aodh's in check. Yes, I know all about Aodh," he added. "And for the first time in centuries, several kin of her direct bloodline live."

"Eliza."

"Not merely Eliza, but you, Holly, the Ellis sisters."

"We are of Mab's blood?" Sweet gods, Sin would be ill.

"The Evernight's and the Ellis sisters are elementals, born ages ago of Mab's blood. Now, Eliza is the most direct of Mab's heirs, which is why Mab is desperate to control her. Because Mab is weakest against those of her blood." Augustus paused and stared at Sin. "You, however, have the distinction of being of her blood and able to control all the elements. What is more? You were born of Isley, a powerful demigod akin to the angels." He smiled, this time with a strange sort of anticipation. "An Egyptian-based god at that."

"Why," Sin ground out, "does that matter?"

"Tell me," Augustus asked, "did Archer ever mention how he'd been cursed?"

Sin swallowed, his gaze darting over Augustus's face. Archer had drunk an elixir, and it had cursed him to a strange living death, locked into immortality while slowing turning into a being of... "Ice," Sin croaked out. "He described himself as looking as though his flesh had been carved from ice."

Augustus's smile was slow and broad. Again, before Sin's eyes, he shifted, his flesh becoming crystalline and pure. It was beautiful and unearthly. "Not ice, but altered. He was not cursed but becoming Judgment."

"Judgment?"

"Yes. A select group of warriors who possess the ability to judge a soul and send it to the afterlife. Archer did not know what he was. Thus he feared it and never learned the ability to control it." Augustus's lashes swept down, and he frowned. "The fault was mine. My acolyte Victoria was damaged, mentally, and she'd stolen my secrets, giving her the knowledge to create others without proper care. I did not know until it was too late. Nor did I know about Archer's change until he was already free of it."

"Have you told Archer?"

Augustus's shake of the head was almost undetectable. "No."

"Why the devil not?"

With a sigh, Augustus sat back. "He is no longer Judgment. Therefore, he cannot know unless he was to take up that task once more." A look of melancholy filled his eyes. "Why would he want to when he has Miranda now? When his life is settled." He gave a bracing sigh. "But enough of that. It is you of whom we speak tonight."

"You want me to become Judgment." Sin laughed. "I'm hardly fitting for the task. Nor do I have the ability to alter my flesh to..." He waved a hand in Augustus's direction. "Do that."

"But you could. Become Judgment, St. John."

This time, when Sin wanted to surge to his feet, he was free to do so. He paced away from the fireplace and then turned back toward Augustus. "And Mab? She owns me. As surely as if I were a piece of furniture." He slammed his fist against a sideboard for emphasis, and the knick-knacks upon it rattled.

Augustus did not blink. "You are blood bonded. Take the elixir and your blood will be irrevocably changed. The debt will dissolve."

"Convenient that."

"It is." Augustus smiled. "I know things that that bitch cannot begin to fathom."

"Then kill her yourself."

"Alas, I cannot. We all have our crosses to bear. Mine is that I can no longer act as Judgment but merely guide those who choose to serve."

"To do your dirty work." Sin ran a hand through his hair and picked up pacing again. "Even if I were to do this, there is no guarantee that I could destroy Mab. Holly managed to destroy her human body but Mab merely popped up again a few months later." Sin could only be thankful that Mab had decided to stay far away from Holly. He supposed she was still smarting over Holly slicing her to ribbons with iron bars.

"Dear boy, there are few more powerful things on this Earth than Judgment. And one with the power of all the elements?" Augustus gave a small shake of his head. "She hasn't a chance. Even better? She'll never see you coming because she believes she is in utter control over you."

The very idea was a whisper of seduction along Sin's skin. To be free.

"Think, St. John," Augustus said quietly. "A chance to live a life of pride, to do good, to be with Layla."

Sin's gaze snapped to the man sitting in the chair. "Yes, what of Layla? Why do you guard her?"

"You do not get to know that until you are Judgment."

Sin ground his teeth. The bastard was blackmailing

him. And Sin would fall for it, because if there was one true thing he held on to, it was the thought that Layla Starling, his childhood friend, lived safe and happy in this world.

With a sigh, Augustus stood. Slowly he walked to him. "Let me give you this." Before Sin could speak, Augustus whipped his own palm across his mouth, tearing the flesh open with the tip of a fang that had suddenly descended in his mouth. Sin didn't have time to flinch as Augustus cupped his cheek, smearing hot crimson blood over Sin's skin. "By my blood," he said, looking into Sin's eyes, "I swear what I say is truth."

Sin felt himself sag, his will crumpling. Perhaps he'd regret this even more than his other mistakes. Perhaps he was consigning himself to more misery. Sin closed his eyes tight and let fate have its go. "Tell me what I must do."

Chapter Twenty-One

Eliza stood in the little living room of the cottage that Adam had secured. It was a warm, tidy room with a separate sleeping room and a good-sized bed. For two. She'd resolutely *not* looked at that bed when they inspected the place. But she was glad to have a haven to stop and rest for a while. Her stomach tightened; they also needed to eat.

But Adam had yet to move from his chair by the hearth. Firelight painted the strong lines of his face in warm gold. But his hair was so raven black that it absorbed the light. A lock of it fell over his brow, dancing just over the bold curve of his nose. Eliza fixated on that sight, waiting for him to brush the tendril away. Yet he never moved. Her fingers began to itch to do the job for him. Perhaps stroke his hair and see the deep lines along the corners of his eyes ease a bit.

Repressing a sigh, she moved toward him, noting the way his shoulders tensed and his wide, mobile mouth thinned. Oh yes, he might have been looking off into the fire, but he'd been aware of her the entire time.

Drawing a footstool with her, she sat and waited, knowing he'd be unable to ignore her for long. He never could.

Soon enough, his gaze sought hers out. And she flinched inwardly. Here was not the arrogant ass who'd chained her, nor the proud yet pained man who'd been chained himself. Not even the sly charmer who'd wrangled a kiss from her this morning. This man was pensive, lost.

Without thinking, she touched his forearm, where the muscles clenched like iron beneath the homespun linen. "What troubles you?"

Adam's gaze slid away. "They recognized me. When we let the room."

"Of course they did."

The GIM had watched him with awe. The innkeeper had insisted that Adam take not a mere room, but led them out to a small but charming cottage a bit of a ways from the inn. *"For privacy and true comfort, my lord."* Eliza suspected that it was the innkeeper's home and thought Adam realized this as well. But the innkeeper would not take no for an answer.

Eliza had noticed Adam's agitation then, but had thought it had been directed at her.

"You are their sire," she went on. "How could they not know you?"

He made a dry sound. "They expected me to have power. To help them." His wide chest lifted on a sigh. "I don't know who I am anymore. For thirty years of my human life, I served God with blood and blade, convinced that I was not a murderer but a champion of Christian right and virtue." He blinked, the thick tips of his black lashes gleaming in the flickering light. "A mere blink of time when considering my life as Adam." A soft snort left him. "I thought, here is a chance to make up for all the lives that I'd cut down. To make life anew. It was such an elegant solution, saving souls while searching for yours." He glanced at her, then away. "But part of me feared, would I be punished for my actions?

"And though I've seen Hell, angels, even played cards with the being you call Lucifer, I've never, not once in all those endless centuries, seen God."

He turned and pinned her with his deep-set eyes. Weariness lined his handsome face, and something close to sadness. "No one has. Not even the angels." The corner of his mouth quirked. "What is one to make of that? Here I am, a man who has all but played God himself, deciding who may live forever and who will stay dead, acts of utter blasphemy, and where is God? Why hasn't He come to smite me for my sins?"

Eliza felt wooden inside, incapable of movement, unable to feel anything other than a strange heaviness. "I don't know."

He bent his head and the lock of dark hair tangled in the long length of his lashes as he blinked. But he didn't attempt to brush it away. Instead he slowly shook his head. "I am nothing now. Not Templar, not Adam. I've no purpose."

Eliza wasn't aware of moving, not until her fingertips brushed over the back of his hand. He did not resist but let his fist uncurl as she twined her fingers with his. "My grandda used to say a person hasn't truly lived life to the fullest if they haven't had cause to reinvent themselves once or twice." Gently she squeezed his warm hand. "I figure, you've just arrived at another crossroads, and it's time to make yourself over once more."

Adam was silent and still for a long moment. When he finally faced her, she wondered if she'd ever become accustomed to the impact of him. He saw too much, made her feel too much. Always. Her stomach clenched, a hot, pleasurable, yet achy sensation that had her breath catching.

But for once, he didn't appear to notice. Instead he studied her, frowning a bit, as though concerned. "And what of you, dove? What do you want of life?"

That was easy. "What I've always wanted. To live it. As a man might. Unfettered and free to roam as I see fit. I think I should like to see the Great Pyramid of Giza, if we're being particular."

His lazy, tilted smile returned as his free hand raised to cup her cheek. His skin was rough and warm, and she felt it down to her toes. "And who's to stop you now? Miss Eliza May of Boston, the most stubborn, willful creature I've ever met."

Her mouth quavered, torn as she was between a laugh and a scowl. "You say that like it's a compliment."

His voice lowered as he drew her closer. "Because it is."

Ignoring the quiver inside of her belly, Eliza squeezed his hand. "Come. Let us go to dinner." She rose, giving him a little tug to prompt him to stand. "Some hot food and a bit of wine, and you'll be square as a quilt in no time at all."

A smile played about his full lips. "I do not believe I'm familiar with that saying."

"That's because I just made it up." Eliza walked to the door, Adam still holding her hand as though she were his lifeline.

Once in the dining hall, however, he did not brighten. They ate their meal in relative silence, the good-natured laughter and conversation of their fellow patrons surrounding their corner table but never quite touching it.

Adam's expression remained pensive, his attention on his meal. Thus it was a surprise when he at last spoke.

"I used to watch that sort of thing, you know." With a jerk of his chin, he gestured over to where a young couple nuzzled each other, uncaring of any attention they might receive.

"You watched people..." She trailed off, horrified. But he merely shrugged and took another bite of his beef.

"I was bored. And it wasn't as though it affected me. Not in any lustful sort of way." He sipped his wine.

"It's perverse," she insisted.

Adam lowered his silver and sat back in his chair with a negligent air. "It was a glimpse of life that I'd been denied. And yes, it was wrong." He looked off, his long lashes casting shadows on his cheeks. Such a harsh profile, yet his lush mouth and pretty eyes softened him. "Eventually, I stopped. What point was there to watch what I could not have?" A frown marred his countenance and then was gone with his next breath. He turned back to her. "I've seen intercourse performed in so many ways and scenarios, I've lost count. Love, the birth and death of it, played out over and over again."

The wooden chair that held his large frame creaked as he leaned forward, bracing his forearms upon the battered table. "Would you care to know what affected me the greatest?"

Would she? Eliza was afraid she did, and she found herself nodding, even as her breath quickened.

"It was in the year 1373. A crofter and his family lived in a one-room cottage. I don't know why I was drawn to their little house, perhaps it was my being in the cold dark and seeing the firelight flickering from their small window. Whatever the case, there they were, four children and their parents, all bundled together in the family bed, limbs intertwined, bodies higgledy-piggledy. They held on to each other in sleep with such perfect trust."

Eliza thought of him, huddled in a dark corner of those long departed crofters, watching them with the same longing that graced his hard face now. Did he know it then? How much he longed for love? She rather thought he knew all too well. It made her heart ache to think of his loneliness. Would she have survived nearly a millennium of such isolation? Of never having felt loved or cared for?

His voice turned soft, reflective. "It struck me that I'd never known that sort of connection to another. Just the simple act of loving for love's sake." Golden eyes framed by black lashes stared at her. "I became a knight to protect the promise of that type of love. Yet all I saw was death. *Cù-Sìth*, the hound of death. That is what they called me."

"Is that how you see yourself?" she asked, quiet in the shared space between them. Not waiting for his answer, she shook her head, and it felt unbearably heavy. "You are so very wrong. So blind."

His thick brows drew tight, that bold, stubborn nose of his lifting in defiance. "On the contrary. I see myself far too well."

The lively strains of a reel lit over the room. Eliza glanced toward the group of fiddlers who had begun to play and then back at him. Bracing her hands upon the table, she rose. "You are life. You create it from death. And it is lovely."

His mouth fell open, a nearly comical expression on one so stern. She fought a smile as she extended her hand towards him. "Come, dance with me."

The look of shock he wore grew. And then he blinked as if shaking himself out of a dream. "I don't dance." It was a croak from the depths of his chest.

"Pity." Eliza shrugged. "As I love to dance."

His darkly beautiful face twisted in a scowl. "Are you mocking me?"

Dear, confused man. "Far from it." Eliza sighed. "You are life, Adam. I suspect that's why you chose the name you did, even if you weren't aware of doing so. You are life," she said again with greater emphasis. "You simply don't know how to live."

Adam sat watching as Eliza May made her way to the crude dance floor in the space cleared before the fiddlers. Immediately she was welcomed into the fold.

His life was lovely? Was she bloody bamming him? Adam had expected platitudes. A bit of "but there is nobility in death" or "you did what you felt you must." He'd have hated it, but at least he'd been prepared to react accordingly.

He rubbed at the tight knot forming beneath his breastbone and watched Eliza May dance. Light on her feet, her lithe form moved as if made to follow music. Cheeks pink and eyes like dark velvet, she smiled at a bloke who'd taken her in his arms. Together they twirled, her frothy skirts swirling about her slim ankles, the man's hand snug on her neat waist.

A growl rattled about in Adam's throat. He swallowed it down. He'd no right to interfere. He hadn't lied. He didn't dance. Because he didn't know how, not any dance that had been invented in the past few hundred years, at least. And he'd be buggered if he'd bumble about, trying to learn here.

She laughed. The lovely sound brought his head up sharply. A waltz played now, melodic and haunting in the fiddler's hand. The big GIM hadn't let her go. His hair was nearly the same shade as Eliza's and, as they moved about, gliding and twirling, they seemed to glow, their heads glinting like gold in the low light. Perfectly matched.

Adam's fingers dug into the arms of his chair. She ought to live in the light, as she was now. And he would not go to her, nor hold her. Eliza's gaze never strayed to him as she danced her waltz. As if she'd forgotten him entirely. Wood cracked beneath his hands. Bugger, would this set never end?

The fiddler playing was an expert, his music haunting and pure, his instrument battered and well loved.

Despite his death grip on the chair, Adam could almost feel the smooth, cool surface of the violin and the bite of the strings against his fingertips. A distant memory. One he did not want to revel in. He'd felt too much already this day.

The GIM moved closer to Eliza, his hand sliding a bit lower. Adam was out of the chair in the next beat. With each step, the floor rose up to meet him. With each breath, a matching protest shouted in his head, *Stop, stop, stop.* He couldn't. They belonged to one another, and he'd be damned if he let another man touch her.

Like gazelles in the plains, the dancers sensed him coming. Heads turned, conversations stuttered. Eliza's wide, brown eyes stared up at him. Waiting? Wondering? He ignored her. One touch would undo him now.

The fiddler halted, his last note screeching unfortunately loud in the tavern. What did they think of their sire? Did they fear his wrath? Or merely wonder why he'd come to beg for scraps of attention from the woman who'd bewitched him? He was Adam, King of the GIM. He was supposed to be dignified, inspiring awe and respect from his subjects. A king did not humble himself.

Though his heart pounded and sweat bloomed over his skin, he used his charm, giving a wry grin and a small nod as he prepared to do the one thing no one on this earth had seen him do. He gestured toward the fiddle. "May I have a go?"

Awkward silence grew and swelled before the man shook himself out of his gaping stare. The man handed over his fiddle. "But of course, sire."

Ah, but Eliza May's expression was rapt now. He gave her a small smile, one that challenged and taunted. He'd been giving her those for months, wanting her to see that his soul and hers were one, and yet now she did not resist. No, she grinned in return, accepting his challenge and acknowledging the taunt.

Anticipation plucked at his innards. Holding her gaze, he tested the strings. Perfect tune. Adjusting his grip, he raised the bow. It held there, and it seemed the room held its breath with it. And then the bow tore across the strings, whipcord fast and violent. From the first note, he poured his soul into the music. No slow dances for Miss May. No peace. No escape.

He did not remember the first time a violin had been placed into his hands. Only that, be it due to a supernatural dexterity or an innate talent, he'd known how to make it sing for him, from Beethoven to Bach. Secret trips to Gypsy camps had taught him other music. The devil's music, his fellow knights would have called it. But they were long dead by the time he'd learned to play.

Nor would he give up his music. It had been his one true joy. Adam would take on the appearance of another man and play. Play on a corner of Hyde Park, in the crowded bowels of a steamer ship, on the rooftops, wherever he wanted. He relished the anonymity of it, that he could be in the moment without judgment or speculation. But now. Now Eliza danced for him.

Her hands were at her hips, her heels pounding out the

rhythm, matching him, pushing him harder. His fingers worked over the strings, his bow white lightning. Blood pumped through him, the music flowing. It was power, lust, the thrill of the chase. His breath quickened. He held her gaze and worked the bow, sweat trickling down his back, his cock hard and his heart racing.

The notes came out sharp, quick, urgent. Only she existed in his eyes. He needed to stop. He pushed it further, his body thrumming with the music, with her movement. He wouldn't last. Her flushed cheeks, parted lips, breasts bouncing. Faster. Harder. He panted, his vision blurring. Need surged. His arm jerked with the urge to throw the fiddle aside and grab her. The music pitched. Stretched too thin. Worked too hard. He would snap. A string snapped instead.

The awkward note died in the air, and both he and Eliza halted. Her breath came out in rapid bursts, her cheeks glowing from the exertion of the dance. They stared at each other and, for the life of him, he could see no one else but her. And then she moved, making him flinch, making him want to launch himself at her. She beat him to it, her slight body slamming into his, her slim arms wrapping about his neck as she laughed. His hand lifted, hovering at the small of her back, wanting to hold her but not daring to for fear he'd never let go.

"Oh, but that was marvelous," she said as his blood raced like fire through his veins. Then she pulled him in closer and her warm breath touched his ear, uttering words that had his throat constricting and his vision blurring. "This is life, Adam. Let the past go to the devil. Let yourself live now."

And so he would.

Chapter Twenty-Two

～～✦～～

Sweaty and pleasantly warm from the dance, Eliza made her way back from the ladies' lounge. She'd washed her face and smoothed her hair. The lively sounds of music and dancing still filled the air, and she felt content. For the first time in years, she was happy. The realization stole over her quick as a fox, making her smile.

She'd taken no more than a few steps when a hot hand clamped down on her wrist and tugged. Eliza collided with a solid chest, the scent of spice and clean sweat surrounding her. "Adam." She laughed up into his face as he wrapped her up in his arms and walked them backwards. "You scared the daylights out of me."

His smile was sharklike, but when she thought he might answer, he cupped the back of her head and his mouth captured hers. Eliza's breath hitched. And he took advantage, opening her lips with his, licking with his hot tongue.

"Adam," she murmured against him, even as she canted her head and sought more. More of his taste. More of his yielding lips.

"Seven…" He kissed her—"Hundred…" His teeth nipped—"Years, love." Another deep kiss had her knees buckling. He grinned against her mouth, even as he tightened his hold to keep her from falling. Golden, glinting eyes met hers as he pulled back. "Do not expect me to refrain from touching or tasting you every chance I have."

Her head spun, it felt as though she were falling, yet he was holding her up, holding her against him. They'd stumbled into a private dining room. Her back met with the wall, his mouth hot on hers with messy, frantic kisses, as though he'd been starved and given a buffet. His large palm, so warm and rough with calluses, held her cheek, his thumb sinking into the corner of her mouth as though he wanted to touch their kiss, experience it with every sense.

Breathing hard, her breasts crushed against his, Eliza let him do as he willed. His enthusiasm was heady, erotic. She became languid in the face of it, hot and boneless and wanting more.

Adam's lips trailed across her jaw and down to the sensitive skin of her neck. He breathed her in, his tongue flicking out to taste her. "Have you any idea," he murmured, "what it's like to touch you?"

Her lashes fluttered, and she gripped his broad shoulders to keep standing. "Tell me."

The rough scrape of his evening beard had her shivering as he nuzzled the crook of her neck, and still his thumb ran along her bottom lip. Always touching her. Feeling her. "It is almost pain, this pleasure." He nibbled her ear lobe. "Only I want to push into it, let it skewer me to the core."

Closing her eyes, she ran her fingers through his silky hair, the heat of his body warming her palms. A pressing

kiss on the tip of her breast had her gasping. He surrounded her with his need.

"And when you touch me," he said, leaning in closer
until his long body rested against hers, "I ache so very
sweetly, Eliza."

On a breath, she opened her eyes. He was staring down
at her, his gaze hot with need. Yet his hold on her cheek
remained soft, tender. Eliza licked her lips, and he dipped
down to taste them again. A smile danced over his mouth.
He was playing. Enjoying her. She'd never had a playful
lover.

"You truly haven't felt anything all these years?"

"Truly," he murmured, preoccupied with stroking her
neck, his expression absorbed. "Like silk, your skin is.
Only better. I could touch you endlessly."

"And when I touch you here?" Eliza could not resist;
she laid her hand against the hard flatness of his abdomen,
and Adam's breath left in a whoosh.

He closed his eyes, his forehead resting against hers.
"God, pet me, sweet dove."

Gently she rubbed his stomach, the action making her
sex clench and her thighs draw tight. He leaned against
her, his elbow braced upon the wall, and he trembled, his
breath agitated. The pained yearning in his expression,
his eyes closed tight, was a beautiful thing to behold. It
made her bold, and her hand slid lower.

He grunted, his hard cock surging within her grip.
Eliza kept a hold on him while her free hand gathered
up the loose folds of his shirt and began to tug it free.
Deftly, she unbuttoned the front of his trousers. "I find,"
she whispered against the corner of his mouth, "myself
wanting to touch you in other ways."

The poor man actually whimpered when she discovered his bare skin. And she smiled, stroking the heated length of him. My, but he was...Eliza's eyes closed for a brief moment, lust threatening to overwhelm her. When she dared look down, her mouth went dry. Dark and thick and long. The bulbous head wept with impatient need. Eliza swiped her thumb over the little bead, slicking it into his skin, and Adam groaned. Running her fingers along his shaft, she stopped at the tip and squeezed, loving the noises he made in the back of his throat.

He pressed his mouth against her temple, his breath a hot, erratic pant. "More."

Just that word. And Eliza wanted to give it to him. She wanted to give him the pleasure he'd been denied for far too long. "Lean against the wall." Her voice was quick and light, as she eased him around. Weakly, his big body shaking, he did as bidden. But his eyes grew wide, his lips parting as she smiled at him and slowly sunk to her knees before him.

He was dreaming. He had to be. Because she'd been in his dream like this—kneeling before him, her slim fingers around his cock, her eyes bright and intent upon his—so many times before. If it were a dream, God help any person who dared wake him.

But then she lightly ran her nails along his length, the sensation so vivid and unexpectedly luscious that he knew it was no dream. She wanted him. Wanted to do *this* for him. He could hardly account for it. A lump rose in his throat, even as his heart raced and his breath grew short. Eliza. She was everything he'd feared wishing for.

Her pink tongue flicked over the tip of his cock, and he felt it down to the soles of his feet. His hands clenched, and it was all he could do not to push his aching cock into her mouth. Patience. Patience.

As if she bloody well knew how badly she affected him, she grinned. Canty, wee temptress. Gently, she kissed him along his length, and he shook with the feeling. Slowly, he was becoming alive. Dead and untouched for so long, and now this. He wanted to weep. He wanted to laugh.

And then she took him into her mouth.

"Holy God." Adam arched back and panted, his body trembling and so taut he feared he might snap. Unable to think, he stared up at the dust rafters of the ceiling. God, her mouth. Hot, wet, tight, her tongue slick silk. Heated pleasure raced down his spine and clenched in his abdomen. His knees were weak. She sucked him hard, drawing it out, until her sly tongue flicked over his sensitized head. Something much like a whimper escaped him, and he clutched at the smooth walls without purchase.

He wanted to thrust himself deep into her throat. To fuck and snarl and lose his mind. And he wanted to stay like this for an eternity, with her slowly and wickedly sucking his cock. She drew him back in, then out. In. Out. Adam's hand somehow found her hair, his fingers snaring the heavy mass and holding on tight.

"More. God... more. *Please*."

And, Lord love her, she made a happy little hum that he felt *everywhere* and smoothed her hands up his thighs. He shivered, swallowed hard. Her slim hand, so very delicate and nimble, cupped his cods. And gave them a gentle squeeze. Adam groaned, heat swamping him. So hot, he'd soon burn up like a fucking torch. He'd been missing *this*? No more. He didn't care if he had to beg for it every day of his life, he'd gladly do so. The sight of her, on her knees, eyes closed, her delicate brows knitted in a little frown of concentration, while her pink lips stretched wide around him...

"Fuck." He was going to come. Hard. Hundreds of years of being denied that singular pleasure, and yet instinct could not be misunderstood.

His shoulder blades pressed into the wall, his grip tightening in her hair as his hips canted, the urge to thrust overcoming any need to draw out this pleasure. "Tell me, lass," he said, panting, thrusting in and out of her mouth. "Tell me this feels good to you."

Her answer was to cup his arse, slipping her hand beneath his trousers and finding his bare skin. She dug her fingers into the muscle there and held him tight, urging him in deeper. Adam nearly lost his wits.

"You like it," he rasped. "Me fucking your mouth." The thought drove him to madness. His cock throbbed to near pain now, and still the need to thrust and plunder. To take everything she had to give. "Will you drink me down, love? Take it all?"

Eliza's eyes opened, and her gaze clashed with his. And his breath caught, sharp and swift. She bloody loved it. High color stained her cheeks. Holding his gaze, she let her free hand move from his cods; he missed the heat, the solid comfort.

A strangled sound tore from his throat as her dainty finger stole beneath his stones and stroked him *there*. Everything turned white. Blinding heat and pleasure. He lost himself, not feeling his body, not knowing where he was. Just pleasure and the sweet pain of release.

He came back to himself by degrees. The sight of the wall before him. The mad beating of his heart. The slick feel of his soft cock slipping out of her mouth. He groaned, his body sliding a little down the wall. But she was rising, pressing her warm and lush body against his, holding him up with her arms about his waist. He hauled her closer, his arm about her slim shoulders as he bent and pressed his lips to her fragrant neck, moist now with perspiration and heat.

"By my vow," he said against her skin. "I'll be returning the favor, Eliza May. And when I get you into my bed, I'll not be letting you out of it again."

Chapter Twenty-Three

The taste of Adam was on Eliza's tongue, as he led her back to the taproom, and she flushed a little when she thought of how she'd taken him in her mouth. She'd loved it. Loved seeing him come undone. It had been beautiful, empowering. Carnal. A pleasurable shiver lit through her at the memory of his expression, tight with ecstasy. She had done that to him. And she wanted more.

At her side, Adam walked along, his hair mussed, his color high, and his shirt clearly tucked in with haste. A man debauched. And content, if his rather badly hidden grin meant anything. He caught her gaze, and his eyes blazed with certain promise to return the favor.

It made her unaccountably shy. Where did they stand? Would they be lovers? Eliza wanted him. She could not deny it. But was it enough? Was he truly her soul mate? And was all this seduction and charm his way of getting her to believe in it? She hated that she had doubts, but trust was an ill-fitting glove that she fought to slip on.

Adam's reappearance in the room garnered attention, as

it always did. Instantly, the innkeeper came out from behind the bar and made his way to them. "Sire," he said, bowing a bit, "would you take a dram with us?" Behind him, a group of men sat around the table with expectant looks.

Eliza smothered a smile, for the tension that shot through Adam's back and the slight twitch at the corner of his eye spoke of utter frustration. Poor man. But he shook it off with a small breath and a nod. "But of course."

With a wry glance at Eliza, he made as if to move, taking her with him. She resisted. "I'll be sitting over there," she said, pointing to the small corner table they'd supped at. When he frowned, she leaned in close, far too aware of the scent of his satisfaction lingering on his skin. "They want to talk to their king. Let them have this."

Adam sighed. "And I want to tup their queen," he groused, then shook his head, his lips quirking. "At least someone shall have their wish." He ambled off, leaving her standing there, open-mouthed and heart pounding. Queen. She nearly laughed at the idea. The GIM needed a leader, a fearless and noble woman to be their queen. Not her.

Frowning, she made her way to her table, and a pretty barmaid came to check on her. "What shall I be getting you then, miss?"

"Ale," Eliza said. "A pint of it."

The barmaid went to fill her order.

"Playing with a man such as that can work up a powerful thirst, can it not?"

Eliza turned to glare at the woman who'd spoken, and found herself face to face with a fae. Eliza sat up straight, her knee banging into the table leg. And the fae leaned in. "Easy now," she hissed, her purple eyes flashing in warning. "No need to kick up a dander."

"I beg to differ," Eliza said. But the sudden knife pressed against her ribs had her refraining from doing more. She glared at the young woman holding it. "What do you want?"

Ivory cheeks plumped. "Mellan sends his regards."

"They aren't returned."

"To be sure," the woman murmured, looking not altogether unsympathetic. "He's expecting you to fulfill your promise to him."

With a deliberate hand, Eliza grasped the blade threatening her side and wrenched it from the fae's hand. The knife was meant for stabbing, not slicing, and thus did not cut her hand. Foolish fae girl, using a dull blade against her. "You listen to me," Eliza said in a low voice. "I am not killing Adam. I am his bride." She leaned closer. "I chose him."

Around the room the air stirred, and from the corner of her eye, Eliza saw the ghostly shapes of spirits. So many of them, crowding the area, all of them watching her. And yet none of the GIM seemed to notice. Nor the fae who sat, tight-lipped and scowling.

"Go," Eliza told her.

"I am but a messenger," the woman said. "The next one who comes will be here for your head."

"Do you know," Eliza said, "I find that threat no longer scares me?"

When Adam finished his drink with the GIM—a novel experience, listening to their concerns and attempting to assuage them that he was trying to regain his powers, and thus their safety—he'd found Eliza nursing an ale and looking pale.

"Are you well, dove?"

Eliza flinched as though she hadn't heard him approach. Her brown eyes were round, almost too large in her face, as she blinked up at him. "Yes," she said slowly. "I am well. I…it is hot in the inn."

"Shall we retire then?" *Jesu*, simply asking the question sent blood surging to his cock and made his breath quicken.

Still not fully roused, Eliza gave an absent nod of agreement and rose. He wasted no time in leading Eliza toward the cheery little cottage a ways off from the inn. His hand rested upon the small of her back, a simple gesture, and yet she quickened her step as though she might outpace his touch.

And it felt as if he'd been slapped. Was his touch so very distasteful? She hadn't been so reserved when she'd lapped at his cock like a cat seeking cream. It had been the single most erotic moment of his long, long life. The mere memory made him hard and his step awkward.

"Eliza," he said, pressing his hand once more against her slim back, "you are practically running from me." She shot him a look over her shoulder, her golden brows furrowed. And he snorted without humor. "Do not scowl. You are, and I'd like to know why." He cleared his throat. "Do you regret it? What we did?" He was not certain what he'd do if she did, but thought it would include punching a wall somewhere close by.

Eliza slowed to a stop, which made him stop too or run over her entirely. Inches separated them. Her scent flooded his senses, and he struggled not to close the gap, to fit his mouth to hers once more, and *take* this time. The warm light of the inn's window shone down upon her, picking up the copper filaments in her bright hair and highlighting the sweet curve of her mouth. That mouth.

He repressed a sigh of longing and focused on his irritation. "Well?" he asked, his tone short.

The little furrow worked deeper between her brows. "It lies between us, our bad beginning."

"What does that have to do with your flinching from my touch?"

"It taints every experience we have." Her lashes lowered a fraction, and her attention drifted to his mouth. Adam's heart began to pound, but she flicked her gaze upwards once more, and her chin lifted. "Adam, I would not have touched you if I hadn't wanted to. As you should well know."

He stepped close to her, his hand wrapping around the base of her throat, because he needed to touch her. The contact settled him, yet his heartbeat kept a hard rhythm. "Then tell me what has upset you."

Her fingers clutched his biceps, their tips digging in, and a surge of protectiveness swamped him. Adam rested his forehead against hers, the difference in their heights making him duck his head low. "Truth, Eliza. Surely we can have that between us."

"A fae came into the taproom."

He lurched, ready to turn and hunt down the fae, but she held him fast. "She is gone, but she had a message for me. She said they would be coming for my head next."

Chapter Twenty-Four

Fear for Eliza held Adam by the cods, hard enough to kill his ardor, or at very least, take the edge off of it. When they returned to the innkeeper's cottage, Adam locked them in tight and then went about securing all the windows. He could only be thankful that the old cottage shutters were decorated with iron laths. Not much iron, but enough to deter most fae.

Task done, he walked Eliza to the tiny bedroom.

"I'll take the couch and keep guard out here," he said somewhat grimly, for the baser part of him still wanted to sink into her warmth and stay there. An eternity just might relieve his need.

Eliza gave him a long look but then sighed. "Very well." She glanced at the door. "Will you be all right?"

"I've my sword and my strength back." Adam ran a knuckle over her silken cheek. "All will be well, dove." He'd keep her safe or die trying.

She left him then, and he stood for a long time in the middle of the cold cottage, listening to the sounds of the night and cursing Mellan to hell and back. To deny sleep was foolish; a tired warrior made for a sloppy fighter. So Adam lay upon the couch, sword by his side, just as he'd done centuries ago. Sleep was a long time coming, but eventually it took him.

He became aware of himself the very moment Eliza slipped into the room. His eyes snapped open in time to see her walk past, her white nightgown billowing behind her like a ghostly sail, her steps steady and sure. She never looked his way.

Huddled into the too-small couch, his body creaked with protest as he slowly rose to follow. He barely paused as he grabbed hold of his sword and back scabbard, strapping them on as he went. Cold floorboards chilled his feet as he moved across the cottage. She was far enough ahead not to notice him creeping up behind her. Out the door she went, never hesitating, looking neither left or right, and into the crisp night air.

Fog rose up from the ground, a soupy swirl, thick and pale green. Fae's fog. The herald of evil. The hairs at the back of Adam's neck lifted, his muscles tensing for battle. Eliza's golden curls bounced, her gown swaying as she walked, keeping that eerie, unwavering pace.

Sleepwalking. She had to be, for she barely blinked, not noticing him in the least. Not that he wanted her to see him. Instinct told him not yet. The fog parted for her as she moved toward the pasture just beyond the barn. It was then he saw them: spirits. His heart began to pound. He'd not seen spirits since Mab had taken him. So many now, hovering and weaving in and out of shape. Shining, translucent shells of those they'd once been in life. And they waited for Eliza.

Fear grabbed hold of Adam, and he strode forward,

pulling his sword from its scabbard with a decisive ring of steel. It did not matter that steel couldn't touch them. Adam simply needed to feel his weapon in his hand. He'd figure the rest out as he went along. But one thing was certain. They would not take her. Even if he had to become a spirit to fight them.

"Eliza." His deep call rang out through the night. She did not falter but moved ever closer to the waiting ring of ghosts. Desperation gave his voice a sharp bite, turned his stride into a jog. "Eliza, stop!"

She paid him no head. Moonlight shone down, illuminating her in brilliant silver-white, and her slim arms rose as if to beckon the waiting dead. They surged forward, swarming her, even as Adam shouted his outrage. Unaffected, she raised her head to the night, tears leaving shining trails down her cheeks, and a laugh bubbling up from her throat. A mad, disjointed cackle.

Adam skidded to a halt, gooseflesh pricking his skin. Eliza laughed with glee, the sound drawing in more spirits. More and more, writhing bodies of the dead, touching her hair, her arms, their diaphanous faces holding looks of rapture.

"*Iosa Criosd.*" Though he had not done since he'd been fully human, he crossed himself. And she did not push the spirits away, but opened her arms to embrace them all. A terrible fear that they would claim her as one of their own swamped him. One that increased when her eyes turned mirrorlike. Possessed.

"Eliza," Adam shouted, lunging forward, though he knew he was too far away. "No!"

Adam's palms grew damp, his grip on his sword's hilt slipping, his heart pounding against his ribs. Transfixed as he was, he didn't see the movement to his right until the fae was almost on top of him, scythe already swinging to slice off Adam's head.

Adam blocked with the flat of his sword, the impact vibrating through his bones. The fae was enormous, stronger than hell. And fast. The fae's strikes were a blur of movement. Sweat bled into Adam's eyes as he parried and riposted.

This was no ordinary fae but a trained assassin. And his weapon no ordinary scythe, or Adam's sword would have sliced through it like parchment. Trepidation took hold of Adam's gut. He was no match against such things, and so he put all his strength into his next swipe, angling the sword for the killing blow.

Wrong angle and too hard a strike. For when their weapons clashed again, they both snapped in half, sending sparks shooting into the sky. The fae's scythe fell from its handle just as the long blade of Adam's sword clattered to the ground.

Adam felt the loss like a stab to the heart. But he wasted no time and, flipping the weapon in his hand, he smashed the blunt end of the hilt into the fae's nose.

Cartilage crunched, blood poured. The fae bared his back fangs and pulled another sword from behind his back. Another fae weapon, and one headed for Adam's gut.

In the near-distance, Eliza's horrible laugh turned into a scream, straight from hell.

The fae glanced back, his face leaching of color. The ungodly sound coming from Eliza had frozen them both in shock.

Adam recovered first and, putting all his strength behind the action, thrust the broken end of his sword into the fae's chest.

At the same moment, Eliza turned, her arms outstretched,

her mouth agape—that never-ending scream ringing out in the night. Spirits swarmed around her in a maelstrom. Eliza's odd, reflective gaze landed on the fae, and as if commanded, the spirits moved as one, flying over the field, coming straight at Adam and the fae warrior.

Terror punched into Adam's heart, even as a blast of breathtaking power knocked him back on his arse. He landed with teeth-rattling force.

As for the fae, he burst into a cloud of grey ash, the remnants of Adam's sword clattering to the ground. As if waiting until the fae was truly destroyed, Eliza gave one last, rasping cry and then dropped in a heap of white gown and tangled limbs.

Strong arms held her tight, warding off the chill in the air. Eliza's cheek was pressed against the fragrant heat of male skin. Adam's neck. She knew his scent, the exotic spice of it, tinged with something like crisp apples and smoky autumn leaves. She burrowed closer, inhaling and feeling safe.

"Eliza?" His whisper held a hint of worry, and fear.

Only then did she open her eyes. She lay cradled in his lap, as wisps of fog dissipated around them. "Why," she rasped, "are we sitting in a field?"

Deep grooves bracketed Adam's mouth. But he answered lightly enough. "Oh, I thought we might take in the night air."

With a huff, she sat up, but quickly grabbed hold of the front of his shirt when her head swam with dizziness. Instantly, he pulled her back down into the crook of his arm where she could hear his heart beating steady and strong. "Easy, lass."

His big hand covered the back of her head. Gently, he

ran his fingers through her hair. "You were walking in your sleep," he murmured.

Eliza tensed. And his touched grew firmer, reassuring.

"What did I do?" she forced herself to ask. And hated the way he stiffened, his breath drawing in as if he were struggling to find an easy answer. Eliza closed her eyes, her fingers curling into his linen shirt. "Did someone die?"

Against her ear, she could hear his heartbeat quicken and his breath stutter. "Why is it that your first assumption was a death?"

Because he looked at her as though he held a monster in his arms. A dull yet pervasive hurt spread through her chest.

"I..." She could tell him. He'd understand. He'd been the keeper of souls for centuries. Eliza found herself sinking further into Adam's warmth. Shockingly, he let her do it, his body curling around hers as though he would block all hurts if he could.

"Tell me, *mo gradh*," he said. "Tell me what has happened to you."

Eliza's breath seized, her heart clenching beneath her ribs. Adam's proper English slipped now and then, and it was clear he thought she was ignorant of Gaelic. But her grandfather, Aiden Evernight, had taught her the language. And all that she could think on now was that Adam had called her *my love*. Not the light and teasing "love" the English liked to toss around. But in a reverential tone.

"Eliza?" He touched her cheek with the callused tips of his fingers.

"I kill."

Adam's brows drew together as he looked off, and she

had the mad urge to trace the sharp line of his jaw, to trail her fingers along the growth of stubble there that heightened the softness of his mouth.

"You do not appear surprised. I killed again, didn't I?"

"Aye." He said it slowly, a drawn-out breath as though he were tired. And Eliza's insides went ice cold. Who had she killed?

She'd always been in control when it happened. She had never killed and not remembered. Curling up closer to Adam, she clung to his shirt. "That is what Mellan used me for. To kill, to instill fear in the hearts of men."

Against her, Adam went stiff and uttered a foul curse. Oddly, Eliza found herself stroking the hard swell of his chest. "I've always been able to . . . I don't even know what it is that I do . . . Only that this black, foul anger comes over me, and I can pull the life out of a man."

"Pull out his soul," Adam murmured. "You're pulling his soul."

"Yes." Eliza ran a finger along the seam of his collar, the action soothing her. "I suppose that's it."

"And you did this for Mellan?"

A sigh left her, and her throat burned. "I was so foolish, Adam. So full of fear and hate. I was alone in the world, and he took me in, made me feel safe and comfortable. He told me that I'd only be killing evil men, those who harmed women and children." She laughed. "Such a horrible cliché. And I believed him, lived to do whatever it was he wanted, until I finally realized that it did not matter who I killed. I was wrong for doing it."

Adam's long fingers sifted through her hair, his touch so gentle that she barely felt it. "In all my years of life," he said, "I have come to discover that, more often than not, we believe what we want to believe. The con-

venient lie, an easy truth, whatever we must to survive."
His hand stilled, cupping the back of her head, and easing her against his shoulder. "Is it wrong? Perhaps. But you broke from those bonds of fear, did you not? You left Mellan."

"And yet," she rasped, "I did it again. At the Rag Fair. A man cornered me, and instead of trying to get away, I killed him."

He let out a breath. "I knew something had happened."

Eliza shuddered. "I reveled in it. And at the same time, I felt soul sick."

He did not say anything to that, but merely brushed a kiss against the crown of her head. And, shockingly, it made her feel, not better, but it opened a small warm corner of her heart.

Adam sat back a little so that his gaze met hers. There was no judgment in his golden eyes, only puzzlement, and a bit of caution. "How is it that you did not kill those men who..." He swallowed hard and a dark rage filled his expression before he spoke again. "The men who violated you that night? The men who killed you."

Eliza's heart gave a small start. "They did not violate me, Adam."

His scowl said he believed otherwise. "Your skirts were up and—" His jaw bunched.

"They tried," Eliza clarified, pressing her palm to his chest where his heart pounded hard. "I had my hand around one of their necks, he was dying, and the others gutted me to save him." She let her hand slid down to rest in her lap. She could not touch him then. "This power I have only works when I touch another. And only on humans."

She grimaced, even as he tensed. "I tried to kill Mellan, you see. And it never worked."

"Hmm…" Adam's breath was warm against her hair. "I think you're changing, Eliza. Your powers. Perhaps this is why he is desperate to control you."

"There is more." Her voice was a ghost in the night.

He made a sound of amusement. "There always is, love."

Eliza cleared her throat. "Death calls to me."

He stilled, his grip tightening in her hair. "As though the dead need you."

"Yes. Exactly." Eliza tipped her head back and met his dark gaze. "Only I cannot hear what they say. And I see the light of souls within a person's body."

At that, he twitched.

"Mab says it is because you made me like you," she said.

He visibly flinched but did not answer.

"Did you?" she pressed. "Am I a GIM without a clock-work heart?"

A lock of his inky hair fell over his brow as he woodenly shook his head. "No. I made you…" A grimace twisted his mouth. "Less than."

Eliza sat up, her mouth agape. Still he would not face her. With a cold hand, she turned him toward her. Defiance was there in his gaze, and regret.

"Less than," she repeated, shaking. She ought not to care. Why, then did she feel let down?

"Aye," he said with clear reluctance. "I gave your body life anew, but you cannot roam in spirit. Nor are you immortal." He winced once again. "You can die, Eliza."

Eliza rose from his lap, her legs stiff, her chest aching. He let her go, tracking her movements but not standing. He simply sat upon the dirt, regal as a king, and waited for her ire. Well, he would have it.

"You made me vulnerable to death so you could hold the promise of life over me, didn't you?"

A bare nod. "That I did."

The metallic taste of blood filled her mouth before she realized she'd bitten her lip. A rough laugh tore from her. "Oh, well played, sir. And you accuse the fae of being manipulative. Forgive me if I choke on the hypocrisy."

Adam sighed, but he did not try to defend himself. Which made it worse. She wanted his fight. Wanted to hate him. Because she felt too much for him now. The thought of needing him terrified her.

Her feet slapped over the cold, hard earth as she paced away from him before whirling back. "I'd call you a rotten bastard, but what difference would it make?"

"Would you rather I had made you GIM?" he asked with quiet earnestness.

"I'd rather you had not used me as a pawn. I've had enough of that in my life."

Still as a lion, he blinked at her. "I told you, Eliza, you were the answer to all my hopes and dreams, to my freedom. I would have done anything to safeguard it. That I went about it the wrong way cannot change the past."

"And now?" she snapped. "Is all this"—she waved a hand between them—"kindness and care merely another bid to secure my affection?" God, he'd been succeeding. Far too well.

His body was moving grace as his long limbs unfolded and he stood tall before her. The breadth of his shoulders blotted out the moon, leaving him limned in silvery light. "Truth, Eliza?"

She nodded, and he took a step closer. Beneath thick, straight brows his gaze burned. "In truth, I want you so badly, the mere thought of you is a hand around my cock."

A strangled sound left her, but he wasn't finished. "I want to sink into your quim and call it home. To learn the taste and texture of your skin, and then do it all over again. Is it because you are my soul mate? I do not know. I bloody well don't care. All I know is that I want this ache"—his fist hit the wall of his chest with a thud—"this need to abate. Will bedding you quench my thirst? I cannot tell you, but I'll gladly put that question to the test."

The way he looked at her, so fierce and angry yet pleading, it licked over her skin like fire. He was too far away. And too close. She wanted to ease his tension, to rub her hands over those broad shoulders and down his bunched biceps. And she wanted to escape. He'd manipulated her, left her vulnerable to his will, all for his own selfish gain.

She took one step, and her foot sank into a pile of something soft and loamy. Eliza gave a start and glanced down. The substance was dark grey and scattered as her foot disrupted it.

"What..."

Adam blanched, his hand reaching out to draw her away from the mess. "Ashes. Fae."

Eliza shuddered. God, and it was all over her feet. She rubbed her soles over the grass, her skin creeping. "There was a fae here?"

"A male." Adam's voice was as tight as his grip on her elbow.

She closed her eyes for a moment. A blur of images went through her mind. Love. She'd been surrounded by love and adoration. Cool brushes of air. It had been the spirits. They'd done her bidding. In her mind's eye, she saw Adam in danger, his face frozen in horror as he stared at her. Eliza's eyes snapped open. "I killed him." *For you.*

His chest lifted on a deep breath. And when he faced her, wariness and dread darkened his golden eyes. "You may not have been able to kill the supernatural before, dove." His expressive lips pinched. "But tonight, you commanded the dead to kill for you."

Chapter Twenty-Five

~~~~~~~~

If someone had once told Eliza that hell would be found in a quaint and cozy country cottage, she would have laughed. Now it was all she could do not to cry. The cream plaster walls pressed in on her, while the rough-hewn timbers supporting the ceiling seemed to sag as if they'd break at any moment. Flights of fancy. As was the feeling of her bed being made not of fine feathers but hard rocks. Yet she could not find peace from her restless, hateful mood.

She'd killed a supernatural being tonight. If she closed her eyes, she could replay the events. The power, the mad laughter that wracked her body. It had felt so very . . . *good.* As if she'd waited the whole of her life to embrace the full extent of her power and use it.

Stranger still, in the midst of that tempest, at the very moment she'd turned and met the fae's eyes, she'd thought of one thing: to protect. The fae had been poised to kill Adam. Did her defense of Adam make it right? She could hardly think it so. Nor did that excuse her from all that she'd done before. Was she evil? How could she deny it in the face of all the evidence?

Stifling a groan, Eliza pressed the cool tips of her fingers against her eyelids until red spots danced before her in the dark. She wanted Adam here. She wanted him to hold her, despite the anger she felt in learning yet another of his machinations against her. But that was in the past, and she'd promised him a new start.

Aodh MacNiall, now Adam of the GIM, had stolen her peace and shattered her illusions. He rested in the room beyond, a mere closed door away. No longer could she deny it; she felt better when she was with him, settled and right, in the same manner she'd experienced when using her power. Away from him, an uncomfortable tugging started within her breast and lower belly, as though he chained her still and was constantly pulling her back to him.

With a curse, she whipped back the covers and left her bed. Cold air chilled her overheated skin, and her feet slapped against the icy floor. *Do not think. Act. Simply act.*

So great was her intent to get to him that, when she opened the door, she nearly barreled right into him. She stopped short, her nightgown swaying about her legs. He'd halted as well, his hand still up as though preparing to knock. For a long moment, they simply stared at each other, and then he slowly lowered his hand.

"What is it?" Eliza whispered, searching his face. Her fingers twitched with the urge to stroke the corded muscles that ran along the thick column of his neck, now exposed by the loose edge of his collar.

"You know," he said in a soft, yet rough voice, "I cannot recall the excuse I'd made up to come to you."

Everything inside her stuttered to a halt, her breath, the blood in her veins. She stared at him, her mouth surely hanging open, and his lush lips quirked with self-deprecation. "Aye, I know you're cross with me just now, and I've no true reason to bother you, Eliza May, save the fact that I cannot stay away." His gaze grew slumberous, lowering to her lips, even as the strong lines of his shoulders grew tense. "I need to be near you, if only to know that you are well, or I become a man unmoored."

Slowly, as if he feared she'd bolt, he raised his hand. Eliza's lids fluttered, her body swaying towards him when the warm, callused tips of his fingers traced the curve of her cheek. His deep voice came to her as from a distance. "Whether you believe in soul mates or not, I think of you as my other half. The better half. And I am not whole unless I am with you."

Shaking deep within herself, Eliza drew in a sharp breath. He saw the movement, and his hand dropped. With a wince, Adam straightened. "Ah, well. It's clear you are well enough. I'll no' bother you a moment more." He moved to step back.

Unacceptable. Eliza caught his fingers with hers. He was so warm, solid, even with the tenuous grasp she had on him. And he stilled, his expression one of granite as he watched her. Oh, but those golden eyes of his shown with fragile hope and dark curiosity.

She couldn't speak, her mouth dry as crust as she held on to him and backed into her room. He waited until their arms were outstretched before taking that first step with her. His eyes never left her as he quietly followed her. And Eliza's heart beat a strong, nearly painful tattoo against her breast. Its fearful rhythm quickened as she drew to a halt by the bed tucked against the wall.

Adam's slow, deep breaths mingled with her lighter ones as they gazed at each other. He did not move, but remained alert and watchful. Waiting, it seemed, for her to tell him what she wanted.

"Stay with me." Her plea came out so thick and low that it was a wonder he heard it.

But he did. He gave a sharp nod.

She couldn't look at him as she crawled back into the bed, now cool and far too small. She had lain with others, men that, despite working for Mellan, had been kind to her. Those acts had been impersonal, born from a basic need to feel something other than numb fear. But Eliza had never felt true desire, the desperate need to simply touch a man or the utter craving to feel a man moving inside of her. Until this man.

In truth, she could barely believe that she wanted Adam. She'd resented him for so long, been afraid of him, of her intense reaction to the very person who'd disregarded her feelings. But it was different now. Everything was different.

The covers rustled as he slipped in, the mattress dipping. But he did not lie down. Instead, he peered at her, his gaze roving over her body before meeting her eyes. This man, the way he looked at her, looked into her, it undid her every time.

Eliza leaned back against the pillows, her nipples tight beneath her flannel gown. And when he reached out, her breath caught. The tip of his finger brushed against the crystal clock lying in the hollow of her throat, and an almost melancholic expression graced his face.

"Will you tell me now," Eliza asked, "what this is?"

"The key to all the GIM." He stroked the face of the clock. "It rests inside here."

Her heart thudded in her chest. "And you let me wear it?" She should not. It was too great a responsibility.

But Adam merely looked at her with serious eyes. "Who else ought to but the other half of my soul?"

For a moment, the world blurred, and then Eliza blinked. "Adam." It was a breath of sound.

Their gazes clashed, and she saw everything in his eyes, his vulnerability, his belief in her, and his need. He needed her, and Eliza could not deny him. She needed him too.

"Could I?" Adam hesitated, a flush creeping up his cheeks. His gentleness, mixed with the overwhelming maleness of his graceful body, made her heart squeeze.

"Could you what?" she whispered.

With the awkwardness of one unaccustomed to such actions, he lowered his head and rested it on the pillow of her breasts. A sigh left him as his body melted against hers, his arms wrapping around her waist as if he'd never let go.

The ache in her heart became tender pain, and she closed her eyes to manage it, even as she softly placed her hand upon his head and cradled him close.

When he spoke, his voice was low and dark. "Is this my night?"

"I-I suppose it is." Simply saying the words left her flushed. Yet he did not move. Tentatively, she stroked him. "Is this how you want to spend it?"

A broken chuckle left him, his body moving against hers. "Ah, lass, I want so much. So very much when it comes to you." Then he stilled. "Truth, Eliza?"

"Always." Her voice cracked.

She thought he might not answer, silent and tense as he was, but then he took a small breath. "I looked down at you, lying here upon the bed so very lovely, your hair unbound as a wife's might be, your eyes on me, so soft and beguiling. It felt as though you were mine ... No," he amended, "it felt as though I was *yours*."

Inexplicably, she wanted to sob. She blinked at the ceiling, her eyes burning, and her hand stroked through his silky hair.

"So many souls belong to me." The wide warmth of his palm slid, slow, almost seeking, down her waist. He paused, just below the curve of her hip, and his grip held. "And yet I've always remained alone."

Eliza's heart pounded against her ribs. She wanted to speak, to assure him that he was not alone. But her voice was caught at the base of her throat. So many people thought to own her, yet no one had ever wanted to be possessed by her.

His lips found the pounding pulse on her neck, and he pressed them there, not a kiss but enough to hold her attention.

"Let me believe it," he whispered against her skin. "That for one night you've claimed me." His movements were careful as he lifted his head and looked at her with his unearthly eyes. Behind his thick, black lashes, they seemed to glow gold, as he spoke with a soft breath of sound. "Let me believe that I am yours."

"Adam." The shell she'd placed around her heart was breaking, and it hurt, even as warmth flooded that cold space. With shaking hands, she cupped his lean cheeks, his evening beard rough against her skin. He watched her, still and silent, and she pulled him closer, closing her eyes only when her lips met his.

Kissing had never been like this, when the mere feel of a man's mouth made her melt, made her body clench with a raw, almost angry need for more, instantly *more*.

As if he felt it too, Adam breathed into her, as he softly groaned and canted his head, opening her mouth with his, and slipping his tongue in deep. A taste. A tease. Her fingers twined into his hair, her body arching as she licked him back, reveling in the way it made him shake.

Adam exhaled roughly and drew back to look down at her. With the tips of his fingers, he traced along her skin, not quite touching her but raising the flesh there and leaving a trail of heat as he moved. But it wasn't enough. He caught her look and a wry smile tilted his lips. "I can't decide."

Eliza licked her dry lips. "Decide what?"

"Where to touch you first." His gaze went dark as melting molasses. "I want it all at once."

"And I just want *you*." The demand was out of her mouth without thought. He had to know this. Of course he did, and yet her words had an immediate effect upon him.

His nostrils flared, and when he spoke, his voice was guttural. "You have me. Always."

"Then let me have you now." Gods, she was burning for him.

He grinned wide, his expression lightening like the dawn. "My impatient dove."

"My wicked tease," she shot back, loving that she'd made him smile.

He eased back farther, resting his head upon his hand, his long body stretched out beside her. With a lazy hand, he plucked at the sleeve of her gown. "Take this off."

The arrogant demand in his tone and the way he looked at her, expectant, almost greedy in his impatience, ought to have annoyed her, and yet heat shot over her skin, and her nipples tightened painfully. Adam saw her reaction, and a dark growl rumbled in his chest, his gaze rapt upon her aching breasts. "Let me see you."

With shaking hands, Eliza reached up. Slowly, she pulled on the tie that bound her nightgown. She watched his face, taking in the tightness there, the way his lips parted. The bow of her gown slipped free, and the fine linen slithered over her breasts.

Adam's gaze blazed hot, but he made no move to touch her. "All of it, Eliza."

Such a blunt command. She flushed hotter, her movements clumsy as she worked to push the gown down over her hips. And all the while, he watched, silent, his dark brows drawn together in concentration.

Silence nearly overwhelmed her as she lay against the cool sheets, her hot skin exposed for his inspection. And yet she'd never felt so wanted. Adam drew in an unsteady breath. And then he moved, the bed creaking under him as he eased forward, his mouth coming for her breast. But he did not kiss her. Eliza's heart nearly stopped as he leaned down and nuzzled the tip of her nipple, his evening stubble rasping over her.

"So bloody beautiful," he whispered. And then his mouth caught her, the flat of his tongue swirling around her breast as if to savor her flavor, and he groaned as if in pain. "So bloody good."

He had to know how much he affected her, for his eyes gleamed hot as his hand eased lower, a light, hot pressure, over her hip. His slipped between her legs to cup her with firm possession. The blunt edge of his thumb ran along her center, seeking the sensitive tip of her sex. And a gurgled sound escaped her as he slowly, almost absently, played with her, until she grew wet and swelled against his touch.

"Luscious Eliza," he murmured, his deep voice rumbling. "Slick as a summer peach." Firm strokes moved along her sex. "Will you taste as sweet? Fill my mouth with your juices?"

Dizzy heat invaded, and her lids fluttered. She couldn't breathe through the need to have him fill her. "Adam. Please."

"Anything, Eliza." His fingers moved in a circle, faster, harder. "Anything."

The orgasm rushed through her, and Eliza stiffened in his arms, her body shaking. Adam watched it all with rapt attention. "Eliza…"

Panting, Eliza grasped the back of his neck and pulled his lips to hers, her hands at his shirt. Kissing her, Adam helped her draw it off. Flush now with health and vigor, he radiated strength, the muscles along his torso tight and defined. His was a warrior's body, faint scars crisscrossing his flesh. She knew every inch of him, and yet this was different. This time she could explore, run her palms down his lean waist, glory in the satiny tightness of his skin.

He shivered as she touched him, his breath exhaling in a rush. Eliza's hands drifted to his trousers. "Let me see all of you too."

Wry humor entered his eyes, as he started to unbutton his trousers. "You've seen all of me, dove. Many times."

Eliza ran a finger across the tight bead of his nipple. "I know," she said in a thick voice, "but not when I knew you were mine."

Adam's gaze flew to hers, and his broad chest hitched. "Ah, lass, then you haven't been paying attention. I've been yours since the moment we met. Every bloody inch of me."

There was no more finesse. He hauled her close, his kiss deep and frantic. Starving for her. Their fingers tangled as she reached down to help him push his trousers past his hips. Breathing hard, Adam kicked them the rest of the way off. And then there was only him, kneeling before her, so very strong, his cock jutting out before him, pulsing and dark with need.

Eliza remembered the taste of him, and wanted another. She leaned down, caught the smooth crown in her mouth and gave it a soft suck. Adam reared as if shot. "Holy God," he rasped, his hand cupping her head as he gave a few quick thrusts. And then he groaned, pulling back, his voice rough as newly hewn stone. "Not this time, dove."

He pushed her back into the pillows, his mouth finding hers. His kiss was hot, his mouth open and wanting. His scent, his touch made her want with a passion that took her reason. "Come into me, then," she whispered against his lips.

Hot skin slid against her own, his body like moving granite. "If I take you now, I'll not be letting you go, Eliza."

A smile curled over her lips as she nipped his earlobe, loving how he shuddered and the way he cupped her breasts, tweaking her nipples with impunity. She arched into the touch. "Maybe you won't enjoy me."

It was Adam's turn to grin, though his attention was elsewhere, his tongue tracing down her neck. "Eliza love, I plan to enjoy the hell out of you."

She shivered at that and parted her thighs to let him in.

He rose over her, his broad shoulders blocking out the light, his warm arms bracketing her. "You asked me earlier what this was between us," he whispered, his lips skimming her cheek.

"Yes."

He canted his head, kissing her soft and slow. "This, Eliza"—he traced her cheek with fingers that shook—"this is everything."

Chapter Twenty-Six

He was going to fuck her. Fuck her first, and when he could think straight, when his cock wasn't about to go off at any moment, he'd make love to her, slowly, gently, for as long as she'd let him.

But for now, Adam trembled like a lad, his entire body undone with want. The tip of his cock slid over her sex, and his gut clenched. Beneath him, Eliza lay flushed, her eyes bright and her pink lips parted. So bloody beautiful it made his heart hurt. Countless times he'd witness this done by others, yet now that he had his woman under him, Adam was filled with a sudden panic. He felt awkward, needy, and wanted to please her. But when her fingers curled around his cock, guiding him back to her, he lost sight of everything save the feel of Eliza.

A low, pained groan ripped out of him as he pushed into her. Heat, warmth, the tight silkiness of her all around him. Heaven. Fully seated, he leaned his forehead against hers and tried to breathe past the mad urge to plough into her with abandon. "Are you well, dove?"

Gently, she caressed him. "Very well, demon."

That was all he needed. Another shiver lit through him as he drew back out of her snug, slippery clasp. With a grunt, he thrust, and pleasure reverberated through his body like a thunderclap. His muscles clenched tight. Sweat beaded on his hot skin.

She held him close, her strong legs wrapped around his waist, one of her heels digging into his arse, prompting him on. He gazed down at her. And she surged up, capturing his mouth, sucking on his tongue as though it was a sweet. Adam lost his restraint. He pumped into her, again, again, each time, the need to do it harder, faster, making him quake.

"Eliza..." His voice held a desperate edge. "Dove... I..." He did not know what he wanted to say, only that he needed her. Needed to please her, needed to fill her with his cock and for it to never stop. But he could not hold on. His cods were drawing up tight, a bolt of white-hot pleasure racing down his spine.

Understanding gleamed in her eyes. "Let go, love. There's time for me yet."

"I don't want it to end."

"The end simply means we can begin again." Smiling, she leaned up, her hand cupping his sweat-slicked nape, and she licked his neck, just as her sex squeezed around his cock. Adam shouted his pleasure, and promptly lost his mind. Pumping into her as though his life might end, he came with such force that his sight went dark.

He paused over her, his body a plank of quivering muscle, before his strength left him, and he fell against her, wrapping her up in his arms, his cock still snug within her. Where he belonged.

* * *

"Spread your legs wider, sweet dove." Adam's deep voice rumbled in her ear like the purr of a lion. And Eliza obeyed, her body no longer under her command, but beholden to his will. And his hard body moved over her, surrounding her with heat and the scent of him.

"I'm tired," she protested in the dark. A lie. And he knew it, for his chuckle was slow and satisfied, his cock stiff and seeking.

"I'll go slow." He eased inside of her, inch by thick inch. And she groaned, her sex tender and swollen, her flesh so sensitive the pleasure was near pain. Adam murmured words of praise as he worked himself in, his hands roaming her body in gentle caresses. "That's it, lass, take me."

Her lids fluttered closed, and he brushed his lips over them. So tender. His breath warmed her skin. "Tell me again, Eliza."

In the dark, she smiled weakly, heat blooming anew. He'd been making the same demand all night. All night as he took her, made her scream her release, and then took her again. And she'd been answering all night.

"No," she said now, still smiling. She'd tease him this time, and he would reward her.

His next thrust pushed her up the bed, and her sex clenched around him. Adam groaned. "Tell me," he murmured, his mouth skimming along her neck. He moved slowly now, so very slowly but with a deliberation that made her feel each stroke, each time he almost left her, only to surge back in.

Boneless and hot, she stretched her arms overhead, as his mouth traced the contours of her breast. "Tell me, Eliza," he said around her nipple. "Say it."

He drew the tender nipple into his mouth and suckled. Eliza whimpered, her hands clenching his shoulder, and she gave him what he wanted. "You are mine."

He kissed her then, open and deep, his breath heavy as he pumped into her with hard, sure strokes. And she lit up like a brand, her body flaring with such heat that she cried out into his mouth. As if he'd been waiting for that moment, Adam bucked against her, all moving muscles and utter strength. They came together, lost and found. And he pulled her close, his damp limbs tangling with hers, his lips resting against the curve of her neck.

Eliza drifted off with his voice whispering in her ear. "And you are mine."

Lust was an ache that had not abated. Not even in the new hours of the morning when the sky had begun to lighten to grey. She could not stop touching him, smoothing her palms down his strong back, along the rippling length of his arms. Nor he her. With languid movements, Adam nuzzled his way along her body, as if he needed to discover her anew.

She kissed his neck, where his skin was sensitive and his scent the strongest. "Was it what you expected?"

She had been his first. His only. Pride and possession filled her. Was this how men felt when they bedded virgins? As though they'd claimed something rare and precious and never wanted to let it go?

Adam released her nipple with a wet pop, and lightly resting his chin upon her belly, he gazed up at her. In the dim of the room, his eyes seemed to glow with a satisfied light. "It was more." His lids lowered, his attention drifting once more to her breasts. "I want more."

Her sex clenched. But he caught her eye, and his

expression grew hesitant. "And you," he asked quietly. "Was it...Did you..." His teeth bit into his bottom lip.

Eliza pushed an inky lock of hair back from his brow. "It was glorious, Adam." And it had been. The power of his body, the force of his need, had taken her breath away. Witnessing him come apart, the almost painful expression upon his gorgeous face, was something she'd never forget.

Still watching her, he made a noncommittal noise. His warm palm caressed her thigh, as if he too could not stop touching, exploring. "And yet," he said, pressing kisses across her belly, "I do believe, I need to return a favor."

The linens rustled as he sank lower, nipping along her skin. A small cry escaped her as he eased between her thighs and his clever mouth found her sex. His voice was a vibration against her sensitized flesh. "Here, for example"—his tongue licked out, making her pant—"has been sorely used. Shall I kiss it and make it better now, sweet dove?"

He did not wait for her answer but proceeded to pay full homage to her with lips, tongue, and, at times, teeth. And Eliza loved every moment of it.

Chapter Twenty-Seven

The air in Mab's room was too thick, too close. Mab longed for fresh fields, green grass, flowers. She longed for the old days when idiot villagers placed sick babes in the woods because they believed in her, believed in the fae—when they thought she would give them a new child. Such fear and devotion. Such power.

And now? Sweat trickled down her spine. Disgusting, agitated sweat. How could this be? Mab strode over the thick silk carpeting, the sound muffled, until all she heard was her own breath and the hard beat of her heart. Plots. Plots abounded. Against her. She knew Mellan wanted her dead. He always had. And now her sweet and biddable Eliza had left her. Taking *her* Aodh.

With a scream of rage, she swung her arm across her marble mantle and sent crystal candlesticks and china maids crashing to the floor. Shards flew, slashing her bare feet. Mab snarled, picking her way over the mess.

Her wounds healed with a slight tingle, when hundreds of years ago, she'd not have been cut at all. Her power was fading. And plots. "So many," she mumbled. The room was too hot. She could not breathe.

Mab glanced at the large French windows. She could open those, let the cool predawn air in. Only Augustus was out there. Plotting as well. She could feel it. His long-ago words haunted her still. *"When you think you've finally won Aodh, you will lose him. And that will be the beginning of the end for you."*

"No!" Her shout rang out in the empty room. No. She would not fall victim to fear. Mab, of all creatures, understood the power behind fear, how it attached itself with wee hooks to the mind, the soul, tearing away at one's strength until all that was left was weakness and doubt. She would not let Augustus win. The bastard had wanted to be rid of her for a millennium. But he could not do the deed. None of them could.

The only one capable of that feat was under her complete control. Just as she'd planned. A smile of satisfaction warmed her insides. The pleasure of seeing the hate in young St. John's eyes while she took him was fast becoming the high point of her day. Without Aodh to play with, she had little else.

Blood pooled in her mouth, and she realized her fangs had sunk into her lip. Licking it away, Mab reached for the gold silk bell pull. From far off, she could hear the little chime, and her smile grew. It stayed in place as she arranged herself on the divan and waited—hell be to the boy if he did not hurry.

But that concern was assuaged when, a moment later, the door opened and young St. John entered. Oh, but he was a beautiful lad. Mother Nature had kissed him with tender lips when she created him, for his was a face of sculpted features: high cheeks, strong jaw, straight but masculine nose, and lips that were nearly feminine in shape, yet firm. Mab loved to bite those firm lips, to watch him wince.

Eyes of green frost swept over the mess upon the floor and then settled on her. She sucked in a delighted breath; his hate was that palpable. St. John had never tried to hide it from her; he merely could not act on it, which made their meetings all the more delicious.

"You rang?" His voice was deeper now, with a low pitch to it that one felt in the pit of one's stomach.

Idly, Mab stroked the neckline of her dressing gown. "Strip and come to me, boy."

He was hardly that any more, tall and broad of shoulder. But he did so hate it when she called him *boy*. He held her gaze as his hands went to his collar. A shiver of excitement rent through her. Yes. This is what she needed. Then she'd take care of Mellan. Yes, him next. He wanted Eliza, did he? Well, he would not have her. Mab would rather see Eliza dead.

Before her, St. John had finished unbuttoning his shirt. It slid from his body, revealing toned flesh and rippling muscle. Such a lovely display. "Mmm…" she purred. "Come here and let me stroke that glorious skin."

He'd ducked his head to take off his shirt, and when he met her eyes again, it was from beneath a lock of his raven hair, tipped with fiery red. He walked forward, his gaze still upon her. The way he moved, like a sleek cat, held her in thrall.

"The trousers," she rasped, as he drew near. "Off with them."

He did not even flinch. With the flick of a wrist, the buttons came free and his trousers hissed down the long length of his powerful legs. He was growing hard. A surprise that. Usually, she had to coax and coax. Pleased, her gaze snapped back to his face, and another smile spread over her lips. Anticipation seemed to vibrate about his form, quickening his breath and parting his lips.

Mab's own lips parted, his eagerness was unexpected but most welcome. He was almost upon her, and the fine hairs at her nape lifted. Gods, his power hummed within the room. The thought barely formed when suddenly his entire form shone blinding white, making her squint. She hadn't time to move before he stood once more, his golden flesh now crystal clear and brilliant. With a flap, a massive set of silvery, batlike wings unfurled behind him, and a sound of shock finally escaped Mab.

Judgment. He'd become Judgment. How?

Terror arced through her, and she tried to move, to lash out, but his arms were already rising, a grin wide on his face. It was the smile Death gave just before he took. A scream of denial tore from her even as the white-hot lightning shot from his hands, slicing through her flesh and wrapping itself around her soul.

And his voice boomed, the power of the gods living within it. "You have been judged, Mab of the Fae. And found wanting." Crystalline eyes gleamed. "Hell waits for you."

Dawn rose, bleeding pink fingers over a pale yellow sky. Adam found himself leaving the warmth of Eliza and their bed. Foreboding and a strange, almost aching anticipation gripped him.

Searching the horizon, his hand clenched the windowpane in the parlor. Nothing moved, not even a slight breeze stirred the leaves upon the trees. And the feeling of unease grew within him. He needed Eliza. Needed to know she was within touching distance. He turned away from the window and headed for the bedroom. He had to reach her. Now. He crossed the room in two strides, but it was not fast enough for the fear that had him by the throat.

"Eliza!" Desperation tainted his tone, making it sharp and brittle.

A cold sweat broke over his skin as he wrenched the door open. He felt as though he were racing a storm, try-ing to get just ahead of it before it broke. She was not in the bed. "Eliza!"

She stepped out from behind the doors of the dressing cabinet, her lovely face drawn in concern, and he nearly sobbed his relief.

"What is it?" she asked, coming for him just as he strode towards her. He needed to touch her. Hold her.

Their outstretched fingertips brushed together, and then the thunder stuck. It boomed with such force that the room shook, and Eliza screamed. The shockwave hit Adam dead center, sending him to his knees. His breath left him. Dimly he heard Eliza calling his name. A red haze clouded his vision, a buzzing filled his ears.

Power, complete and white-hot, rushed over him, curl-ing him in on himself. He could not breathe, not move. Eliza cried for him.

Eliza.

Another wave of power struck; this one cool as lake water. With a great gasp, he drew a breath, his back arch-ing and his sight returning. For a moment, he hunched upon the bedroom floor, his heart threatening to pound out of his chest, and Eliza kneeling beside him, her soft hands touching his cheeks. Then he blinked, and it was as if the world had been repainted with the saturated colors of a Van Gogh, the edges of objects shimmering with strange light.

Oh, but he knew this world. A shocked laugh left him as he turned towards Eliza, who gazed up at him with worry.

"Eliza." He whispered it but his voice rang like bells in his ears. Joy and relief surged through his bones. He cupped her cheek with one hand while wrapping his arm about her slim waist to pull her tight against him. She felt so bloody good, just right. Her pink lips opened to question him. He captured those lips, licked away those words with his tongue, and she melted into him. Just so.

He kissed her deeper, his thumb caressing her plump lower lip so that he might feel her mouth even as he tasted it. And she moaned, her breasts pillowed against his chest, the sweet valley between her thighs cradling his cock. Never in all his long years had he felt anything better. But she pressed her hand against his shoulder with enough force and intent that he knew she wanted him to stop.

He didn't like that, wanted to growl his protest, but he eased back. Lips swollen and her cheeks flushed, she was so enticing he nearly kissed her again.

"What has happened?" she asked, searching his face for answers.

His grip upon her waist tightened. "Eliza"—he swallowed hard as elation went through him again—"my powers are restored. But Mab's curse is gone. I felt it break."

Had he not been so close to her, he might have missed the shadow of fear that flickered through her eyes. Slowly she sank to the floor, and he realized they'd been kneeling this whole time. He followed her down, gathering her up and pulling her into his lap. That she didn't resist but rested her head against his chest made his old heart ache.

Adam closed his eyes and pressed his lips to her temple. She was his. *His.*

"What does it mean?" she whispered, her nimble fingers tracing patterns over his chest.

He might have told her what he suspected, but her shocked gasp had him tensing. Only then did he become aware of the sound of rain. It came in a great downpour, beating against the roof as if trying to break in.

"Adam, look." With a shaking hand, she pointed to the window.

It was not rain, however, that streaked over the windows. But blood.

Chapter Twenty-Eight

Sin left Mab's house on legs that shook. He'd done it. He'd destroyed the bitch. Above him thunderclouds began to gather, the rumble in the sky deep and ominous. The clear morning sun fled in favor of darkness. And yet he'd never felt lighter. He grinned, wanting to laugh. He was free.

The faint rumble of thunder lingered as the tiny hairs on the back of his neck lifted. Slowly he turned. A shadow broke from the garden wall. Sin's back tensed, a crackle of power dancing over his fingertips. But he hesitated in striking out. Slim and lithe of movement, the figure stalked toward him without pause.

The clouds parted, revealing his guest, and a punch of hot dread hit him hard enough to set his skin to prickling. Miranda, dressed as a boy beneath the billowing cloak she wore, stared right back at him. Her expression was not one of love, but of disgust.

At first her voice was calm, almost regretful. "I've been following you. You've seemed so...lost."

Because he was lost. A strangled sound left him, but he could not give voice to his pain.

"I saw you." She nodded up toward Mab's window, the curtains open wide as always. "Undressing for... You are her lover?"

No. No. No. He willed the ground to open up before him. But his powers, like him, were frozen with fear.

"St. John." Her honey-rich voice was curt with displeasure. "Tell me that what I saw is not true." Closer she came, little flames dancing along the ground in her wake. "Tell me you have not betrayed us all."

Christ, he wanted to cry. He couldn't even make his mouth work, but merely looked at her with all the regret and shame in the world. Because it was clear she did not see him slay Mab. Even worse, he'd given a vow never to reveal what he was. It was the price of Judgment. He was a secret slayer. His deeds never to be revealed, or he would die.

She cocked her head, peering at him as though he were an insect she'd soon smash. "The GIM are dying. *Daisy* and Mary are dying." The bush beside him burst into flames. And Miranda's eyes flared with ire. "Yet you are in bed with the very bitch who is causing this."

"I..."

Miranda took a hard step closer. "Holly is like a sister to you. How..." She took a sharp breath. "How could you? And for what? To...to swive that..." Her teeth ground, and another bush exploded in flames.

"Miranda—" Sin winced as his throat clamped shut. He literally could not give an excuse. And it was agony. As was her disappointment and disgust in him. "I am not worth your regard."

It was all he could say. And it was the truth. His stupidity had put him in this predicament. It did not matter if he was free, if he'd destroyed the fae queen. He'd let them all down long ago.

She flinched. "I wanted so badly for you to feel as though you belonged."

He would not cry. Nor throw himself at her feet and beg for her to make it all better.

Her voice went soft, but no less angry. "I believed you to be a true brother to us, as we were your true sisters."

I am. But he wasn't. The truth was he might have ended himself and spared them all. But he'd been too much of a coward.

Her red-gold locks slithered over her slim shoulders as she shook her head. "But you never were. You always held yourself apart."

"Yes." Because all of it was true. He was never a true brother to his blood sisters. He'd failed them long ago.

"Have you nothing to say for yourself, St. John?"

I hate that you no longer call me Sin. I hate that you've seen the worst of me. I hate myself most of all. He gave a stiff shake of his head.

Her eyes, which had always been filled with warmth and love for him, were chips of glass. So empty he wanted to sob. Worse when she spoke in that terrible, flat voice. "For your sake, I will not tell Ian or Jack what you've done. I've no wish to see you slaughtered. However, I think it best that you no longer come around the family."

He could only blink back tears burning in his eyes and watch as, with a swirl of her cloak, she turned and left him standing alone, and the rain began to fall.

Armageddon, some were calling it. The end of days. Others called the rain the devil's tears. Even practical, scientifically minded men and women looked towards the skies with trepidation, for no one could account for the blood-red rain that continued to fall from the sky.

Fear ran rampant, people went to church or stayed locked firmly behind doors. Officials tried to assure residents that the rain, while red, was in fact water and not blood. It did little to quell the fear. Not with the steady rainfall, staining clothes pink, and running in little, crimson rivers along the cobbles.

It was a macabre sight. Unsettling to say the least.

Adam's jaw stayed bunched as they kept riding at a steady clip down the high road toward London. Rain dripped from the wide brim of his riding hat and ran in red rivulets down his lean cheeks. It was as if he were bathed in blood. Eliza shuddered, knowing she likely looked just as gruesome. No one would drive a coach so they were forced to ride horses.

And while normally Eliza would not mind riding, she loathed being out in the unnatural rain. Adam had suggested she stay behind. He had to discover what had occurred. Eliza would be safer tucked up in their little cottage.

Perhaps, but she was not going to be left behind. And perhaps he knew that, for he'd merely given her a nod and packed up their saddlebags. Now she could only duck her head, press her lips together, and hope none of the rain would get into her mouth.

Perhaps it was an irrational fear, but it could not be helped. The very air about her seemed malevolent. At least, they made good time, for the roads were deserted. And soon enough, London loomed before them. Black clouds limned in swirling, light-grey bundles sat like fat toads over the great city. Even here, nothing stirred. It was as if the rain held siege.

They rode down Hammersmith Road, heading into Kensington, their horses' hooves clopping upon the cobbles, a strange counterpoint to the patter of rain. Usually, the clatter and rattle of endless cabs, drays, and omnibuses would compete against the cries of the costers and the distant whistle of the railways. Now, silence and rain.

Pale faces hovered behind grimy windows, wide eyes watching them ride along. Just ahead of her, Adam sat tall on his horse, his broad shoulders and straight back a familiar and comforting sight. She urged her mare alongside of him, needing to keep close. He glanced her way, and his expression was grim. "Unnerving, this."

"Everyone has gone to ground."

His eyes scanned the streets. "I don't detect any supernaturals out and about either."

Eliza sat straighter on her mount, a bolt of shock catching her breath. "That is it... Adam, the spirits. They've gone as well." She'd yet to see a single soul. The lack of them was what had unnerved her far more than the lack of people. For spirits were not ones to flee. Ever.

Eliza shivered and huddled farther inside of her mackintosh cloak. She'd dressed in trousers. They were more comfortable for the ride. And no one was around to gawk at any rate. "Where are we going?" She hadn't asked Adam for specifics. There wasn't time.

"To Mab's."

Her horse shied as she half-spun in her saddle. "Have you gone mad?"

His mouth tilted up at the corner. "Not that I can tell, no."

Eliza slowed her horse, and thus he did as well. She could only gape at him, no longer caring about the blood-rain. "Then tell me why on earth you'd be willing to return to her?" Something odd and ugly, like jealousy mixed with fear, twisted inside of her.

As usual, he read her too well, and a slow grin broke over his face. The bastard really was breathtaking when he smiled in that manner.

"I've no desire to see the fae bitch. I do believe she's gone, love."

"Gone?" Eliza frowned.

"Aye. I don't feel her anymore." He grimaced, crimson rain mixing in his afternoon stubble. "Always I've felt an echo of her, like the annoying buzz of a mosquito just out of sight. Now ..." He turned his attention back to the road, his profile stark. "It's as if all is silent."

He did not appear precisely pleased, but thoughtful. Which bothered her even more. "And Mellan? How will you fight him, when your sword has been destroyed?"

It had been an unfortunate loss, Adam's sword. The assassin's weapon had been fae-made and thus able to cut through Adam's sword.

A shadow of regret fell over Adam's face, but he spoke with calm authority. "I'm considering our options."

"Adam." She reached out and plucked at his arm. "Stop and explain yourself or I won't go any farther."

Adam reined in his horse. Wariness lined his face, hesitancy darkening his eyes. "All right. I'll start with Mab. You'll remember when I spoke with Lucien? And you asked me what I'd said to him?"

"Yes." She said it tentatively because she couldn't fathom what that had to do with anything.

As always, he read her well, and his lips curled in a half-smile. "I told Lucien to inform Augustus that St. John Evernight was blood bound to Mab's will. I knew Augustus would seek out St. John."

Outrage had her nearly shouting. "Why? How could you put Sin in danger—"

"If you'd let me finish," Adam cut in placidly, though hurt darkened his eyes. She hadn't trusted him. Again.

With a pang of guilt, Eliza gave a curt nod. She'd hear him out.

"I am trying to help him. St. John is an elemental of untold power, which is most likely why Mab acquired him in her collection." Adam's lips curled in distaste. "In all truth, I see myself in him, what I might have become had I been younger when Mab got her hands upon me. St. John deserves his freedom."

"And you believe Augustus can give it to him?"

"If there is anyone who can work around Mab's curses, it is he. But more important, Sin is a worthy soul. Augustus needs souls such as his."

"Why? What will he do with him?"

Slowly Adam shook his head. "That I cannot tell you."

Eliza huffed out a breath. "Cannot or will not?"

Adam's eyes gleamed gold as he met Eliza's gaze. "Some secrets are not mine to tell. Will you trust me, sweet dove, when I say that, if St. John goes to Augustus, he will not be harmed?"

For a moment, the only noise was that of the horse hooves clomping against the pavers, as they stood impatiently waiting to move again. And then the stiffness left Eliza's shoulders. "Yes, Adam, I will."

All at once, he leaned across the small divide between their horses. His lips caressed hers in a soft, melting kiss, his mouth warm and his cheeks wet with rain. "Thank you, Eliza May." He kissed her one more time before sitting back.

Eliza smiled a bit but then wavered. "Tell me now how this has to do with Mab being destroyed."

"Ah," said Adam, resting a hand upon his pommel. "Mab had to be fighting mad at our evasion. She wouldn't be thinking clearly, especially if Mellan was, as I suspect, after her as well. She'd trust that St. John would be under her complete control. Which would leave her vulnerable."

Eliza licked her dry lips and stared down at the cobbled bricks, stained now with crimson rain. "You base all this on the hopes that Augustus will somehow enable Sin to fight Mab, and that he will win."

"I base this on my knowledge of the situation and how best to maneuver certain players into the most probable outcome." He turned and the strong line of his neck peaked out from his grimy collar. "Yes, there is risk involved but, using what I had, it seemed the best play to make." A small laugh left Eliza, and he frowned at her. "Why are you amused?"

"You really cannot refrain from plotting and playing with the lives of others."

His thick brows knitted, a dark flush coming over his high-cut cheeks. "I told you, one cannot win against the fae unless you treat it like a game of chess. Mab needed to die. I could not destroy her, so I sought a way to see the job done. And, hopefully, free a man who has been ill used."

"Adam," Eliza said softly, "I do not fault you for it. I simply am in awe of your working mind."

The flush on his cheeks deepened. He sat higher in his saddle, clearing his throat. "Yes, well, that is what I hope has occurred."

"As do I." Eliza took a better hold of her reins but paused. "Adam? My powers are increasing. Might I have killed her?"

His lips pursed before he spoke. "Perhaps. And perhaps,

had I known then that you were capable of defending yourself against a fae, I'd have planned differently." But his bold nose lifted a bit as he eyed her slantwise. "Then again, I'm not of a mind to lose you, Eliza."

"Oh that is rich," she snorted, "and does it occur to you that it is not your decision to make?"

"Of course it does," he said lightly. "Just as it is my decision to be a boorish, over-protecting, primitive male." He arched a brow and gave her a smug look. "Have I left out any adjectives?"

" 'Smarmy' and 'arse' come to mind," Eliza muttered. "And if I do the same? If I try to protect you?"

"Why, my love, I'd take it as a sign of your single-minded devotion to me." His eyes began to glow. "It would be a highlight in my life, to be sure."

She could not help but laugh. "You are one twisted root."

He laughed too. But they grew quiet as they began to ride once more.

"Will you answer me a question, dove?" Adam asked as they neared their destination.

"Of course."

His eyes crinkled at her immediate response, but his tone remained somber. "What did the oracle tell you?" When she opened her mouth to speak, he hurried on. "If it puts you in danger to reveal anything, pray keep your council."

She wanted to kiss him again. "The oracle saw you in possession of the horn. However, only I would know how to use it. And that..." Shy heat flushed her cheeks. "That is to say, I'd only know how to use the horn when I let you into my heart."

Adam's face was blank for a long moment. Then his set expression broke on an indrawn breath. He closed his eyes, and appearing almost pained, he asked her, "Have you let me in, Eliza?"

Tender emotion was a lump deep within her throat. "You are in my heart, Adam."

Nostrils flaring, he jerked his head as if her words had struck him. When he opened his eyes, they glowed with a gold light. It bathed the area around Eliza as if the sun had come out to shine upon her. His husky promise was filled with power. "That is all that I needed to know."

The moment they set foot on Mab's front walk, Adam pulled Eliza close. Were he to listen to his heart, he'd insist she went to Lucien's barge and wait for his return. But he knew precisely how that would go. She'd fight him come hell or high water. And he'd not chain her spirit ever again.

He had her heart. His own swelled at the thought. It made him feel immense, powerful, terrified. She owned his as well, and he was about to literally put it into her keeping. So many things could go wrong, but he had to trust in Eliza.

Taking her hand in his free one, he felt marginally better. Especially when she twined her fingers with his and gave him a squeeze. She was his now. And he hers. He'd make that perfectly clear as soon as this was over.

"It looks wrong," said Eliza.

He knew what she meant. Like the rest of London hiding away, the house appeared abandoned. Too dark behind those mullioned windows. But he knew who would be waiting. He held Eliza more securely.

When no one answered the front door, Adam tried the handle. The door swung open, revealing Mab's front hall, now dark and still. He spoke not a word, but gave Eliza a look. *Caution.* Her blink of understanding was all he needed.

Their steps sounded small in the cavernous silence of the house.

"If you came looking for tea," said Mellan from behind, "I'm afraid you'll find the staff has gone."

Adam spun himself and Eliza around. God, but his sword hand felt too empty, and he experienced the loss of his weapon anew.

"Flown the coop, as it were," Mellan continued as if he hadn't a care in the world. Adam was not fooled. The fae prince was wound tight. The blond length of his hair had been bound at his temples by intricate braids. An exotic counterpoint to his suit that was cut to perfection and a dark, forest green, lacy jabot at his throat. Formal attire, as though he were in a celebratory mood.

Just as Adam suspected.

"And Mab?" Eliza asked at Adam's side. Her fingers curled around his arm as if anchoring herself to him. He approved.

Mellan shrugged as he strolled closer. "Alas, she has left this mortal coil." He chuckled. "And lost her fae immortality as well."

"So then St. John destroyed her," Adam said.

Mellan stopped short, eyes narrowing, and it was Adam's turn to laugh. "Did you think it was a happy coincidence?" It was petty to rub it in the fae's face, but necessary. Mellan had to attack first.

"Honestly," Mellan finally said, "he did me a service." He turned his attention to Eliza. "I needed to control the fae. Without my sister's interference."

"And now you are what?" Eliza asked. "King?"

Black fangs glimmered behind Mellan's pale lips. "Just so."

"Congratulations," Adam said without feeling. "And

yet I do wonder why it is that you've been so keen to track down Eliza." Oh, but Adam knew. Understanding sang through his blood. It all fit, and he was about to call checkmate.

Not a flicker of emotion went through Mellan. "I had thought that Eliza and I had an understanding."

"That I would kill Adam?" Eliza scowled. "Why not do the deed yourself, and leave me be?"

"Because," Adam said, "he wanted my sword first. Fae-made weapons are rare, true, but my sword—"

"It was *my* sword," snarled Mellan, his color high. "My battle sword, stollen by a foul and God-fearing human. I was not going to send you to hell before I had it back in my hands."

"I'm afraid to report," Adam said, "that your assassin destroyed the sword."

Ice crackled over the floors and up the walls as Mellan inhaled with an audible breath. "For that," he ground out, "I shall make your death an agony."

Now, Adam thought. Fight me now. He was not afraid of death. Not anymore. But Mellan blinked and his anger seemed to fade as he looked at Eliza. Which meant he wanted her more. Adam's determination increased. He knew with utter certainty that what he'd planned was in the right.

"I did want you," Mellan said to Eliza, as though his anger had never happened. "Were I to marry Mab's grand-daughter, I'd have a stronger claim to take over the throne."

Adam did not believe it for one second. "And the Horn an Bás?"

Mellan's expression turned peevish. "A myth I used to distract Mab."

"As I thought," Adam lied. Oh, he had thought that

before, but now he knew better. At Adam's side, Eliza stood, warm and trusting. He wanted nothing more than to draw her nearer and hold her tight. *God keep her, make her strong when he couldn't hold her.*

Mellan watched them with a hawkish fervor, his gaze darting between them. "It appears that Mab's curse upon you has ended as well, Aodh."

Adam found he hated that name; it felt as though it belonged to the fae, to that time when he'd been young and foolish. "I am Adam, King of the GIM," he said. "And yes, I have my power. Pray, do not test me, Mellan." *Test, me*, he thought. *Challenge me, you wily bastard.*

"I would not dream of it," Mellan drawled, yet there was satisfaction in his eyes.

"Then I'll have your word that you'll leave Eliza alone from now on."

Eliza tensed, and Mellan froze. It seemed the fae would snarl and lash out, but he held still. Adam did as well, ready to fight this man with the one thing he had left: his life. For Eliza.

Mellan broke the tense silence. "Mab is out of my way. Thus I no longer need you, Eliza." Mellan looked her over, his gaze roving. "Though I am not averse to keeping you as my concubine."

Eliza's face twisted in disgust. "You do realize how very disturbed that is. You are my granduncle."

Mellan gave a negligent shrug. "My sister birthed some brat decades ago, and you are the final result. What does it matter to me? I am not human, nor bound to their customs. In truth, were I to get you with child, our combined blood would only serve to strengthen the child."

Fucking bloody fucking bastard. Adam's only wish was to see the fae king die. But understanding lit through him; while Adam was trying to bait Mellan into a fight, Mellan was trying to bait Eliza.

Eliza's expression iced over as she spoke to Mellan. "Let me say that, at this moment, I'm not averse to gelding you."

Adam could not help it, he laughed, glancing down at his beloved. That mouth of hers, always quick to say the most cutting thing, and he loved it. He loved *her*, Eliza May of the tart tongue and sweet lips. He almost said it there and then. Except he heard Mellan snarl, saw him move out of the corner of his eye. Too soon, and attacking the wrong person.

The world around him did not slow down, but sped up. Mellan's clawed-tipped hand shot out, terror ran down Adam's middle, and Eliza froze. He did not have time to shout, to push her out of Mellan's path. Adam threw himself forward, into Mellan's lashing hand, protecting Eliza with the only thing he had. His body.

He knew it instinctively, knew that this was it, that he would die. *Let her be strong.* And all of it happened in a second.

The impact shook him to the core, pushing the air from his lungs. Adam curled into it, his sight going hazy, as agony exploded over his chest. His body arched back as something tugged at him.

Eliza's scream came as if from a great distance, a buzzing, indistinct sound, drowned out by a huge whoosh of white pain. He could not move. Numb, he glanced down.

His chest was a gaping cavern of blood and gore. Odd. Had he...Mellan grinned at him, his pale face splattered with little crimson dots. He held out his hand to Adam as though offering him something. Adam could not focus on it.

Cold. He was too cold. He could not feel his legs. Was he falling?

The floor greeted him with a jarring smack. Grief clamped the sides of his head with hard hands. Or was that Eliza? Was she speaking? She made an awful racket, and his head hurt. *Be strong, love. Win this.* Mellan still grinned. Holding out his hand. Something in that hand. A throbbing dark mass, dripping with blood.

Oh.

It was his heart.

Chapter Twenty-Nine

Jack Talent was not in the habit of retiring to bed early. Unless it was to tumble about in it with his wife. He pulled his shirt over his head and tossed it on a nearby chair. No, he had no desire to lie about in bed at—he glanced at the ornate clock on the mantle—four in the afternoon. But his wife was tired, so he would keep her company.

A heavy fear weighed down his heart. Mary was often tired now. Sleeping more than she was awake. Weakening. He ran a hand through his hair and grabbed the back of his neck. Would she soon be like Daisy? Vacant and motionless upon her bed?

For a moment, the fear threatened to rip out of him. He reined it in. For her, he did this. He had to remain strong for her. Jack stared into the fire, watching the flames dance and crackle and he tried not to cry like a lad.

Ian was already lost to fear, snarling at anyone who came near Daisy, and growing weak from lack of sleep and food. Jack worried that his foster father might soon lose control of his inner wolf. And a mad lycan was a danger to all. It would destroy Jack's soul if he had to kill Ian in order to protect the people of London.

"Christ." He sat heavily upon the edge of the bed and held his head in his hands.

He could hear Mary puttering around her dressing room, washing her face and brushing her hair. He rose to join her, perhaps help her out of her gown and make love to her nice and slow, when the floor shook. Hard. A silent boom seemed to rush through the air, making Jack stumble. An earthquake? He'd never experienced one, but it was the first thought that came to mind. Only the air had felt ice cold.

And then he heard Ian's roar, filled with utter terror. Jack moved to go to him, but then halted. Mary. Secure Mary. On unsteady limbs, he rushed to the dressing room, his heart pounding and his father's screams ringing in his ear.

Wrenching the dressing room door open, he skidded to a halt. "Mary!"

She lay in a tangle of limbs, her eyes open and staring. Jack was at her side in an instant. "Mary."

God. God. He'd seen her like this once before. When she'd died for him. Terrified, he pressed his head to her breast, frantic to hear the steady churn of her clockwork heart. But only found silence. Jack's breath came out in hard gasps. His eyes burning and his mind frozen in fear. And then the second blast came, a great boom of noise that shattered all the windows.

Jack didn't look up, but held his wife close, and wept.

Eliza could not recollect what played out before her. She saw it unfold but it could not be true. It could *not*. Yet it was.

Adam toppled to the floor, his chest ripped open. And

his heart. That powerful organ that held his life's blood. It was in Mellan's hand. He'd pulled it from Adam's chest.

Eliza snapped out of her terror. "Adam!"

She fell to his side, scrambling to hold him. What to do? What could she do?

His mouth hung open as if in surprise. A fine sheen of sweat covered his greying skin.

"Adam." With frantic hands she touched him, stroking, begging with all that she had that this was a nightmare. "Love. Adam."

What to do?

His eyes, once brilliant and golden and filled with eternal life, grew dull. Frantic, she cupped his cheek, the skin slack there, and peered into his eyes. "Adam." There was nothing else to say. He couldn't even focus on her. Because he was dead.

Eliza remained hunched over his form, her body locked tight in horrified shock.

And then Mellan laughed. "That was far easier than expected."

Though her fingers felt like ice, a fine, fierce heat began to coil within her. Slowly, carefully, she eased Adam's shoulders off her lap and placed him on the floor. Mellan watched her with amusement. "His curse broken and still he hadn't claimed you as his soul mate. For here you stand, and there he lays."

The rage grew, pumping like a bellows, filling her up.

Mellan continued on, not realizing the danger. "There is no one left to you, Eliza. Save me. The only one who knows of what you are capable. The only one to teach you how to use your talents."

On strong limbs she rose. And the air about her seemed to crackle and spark. Bastard. Eliza sneered, showing her teeth.

"I will control you, Eliza May. And thus control death. Oh, the possibilities—"

A screech flew from her lips, louder than anything she'd ever heard. With the force of a locomotive, it rushed from her. Endless screaming. Mellan blanched, his skin sinking and cleaving to his bones as he stood rooted to the spot.

Eliza's scream grew in volume. In strength. Windows shattered, Mab's fine crystal chandelier crashing to the ground. And it was power. A rush surged through Eliza's body and outward. She lifted her hand, her pale fingers stained scarlet with Adam's blood. The sight gave her direction. Mellan's mouth worked on a wordless cry as she came for him, wrapping her fingers around his throat and lifting him high.

And the endless scream took on a life, swirling about him with black fingers that invaded his mouth. His body arched, thrashing within Eliza's grip. She did not let go but squeezed tightly, her mouth stretched open with the terrible screech of her rage. Then the black fingers yanked the soul of Mellan out of his body.

And Eliza let the lifeless body drop. All at once, her scream died.

She stood, swaying, her body weak and her heart broken. At her feet Adam lay. The sight of his empty eyes brought her to her knees. And then all went black.

Eliza woke with a gasp. She hurt. Everywhere. But it was her heart that felt broken and bleeding, as though she'd swallowed shards of glass and they'd collected in that tight space. A sense of horrible, black dread consumed her, and she stared up at the ceiling, her gaze stuck on a tattered cobweb dangling from one plaster rosette. What place was this?

And then she realized that she was not alone. The slight warmth of a body came from the right of her. And on her left? Coldness. Dread. A sob, unbidden, wracked her aching chest.

"Eliza?" It was a soft, feminine whisper. And Eliza jerked, wrenching her head toward the sound.

Holly Evernight knelt next to her with an expression of abject sorrow. Just over her shoulder hovered Will Thorne. His black eyes were threaded with strands of silver, and as he stared down at her, the silver grew stronger. He looked as if he might weep for her.

And then it all came back to her.

A wail tore up her throat, thrusting her upright with its power. The cold weight by her side jostled, and she turned, feeling her entire soul shrivel with utter grief. Adam.

He lay, bone white, dull eyes staring into nothingness, a gaping hole in his chest.

"Eliza." A hand settled on her shoulder. Holly.

"He's gone," Eliza said unnecessarily. She wanted to cry, hot tears of pain. And yet her eyes remained dry. This one time in her life and she couldn't shed a damn tear.

"I'm so sorry, Miss May," said Thorne, and when she began to shudder with dry sobs, he eased around Holly and embraced her, holding her head against his shoulder. Eliza did not really know this man, his scent was unfamiliar and not the one she craved, but he was warm and offering a sorely needed comfort. She let him hold her as she shook. So very cold.

Holly looked on in concern, holding Eliza's icy hand in her own. "Who did this?"

There was a strange urgency to her question, one that went beyond Adam.

Eliza squeezed her eyes shut. "Mellan. The fae ... Well,

I suppose he'd been king for a day." An unhinged laugh escaped her before she took another breath. "Adam...he was trying to protect me. And now..." She pressed the heel of her hand against her brow. "At least Mellan is no more."

She pointed in the direction of the human-shaped mess of loamy ash that had once been Mellan's body.

"Christ," muttered Thorne, his hand tightening on the back of her head. She felt him turn slightly and knew he was looking at Holly.

Eliza eased herself back and took in their twin expressions of fear and grief. "It is good of you to care for me. But neither of you has any cause to grieve..." She could not say his name, but forced herself to go on. "There is more, isn't there?"

Thorne sat back on his haunches. "The GIM, all of them, have collapsed. London is in an uproar. First the blood rain, and now this. Humans are thinking it is the end of days. And the rest of us..." Thorne ducked his head.

Holly's dark blue eyes filled. "They are dead, Eliza. Or give every appearance of being so."

Eliza's body went hollow. Not only Adam. But Lucien. Mary and Daisy, who had saved her. Kind Mr. Brown, who had harbored Adam and her. All of them. Adam's children.

"He dies," Eliza whispered. "They all die."

A terrible stillness settled over the room. "I fear it is so," said Holly after a moment.

Eliza pressed the heels of her hands over her aching eyes. She could not bring herself to look down again. To acknowledge that he was gone. And her soul was torn in half. Yes, he was her other half. She knew that implicitly now. He was gone, leaving behind a terrible sense of wrongness within her.

She felt Thorne stir, heard the shushing of fabric. From the corner of her eye, she saw him move to cover Adam with his coat.

"No!" Eliza rose to her knees, pushing him away, and curling herself over Adam's cold body. His life's blood, now sticky and thick upon the floor, seeped through her clothes. "Do not touch him."

Silence.

"Miss May—"

Holly hushed Thorne with a small sound. When she spoke, her voice was even and low. "Eliza, I know this pain. I know you do not want to let him go." She swallowed audibly. "But let us take him to a better place. Not here."

No, not left disgraced upon the floor. With the stiffness of an old woman, Eliza moved away from Adam's body. She didn't look down. He wasn't there at any rate. Not the soul that lit him up. A steady burn grew behind her eyes and prickled at the bridge of her nose.

"Will you..." Her breath hitched. "Will you help me take him to Lucien's barge?" Eliza did not know where else to go. And Adam had loved Lucien as a father to a son.

Holly's voice came as though through a fog. "Anything, dearest."

Eliza stood. She would take care of Adam. And then she did not know. The endless possibilities of life had simply stopped.

Chapter Thirty

———— ❧ ~❧ ————

They'd placed him on a pallet under the window of Lucien's great dining hall. Dressed in a simple tunic and resting on a bed of black velvet, his hands clasped on the hilt of his broken sword, Adam looked every inch the fallen knight. But peace had not eased his features.

Eliza sat by his side. The room was too hot, the light of hundreds of candles—a flame for each GIM—burning too bright for Eliza's eyes. Yet she did not mind. She did not think on much at all. Only him.

Her hand curled around his cold and unmoving one. "Descartes said that it is easy to hate and it is difficult to love. I suspect he is right in some regard." Eliza ran her thumb over Adam's knuckles. "It was easy to hate you." A strangled, half laugh, half sob left her. "I did it so well. And yet, it was so very easy to love you too, Adam."

The light of the candles blurred as Eliza's eyes filled. "Oh, I fought it, like a cat to a water bath. But it was of no use. Love you, I did." Gently she stroked the back of his hand. A fighter's hands, wide and strong. "And you must be my soul's other half, impossible demon, for I feel so . . . broken."

As if a damn had burst, she cried, tears falling fast and hot. The pain in her heart had her curling over Adam, resting her head upon his hard shoulder. And she cried. So hard that she nearly missed the faint hissing sound beneath her cheek. It grew louder, and Eliza sat up.

"Oh no." Adam's fine wool tunic began to disintegrate, spreading out from a patch by his chest. "No, no, no." Eliza slapped at the slow burn, but it did not stop, and she hissed in pain when the cloth singed her fingers.

And then she froze, for it seemed as though Adam moved. Heart pounding furiously, Eliza sat, her gaze riveted to his chest and the spot where his clothing still burned away, enough now that she could see the smooth skin beneath. Skin that began to turn a healthy, golden shade.

An inarticulate cry left her as she lurched up, her chair clattering to the floor behind her. His chest moved again, a deep rise and fall. A breath.

Wordlessly, she stood. Watching. Blood rushed in her ears. *It could not be.*

And yet . . . His dark brows twitched, a frown.

"Ahh . . ." Eliza stumbled forward, her hand going to his shoulder. "Adam?" Her lips felt numb. Hope was a choking thing within.

The thick fan of his black lashes fluttered, and then his eyes opened. His gaze locked on her. There it was, that visceral hit that took her breath. Every time he looked at her. Eliza found herself laughing and crying all at once. She threw herself upon him. Kissing his face, his big, stubborn nose, his soft, pliable mouth.

He lay slack, his breath coming out in weak pants,

and then his strong arms crushed her to him, his fingers threading through her hair, pulling out strands in his haste. "Eliza."

She kissed him, holding his beloved face in her hands. "Adam." Another kiss. "How can it be?"

Adam pressed his forehead to hers. For a moment, they simply breathed. Eliza slid her finger under the ravaged edge of his tunic to stroke his smooth skin, smiling at the way his breath hitched.

He eased her back so that their eyes met. "*Bean sídhe,*" he said.

"W-what?" Eliza blinked away the tears and stared in confusion.

His mouth canted on a smile. "You. A wee and fey banshee."

Despite her joy, indignation rocked through her. "You mean one of those ghoulish ghosts that screech and terrify villagers?"

Adam's laugh was a deep, rolling rumble. "Oh, aye. Just as fae are tiny creatures with crystalline wings and death is eternal."

Eliza let out a huff, but nuzzled into his warm, rough palm. "Then what? You believe me to be a banshee?"

His thumb stroked the curve of her cheek, and he gazed upon her with warm happiness. "Aye. The banshee. A rare and wonderful creature once thought to be myth. She whose mad laugh announces death, whose screech can cause it, and whose tears of sorrow can call the dead back to life."

He gave one of her curls a gentle tug. "A golden-haired banshee, whose shout is a trumpet, heralding death."

At that, Eliza sat up, her hand falling to his chest where his heart now beat a steady rhythm. Alive. Restored. "You think I am the Golden Horn an Bás?"

"You do not?" he countered.

Eliza stroked a lock of his ink-black hair back from his brow. "Well, I suppose you're alive." With a flush of discomfort, she glanced down at her hand. A banshee. It felt right. "When Mellan killed you, I screamed. Adam"— she looked at him—"I killed him without any effort, as if the scream itself held power."

His face remained expressionless for a moment, then broke into a wide grin. "As I said, banshee." With a small laugh, Adam eased upright, groaning a bit. "Feels as though my heart has been ripped from my body."

Eliza smacked his shoulder. "Don't you jest. I saw you die." On a breath, she wrapped herself around him, pushing between his thighs where he sat upon the pallet and burying her head in the crook of his neck. The scent of spices and luscious man filled her. Adam. Eliza held on tighter. "Don't do that again."

"All right, *mo gradh*," he whispered. "I will not." The press of his lips at her crown was warm and tender.

A thought occurred to her, and she went stock still. "Adam," she said, slowly moving away from him, "when did you suspect I was banshee?"

He winced, contrition warring with defiance in his eyes. "Love..." He ran a hand through his hair. "When you destroyed that fae with your scream, I suspected. But when you told me what that wee shite oracle revealed, I knew you were the Horn an Bás that Mellan sought."

Eliza's breath left her with a hiss, her body going ice cold. "You planned it," she ground out. "You let Mellan kill you!"

"Aye," he said. "I did. Though I didn't think he'd do it in such a painful manner." Again he winced, and it was all Eliza could do not to clout his thick head. He rubbed his chest. "Having your heart ripped out hurts like the devil."

"Arse," she shouted, slapping his shoulder once more. "How could you?"

He caught her arm and pulled her close, wrapping his arms about her in a secure hug. "Because I knew that you would bring me back. And there was no other way. Mellan had to be utterly destroyed. A banshee could do that. I could not."

She shivered, her heart hurting at the risk he took. "You might have been wrong about me."

"But I was not."

"You might have told me," she countered with ire.

He snuggled her closer. "If you knew what I had planned, you'd have talked me out of it. And you needed to act out of instinct not reason, sweet dove. End game, Eliza. I told you I'd do whatever it took to win this time. Because you are my end game, and you are too important to lose."

Eliza pressed her nose against the smooth skin at the base of his neck and let out a breath. "If you ever risk yourself in that manner again, I shall kill you."

"Not a very good threat, love, when I know your tears will restore me."

"Bastard." She pinched his side, but it was a half-hearted effort that she abandoned for kissing her way up his throat.

Adam stroked her hair. "You are in my heart too. I'll never be sorry that I died for you." He said it so quietly, his voice ragged and raw with emotion, that Eliza's body responded with a rush of warmth. She lifted her head, and he touched her jaw, his golden eyes glowing. "Eliza—"

The door to the dining hall burst open, and Lucien

Stone strode in, his hair falling about his shoulders, his lacy dressing shirt open to the waist. His jade green eyes were wild until they locked onto Adam. And then he seemed to sag on a sigh. "Sire. Adam... You are well."

Adam's smiled at his friend. "As are you."

For a moment, Lucien simply stared and then he pressed his hand against eyes that grew red and watery. His shoulders shook as he stood at the entrance to the room. Gently, Adam moved Eliza to the side and went to Lucien. As if the GIM were his child, Adam pulled him close, and Lucien grasped at the back of Adam's tunic, hugging him tight. His words were muffled against Adam's shirt. "I missed you."

When Adam rose from death, so too did the GIM. Which, in turn, scared the wits out of human Londoners. Even from the relative solitude of Lucien's barge, one could hear the commotion running amok throughout London. The SOS was working overtime with the queen to contain the problem, using false news reports about a gas leak to pacify the fear. Not that leaking gas was anything to smile over, but at the very least it was something logical to the human mind. Better that than explain that there were those who walked about with clockwork hearts in their breasts.

As for the supernatural population of London, they breathed a sigh of relief. Or most of them did. Some demons were not at all happy that the GIM had been reborn. To which Adam replied, somewhat sardonically to Lucien, that the demon rabble could "kiss his left nut."

"Only the left one, sire?" Lucien teased.

Adam huffed, his attention set on placing a tiny cog into the clock he'd been fixing for the past hour. "It hangs lower, and I wouldn't want them too far up in my business."

"Charming," Eliza murmured. "Truly, Adam."

He merely winked at her, his grin wide and mischievous.

Fortunately, Daisy and Mary arrived, putting an end to discussions of Adam's lower anatomy.

Eliza rose to embrace them.

"It gladdens my heart that you are here," she whispered when they hugged as one.

Daisy gave a wry chuckle and kissed Eliza's cheek. "As it does mine, sweet dear."

Mary, who was more reserved, simply nodded in agreement. "Though I am not certain who was more happy, myself for being alive once again or my husband for seeing me wake."

"Your husband, to be sure," Daisy murmured, her plump cheeks pink. They went deeper pink, even as her eyes crinkled with a saucy look. "If he behaved anything as mine did?"

Mary gave Daisy an exasperated look, but did not reply.

She hadn't an opportunity, for Ian Ranulf, the lycan king and Daisy's husband, stepped up to Eliza. He'd been quietly talking to Lucien and Adam, but now he faced her. He was a handsome man, undeniably so. Vivid blue eyes, fine features, and rich auburn hair that fell down around his shoulders. It ought to look feminine but he looked every bit the warrior Adam did.

In truth, he was a tad frightening, his expression fierce with concentration. High color darkened his face as he stared at Eliza with an intensity that was slightly unnerving. The room fell silent. But Eliza did not look around. She kept her attention on the man capable of turning into a wolf and tearing her throat out on a whim.

His nostrils flared on a sharp breath. And then he fell to his knees. His hair swung forward as he bowed his head.

"My lady," he said in a deep burr, "you restored my wife to me, and that of my kinswoman. I am in your debt. Beyond measure. Beyond price. Consider me your servant, and I shall gladly do as ye bid."

Eliza looked around, helplessly. Adam's gaze met hers, his solemn yet gleaming with a bit of humor. He gave her a nod of encouragement. Just beyond him, a massive, younger man with light brown hair stood, his hand upon Mary's shoulder. "It is so," the man said in a voice deep with emotion.

"I..." She gaped down at the man before her. "I would not be here were it not for Daisy and Mary coming to my aid and calling Adam to me. Thus we must be even in gratitude."

Ranulf lifted his head. "Aye, well, I'll be contesting that claim, Miss May. You brought my world back to me. I'll not be forgetting that, nor taking it lightly." A spark of good humor lit his eyes. "Will you accept my thanks then?"

Eliza would not blush. Her cheeks went warm. "Of course."

With great formality, Ranulf took her hand and pressed her knuckles to his forehead. He held her there for one long moment, then placed a kiss on the air just above her hand. With that, he rose, a graceful and lithe move Eliza had come to expect from supernaturals.

"Now then," said Daisy, bustling over. "Enough with emotional displays. You'll soon give poor Jack the vapors."

Jack turned out to be the massive man with the brown hair, who snorted at this and rolled his eyes. "Only you are capable of doing that to me, Daisy."

Then they all enjoyed a lovely dinner, in which Lucien entertained them with stories of New Orleans as it was in the last century. Then it was Ian and Adam's turn to tell stories of the past.

It wasn't until the dawn neared and their visitors had gone home that silence descended, and only Lucien remained, sitting opposite Eliza. As for Adam, his body was draped in a large black chair, adorned with mother of pearl, that sat at the head of the table. From the surprised looks the others had when Adam sat in it, Eliza had gathered that this was Lucien's special chair. Lucien, however, had been the one to insist that Adam sit there.

Now, the candles burned low, leaving the table aglow with mellow light. Lucien had been quiet for some time, taking slow sips of his wine, his eyes watching the little candle flames flickering. Now his gaze went to Adam, and Lucien's expression grew pensive.

"Out with it, Lucien," Adam drawled, not bothering to look up.

Lucien glanced at Eliza, and his mouth tightened. With deliberation, he set his wine glass down and braced his forearms upon the table. "All right then, *mon ami*. We need to discuss what has happened."

Adam arched a brow. "What of it?" There was a hint of belligerence in his tone that Eliza did not understand.

But Lucien clearly did for his expression softened. "Do you remember where you went when you died?"

Adam's lush mouth tightened a fraction. "Darkness. That is all. Just darkness."

"As did I," admitted Lucien. "And the others. I have spoken with Daisy, and a few more. They all say the same. Darkness." Lucien's lacy sleeves rippled as he leaned in farther, his voice growing deeper. "It was true death. Not a simple leaving of our bodies. We *died, mon capitaine.* You. I. The whole of us."

"I am aware, Lucien." Adam resolutely did not look Eliza's way.

Eliza was unable to keep quiet any longer. "What is it that you are implying?"

Lucien's eyes held regret yet resolve. "From what my sire has told me"—at this he gave a pointed look at Adam—"he is soulbound to death. To the GIM, to be precise. Whatever is between the two of you does not negate that."

Adam's lips pressed together. "You cannot be certain—"

"Oh no? And what is it, then, that occurred this day? Merdé, but you cannot be stubborn on this." Lucien's fist pressed against the heavy wooden table. "If you do not take back control, continue as you have been all these years, the GIM will die out."

Eliza felt Lucien's words like a punch.

"I gather," Eliza said to Adam, "that you did not think about your connection with the GIM when you let Mellan rip your heart out."

Adam shot her a glare, but it faded fast. "No," he admitted through his teeth. "I did not then realize that the GIM were bound to me so completely. If anything, I believed that my physical death would set them free." With a sigh, he leaned his head back against the chair. "I erred in judgment."

"Very well," she said. "So you must take control over the GIM once more. Why is this a problem?"

Adam's scowl was dark, but it was Lucien who answered.

"Because he wants an ordinary life. To live it with—"

"Enough." Adam's order rang loud and deep over them.

When Lucien merely looked at Adam as though daring him to deny a word, Adam's broad chest lifted on a sigh. "It isn't so simple, dove. As king of the GIM, I cannot solely live here. I must reside There."

"Here." Lucien gestured towards the window and the lights of London, glimmering off the waters of the Thames. "There, being an alternate reality where spirits, angels, and some primus demons dwell. And then Nowhere." A hint of a smile touched his lips. "That place that your culture would call Hell."

Adam nodded without enthusiasm. "In truth, the time I spent with you"—he grimaced—"when I'd chained you to me, was the longest I'd spent on this plane."

"But why?" Eliza would not allow the panic to creep farther up her back. She'd forge ahead, solve the problem. "Why must you live There?"

"My power regenerates There. And I don't merely create GIM. I collect souls. Of those who refuse to pass on to..." He hesitated then, his dark brows knitting.

"To wherever it is that those who truly die go," Lucien finished for him. "It is hard for Adam to explain because none of us, not even the angels, truly know where that is." The thoughtful expression did not leave him as he reached out and refilled their three glasses of wine. "What Adam forgot, I suspect in his joy of being free from Mab, is that by being soulbound to the reluctant dead, he draws them in. If he is here, so shall they be. In far too great a number."

Eliza's fingers curled tight, lest she reach out for him, demand that he stay precisely where he was. She'd never felt more alone. Blinking rapidly before tears could flow, Eliza turned away, running a finger along the carved rosette on the arm of her chair. She didn't believe in soul mates or fate. Adam was clearly never meant to be hers. Why then did she feel so...defeated? Lost.

"So then," she said slowly, the words fighting past the lump of emotion in her throat. "So wherever you are, so shall the dead be."

Adam gave her a black look, his golden eyes glowing with fierce light then abruptly dulling. "Always."

Chapter Thirty-One

She found Adam in Lucien's dining hall. He sat alone upon the ornate ebony and pearl chair. She walked farther into the room, her heels echoing in the silence.

"I picked this chair up in China. Brought it as a gift to Lucien after he became my eyes and ears for London." Adam's voice was low with melancholy, and the fine curve of his mouth curled. "He fancies it his throne now."

"And yet he wants you to sit in it." Eliza's throat hurt when she spoke. Everything hurt within her.

He stilled, the blunt tip of his finger poised above a pearl star. Golden eyes, now glowing once more with power, met hers. In them, she saw her own sorrow and need. "And so here I sit," he said.

Her limbs ached as she went to him. And he watched her, his big warrior's body unmoving but tense. Eliza stopped just before the arm of his chair, close enough to feel the heat of his body, close enough to touch. "You are their king once more."

Adam didn't reply. His expression was hard, his thick

brows knitting over his strong nose. The scowl he wore grew, his nostrils flaring, and then he hooked his arm about her middle, hauling her in front of him. Before she could breathe, he pressed his forehead against her ribs. "Eliza." Such pain in his voice. He gripped her skirts, his breath heating the fabric of her bodice, but said no more. Eliza's fingers threaded through the silk of his black hair, and he sighed.

What was there to say? Their time together was at an end. "You'll be leaving soon?" Her question came out garbled and rough.

Adam burrowed in closer. "Yes." Did he want to stay? It did not matter; the GIM needed him, and they both knew as much. Eliza looked towards the windows, thick, green bottle glass windows that let in light but no view. The back of her throat prickled. *Ask me to go with you.*

She almost said it aloud. But she couldn't. Everything had been thrown off kilter. And he no longer needed her. Perhaps he never truly had.

Eliza moved, intending to back away, when Adam lifted his head. The look in his eyes took her breath, and she tensed with sweet pain. He watched her as though he'd devour her bite by bite, taking his time, making her feel it.

Neither of them spoke. His gaze trailed down her throat and honed in on her breasts. Those strong hands grasped the edges of her sleeves, pulling the fabric painfully tight against her flesh. Her breasts swelled against the constriction, and then he yanked. The bodice tore like paper, the sound sharp. And she bobbled forward, braced up only by his hands upon her corset. His angry scowl stayed set as he made short work of her undergarments, shredding them with nary a flinch.

"I see you've regained all your strength," she murmured, a low and steady throb building at the sight of her unbound breasts bare before his gaze.

He didn't answer, but merely slid his hand up her ribs, trailing a fine heat in its wake, until he cupped her breast with firm fingers. He held her where he wanted her, his grip possessive, and then he leaned forward and licked her. Eliza whimpered as the warm flat of his tongue dragged over her nipple. Dear God. The way he tasted her. Melting heat spread over her heavy breasts, licked between her thighs. Her knees grew weak, but he had her, one hand gripping her waist, the other holding her breast captive.

His lids lowered, a small sound of need escaping him as he drew her nipple into his mouth to gently suckle it. So gently, a counterpoint to the firm way he touched her.

"Adam." She cupped his head and held him close.

With a muffled sound, he wrapped his arm about her waist and brought her down upon his lap, as he kissed his way up her neck. Soft lips and warm breath. He found her earlobe and nipped it, even as his strong hands drew her tattered skirts over her knees.

His fingers traced the soft curve of her thigh, raking over tender flesh. Such a hard touch with his warrior's hands. Hard touch, gentle mouth. Eliza wiggled closer, needing him too. She pulled at his shirt, desperate to get at the solid heat of his chest. His skin was tight satin, and touching him did nothing to satisfy her hunger. It merely made her want him more. She wanted to touch him endlessly, taste him, fuse her flesh with his. Anything to ease this agitation. This want. Something near a growl rose up within her as she reached between them and freed his cock, wrapping her fingers around its hardness and giving it a firm tug.

Adam hissed, his hips canting. Just as frenzied, his mouth moved over her, biting kisses, licks of his tongue. His wide chest rose and fell with each breath. She pressed against it, antagonizing the throbbing ache in her breasts. Adam grunted, his big hands finding her bottom. With an impatient noise, he hauled her against his cock. They both shuddered. Stilled a little.

His mouth was at her ear, his breath a pant, as he slowly lifted her, sliding her wetness over his length. Adam trembled, his massive thighs tensing. "Take me into you, dove."

Eliza's head fell to his shoulder, lust making her bone-less. Hand wrapped around the root of his cock, she lifted a little, guiding him to her entrance and biting her lip as the thick, round crown pushed into her. A broken, weak cry left her.

And then he gave her no mercy but ploughed into her. There was no more thinking. Just mindless want as he worked into her, his hands upon her arse. She found his lips. Their kiss was messy, an uncoordinated meeting of lips and tongues.

"Adam," she said into his mouth. "Please. Please." She didn't know what she was asking for, only that she needed more. It couldn't stop, this feeling. It couldn't end. Fear that it would rode her hard. She twined her arm about his neck, desperate to get closer still.

And he held her secure, one hand holding the tumbled-down hair at her nape, the other clasped on her bottom. But he suddenly slowed, his movements becoming more steady, yet no less intense. And she quaked, her eyes closing, her forehead pressed to his sweaty cheek.

"Look at me," he rasped. "Look at me."

He cupped her chin, bringing her head up, holding her

there. Golden eyes glowed with the power of the GIM. His power. It took her breath. His expression was near pain and filled with a tenderness that battered her heart. "There will never be another, Eliza." His cock moved within her, slow, steady, deep. Her eyes fluttered, but he held her tightly, not letting her break eye contact. "Do you hear me? You are my first"—he thrust—"my last"—he kissed her jaw—"my forever."

She kissed him, her lips barely brushing his, her tongue lightly licking along the edge of his mouth as they shared a breath. "Yes, Adam." She suckled his bottom lip. "Yes."

He swallowed audibly, his big body trembling, his movements becoming disjointed once more. "Eliza."

He sounded broken.

And so she kissed him again as she clenched her inner walls, clamping down tight on him. "Come home, Adam. Come home to me."

She hardly knew what she was saying, only that she would be his home if he'd let her. But he understood. On a loud groan, he thrust into her, the tip of his thumb finding her sex and worrying it as he pumped. That touch, and the feel of his open mouth against the sensitive skin of her neck, sent her spiraling. Cool heat pushed through her, and Eliza tensed with a whimper of pleasure.

He held back no longer. Shouting his release, he bucked into her, frantic, violent. Until he finished, his hips grinding into hers, his body rock hard. And then he collapsed back against the chair, taking her with him.

Shaking, she clung to him, her breasts crushed against his damp chest. Despite the way he panted, sweat slicking his skin, he was solid, eternal in his strength. His wide palm, roughened by calluses, explored her back with long strokes. He held her as if he'd never let her go.

And yet she could feel him mentally drawing away. All those pretty words, and she knew he wasn't making promises. But saying good-bye.

Eliza's fingers dug into the hard curves of his shoulders. "Ask me to go with you. Ask me to be yours."

She hadn't meant to say it. And yet she wanted it with her entire soul.

He froze, the corded muscles of his arms clenching tight, and his palm stilled. Gods, but she could feel the tension gathering within him, making her insides seize. Tears burned in her eyes even before he spoke. And when he did, his voice held the finality of death. "No."

Eliza left him. Adam did not blame her in the least. He'd been a cruel bastard. He'd turned her away. And ripped out his own heart in the process. Alone, he sat in the chair he'd made love to her in. Echoes of what they'd done, of her passion, the ripe warm feel of her body, haunted him. He ached for her. In a way he'd never thought existed. All these centuries, he believed loving a woman would be the making of him. How wrong he'd been.

He wanted to die. He, the king of death. Adam snorted, and it came out as a pathetic dark sob.

"I see we are not our best at the moment."

Lucien's voice had him jumping within his skin. Adam winced at the sight of him, resplendent in cobalt blue and sunshine yellow.

"Christ, you look a parrot."

Lucien lifted an elegant brow before running a hand down his satin coat. "Admit it, *mon ami,* you've always been jealous of my plumage."

"Oh, aye," Adam drawled. "I'd look a treat kitted out like a pretty dandy."

"That you would," Lucien murmured, eyeing him with frank appreciation. A rare show of his true appetites and one designed to discomfort Adam. It didn't, but Lucien's constant needling did.

Scowling, Adam shifted in his seat. "I'm in no mood to spar with you today, Lucien. Tell me what you want and go."

"Ah," said Lucien lightly, "but of course, you'd rather sit here and wallow in misplaced pride."

A haze of blackness rushed over Adam's vision. "You think this is about my pride?" His shout reverberated throughout the room. "Smarmy arse! I've no pride left when it comes to her." Adam's fists pushed against the table until it groaned in protest. "It is about my children, my GIM. It is about *you*, Lucien. You and every one of my GIM will die if I do not return to what I was, as you so kindly pointed out last night. So do not presume to come and lecture me now!"

Lucien's pale green eyes remained pallid. "So then, you shall sacrifice your love for the greater good, is that it? Most noble of you, *mon capitaine*."

Adam's teeth met. "My patience wears thin, imp."

Lucien's soft chuckle rumbled. "I have that effect." He shrugged, the cascade of lace at his throat sliding over his cobalt waistcoat. "So make her your queen. Bring her with you."

"Jesus." Adam raked his fingers along his aching skull. It was either that or punch his old friend in the throat. "Have you gone completely daft, Lucien? Or has love addled your brain as well?"

Lucien went milk white, his fine nostrils flaring on a sharp breath as his irises began to glow with green light.

"Oh aye," Adam went on, wanting to hurt. "You think

I don't know. You talk of making difficult decisions as though it were so very easy. When you turn your back on the sacrifices you must make for your own happiness."

"We are not discussing me," Lucien shot back, his usually smooth voice a near roar. Red faced, he pounded his walking stick into the wooden floor of the barge. "And my dilemma is nothing like yours. She loves you. And you her."

"You know damn well that if Eliza were to come with me, she'd have to *die*." The very thought was a spear through his heart. "Death, Lucien, when she's fought to live for so long."

And they both knew Adam could not even make her a GIM. She was too much fae, the one creature who could never be turned. And she was his soul mate.

"She loves you." Lucien's voice was a ghost. "That means...everything."

Guilt and shame punched into Adam. Lucien sounded as torn as he.

"I struck low and dishonorably," Adam said. "Forgive me."

Lucien gave him a short nod. "And I pushed you hard. But it is done out of my love for you." He leaned in, his expression earnest. "Can you not see? All is not lost if she were to—"

"She'd be stuck There. And I..." His voice left him for a humiliating moment. "I'll not see her fade away, lost to life, solely because of me." Adam blinked down at the rough, worn edges of Lucien's table. "I'm giving her up. Because I love her."

The distant clank of a ship's bell drifted over the room, and Lucien sighed, as he moved to the sideboard and poured them both a glass of claret. Adam accepted it with a numb hand and then drank it down in one gulp. He'd have preferred whisky, but suspected Lucien was still cross enough with him not to have offered it.

Lucien sat across from him and took a sip of wine.

"You want to know the worst of it?" Adam murmured.

"Oh, there's more?"

Adam glared but then his shoulders sagged, and he rubbed a hand over his face. "I'm tempted to choose her." So very badly.

"It shames you that you'd prefer love and happiness over holding up the lives of thousands." Lucien shrugged again. "And here I thought this is what makes you so very human. For once."

A snort left Adam, and he slumped in his chair, pressing his fingers to his eyes. "All too soon, I'll be as far from human as one can get, my friend." And he'd have an eternity to remember Eliza.

Chapter Thirty-Two

Adam left London on a sun-filled day. No rain for him, only clear skies and that rare and lovely weather that made Londoners flock to the outdoors. Cursing the weather, and heavy of heart, Adam moved away from the hot sunshine and stepped into the shadows provided by a large elm tree. Across the lane, Eliza sat in the window seat of Mab's grand house. Lucien had told him that Mab's possessions would go to Eliza. Good.

Adam had left all his worldly goods to Eliza at any rate. He'd amassed a king's fortune several times over, and he wanted her to have it. He would not be returning to London. He wouldn't be able to stand it, not when he knew she'd be here, within reach but never obtainable.

Under his collar, his clock rested against his skin. Eliza had taken it off just before they'd parted, her expression void of any emotion. *I no longer need to keep this safe. It is yours once more.* And it had felt as though she'd torn his heart out all over again. But he'd said nothing, nor protested when she walked away.

The clock ticked a steady rhythm, power flowing through it and into him. Once more, he felt each and every soul he'd saved as if they surrounded him. With stiff movements, he pressed his hand to his chest. He'd literally experienced having his heart ripped out, and yet this was worse. Physical pain eventually ended, the lights dimmed, and the mind shut off. Enduring without happiness or hope, that was the true hell. And his happiness sat across the way. She lived, and he would hold that thought close to him. She'd live a full and adventurous life, just as she'd dreamed of doing.

Behind the window, Eliza stared out onto the street. She could not see him now; he was invisible to the living. Even so, he hid in the shadows, afraid that she might catch a glimpse of his spirit. If he stopped to say good-bye or explain himself, he would never leave.

Logically, Adam understood that he ought to lay the choice at her feet. But everything in him protested at asking her to leave this world. For centuries he'd wanted nothing more than to be a normal man once more. He would not, could not, offer her anything less than a normal life.

Eliza stirred, sunlight gleaming in her hair and caressing the curve of her cheek. A lump rose hard in Adam's throat, choking him. And he turned away, unable to look upon her a moment longer. It took but a thought and the black door to his own personal hell opened up before him. Adam stepped into it without looking back.

He'd left without saying good-bye. It ought to have hurt the most, this slight, but it did not. No, Eliza was far more hurt by the simple fact that Adam had left her. The when and how of it meant little in the face of that rejection.

Alone, she sat, as she'd done every day for the past few months, in the window seat of Mab's house. Her house now.

Shortly after Adam had disappeared from Lucien's barge, from this world entirely, a solicitor came to visit Eliza. A fae solicitor as it turned out. The little man, dressed in a velvet suit of forest green, had given her a neat bow and introduced himself as Mr. Marcus. Combined with his bright red hair and smattering of freckles across his nose, he bore an unfortunate resemblance to one of those cartoon leprechauns that merchants liked to paste up in their shops come St. Patrick's Day. Or they did in Boston. Eliza did not know if anyone celebrated here in London.

"I did not realize that fae occupied such professions," Eliza had mused.

"I can't see why not," Mr. Marcus had said sensibly. "We've claims and courts just like any other."

Well then.

And it turned out that she now owned all of Mab's estate. Eliza was also the most natural candidate to take over the throne. "However," Mr. Marcus went on to explain, "should you not take up the claim, there are many others most willing to do so."

Eliza could just bet. "Let them at it, Mr. Marcus. I'm of this world, and here is where I intend to say." Eliza might have gone to Adam's domain, if he'd but asked. No. She would not think of that.

And so she took up Mab's estate, despite the fact that the house felt repugnant to her. For where else was she to go? She might stay with Daisy, or one of her sisters, Poppy or Miranda, who were also Eliza's distant cousins. And Holly Evernight had extended an offer as well. But all of them had families, husbands who loved them. And Eliza was in no mood to live amongst marital bliss, thank you very much.

As for Sin, he'd disappeared. Not a soul knew where he had gone, though his sisters seemed quite tight-lipped and cagey about the subject. Now Eliza had a fine home, one on which she'd spent a fortune—Mab's old fortune—to have redone. Gone were the gaudy trappings, the endless greens and ornate flowering brocades.

Eliza gravitated toward simple luxury now. Understated creams, blues, and golds. Calm and peaceful. Nothing like how she felt inside, empty and aching.

"Don't you look a sight," said a man's voice.

Eliza nearly jumped out of her skin, her heart rearing up into her throat. Pressing her hand upon her breast, she turned and glared. "St. John Evernight, you gave me a fright."

Sin, looking far too pale and thin, gave a small smile. "Apologies. I've been told I walk on cat's feet." His expression dimmed at that, and he gave a negligent shrug. "I thought you might like some company."

"I would..." Eliza shook herself out of her shocked state. "I was just thinking of you."

"Not too terrible thoughts, I hope?" He appeared to expect the opposite.

"Don't be ridiculous. But where have you been? Everyone is concerned."

He shook his head, appearing bemused. "I've grave doubts that *everyone* is. In truth, my sisters are not happy with me at the moment."

"They found out about your bond with Mab."

"Close enough." He winced and rubbed a spot over his chest.

Eliza hurt for the way he so clearly hated himself. "Well, I worried. I care."

"You're too good to me, cousin." But his shoulders relaxed a bit as he sat in the chair opposite her and offered a small, weak smile.

"Nonsense. I could be better." Eliza leaned forward. "Stay here with me, Sin. As you can see, I've cleaned house."

"Yes," he said, glancing about, "and quite nicely at that. I approve. But I cannot stay."

"Mab is dead. Do not let her memory hurt you."

He made a small sound of dry humor. "Believe me, no one is more glad of that fact than I."

"Which means you are free."

"Yes." He did not sound happy but weary.

"Then why haven't you returned home? Why can't you stay?"

He glanced towards the window, and the morning sun cast his fine feature in harsh light. "I think it best if I go away for a while. See what there is of the world." He turned back, his green eyes searching. "You could come with me, if you'd like. We could have an adventure or two."

It was just the thing Eliza had always yearned to do. But she no longer wanted to do it with anyone else but the man who'd left her behind. Perhaps that knowledge was clear upon her face, for Sin's hopeful expression dimmed.

He slouched in his chair. "I've heard Adam has gone for good." His tone was gentle.

Not that it mattered. It still hurt. Far more than Eliza wanted it to. Blasted Adam. "Yes."

Sin peered at her. "So then you never warmed to him?"

"Must we discuss this?" Eliza plucked at her sleeve,

then curled her legs up and under her within the well of her comfortable chair.

"We might talk of other things, yes." Sin shrugged. "Only you appear...sad, cousin. Like your heart's been broken."

Before she could stop it, her eyes instantly watered, and a horrible sniffle broke free. "Oh, well, it's better to have loved and lost...Hell, I can't even finish that nonsense." Eliza wrenched herself from the chair and went to the window, only to walk away. She was pacing. Which was never a good sign.

"You love him, then."

Sin's quiet conviction slashed into wounds that had yet to scab over. Eliza sucked in a breath. "What does it matter? He did not want me to go with him."

The mantle clock ticked merrily away, a rapid click, click, click. Eliza was of a mind to toss the timepiece out the window.

"Eliza," Sin said softly, "you do realize that for you to have gone with Adam to his world, you would have had to leave this one?"

Eliza's breath stilled. Slowly she turned. "What do you mean?"

Sin's handsome face was somber. "I mean, dear girl, that Adam's realm is of the dead. The living cannot go there."

"So I would have to die?"

"It isn't really death though, is it?" Sin ran a hand over his mouth, his brows drawing close. "I mean, you are not of this body, but of the soul that resides within?"

"I've been a spirit, Sin," Eliza said through dry lips. "It was not very pleasant." She'd felt nothing, just as Adam had felt nothing for centuries. Adam. She missed him so very much.

"That is because you were hovering here. From how Daisy tells it"—a shadow filled his eyes upon the mention of his sister—"when you are There, you feel as whole and as real as you were on this side of the coin. As if you were alive There and a spirit Here."

"So I would be as I am here but with—"

"Him," Sin finished for her. "Yes." He hesitated, wincing slightly. "But you wouldn't be able to come back here. I don't believe so, at any rate."

Eliza pinched the bridge of her nose, tears pricking at the backs of her eyes. "Not every soul goes to him. Some move on." True death, Adam and Lucien had called it, to a place no one living had ever been. What if she were to end up there?

"You are Adam's soul mate, are you not? His other half? You'll go where he goes." Sin stared at her. "Or do you believe that was all Mab's nonsense?"

Eliza sagged against the arm of her couch. "He let me go," she said helplessly. "What is to say he even believes in us?"

"Or maybe he let you go because he loved you too much to ask you to leave this life behind?"

"That ought to have been my decision, if that were so."

"Then there's naught for it," Sin said decidedly. "Make the decision now. Do you love him enough to risk everything?"

Lucien was reading a book when Eliza arrived. The sight of him, sitting in a reading chair, a pair of spectacles perched on his perfectly shaped nose, was so incongruous with how he usually presented himself to the world that Eliza stopped short.

As for Lucien, he closed the book with a muted thud

of the pages and set it aside. His smile was genuine if not sad as he took off his glasses and stood. "This is a nice surprise, *ma chère*."

"I hope I have not intruded upon your quiet time." Eliza took another step farther into the room, near the drinks table placed against the wall.

"Hardly," he said with a slight wave of his hand. "And I shall always be here for you, my lady."

She wasn't a lady. But she supposed he was trying to be kind.

"What brings you here, Eliza?" The rare use of her name was soft and searching. He must have known she wanted to speak of Adam.

"I wanted to ask you a question."

"Only one?" His full lips curled. "How rare."

"Well, perhaps a few more than that." She gestured toward the drink. "Might I have a drink with you?"

"But of course. Let me—" He moved to come pour her a drink, and Eliza waved him off.

"I'll get it." Eliza selected a crystal glass and, turning her back on him, filled it. Her hand shook only a little when she made her way over to him.

Lucien had pulled out his favored chair—the very damned chair that she'd made love with Adam on—and another for her. She ground her teeth together and accepted a seat, waiting for him to sit upon the chair that she could barely look at anymore.

"So then," he said picking up his own half-filled glass. Deep amber liquid swirled about there. Brandy perhaps. He took a sip, then gave her an expectant look. "You have questions. I hope I have the answers, my lady."

As did she.

"You know," she said in a low voice, "I am not a lady."

Lucien gave a lazy smile. "Ah, but you are, for you are Adam's queen."

Eliza snorted, a most unladylike sound. "If that were so, I'd be with him."

"You speak of geography," Lucien answered easily. "I speak of the heart."

Her own heart quickened at that. She tapped the hope down. "What is his realm like?"

Lucien's glass froze halfway to his lips. Carefully, he set it back down. "Just as it is here. Call it an alternate version of our world. Only the ghosts you see there—and you, *mon amie*, will see them—are the souls of the people who live here."

"Is he all alone then? Without friends?" Her heart ached at the thought.

"Not entirely. Any GIM may travel there. He need only give permission. He hasn't in the past." Something like sorrow rested in Lucien's pale green eyes. But he blinked it away. "Do not fret, *amie*. It is not a horrible place."

"Hmm." Eliza toyed with the stem of her glass. Part of her wanted to fling it across the room and leave this barge. But she'd never outrun her need for Adam. He was part of her, and she was soul-sick without him. "And his home? Has he a place of comfort?"

Oddly, she could not picture Adam in a home. Nor a castle. She could not picture him anywhere but at her side. Whether driving her mad with irritation or out of her head with lust.

Lucien began to chuckle, the sound grating. Gods, had he guessed her thoughts?

Eliza's face heated as he continued to laugh. "I'd like to know what you find so amusing."

"It is Adam." Lucien waved an idle hand, sending the

cascade of lace at his sleeve swaying. "He has his little jokes, and I find they amuse me greatly at the moment."

Eliza scowled. "Have you taken leave of your senses?"

"Oh, how I wish to do just that one day." Lucien straightened his expression. "The fact is, *chère amie*, that in his realm, this barge is Adam's." One long, tanned finger tapped upon the pearl-inlaid chair. "This chair is his chair."

"So...if we were to go there at this moment," Eliza worked out slowly, "we'd find him in this barge?"

"Just so."

Eliza could not quite wrap her head around it, but she trusted Lucien. Sitting back, she picked up her wine glass. Her heart began to pound a frantic, fearful rhythm. She was afraid. Utterly. How could she not be? Her fingers turned to ice, a fine, slick sweat breaking out over her skin.

Lucien frowned as if just noticing her terror. "*Chère...*"

Eliza's hands trembled, sloshing the ruby red liquid about in her glass. Mustn't spill a drop. She gave Lucien a wobbly smile, as if she were not about to be ill. "Thank you, Lucien. Your information was most helpful and makes this much easier."

His brows rose, the heavy chair screeching as he lunged up.

But Eliza was quicker. She lifted the glass to her lips and swallowed the contents down in a painful gulp. Bitterness filled her mouth, her breath stopping short. Lucien may have shouted. She did not know. She was gone.

Chapter Thirty-Three

Loneliness was much easier to bear when he hadn't felt a thing. Adam had been numb, and life had been tolerable. Now, loneliness was an agony of the soul. It shredded his heart and bled into his limbs. Eternity stretched around him as a dark and bottomless hole. And he felt as though he were forever falling.

A king alone. And wasn't that quite pathetic? True, he had his subjects here, and Lucien often came for a visit. And because Adam could no longer tolerate being alone with his thoughts, he'd let Daisy Ranulf and Mary Chase come round as well. Which was all very good. But they were not *her*.

Slumped upon his chair—the very same version of the chair he'd last made love to Eliza upon—he toyed with the stem of his glass of port. Eliza. He squeezed his eyes shut, not wanting to think about her. But she was his every thought. His waking breath. His endless torment.

"Lord above but you look worse for wear."

Adam's blood stilled within his body. For a moment,

he could not breathe. No. It was just a trick of his mind. She couldn't be here. It was impossible.

"I see," said Eliza's voice in his head. "You're going to ignore me now? How very ironic."

Adam's fists clenched reflexively. He forced his eyes open. And promptly lost his wits. The glass toppled to the floor, shattering upon impact. He paid it no mind.

There, dressed in a simple gown of deep brown, stood Eliza May. As a man starved, he drank in the sight of her. Lamplight caught the golden filaments of her hair and highlighted the cast of her creamy skin. Her wide, brown eyes gleamed, alive and quick, and the gentle curve of her cheeks were flushed.

When he did not speak, she propped her fists upon her lovely hips and narrowed her eyes. "Has the cat got your tongue? Say something, for god's sake."

It was the fear in her eyes, and the hurt lingering beneath it, that gave him his voice.

"You... you're... here?" Very intelligent, that. But Adam was at a loss for words. In truth, he wondered if he might soon weep. Perhaps it was a dream. *If so, let me never wake.*

"Would you rather I leave?" She made as if to turn away.

"No!" He nearly shot out of his chair but found he could not stand. His legs, nay, his entire body was all at once weak as a babe's and yet heavy as a stone.

Eliza let out a small breath. "Right. Well then... yes, I'm here." She winced, her cheeks coloring a bit. "Haven't you anything to say?"

Adam licked his dry lips. "How did you..." He trailed off, afraid to ask. Afraid this was all an illusion of his desperate mind.

"I drank a glass full of cyanide."

"Jesus Christ." Adam smashed his fist against his chair. "How could you—"

"Well I had to, hadn't I?" Eliza shouted back. "How else was I to get to you?"

"You died." His voice broke, and he took a deep breath. "To get to me."

Eliza shrugged. "To tell you the truth, I don't feel dead at all. I feel quite fine, actually."

Adam dragged a hand over his jaw, the action sending a rasping sound into the silence. Heat and need and hope were a volatile mix within his veins. "Eliza," he said, carefully. "You can't go back."

Her lovely brown eyes darkened. "I know."

Again he swallowed, his body trembling. She was here. *Here.* He was not alone. No more.

"Why?" It came out a rasp. "Why come for me?"

No one had sacrificed themselves for him. Nor claimed him. And though he suspected, *hoped*, he needed to hear the words.

Her golden locks tumbled about her shoulders as she shook her head in apparent exasperation. "Because, you thick-headed man, I love you."

Adam's heart seized, terrible joy swelling within him. "You..."

Eliza tilted her head, her brown eyes narrowing. "Would it have made a difference if I had said it before? Would you have wanted me then?"

"I've always wanted you. I always will."

Absently, she nodded. "And do you—"

"I love you," he shouted, his voice wild, not his own. "Utterly. With all that I am."

At this, she frowned. "Then why do you sit there, as if made from stone?"

He gave a disjointed, weak laugh. "Madam, I fear I've lost the ability to move. You've rendered me senseless."

A slow, pleased smile curved her lips. "Mmm. I must admit, I rather like you at my mercy."

With a groan, Adam launched out of his chair. In two strides, she was in his arms, her slim, warm length pressing against him. The action soothed him to the core, and his soul lit up with a sense of rightness and of peace. Finally, peace. Tears burned in his eyes. And then he claimed her mouth. Sweet, soft, luscious Eliza May.

She wrapped herself around him, her tongue seeking the same comfort. God, to kiss her again. It was better than anything else in this world or the other. He'd endure every single century all over again if he knew this waited for him at the end.

"Mercy," he whispered against her lips. "Have mercy on me, sweet Eliza."

She smiled, her teeth nipping at his lower lip. "Never."

He chuckled, his hand moving to cup her plump arse. "Then torture me some more, for I am yours."

Epilogue

————————— ❦〰❦ —————————

In the sunlit cloisters of Westminster Abby, Sin walked alongside Augustus. Tourists strolled around them, some stopping to peer at the tombstone of a long-dead priest or valiant knight who'd been laid to rest on this hallowed ground.

As for Sin, he passed the letter he'd just received to Augustus and then pushed his hands into the pockets of his cashmere overcoat. His breath came out in a puff as he spoke. "Eliza left it all to me. Mab's old house, her fortune, everything." It made his skin crawl and his heart hurt. He did not want anything of Mab's, and yet it touched him that Eliza had wanted to see him provided for. Not that he needed it; he was comfortable enough. But Eliza was the only true friend he had left, and she was far off in another world.

Augustus read Eliza's letter with a fond look upon his face. "She is happy and well with Adam." He lifted the little photograph that Eliza had sent along, and a smile pulled at his mouth. The grainy image showed a grinning

Eliza and a stern but pleased-looking Adam standing before the Great Pyramid of Khufu at the Giza Necropolis, Eliza's white frock blowing in the desert breeze.

Sin frowned as he looked at the photograph. "How is it that she's in Egypt when she's stuck in Adam's realm?"

"You ought to understand this," Augustus said, adopting his "professor tone" as he handed Sin the letter and photograph. "Theirs is a parallel world to ours. Therefore Khufu's tomb stands as majestic and solid as it is here."

Sin used care as he tucked Eliza's letter into his pocket. His strength was immense now, and he'd yet to become accustomed to it, tearing many an article of clothing or hinges off of doors without thought.

Augustus glanced around the cloisters, and a look of melancholy softened his hard features. When he turned back to Sin, however, it was gone. "You've much to learn, St. John, and I've little time to teach it." Deep brown eyes bore into Sin's. "The question is, are you ready for the next chapter in your life?"

It wouldn't be easy. Sin had been warned. He couldn't tell a soul what he was. And he'd have to watch over the one woman he wanted more than anything in this life. He thought of Layla. Lovely and fresh and utterly out of his reach. And yet he'd endure anything to keep her safe. Sin stared up at the lapis blue sky, the sunlight warm on his face, and drew in a deep breath of the frosty, late autumn air.

"I am."

Read on for a sneak peek into Kristen Callihan's other dark, sensual tales of Victorian London – where magic and passion lurk in every shadowy corner...

FIRELIGHT

London, 1881

Once the flames are ignited...

Miranda Ellis is a woman tormented. Plagued since birth by a strange and powerful gift, she has spent her entire life struggling to control her exceptional abilities. Yet one innocent but irreversible mistake has left her family's fortune decimated and forced her to wed London's most nefarious nobleman.

They will burn for eternity...

Lord Benjamin Archer is no ordinary man. Doomed to hide his disfigured face behind masks, Archer knows it's selfish to take Miranda as his bride. Yet he can't help being drawn to the flame-haired beauty whose touch sparks a passion he hasn't felt in a lifetime. When Archer is accused of a series of gruesome murders, he gives in to the beastly nature he has fought so hard to hide from the world. But the curse that haunts him cannot be denied. Now, to save his soul, Miranda will enter a world of dark magic and darker intrigue. For only she can see the man hiding behind the mask.

'Callihan pens a compelling Victorian paranormal with heart and soul'
Publishers Weekly

MOONGLOW

Once the seeds of desire are sown ...

Finally free of her suffocating marriage, widow Daisy Ellis
Craigmore is ready to embrace the pleasures of life that have
long been denied her. Yet her newfound freedom is short
lived. A string of unexplained murders has brought danger
to Daisy's door, forcing her to turn to the most unlikely of
saviours ...

Their growing passion knows no bounds ...

Ian Ranulf, the Marquis of Northrup, has spent lifetimes
hiding his primal nature from London society. But now a
vicious killer threatens to expose his secrets. Ian must step
out of the shadows and protect the beautiful, fearless Daisy,
who awakens in him desires he thought long dead. As their
quest to unmask the villain draws them closer together, Daisy
has no choice but to reveal her own startling secret, and Ian
must face the undeniable truth: Losing his heart to Daisy may
be the only way to save his soul.

'A sizzling paranormal with dark history and explosive
magic! Callihan is an impressive new talent'
Larissa Ione

WINTERBLAZE

Once blissfully in love ...

Poppy Lane is keeping secrets. Her powerful gift has
earned her membership in the Society for the Suppression
of Supernaturals, but she must keep both her ability and her
alliance with the Society from her husband, Winston. Yet
when Winston is brutally attacked by a werewolf, Poppy's
secrets are revealed, leaving Winston's trust in her as broken
as his body. Now Poppy will do anything to win back
his affections ...

Their relationship is now put to the ultimate test.

Winston Lane soon regains his physical strength but his face
and heart still bear the scars of the vicious attack. Drawn into
the darkest depths of London, Winston must fight an evil
demon that wants to take away the last hope of reconciliation
with his wife. As a former police inspector, Winston has
intelligence and logic on his side. But it will take the strength
of Poppy's love for him to defeat the forces that threaten to
tear them apart.

'Like all good things, Callihan just keeps getting
better and better'
RT Book Reviews

SHADOWDANCE

Once a heart is lost in shadow . . .

Jack Talent is tormented by the demons of his past. Though
Jack loves his position in the SOS, he cannot forget what was
done to him. And so he hunts down the remaining demons
that tortured him and metes out his own brand of justice as
the Bishop of Charing Cross. The only things that soothe him
are his secret visits to fellow agent Mary Chase. But while
something about Mary calms him, she is also his greatest
torment, for she is a reminder of his worst crime – the night
he lost his soul by taking her human life.

Only someone who lives in darkness can find it.

Mary Chase is now free. After years of service to the Ghosts
in the Machine, she now assists the head of the SOS and is
finally enjoying life – except for the one thorn in her side:
Jack Talent. The temperamental shifter unsettles her and
awakens a need she's never felt before. But when a copycat
killer begins to mimic the Bishop's signature and Jack is
assigned to the case, Mary volunteers to join him, eager
to unravel Jack's mysterious façade. Can Jack protect his
secret – and his heart – from the one woman who could be
his ultimate ruin?

'[A] tale so powerful, so compelling, that I had no choice but
to follow it through to the end'
NightOwlReviews.com

EVERNIGHT

Once the night comes ...

Holly Evernight belongs to a very special family of inventors. They have nobly served the Society for the Suppression of Supernaturals for generations. And Holly may have the most special creative powers of them all. But her skills are about to be tested as she tries to save the life of a half-man-half-machine whose clockwork heart is ticking down to the bitter end ...

Love must cast aside the shadows.

William Thorne was a rebel, a hired assassin for the SOS's greatest rival, before he was taken, tortured and transformed. Now his mind and soul battle with his body as he becomes less and less human. But the true fight for his humanity will be waged within his heart.

'[A] perfectly paced, tremendously sexy romance set against a beautifully wrought backdrop'
Washington Post

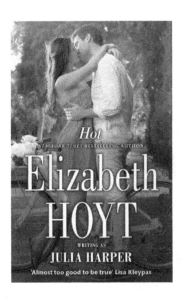

HOT
by Elizabeth Hoyt writing as
Julia Harper

For Turner Hastings, being held at gunpoint during a bank robbery is an opportunity in disguise. After seeing her little heist on tape, FBI Special Agent John MacKinnon knows it's going to be an interesting case. But he doesn't expect to develop feelings for Turner, and when bullets start flying in her direction, John finds he'll do anything to save her.

FOR THE LOVE OF PETE
by Elizabeth Hoyt writing as
Julia Harper

Dodging bullets with a loopy redhead in the passenger seat is not how Special Agent Dante Torelli imagined his day going. But Zoey Addler is determined to get her baby niece back, and no one – not even a henpecked hit man, cooking-obsessed matrons, or a relentless killer – will stand in her way.

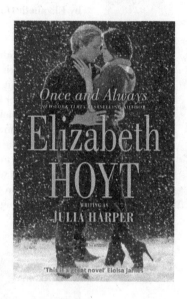

ONCE AND ALWAYS
by Elizabeth Hoyt writing as Julia Harper

The newest contemporary from *New York Times* bestselling author Elizabeth Hoyt writing as Julia Harper! Small-town cop Sam West certainly doesn't mind a routine traffic stop. But Maisa Bradley is like nothing he has ever seen, and she's about to take Sam on the ride of his life!

Do you love fiction with a supernatural twist?

Want the chance to hear news about your favourite
authors (and the chance to win free books)?

Keri Arthur
Kristen Callihan
P.C. Cast
Christine Feehan
Jacquelyn Frank
Larissa Ione
Darynda Jones
Sherrilyn Kenyon
Jayne Ann Krentz and Jayne Castle
Lucy March
Martin Millar
Tim O'Rourke
Lindsey Piper
Christopher Rice
J.R. Ward
Laura Wright

Then visit the Piatkus website and blog
www.piatkus.co.uk | www.piatkusbooks.net

And follow us on Facebook and Twitter
www.facebook.com/piatkusfiction | www.twitter.com/piatkusbooks

piatkus